The Unpredictable Past

Lyn Behan

BehanPublishing

First Edition 2022

Contents

Prologue

How could Edward Turner have guessed that the eruption of a distant volcano, the end of a war and a corrupt government would lead to him being charged with high treason and transported to Australia for the term of his natural life?

Well, this was before the days of the telegraph, so very few people at the time heard about Mount Tambora in Indonesia, whose eruption was one of the most explosive forces in history.

The volume of ash was so great it sank small boats and the sea became a choking mass of pumice. Most of the ash was spewed up into the jet stream, and eventually carried to the Northern Hemisphere. The following year became known as "The year of no summer".

Edward only knew that the sun hadn't been visible, the weather had been appalling and there'd been no harvest that year; crops failed and people starved.

He did know of the defeat of Napoleon – it led to an influx of returned soldiers – many disabled and missing limbs – who returned to England only to find there was no future and no work for them.

The end of the war meant that many tradespeople had no outlet for their goods and the introduction of machines put many craftsmen out of work.

England was ripe for rebellion ...

Wambecarra, Australia - March 2020

Elizabeth Turner paused at the *No Through Road* sign at the corner of her street, for her dog to have her usual sniff.

'Goodness, Molly,' she murmured, pulling on the dog's lead. 'What's been happening while we were out?'

A tipper truck had lowered its tray and was reversing out from the house opposite hers. The truck passed her as she neared her next-door neighbour's house.

She smiled to herself when she saw Merv move from his usual position on an old couch on the veranda, and shuffle towards his front gate.

'Hello, Elizabeth,' he exclaimed, 'Seems like something's happening across the road.' He waved his walking stick towards a pile of rocks. 'You missed it! A big truck just reversed and dumped a load of rubble right inside the gate.'

She was torn between wanting to get a closer look and not appearing nosy. 'Maybe someone is moving in.'

'Hope so,' said Merv, turning to his wife who was hobbling out the front door. 'Look here Mabel, load of rubble just been dumped across the road.'

'Dearie me,' she said, 'a lot of work for whoever's going to move in.'

'About time,' Merv frowned. 'More than two years it's been empty and the place is in a woeful state!'

Elizabeth could sense that he was about to tell her yet again about poor Kathleen who used to live there, when she forestalled him.

'Sorry Merv, Mabel. I must dash, expecting a phone call.' *That wasn't really a lie*, she told herself, she was always expecting a phone call from telemarketers - apart from her daughter they were the only calls she received.

Back in her own house, she fetched her binoculars and went to her bedroom which faced the street. From behind the net curtains, she studied the pile in the driveway opposite; it looked more like a heap of stones; they seemed regular in shape. Then she chided herself, *Really, Elizabeth, you're turning into a nosy old woman! Getting as bad as Merv!*

Then she thought about the pond she was making in her garden. Those stones would be perfect around the edge to keep the pond liner in place ...

Derbyshire, England - June 1817

Edward Turner listened carefully as his older brother, William, told him about a meeting planned for the eighth of June at the White Horse Inn in Pentrich. The two men were walking through the woods to William's cottage.

'Ed, you've got to come to the meeting.' William's voice was filled with excitement. 'There's a march being organised; we're going to meet up with reinforcements in Nottingham and march to London. There're thousands of men waiting to join us there.'

Edward nodded, 'I'll go with you.'

William smiled, turned to his brother and extended his right hand. Edward shook it, and grinned. With a spring in his step, he continued on home through the bluebell woods.

***

Edward's wife, Sarah, sniffed when he told her of the planned meeting. 'You're not going all that way 'cross fields to listen to that old blatherer, Thomas Bacon, are you?' she demanded as he tied the laces on his worn boots. 'Wasting good boot leather on an old trouble stirrer! He caused enough problems starting those Luddite attacks all around here. And his sister, that Nan, she's no better!' Sarah wiped the sweat from her brow with her apron as she turned from the fire where a pot of thin soup simmered.

'We've got to do summat! We're starving and there's no work, while the gentry's eating meat every day,' he replied.

'You still have work. There's always a bit of work for a mason,' she snapped.

'Hmm, but barely enough to put food on the table and most of the people around here are starving.' He finished tying his laces and stood. 'An' I feel for the stockingers now machines have taken over. Poor quality stockings too,' he grimaced.

Sarah studied her husband. He was still a handsome man, she thought, tall and strong, with his kind brown eyes and thatch of thick black hair. She moved towards him and wrapped her arms around his thin frame.

'Traipsing across the fields to sit in that woman's public house, plotting treason with her mischief-making brother. I hope that son of hers has more sense,' she muttered into his chest.

'Nan Weightman's all right, and George said he's joining us.'

'George! You'd think he'd have more brains than that and him just lost a baby son last year.' Sarah sniffed. 'Anyways, I still don't want you to go.'

'What's the alternative?' Edward demanded, holding her tight. 'What have we got to lose?'

'Yer life,' Sarah retorted. She broke away from her husband. 'Oh, Ed, my love, I don't have a good feeling about this march.'

'Oh, you and yer feelings! It'll all be right, love, Jeremiah Brandreth said there are scores of men waiting to join us at Nottingham. And Willum'll be leading us.' He gave her a quick kiss and a hug and went out the door. 'Go and fetch water for your mother,' he instructed his eldest daughter, who was outside playing with her sister.

Sarah wanted to say that just because his brother, William, had fought in the war against Napoleon, that didn't make him an expert in rebellions. But she stayed silent. Forty-six-year-old William could do no wrong in Edward's eyes.

Edward trudged across the fields to the White Horse Inn, his mind so full of the ideas his brother had been telling him, that he barely noticed the spring growth that was happening after the previous summer when all the crops had failed.

Habeas Corpus had been suspended after rocks had been thrown at the window of the Prince Regent's coach in January. William had explained to his younger brother that it meant anyone could be imprisoned without a trial. The Gagging Acts were rushed through parliament banning meetings of more than fifty people and giving magistrates the power to arrest anyone suspected of spreading sedition. Although normally mild-tempered, Edward began to get fired up by the injustices meted out to the common man.

He reached the old stone-built inn where a crowd of men gathered outside, trying to enter. Edward pushed through and elbowed his way into the noisy, smokey bar until he saw Thomas Bacon.

In his sixties, with a flowing white beard and a limp, Bacon was a known agitator, suspected of being involved in machine-breaking in the area. He rose and spoke about having met with a William Oliver, who had told him about the thousands of men around the country who were committed to the cause and ready to march into London and overthrow the government.

Bacon then introduced Jeremiah Brandreth, a bearded, charismatic man with an unkempt mop of curly black hair. Brandreth stood up and spoke convincingly to the half-starved group of locals. He explained the route the march would take and held up a roughly drawn map. The meeting lasted several hours and all the men were instructed to stop at every farm, cottage and factory along the way and enlist men to join. They were told who had firearms or other weapons and instructed to requisition them. Brandreth promised them bread, beef and ale when they reached Nottingham. Once there they would link up with Yorkshire men and make their way to London. The government would be overthrown and replaced with the principal reformers.

The leaders of the Pentrich group were to be Jeremiah Brandreth, William Turner and Isaac Ludlam.

After the meeting, Edward hurried home, anxious to tell Sarah the plan was foolproof.

Sarah just shook her head, as her husband told her all the details, his words tumbling out with excitement. 'Tom Bacon met one of the top organisers, William Oliver, and it's for tomorrow night, and Willum is to be one of the leaders,' he exclaimed.

'And who is this William Oliver? I don't trust that Thomas Bacon, he's all good to get men stirred up but will he be going?'

Edward paused. 'No, but remember he's over sixty and there's already a warrant out for his arrest.'

'Hah!' Sarah snorted. 'And what about young Manchester?' she asked. Joseph "Manchester" Turner was Edward and William's eighteen years old nephew, who had recently returned from Manchester, hence his nickname.

'He's coming with us.'

'Hmph, he's too young and foolish, you shouldn't be encouraging him,' she grumbled. 'And him with only the one good eye.'

Edward shrugged and turned away.

The following night at ten o'clock he joined the fifty or so other men and armed with pikes, scythes and any other makeshift weapons they could find, they set off on their march. George Weightman, a nephew of Thomas Bacon, and son of Nan Weightman had been sent ahead, on a “borrowed” pony, as a scout to assess the situation in Nottingham, sixteen miles distant.

As the rebellion gathered momentum, the rebels recruited more men from houses and farms en-route, stopping at houses where they knew the occupants had guns, to collect weapons and men. The onset of heavy rain delayed them and they were forced to find shelter in barns and sheds.

Edward tried not to think of his warm bed and his wife as he shivered in the barn. Eventually, they started marching again. Some of the marchers banged on the doors of houses they passed, demanding the menfolk come out and march with them or hand over their weapons. Shots were fired.

Brandreth stopped at the village of Codnor and divided the group into three, sending them to different taverns for food and drink and a short rest. Edward’s group went to The Glass House, with Brandreth. As they prepared to resume the march, Brandreth refused to pay the bill.

‘This currency will be worthless soon,’ he shouted, punching the air with his fist. ‘We’ll soon have a new one!’ And he strode out of the inn and led his men away.

Edward frowned, but he kept following Brandreth.

At Langley Mill, they were met by George Weightman, their scout, who dismounted from his pony. He and Jeremiah Brandreth separated from the men and conferred together in low voices. Brandreth nodded, and Weightman straightened his shoulders and addressed the marchers.

‘All’s going well in Nottingham!’ he shouted. This helped the marchers recover their spirits and keep marching. They didn’t know that after Weightman left Nottingham most of the men gathered there had dispersed, thinking the Pentrich contingent had abandoned the march because of the weather.

At Eastwood, just over eight miles from Nottingham, some village people said a magistrate had been called out to bring soldiers to the barracks to confront the rebels. Edward scowled when he heard this. 'Who says so?' he asked the man who'd passed on the rumour. The man shrugged. 'Dunno, just overheard someone say it.'

Edward tried to stay positive. It was sixteen miles from Pentrich to Nottingham, and they were only halfway there. The light was beginning to fade as the marchers reached Giltbrook Stream. Then someone shouted 'Redcoats!' and suddenly, there was chaos as the insurgents flung down their weapons and fled. Edward ran back the way he'd come, eventually reaching Langley Mill. Breathless, he hid in a ditch and then saw the shadow of a man who he recognized as his brother, William.

'Willum!' he called in a loud whisper. 'Over here!' William stumbled towards Edward's voice. He slipped on the wet grass and fell into the ditch beside his brother. 'Sorry, Ed,' he managed to gasp. 'Shouldn't have encouraged you to join us. Seems someone's informed on us. Most likcly that William Oliver.'

'My Sarah had her suspicions about him.'

William merely grunted.

The brothers huddled together in the ditch. 'Bloody nettles,' muttered William, rubbing his hands. 'Hope the Redcoats won't find us here. We'll creep out once it gets light.'

Edward mumbled an assent and pulled his collar up against the rain. 'Sarah won't be happy when she sees my coat covered in mud.' He had every faith that his brother, thirteen years his senior, would get them safely home.

'Sorry, Ed,' William repeated.

'Ah, Sarah won't mind, as long as I get home.'

William was silent. It seemed the state of Edward's coat wasn't what he was worried about; this was not the way the march was supposed to work out.

At dawn, the brothers froze when they heard the noise of approaching soldiers. Soaking wet and stiff from lying in the damp ditch they were hauled up, tied and bound.

Together with some of the other marchers, the brothers were forced to lie in a cart along with an assortment of their weapons. Guarded by a party of Hussars, they proceeded to Derby Goal.

Wambecarra - March 2020

Elizabeth kept watch on the house opposite. Still no vehicles outside when she went to bed. Would it be so wrong to take a few of the stones? There were plenty there, and anyway, they were only stones. In bed, she tossed and turned, trying to sleep. Eventually she glanced at the clock on her bedside table. Nearly midnight. She sighed and sat up, feeling for her slippers with her toes. She rose and crept to the window. The house across the road was still in darkness, as were all the houses that she could see. At the end of the cul-de-sac was just one house which bordered hers on one side and the house opposite on the other. A street light in front of it cast a dull glow over the stones. Before she lost her nerve, she pulled on her dressing gown. Molly raised her head.

'No, you stay here, Molly. I won't be long,' Elizabeth whispered as she padded to the front door followed by Molly.

'Stay home, Molly,' Elizabeth repeated. She stood outside her front door and looked up and down the road. No-one. No lights in any of the houses. Stars studded the sky; at least it wasn't a full moon, she thought. Squaring her shoulders, and taking a deep breath, she strolled across the road. Furtively, she bent to pick up a stone, then yelped as she stubbed her toe on one of them, *Stupid woman, coming out in slippers and dressing gown,* she told herself as she heaved the stone up into her arms. She carried it back and around the side of her house. Feeling more confident she made three more trips.

She loved her garden; since moving in, she'd spent hours making it bird-friendly, planting native shrubs and bee attracting flowers, and the pond in one corner would hopefully attract frogs. She was proud of her efforts; she'd dug out the pit for the pond, moving the earth to make a mound at one side; bought plastic pool liner and bags of sand and it was all ready, just needed rocks to secure the plastic and make a nice edge. She'd need at least another half dozen.

***

The house across the road remained empty, with no sign of life, so for the next few nights she changed her slippers for shoes and wearing an old coat and gardening gloves "borrowed" more stones. She carefully selected them from different places so it wouldn't appear too obvious some were missing. There must be hundreds there, she thought. Surely no one would miss a few. And anyway, they were just lying there - probably just dumped – she tried to convince herself.

She laid the stones and filled the pond with water, then drove to the local garden centre to get rockery and pond plants. On her return she positioned the plants and stood back, admiring the effect. She made a few small adjustments before digging holes and planting. From her kitchen cum dining room window, she'd be able to see the pond and the birds. A bird bath would complete the setting, she thought. Next time she went to town she'd buy one.

The sound of the phone ringing interrupted her thoughts and she hurried indoors, taking off her gardening gloves as she went.

'Hello?' she gasped as she picked up the phone.

'Elizabeth? Are you all right? Sounds like you're out of breath. I hope you haven't caught this Corona virus - all the deaths so far have been in the elderly.'

'Just run in from the garden,' Elizabeth replied, irked, as usual, by her daughter's use of her given name, rather than "Mum".

'I'm just ringing about your birthday at the end of the month.'

'Oh. Right.' Elizabeth's heart sank at the note of disapproval in Bronwyn's voice.

'Well, I was planning on having a big party, after all, it'll be your sixtieth.'

'Hmm.' Elizabeth didn't need reminding.

'But now, because of these Covid restrictions, we can't travel, so that means we can't come down to you, or you come up here.'

'Oh, dear,' said Elizabeth, trying to hide a sigh of relief.

'And I was intending to have a big surprise birthday party for you, even Dad was going to come! And then treat you to a cruise to New Zealand,' continued her daughter.

'That was a lovely thought,' Elizabeth said, hypocritically. She couldn't imagine anything worse than being at a party with her ex-husband and his new wife and then being trapped on a ship with hundreds of other people. And how was it Bronwyn didn't call her father by *his* given name?

'So, I've postponed the cruise until next year, and in the meantime, I've bought you a subscription to a website where you can trace your ancestry.'

'That's nice dear.'

'Yes, I thought it would be something to keep you occupied during the lockdown. I'll send the details with your birthday card. For heaven's sake, Elizabeth, why did you go and bury yourself

in the countryside? It's so inconvenient! And you've hardly seen Chloë and Alison since you moved ...'

Elizabeth spotted a blue wren in the birdbath; she reached for her binoculars, and barely listened as her daughter continued to lecture her about her failings. Bronwyn was so like her father, Elizabeth thought. Graham had always talked over her, never listened to her opinions. It had been devastating when she'd found out about his infidelities, but since she'd escaped from the city after the divorce, and the death of her mother, she'd never been happier.

She made appropriate noises every time Bronwyn paused.

'Are you listening, Elizabeth?'

'Yes of course ...'

'Well, I'll post your card and all the details of the Ancestry stuff today. I know you love history and the girls would be so interested in their ancestry. I thought you could write it all out for them. They're so busy,' she droned on.

Busy on their iPads and game sites, thought Elizabeth cynically.

'And have you made any friends yet?' Bronwyn's voice rose. *'Really, Elizabeth, you're turning into a recluse. It's not good at your age. You're still young and very attractive. You should go back to that blond rinse in your hair. Darren has several older men friends who're single, they'd be perfect for you. I was going to invite them to your party. You need to move back to Sydney; you won't meet any eligible men down there in the bush.'*

Elizabeth rolled her eyes. 'Well, it's difficult now with all these restrictions.' Perfect excuse she thought. And she liked Bronwyn's husband, Darren, but who was he to determine what kind of man she'd like?

'Hmm. Right, well I'd better go now, I'm on my way to work, lots to do. Love you, bye.'

'Bye dear, love you too.'

Elizabeth put down the phone and resumed watching the blue wren in the birdbath. *In the bush! Eligible men!* She didn't live in the bush, just a small village, and eligible men? She was happy with her own company. 'And yours, of course, Molly.' She smiled and patted her dog. She knew Bronwyn meant well and cared about her mother, but really, she treated her like a child.

Derby, England - 16th October 1817

The men held in Derby Gaol were fed only bread and water. Their trials were delayed until after the harvest season as none of the local farmers could spare the time to serve jury duty during harvest time, particularly after the previous disastrous year. When it seemed as though the men would die of malnutrition, the authorities reluctantly agreed to provide small amounts of meat and vegetables to the prisoners. Their conditions were deplorable, six or seven men crammed in a cell meant for one inmate; unable to lie down, they only had room to sit.

Edward despaired. How would Sarah manage if he was convicted of treason? He couldn't come to terms with what had happened. It had all sounded so feasible. Brandreth had convinced them that the revolt was infallible. His thoughts went around in his head. Few of the inmates spoke; they were each preoccupied with their own problems.

The stench in the cell turned his stomach. Crammed in with the six other men, no privacy, and only one chamber pot between them, it was as much as he could do to keep his ration of bread and water down. There was no room to even lie down, his back and legs were stiff from sitting in one position.

At last, the day of the trials came. All thirty-five prisoners pleaded not guilty. Their families had sold whatever they possessed to pay Mr Cross, a lawyer from Manchester, who had demanded

£100 in advance to represent them. But on the day, Mr Cross was useless in his defence of the prisoners. The prosecution cleverly did not charge Thomas Bacon at that point, even though he was one of the ringleaders. Bacon would have mentioned Oliver and revealed the whole plot by the establishment.

The three other leaders of the revolution, Jeremiah Brandreth, Isaac Ludlam, and Edward's brother, William, were all found guilty of High Treason and condemned to be hanged, drawn and quartered.

The remaining prisoners, including Edward and his nephew, Manchester Turner, were told if they pleaded guilty their sentences would be reduced. Of those men who did plead guilty eleven were sentenced to transportation for life, three were sentenced to transportation for fourteen years and the rest were jailed and forced to serve hard labour.

On the seventh of November – the day of the executions – a detachment of the Enniskillen Dragoons was present to stop any vehicles from passing the gallows; the authorities were afraid there would be an attempt to rescue the three men.

The other prisoners were taken to the gallows and forced to watch the executions. At the last minute, the sentence was changed from being hung, drawn and quartered to that of hanging and beheading. On hearing his brother's last words: "*This is all Oliver and the Government, the Lord have mercy on my soul*", Edward screamed and collapsed in a fit and was carried away.

The bodies of the three men were cut down from the scaffold while still half alive and thirty minutes later, Brandreth's cap was removed and his neck pressed against the block, his still open, bulging eyes faced the crowd. The executioner raised his axe and struck. Brandreth's head was not immediately severed from his body, causing the crowd to groan in horror. Then an assistant with a knife finished the task. Brandreth's head was held up by his hair and waved in front of the crowd.

'Behold the head of a traitor, Jeremiah Brandreth,' shouted the assistant.

Isaac Ludlam's and William Turner's bodies received the same gruesome treatment.

The rest of the prisoners, sick to their stomachs from witnessing this hideous scene, were returned to Derby gaol, and from there, eleven of the fourteen who were awaiting transportation were sent to the port of Sheerness near London and incarcerated in the hulks of old war ships, to await the arrival of the convict ship, *The Tottenham.*

Edward Turner, along with three other prisoners, was too ill to be sent with the others. Only when well enough, and when they were considered free from any infection which could be passed on to the other convicts, were they moved to the prison hulk, *Retribution,* until the arrival of the next convict ship.

On the hulks, each morning at seven o'clock, after a breakfast of boiled barley the prisoners were put into irons, taken ashore and set to work labouring, each group of men overseen by a brutal guard who took advantage of the slightest opportunity to beat the men with the heavy club he carried.

The men returned to the ship for the midday meal – a scant serving of stale bread and mouldy cheese – after which they were taken back ashore to resume their work. At night they received the same meal, except for meat days, when a few lumps of beef from tough old animals were boiled with yet more barley to produce a hardly edible soup. The prisoners were then sent below deck and the hatches battened down.

Edward was sickened by the brutality and unnatural acts he witnessed amongst his fellow convicts. On one occasion, in the gloom below, he saw two men molesting a young boy. He couldn't tolerate the sight. He grabbed one of the men and punched him in the jaw; the man fell to the floor, blood coming from his mouth. Immediately Edward was surrounded by an interested crowd of men egging him on. The other man let go the young boy, who hastily pulled up his trousers and disappeared. Someone yelled, 'Let's have some sport!' Edward dropped his hands, scowled and shouldered his way through the gathering crowd. Despite his lack of food and incarceration, compared to most of the starved and puny felons he was still a strong and muscular man; none were prepared to challenge him.

At the end of February, he was lined up with the other inmates for an inspection by Surgeon John William Hallion who was selecting men to take on board his next shipment of convicts. Edward stood straight and tried to look healthy as he knew ship's surgeons only wanted to take convicts who were healthy enough to withstand the voyage to Australia. If there were many deaths and outbreaks of sickness the surgeons would find it difficult to receive their pay for the voyage and their passage home.

It was a relief when, on the fourth of March, along with two hundred and twenty-nine other convicts, he was marched on board the *Isabella*, a brand-new ship of five hundred and seventy-nine tons which had been built on the Thames and was now captained by a Robert Berry. Also on board was a Military guard - a detachment of the forty-eighth regiment under the orders of a Lieutenant Reeve.

Anything was better than being incarcerated in the hulk, Edward thought.

The prisoners were grateful to have been issued with a set of what was called "slops" - inferior quality clothes - as the weather that winter was the coldest in England in living memory. Severe gales and storms delayed the sailing, but on the third of April 1818, the *Isabella* left Spithead, at the entrance to Portsmouth Harbour. Three days out disaster struck - the prison quarters were flooded by the high seas. It took many days for the convicts to get their bedding and clothes dry. It was a wonder none of them died of a chill, Edward thought.

Eleven days later, John Lovett, one of the guards, who had been put in irons due to insolent behaviour, committed suicide by throwing himself overboard while the ship was in full sail. A boat was lowered but Lovett's body was never recovered.

The ship's surgeon, John Hallion was an enlightened doctor, believing that men needed exercise and mental stimulation to prevent their natural inclinations to wickedness. Thus, the men had regular periods of fresh air and exercise, and their quarters were cleaned and disinfected every few days. The addition of lime juice to their rations prevented scurvy.

Edward was plagued by a rash of psora[1] and the coarse cloth of the "slops" made the itching unbearable, but otherwise, he found the voyage was not as horrific as he'd feared. The surgeon asked those who were literate to help other convicts with reading and writing. Edward was happy to be able to do this for the less educated inmates.

There were rumours of a possible mutiny on the voyage. Two prisoners each received thirty-six lashes for concealing knives made from hoop iron.

One of the convicts lost a leg when he was shot by a soldier, but only three of the convicts did not make the journey to Sydney; two died of disease and one of drowning by jumping overboard.

---

1. Psora from the Greek meaning itchy. It's not clear if Edward had what is now known as psoriasis, but there are no further references to his being afflicted with the condition.

Wambecarra - April 2020

Elizabeth wheeled her red bin to the path in front of her gate. Too late, she noticed Merv with his bin, chatting to the man who was now living across the road from her. She'd seen him once or twice in the past few weeks going in and out of his place. Merv waved his walking stick at her and shouted, 'Elizabeth! Come and meet our new neighbour.'

She couldn't pretend not to have heard him; she parked her bin and walked towards Merv.

'Elizabeth, this is Will,' Merv said, gesturing towards the man beside him. 'He's just moved here.'

Will held out his hand. 'Pleased to meet you. Will Barnes.'

Elizabeth gave a slight start at the sight of his outstretched hand. She looked up into a pair of smiling brown eyes.

'Oh, sorry, I keep forgetting we mustn't shake hands now with the Covid restrictions.'

Elizabeth nodded. 'Elizabeth Turner. How do you do?'

Merv sniggered, then turned to Will. 'Elizabeth moved here about two years ago.' He paused, then turned his attention to Elizabeth. 'Mabel and I reckon Will must have paid a lot less for poor old Kathleen's place than you did for yours, Elizabeth, considering how run down it is. Remind me again what you paid for your place, Elizabeth.' He raised his eyebrows.

Elizabeth stared at him. She'd barely spoken to Merv, except for saying "hello" as she passed his house, and certainly hadn't told him how much she'd paid for her house.

Just then an elderly woman appeared across the road with her bin. 'Iris,' bawled Merv. 'Have you met Will, your new next-door neighbour? He was telling us what he paid for Kathleen's place.'

Iris, a tiny white-haired lady, with a dignified stature, walked over to them. 'Not yet,' she quavered. Will looked at Elizabeth and winked.

Elizabeth blinked and gave a weak smile. 'I'd better go,' she said. 'Must take Molly for her walk. Hello, Iris.' She nodded at Iris and started to walk away. She'd just reached her gate when she heard Merv's loud whisper, 'Bit up herself, that Elizabeth. Speaks posh. Doesn't mix with us plebiscites!'

Elizabeth half turned in time to catch Will trying to hide a smile.

Five minutes later, she came out with Molly. To her annoyance, she saw the little group still at Merv's gate. As she approached and was about to move into the road to avoid them, Merv spotted her. 'Ah, Elizabeth,' he shouted. 'I was just telling Will all about Kathleen, the previous owner. Think she passed away before you moved here.'

'Yes,' Elizabeth nodded.

Merv's wife, Mabel, who had joined the group, interrupted. 'Kathleen was a lovely lady, Will. Word was they had a daughter who'd run away to England and they never saw her again. Don't blame her, the old man was a right tartar. Poor Kathleen had a hard time with him; I think it must have been a relief for her when he passed away. That was several years ago, wasn't it Iris?'

'About six, maybe seven.' Iris's face puckered as she tried to remember.

Mabel appeared sad. 'I used to help poor Kathleen, shopping and so on until she had that bad fall and Merv had to call the ambulance. She never came out from hospital. Well, she was over ninety but sharp as a tack.' Mabel sighed. 'I had a key and went and tidied up a bit but we couldn't visit her. The hospital is too far away and Merv can't drive anymore ...'

'Yes,' Iris said, 'she was a lovely lady, so kind and gentle.'

Elizabeth noticed Will looking intently at Iris.

'You've got your work cut out there, I reckon,' Merv said, turning to Will, 'Suppose you want to get it all ready for your wife.'

Will stared at Merv for a second. 'No wife.'

'Ah, well no rush then.' Merv scratched his nose, then continued, 'The old man wouldn't let Kathleen do anything to the place, and after he died, well, I don't think she had the heart. Didn't see any "For Sale" sign go up, so you must have bought it privately, executors sale, deceased estate ...' He cocked his head as if waiting for Will to explain.

Elizabeth made to move on, she'd heard the story about poor Kathleen so many times. 'We'd better keep going,' she said. 'Molly needs her walk.'

'Nice dog.' Will bent to pat the dog.

'She's a bit nervous of men,' Elizabeth said as Molly licked his outstretched hand.

'So, you must have got the house for a good price, Will?' Merv persevered.

'Indeed.' Will straightened. 'Well, I'd better get going too. Lots to do; nice to meet you all.'

Elizabeth smiled to herself. It seemed this Will wasn't going to satisfy Merv's curiosity. Then the smile spread across her face. *She could now inform Bronwyn that a tall, dark, handsome* ***and*** *eligible man had moved in across the road.*

A few days later, out on her front lawn, Elizabeth tried to start her lawn mower. Nothing. Not even a cough. She grimaced, straightened, and raised her eyes to see Will from across the road standing by her gate, his lips moving. She took an earplug from one of her ears. 'Sorry, what did you say?'

'Just wondered if you needed a hand.'

'No, thank you; just trying to start the mower.'

'It's Elizabeth, isn't it?'

She nodded. 'Yes, Elizabeth Turner.'

Will watched for a few minutes, then opened the gate and came into the garden. He patted Molly who'd come ambling over to greet him. 'Hello, Molly.' He indicated the mower. 'Can I try?'

She shrugged. 'If you like.'

'Perhaps it just needs a new spark plug.'

She frowned. 'The mower was in the shed when I moved here. Um, two years ago.'

'May I?' Will moved towards the mower and checked it. He looked up at Elizabeth. 'I'll just get some tools.' He stood and crossed the road to his ute.

Elizabeth frowned as she watched him. She really didn't want to be beholden to a neighbour. She could take the mower to the mower shop in town and get it serviced.

Will returned with a spanner and a few other tools. He bent down and took out the spark plug. 'Looks like it's dead.'

'I'll get a new one next time I go to town,' Elizabeth said.

'I'm just on my way there now, how about I get one for you? And maybe you need new blades,' Will continued, turning the mower onto its side. 'These are pretty blunt.' He took out his mobile phone and took pictures of the mower, then looked up at her as she stood watching him. 'That okay with you?'

Elizabeth straightened her shoulders. 'Thank you, but I can get them myself.'

Will stared at her, then shrugged. 'As you wish, but as I said, I'm going to the mower shop anyway.' He righted the mower and stood up. 'I've had new business cards printed and I'm just taking some to the local shops. And dropping off some stuff at the tip.' He indicated his trailer which contained an old mattress and other rubbish.

She bit her lower lip. 'Well, okay then, if it's not too much trouble. Thank you. Can I give you the money now?'

'Wait 'til I get back.' He smiled at her, took one of his new business cards from his wallet and held it out to her.

She took it. 'Thanks.'

Will studied her then nodded. 'Right. I'll be off then.'

She stood and watched him as he jumped the low gate and went over to his ute. She stared at his card. *All gardening and odd jobs. Nothing too small.* She left the mower and went inside.

She'd nearly said Elizabeth Wright when she'd told him her name. She'd reverted to her maiden name after the divorce; she didn't want to be confused with Graham's new wife, but her mother had still insisted on referring to her as Mrs Wright. 'Don't be ridiculous, Elizabeth,' her mother had said, 'as far as I'm concerned, you're a married woman.' She'd never come to terms with her daughter's divorce.

Elizabeth wondered if she'd been a bit abrupt with this Will. She'd become so used to being aloof around men all her married life that it had become a habit. Graham had been incredibly jealous; he'd been convinced something was going on between her and a violinist in her quartet group. There hadn't been, of course. But her life became very restricted after Bronwyn's birth.

When she'd first moved in a few of the neighbours had called by to introduce themselves, but she'd opened the front door, gone outside and closed the screen door behind her. That way she didn't need to invite them in. 'Don't want my dog to get out,' she'd said as an excuse. Then smiled, and said 'Hello, nice to meet you' and apart from her name, didn't volunteer any information.

Sometimes when walking Molly, she'd pass a neighbour in their garden. She'd smile and say hello and keep walking. Bronwyn kept on at her about making new friends, but she wasn't good at small talk. She'd had enough of that whenever she'd had to go to some function or other with Graham. He'd given up taking her after a few dinner parties when she'd sat, not knowing what to talk about. 'Might as well take a stuffed dummy,' Graham had grumbled more than once. She didn't find it easy to make friends; she'd never felt close to the few acquaintances she'd made in Sydney.

Her neighbours on the other side were a young couple with small children. They were quiet and seemed quite nice; the woman had called around at the start of the pandemic and given Elizabeth a piece of paper with her name and phone number on it. 'In case you need anything,' she'd said. 'Shopping, or anything.'

Elizabeth had been puzzled, then realized the woman considered her as elderly and confined to the house. She'd smiled and murmured her thanks.

That evening, she'd washed her hair and stood in front of the mirror drying it. *Was she elderly?* Her silver-coloured hair framed her face in a page-boy style. She'd gone grey very young. Graham had insisted she had her hair coloured to appear blond, but when she'd gone to live with her mother her hairdresser had said her natural silver colour was beautiful, and not to put any colour in it.

Now, she considered her looks. Graham had always said she was beautiful and she did have nice features, she had to admit. And they did say sixty was the new fifty... She smiled at her reflection. *Get over it, Elizabeth.* She told herself. Who cares anyway?

***

Later that afternoon at the sound of the bell, Molly rushed to the door. Elizabeth opened it to see Will on the doorstep.

He smiled. 'Hi Elizabeth, I've got the parts for the mower. I can fix it now if it's okay with you?'

She gave a slight smile. 'Thank you, Will, I'll just get my purse to pay you.' She turned to the dog who was trying to push past her. 'Molly, go back inside.'

'She's okay,' Will said as he bent to pat her. 'Like her name.'

'I didn't name her. She's a rescue dog.'

'Right. I'll make a start,' Will said. 'Here are the invoices.' He held out the papers.

'Thanks, I'll get the money now.' Elizabeth closed the screen door and disappeared inside. By the time she came out, Will had already changed the blades and the spark plug and got the mower going.

'All good,' Will said, turning off the engine.

'Thank you, Will. This is for the blades and spark plug; how much do I owe you for your time?'

'Why nothing!' Will smiled.

'But I must give you something for your time.'

'Really, it's not necessary.'

Elizabeth hesitated, perhaps it would be churlish just to say thanks and walk away. 'Can I offer you a cup of tea? Or coffee?' She raised her eyebrows then frowned, remembering the Covid restrictions that were in place. 'I think it's all right if we sit outside.'

'A cuppa would be lovely.'

'This way.' Elizabeth led him round the side of her cottage, to a covered outdoor area.

'Nice place you have here.' He waved his hand at the sliding glass doors leading to Elizabeth's kitchen.

Elizabeth nodded and indicated the table and chairs. 'Have a seat,' she said. 'I'll put the kettle on.'

Elizabeth watched him out of the window as she filled the kettle. Instead of sitting, he was walking around the garden looking at the plants. He stopped at the pond for what seemed a long time. Her heart started to thump. The stones were glittering in the sunlight. She thought they must be granite. He couldn't possibly miss them ... what would she say if he asked where she'd got them? She'd have to tell the truth ...

'Lovely garden,' he remarked as she came out with tea things on a tray

'Yes. It was mostly grass when I moved in, apart from the apple and lemon trees. I'm trying to make it bird and bee-friendly. Planted lots of native shrubs.' She knew she was gabbling, trying not to pause and give Will an opportunity to ask about the stones.

'You've done well.'

She placed cups and saucers, sugar and a jug of milk on the table.

She felt Will watching her as she poured the tea.

'Sorry I don't have any biscuits or anything,' she said, 'I rarely have visitors, so don't keep them in.'

'That's okay, I'm not a big biscuit fan, actually.'

Elizabeth picked up her cup, added milk and stirred it. 'Help yourself.' Her pulse slowed. Hopefully, he wasn't going to mention the stones.

'Thanks.'

Elizabeth wracked her brains to think of something to say. There was an uncomfortable silence, then Will indicated the bird bath. 'You're into bird watching?'

Her eyes lit up. 'Yes! It's one of my hobbies.'

He nodded, it seemed he too was trying to think of something to say. He took a sip of tea, then looked up. 'You said "one of my hobbies", what are the others?'

'I play the cello.'

'Oh! Lovely.'

They were both silent for a few minutes, then Will finished his tea and stood up. 'Thank you, Elizabeth. That was good. I'd better get going now. Give me a shout if you need help with anything.'

She got to her feet. 'That's kind of you, Will. But I'm pretty self-sufficient. Thank you for getting the mower going.'

'No probs.'

Elizabeth followed him around the side of the house, Molly at his heels. Will stopped and rubbed the dog's ears. 'Bye Molly,' he called as he walked across the road to his house.

Elizabeth watched him go, then wheeled the mower into the garage. She no longer felt like cutting the grass.

Sydney Cove - 1818

After a journey of nearly seven months, the *Isabella* arrived in Sydney Cove on the fourteenth of September 1818. The convicts were not allowed to disembark until they'd been mustered. *Like an army!* Edward thought. The Governor's secretary, John Campbell, and the Superintendent of convicts, William Hutchinson, boarded the ship and on the quarter-deck, in the presence of the captain and the ship's surgeon, they began the long process of examining each of the two hundred and twenty-seven convicts. Edward waited his turn to be called. It took two days for the information for all the convicts to be recorded and compared with the ship's records.

The Superintendent recording Edward's details peered at him. 'Name?'

'Edward Turner, sir.'

'Date of birth?'

'First of November, 1785, sir.'

'Where were you born?'

'South Wingfield, Derbyshire, sir.'

'Hmm.' Laboriously, the Superintendent wrote down the details. Then looked up. 'And when were you convicted? And what was your sentence?'

Edward replied and then his height was measured and recorded.

The Superintendent glanced at Edward, 'Colour of eyes, dark,' he mumbled to himself as he wrote, 'hair black. What is your trade, Turner?'

'Stonemason,' Edward replied.

Lastly, the Superintendent surveyed Edward. 'Any distinguishing marks? Birthmark, old scars?'

Edward shook his head. 'No.' Then he was taken aback when asked how he'd been treated on the voyage. Seeing the glare of the Captain and the Surgeon, what could he say except that he had been treated fairly?

He was even more amazed to be given a complete set of new clothes, a yellow jacket made of inferior quality wool, a pair of canvas trousers, shoes, two cotton shirts and a neckerchief, and a pair of woollen stockings. The stockings he soon discarded when he found they caught on the native grass seeds whose barbs penetrated the skin and were impossible to remove.

Shaved by barbers and in his fresh clothes, he waited on the main deck for his turn to be rowed ashore; he gazed around at the new settlement. Spread out over low windmilled hills, with gardens, slab huts and some stone buildings, the rocky coastline was studded with low scrubby bushes. He thought the new colony might be the same size as Derby, the only large town he knew, except London, where his sojourn had been brief. But Port Jackson as it was now called, appeared more spread out than Derby. Apart from a short stop at Rio de Janeiro, where the prisoners had not been allowed off the ship, indeed they'd been locked below decks, this was his first sight of land since leaving London.

Edward got into one of the rowboats used to take groups of convicts ashore. He settled onto a bench and spoke to one of the oarsmen. 'Been doing this for long?' he asked.

The oarsman made a face. 'Long enough. Worked on the Thames before being transported.'

Edward and the other passengers disembarked at Kings Wharf. Edward managed to cast a quick look at an imposing building, which he later found out to be the Commissariat Store, before being marched to the yard of the Sydney Gaol in George Street. Here he was lined up for inspection by the Governor, Lachlan Macquarie. Together with several other stonemasons Edward filed past the Military Guardhouse and St. Phillip's Church and down to the Government Quarry overlooking Cockle Bay - this was to be his place of work.

He was shown the stone hut that was to be his accommodation. He looked inside and saw two rooms which he would have to share with several other men. Hammocks made from recycled sails and ropes were slung from the walls. Not much room for privacy, he thought.

He had to work in the quarry, close to an area known as The Rocks, from first light until two in the afternoon. It was October and the beginning of summer.

'You'll be assigned to Mr Cureton, who is the Principal Overseer of stonemasons.' Edward was told.

'You're lucky,' one of the gang of seventy-eight masons said. 'Edward Cureton's pretty fair. He was a convict himself and he's a good stonemason.'

'What's his story then?' Edward asked.

'Apparently he was press-ganged into the Dragoons and sent to fight Napoleon in Flanders. Usual story, when they were discharged and returned there was no work and he took to stealing. Well, he had to, he was starving.'

Edward nodded, it sounded like what had happened to his brother, maybe they'd fought together! But at least Willum had made it back to live with their mother and father. 'So what happened?'

'He was caught and sentenced to be hung but then it was commuted to transportation for life.'

Like me! Edward thought.

'Anyways, us masons get one and half times the usual convict rations, because of the hard physical work we do,' the man continued.

Edward appreciated the extra rations. After the long sea voyage, it took him several weeks to regain his strength. He wasn't used to the heat and there was no protection from the merciless sun.

He welcomed Saturday afternoons when they collected their rations from the Government store and spent the rest of the day grinding their wheat into a coarse flour, washing their clothes, and airing their hammocks and blankets.

At least they were in the fresh air, thought Edward, not in the fetid atmosphere of the *Isabella*.

Vegetables were supplied from the Convict Garden near Hyde Park barracks. Edward was grateful for fresh food; he'd had problems with his bowels due to the diet on board.

He scratched his chest; the inferior shirt he'd been provided with itched his skin. But, hopefully, the psora would improve with time.

Now he could cook his food in the cast-iron pots which hung by chains from the chimney of the hut. He watched how the other convicts made their damper – mixing the flour they had ground with water and baked in the ashes of the fire. He thought about his wife, Sarah, as he washed his clothes - work unfamiliar to him. The same with the damper. The first few loaves he'd made were either burnt or uncooked in the middle. He wanted to write to her; ask her how to make bread, and tell her he was safe. He'd heard other men say it was possible for wives to come out to the colony, but he had no means of getting writing paper and ink.

On Wednesdays and Saturdays, Edward, along with other quarry workers were shaved by the barber attached to Hyde Park Barracks. The Saturday shaves were to allow the men to appear clean for church on Sunday.

He discovered his nephew, Manchester Turner had arrived on the ship *Tottenham* and sent to work as an overseer at the building of the Liverpool Hospital. That would be another thing he could write and tell Sarah to cheer her up.

When they'd finished their government work each day, they could then earn money for themselves in other employment. Edward took advantage of this and soon found extra work. He managed to find lodgings with an old childless couple. The man, Henry Bruton, was a constable to the Governor. Edward soon became like a member of the family. He was elated as it meant that he was now able to write to Sarah, asking her to come out to join him, and bring their daughters and other family members. He thought she would survive the long sea voyage. At least as a free settler she wouldn't be subjected to the rigours of convict life. He dreamed of Sarah at night ... she'd been right about her feelings – he should have listened to her ...

***

A year later and Edward had been taken off his work in the quarry and assigned to Dennis Bryan's convict gang, working as a stonemason on some of Sydney's early buildings and infrastructure. He was becoming a respected stonemason and was gradually saving money. The old couple had managed to get him paper and ink; they were impressed with his ability to read and write.

He was grateful to them. The old woman stood looking over his shoulder as he wrote.

'Dunno what those marks mean,' she mumbled.

Edward smiled at her. It seemed a lot of the convicts and emigrants were illiterate. He'd told Sarah food was plentiful, and that after he'd finished his government work, he could earn in one afternoon what it would take him a whole day in England. He'd also told her if she came as a free settler the voyage would be pleasant, and the girls would enjoy it.

He was happy once he'd sent the letter. He realised it would take perhaps four months for the letter to reach Sarah and the same amount of time for her reply to arrive. He counted off the months as they passed and his savings mounted, but after a year and still no word from her, he despaired of ever seeing her and his daughters again. He went on his knees and prayed every Sunday for their souls and that they were healthy. But he missed Sarah, missed lying with her ... He'd been sure his wife would want to come to the colony to be with him. He wondered how his daughters were, they'd be starting to grow up, becoming women. He sighed.

WAMBECARRA - JULY 2020

One night, a few months after Will's visit, the sound of Molly's noisy breathing woke Elizabeth. She jumped out of bed and ran to the dog, who was panting and not her usual self. 'Molly?' she asked, 'What is it, Molly?' The dog tried to get to her feet, but her back legs gave way. *A tick!* Elizabeth checked Molly every evening for ticks, maybe she'd missed one. She ran to her phone and rang the vet in town. She got an answering machine giving a number for after-hours emergencies. Trembling, she dialled the emergency number and explained the situation.

'Bring her in immediately,' the vet on duty said and gave her the address.

Elizabeth hurried to the garage, reversed her car out into the driveway, opened the gates and went to get Molly. She bent down and tried to lift her dog, but then realised she wasn't strong enough to lift the lifeless Molly. There was no way she'd be able to get her into the car. She panicked. *What to do?* Suddenly she thought of Will. She ran to the fridge where she'd put his card. Her hands shook as she punched in his number, praying he'd answer.

After what seemed like ages, a sleepy voice said, 'Hello.'

'Will, it's Elizabeth Turner from across the road. Would you help me, please? My dog is sick, I think it's a paralysis tick. I have to take her to the vet in town. Could you help me lift her into the car?'

'Of course. Be right there.'

Elizabeth breathed a sigh of relief. She suddenly realised she was still in her nightdress. Hurriedly pulling on jeans and a cardigan over her night clothes, she rushed to the front door and as she opened it, saw Will striding across the road, doing up his jacket.

'She's in my bedroom, in her bed,' said Elizabeth, heading inside. Will followed her.

When he saw Molly, he bent down and stroked her head. 'It's all right, Molly, you'll soon be better,' he spoke soothingly as lifted her up into his arms. 'I think I'd better come with you,' he said as he carried her out to the car. 'I'll sit in the back with her.'

Elizabeth nodded and opened the car door. Will ducked down and slid in the back seat, cradling Molly in his arms. 'Do you know the way?'

Elizabeth was about to start the engine when she realised that she didn't know the exact address of this emergency vet. 'Um ... actually no ... I'll get the directions on my phone, thanks, Will.'

Elizabeth started the engine and turned on the headlights. The twenty-minute drive in the dark seemed to take forever, her instinct was to drive fast, but she didn't want to jerk Molly in the back. In the rear-view mirror, she could see Will gently stroking Molly's head and heard him murmuring reassuringly to her.

At the surgery as she parked, Will said, 'jump out and get the vet. I'll wait here, we don't want to disturb Molly more than necessary.'

Elizabeth obeyed, and a few minutes later returned with the vet, who took one look at Molly and said, 'Bring her in. Can you manage?'

Will nodded. 'I think so.' Elizabeth held the car door open as Will slid out, cradling Molly in his arms.

'I'm Andrew,' the vet said over his shoulder, leading the way into the surgery. 'Bring her in here. Lay her on the table.'

'I'm Will, and this is Molly.' Will gently placed the dog on the examination table.

Elizabeth stood silent, her arms folded tight across her chest, as she watched Andrew examine Molly. He removed her collar and felt around. 'Here we are,' he said. 'Classic place ticks love. Under the dog's collar.' He used his thumb and forefinger nails to expertly remove the tick. 'I know I should use the tick removal tool,' he grunted, 'but by the time I get it I've lost the spot ...'

Elizabeth bit her lip. She could see Will looking at her. She thought for a moment he was going to come and put his arms around her. She moved slightly away from him.

Andrew peered at Will. 'Can you check her for any ticks still on her? I'm going to give her an injection of anti-venom and then put her on a drip. She'll have to stay here for a few days, I'm afraid.'

Will nodded. He went to Molly and started to explore all around her neck and ears.

'I checked her last night,' Elizabeth said tearfully. 'I do it every night when we've been out walking in bushy areas, but it's winter, I didn't really expect that ticks would be around.'

Andrew grimaced. 'Any time of the year, unfortunately, and it's easy to miss them, especially when they're very small.' He smiled, as he pinched up the skin on Molly's back and inserted the syringe. 'Don't beat yourself up about it. She's going to be all right. You're doing a good job keeping her fit, and not over feeding her.'

Elizabeth nodded. 'Thank you,' she managed to whisper.

'Now, you two just go home. The vet nurse is on her way here. Nothing you can do. Leave your name and telephone number. We'll ring you with any news.'

Elizabeth hesitated. She didn't want to leave Molly.

Andrew noticed this. 'It's best you go,' he said.

'Come, Elizabeth,' Will said, taking her arm.

Reluctantly she followed him to her car. He held open the driver's door for her and they drove back in silence. Elizabeth parked the car in front of her garage and got out, as did Will. She turned to him. 'Thank you Will,' she said and burst into tears.

Will put an arm around her. 'Come over to my place, I'll make us coffee.' Gently he guided her across the road, unlocked his front door and led her through to the kitchen.

'I'm so sorry,' Elizabeth sobbed. 'I'm just so upset. She's my first dog. I always wanted a dog when I was growing up, but my mother wouldn't have one, said they were too much work, making a mess everywhere. And then my husband, ex-husband that is, doesn't like dogs.' She gulped and wiped her eyes. 'After my divorce, I moved back in with my mother to care for her when she had a stroke. She died three years ago.' She sniffled and took a breath. 'I was anxious to move out of the city. When I was young my parents used to come to Kiama for holidays. I always loved this area, so I decided this was where I wanted to be. I found this place and the first thing I did was go to thc animal rescue place. As soon as I saw Molly, I knew she was meant for me.' She was overcome with a fresh bout of tears. 'Sorry, Will,' she managed to say. 'I didn't mean to blab all that out and bore you.'

'You're not boring me.'

Elizabeth took another deep breath and blew her nose. 'Sorry.'

'Sit down.' Will indicated the kitchen table and chairs as he moved to the kitchen sink and started to fill a kettle.

Elizabeth sniffed, her gaze fixed on her hands then she raised her eyes and became aware of the kitchen. 'I think this house must have been built at the same time as my place,' she remarked in a shaky voice, 'the layout seems similar to how mine was before I made changes.'

He put two mugs of coffee on the table. 'Help yourself to milk and sugar.' After a pause, he continued, 'Your place seems very nice from what I could see.'

'Yes,' Elizabeth replied. 'When I moved in, I had renovations done, knocked out the wall between the lounge room and the kitchen dining room and put that big glass sliding door to the back garden. I could give you the plans if you like. I think you might be able to do a lot of the work yourself.'

'That would be great. Thanks.'

Elizabeth frowned at her mug, stirring milk into it. She was silent.

Will studied her. 'The vet said Molly's going to be fine.'

She nodded, just as her mobile phone rang. She snatched it up. 'Yes?' There was a pause. Her face lit up. 'Thank you. Yes. Of course. Thank you again.'

She turned off the phone and smiled at Will, her face aglow. 'That was the vet. Molly's comfortable and they think everything will be ok. I'm to ring again this evening.'

'Great news,' Will smiled.

She finished her coffee and stood up. 'Thanks, Will. And for the coffee.'

'No probs.'

Elizabeth moved towards the front door. 'Thanks again, Will. I'll look out those plans for you. Bye for now.' She walked across the road and as she paused at her front door she turned back to see Will watching her. She gave a slight wave and went inside.

***

Elizabeth was surprised to see Will standing on the porch when her doorbell rang later that evening.

'Just came to ask how Molly is,' he smiled.

'Much better, thank you, she's out of danger.'

'That's great news. Right, okay, well, great.' He paused and half turned to go.

'Thank you, again Will.'

'Called earlier, but I could hear music being played; it was very nice. I didn't want to interrupt you.'

'Thank you, my cello.' She hesitated, not wanting to seem rude. 'Er, would you like to come in? I usually have a glass of wine about this time.'

He seemed a bit surprised. 'Thanks, that would be nice.'

She held the door open while he took off his boots and followed her through the hallway and into the kitchen.

'Red or white?' she asked, 'I'm sorry I don't have any beer to offer you.'

'Red wine would be lovely.'

'Please, sit down.' Elizabeth indicated a kitchen chair, then fetched wine glasses. She poured red wine into two glasses. 'Some nibblies, nuts?' she said, going to a pantry.

She came back with a dish of nuts and sat opposite him. She lifted her glass. 'Thanks again, Will.'

'No probs.' There was an awkward silence, then he said, 'have you been playing the cello for long?'

'Since I was eight,' Elizabeth was relieved to be able to answer. 'I studied music. I was in a string quartet until I got married ...' her voice trailed away and she looked down at her glass.

'But you still kept playing?'

'Yes and no. My husband didn't like me being out in the evenings, and that's when most concerts take place. And then when our daughter was born it became impossible.' She sat, apparently deep in thought until Will lifted his glass.

'Cheers. Here's to Molly's complete recovery.'

Elizabeth came out of her reverie and lifted her glass, 'Yes, cheers, Will, and thank you again for coming to my rescue.' She tried to think of something else to say. 'Um, you like classical music too?'

Will shuffled in his chair. 'Well, I don't really know. I've never really listened to it.' He paused. 'But I liked what you were playing.'

Elizabeth smiled. 'It's one of my favourite pieces.'

'I'm afraid my musical education is sadly lacking.' He made a face.

Elizabeth thought he seemed uncomfortable. 'There's lots of information on the internet these days.'

'Yes, where would we be without it?' Will finished his wine and stood up. He surveyed her kitchen. 'Your kitchen is very nice – what you've done to it.' He smiled. 'Thanks for the wine, Elizabeth. Please let me know when Molly's coming home and I'm happy to come with you and carry her.'

'Thanks, Will. That would be great.' She followed him to her front door and watched while he put on his boots. She could see the curtains twitching at the house across the road, next door to Will's. *This would set old Iris wondering.*

'See you,' Will said.

'Yes.' Elizabeth closed the front door and slowly returned to the kitchen. She rinsed Will's glass and then refilled her own. She went to her favourite chair by the window and focused on the pond. *I must find those renovation plans.*

The next day when her phone rang, she hurried to pick it up, thinking it was the vet.

'Hello Elizabeth, how are you?'

'Fine, thanks, Bronwyn.'

'Just wondered how you were going with the ancestry stuff.'

Elizabeth grimaced. She'd only managed to log in to the site. Hadn't actually done anything.

'So, what have you found out so far?'

'Not a lot, just feeling my way, getting used to it.' Elizabeth wondered should she tell Bronwyn about Molly, then decided not to. Bronwyn didn't like dogs; she'd only make some dismissive remark.

'It's a pity you don't live closer, I could have helped you.'

Elizabeth's attention was diverted by a small bird perched on the bird bath. She turned the phone to speaker, took her binoculars and tried to focus on the bird as her daughter began her usual litany of how silly it had been of her mother to bury herself in the country.

'Are you listening, Elizabeth?'

'Yes dear, of course. Now, tell me, how are you all after the Covid restrictions?'

'They eased weeks ago, I told you.'

'Of course. How the time flies.' Elizabeth wished her daughter would get off the phonc so she could get a proper look at the little bird. 'Well, I'd better let you go, Bronwyn, I know how busy you are.'

'Yes, I am busy, very busy these days.' Bronwyn sounded disgruntled.

'Right, dear. How's Darren?'

'Oh, the same as ever. Seems to spend all his time over at the bank.'

'Oh, right, well I suppose being a bank manager carries a lot of responsibilities ...'

'Hmph.'

Elizabeth smiled to herself; she'd suddenly wondered should she mention the tall, dark, and very handsome man who had moved in across the road, apparently single; he'd said there was no wife and she hadn't seen any women around his place.

'Well, give my love to everyone. Bye for now.' Elizabeth gently pressed the end call symbol on her phone and breathed a sigh of relief. But she'd better look at this family tree stuff, Bronwyn would keep nagging at her, and would probably end up driving down to check on her if she couldn't give a progress report.

The little bird flew away. With a groan, Elizabeth got up and went to the small third bedroom which she had turned into a study and music room. Just as she opened the door her phone rang. It was the vet's surgery to say Molly would be well enough to leave the next day.

Elizabeth immediately sent a message to Will, asking him if the next morning would be convenient to get Molly, maybe nine o'clock.

A message came back straight away to say, yes, he'd come over at nine.

Pleased, Elizabeth looked around her study. She'd forgotten for the moment the reason why she was there, then she remembered the ancestry stuff. She stared longingly at the cello, but took her laptop and carried it to the kitchen; she resolved to spend at least half an hour at the ancestry website.

An hour later and she had entered her name and date of birth, and that of her parents. She entered her grandparents' names and saw the details appear as a family tree. With a sigh of satisfaction, she sat back. Maybe it could be interesting.

The next day, Will arrived at her gate as she was backing her car out of the garage.

'Good morning,' she smiled.

'Great news,' he smiled back.

'Yes, I can't wait to have Molly back home. Jump in,' she said, stopping her car outside the garage.

'Want me to close the gates?'

'No, it's okay, we won't be long. Thanks, Will.'

They were both silent on the drive to the vet. Then Elizabeth suddenly spoke. 'Have you managed to get much work, Will? You mentioned you were looking for handyman work around the area.'

'Yes, I seem to be getting enough to keep me busy. And now I've got the outside of the house tidy, I'm going to start on the inside.'

'That's good.' She'd noticed him moving all the stones from his driveway, making numerous trips with a wheelbarrow round the back of the house.

Elizabeth was overjoyed to see her dog. Tears filled her eyes as she got down on her knees to hug Molly.

'She'll be a bit weak for a few days,' the vet told her, as Molly tried to stand and wag her tail.

'I'll carry her out to the car,' Will said, waiting while Elizabeth paid the vet.

In the back seat of the car, Molly rested her head on Will's lap; she half-closed her eyes as he rubbed her ears.

He's kind, Elizabeth thought. She wondered what she could get him as a little thank you gift.

Back at her house, Elizabeth opened the door of the car for Will to get out, then hurried to unlock the front door.

"Where will I put Molly?'

'In the kitchen.' Elizabeth gave a half-smile. 'She has a bed there as well as in my bedroom. I guess she's a bit spoilt.'

'Not at all. Just a lucky dog.' Will gently lowered Molly onto her bed in the kitchen and stood up. 'I'd best be off then.'

'Would you like a cup of coffee?' Elizabeth invited.

'Love one, but I have a job this morning. Perhaps a rain check?'

She felt her face grow warm. 'Yes, of course.' She went with him to the door. 'Thanks again, Will.'

'A pleasure.' With a wave of his hand, he strode across the road to his house.

Elizabeth checked on Molly, made herself a coffee, then went to her study to get her laptop, determined to work on the ancestry stuff. She'd just spend half an hour with her cello first to settle herself, then get going with this family tree stuff. After all, it had been a traumatic few days.

She played her favourite sonata, then feeling calmer, sighed, put away her cello, picked up her laptop and took it to the kitchen.

An hour later, she'd managed to display her paternal grandfather, William Turner, who she could remember and when he'd died. The website displayed an Edmund Joseph Turner as the father of her grandfather, born in 1862, to Edmund Turner and Annie Marchant. She went onto the NSW births, deaths and marriages and searched for an Edmund Turner. After some toing and froing, she was pretty sure that this Edmund Turner was the son of an Edward Turner and an Ann Cawson.

Tired from sitting at her laptop and concentrating, she stretched and decided to stop for a break and take Molly for a walk. But it was getting interesting ...

***

The evening after Molly's return from the vet, when Elizabeth saw Will's ute in his driveway, she walked over to his house and rang the bell.

'Plans,' she said, holding them up when he answered the door. 'I've brought them over for you. I think it would be pretty straightforward to apply to the council to do the same as I did. You only need to copy the plans and change the name and address.'

'Great!' Will smiled, holding open the door. 'Come in.'

'Um, well, I left Molly at home. She's still a bit weak.'

'Just for a minute.'

'Okay.' Elizabeth stepped over the threshold and held out the plans.

'Is it all right if I photocopy them and then perhaps, we could discuss them another time?'

Elizabeth smiled. 'Of course.'

'I'll take good care of them,' he said, as he took the folder.

For some reason, she could feel herself blushing. 'No, problem, Will. Um, well, I'd better get back to Molly. Thanks again, Will.'

As he held the door for her, she suddenly remembered she'd meant to get him a small thankyou gift for helping her with Molly. Perhaps he'd like a CD of cello music ... she'd order one online.

***

She was so engrossed in her research, that when her doorbell rang the following Sunday morning, Elizabeth got up with a jolt and was still a bit dazed when she opened the door.

'Oh! It's you!' she exclaimed.

Will seemed surprised and took a step back. 'Sorry to disturb you.' He straightened his shoulders, held out a folder and turned to leave. 'I was just returning your house plans.'

'Oh, Will, I didn't mean it like that, I was miles away, sorry. Um, do come in.'

Will bent to pat Molly, who had come rushing out at the sound of the doorbell. 'Miles away?' he queried.

'Back in the nineteenth century.' She led the way to the kitchen and her open laptop. 'My daughter bought me a subscription to an ancestry website and I think I'm descended from a convict. I was just reading the history of the Pentrich Revolution.'

'Goodness,' Will exclaimed, glancing at the laptop screen.

'Would you like to read about it? I'll put the kettle on and make a pot of tea.'

'Great. Thanks, sounds interesting.' Will took a pair of reading glasses from the top pocket of his shirt and sat in front of Elizabeth's laptop.

He read, absentmindedly rubbing Molly's ears as she lay slumped against his legs.

Elizabeth studied him as she made tea and brought the cups to the table; she sat opposite him. 'What do you think?'

He shook his head. 'This is appalling; that the English would have set that William Oliver to lie and encourage those men to rebel. Horrible. And the circumstances that led up to the rebellion. I'd never heard of Mount Tambora and the year of no summer. Don't they mean Krakatoa?'

'No, apparently Tambora happened before the days of telegraphs so the news didn't get through for several years. Ships actually sank from the weight of the ash that was spewed out. It was far more catastrophic than Krakatoa.'

Will looked up. 'Wow! But how did you come to be descended from Edward Turner?'

'It was lucky he wasn't executed like the rest. I'm still researching the whole story. I think I'm descended from his son Edmund. I found a death record for an Edmund Turner, who died in Inverell in NSW in 1874, and his parents were Edward and Ann Turner. I couldn't find a marriage certificate for Edmund, but my great, um,' she consulted her records, 'great, grandfather's birth record shows an Edmund Turner and an Annie Marchant as his parents. I think it has to be him.' Her eyes shone. 'It's fascinating.'

'It must be,' he said slowly. 'I'd like to know more about my ancestors.'

'Maybe I can look them up for you.'

Will shifted in his chair. 'Another time, perhaps,' he murmured.

Elizabeth observed him more closely. He seemed a little uncomfortable. Thinking it best to change the subject, she enquired, 'How did you go with the house plans?'

'Yeah, all good. I photocopied yours and you were right, my place is a replica of your original house. I changed the name and address, and aspect and submitted them to the council. Hopefully, it won't be too long before I hear back.' He smiled at her then studied his hands. 'I was wondering perhaps if you would help me choose colours for the paintwork and furnishings ...' He raised his eyes. 'I'm great with garden design and plants but with interiors, well, it's a different story.'

'Love to!'

'Thanks, Elizabeth. You've really helped me,' he stood. 'I didn't know what to do with the house but you've motivated me to make a start.' Elizabeth also stood as he held her glance until she dropped her gaze.

'A pleasure,' she mumbled.

'Right! I'll let you get back to your what? How many great, great grandfathers?'

'About four, I think. I must check.' She smiled. 'I had no idea about this family line.'

Will took a deep breath. 'It's nice, you can trace your lineage back that far.' He moved towards the front door followed by Molly. 'Bye Molly.' He bent to pat the dog.

'Bye Will,' Elizabeth echoed as she closed the door after him. She leaned against the closed door and frowned. Will had been a bit strange when she'd suggested she could help him trace his ancestors. She shrugged, then returned to the kitchen and shut down her laptop. 'Time for walkies, Molly.'

As she walked out her gate, she spotted Merv, sitting on his porch. He got up when he saw her and was at his gate as she walked past.

'I see you've become very friendly with the new neighbour,' he winked at her and cackled. 'Getting on well with him, by the look of it.'

Elizabeth stiffened. 'Yes, he seems nice and helpful.' She moved on.

Behind her back, Merv made a rude gesture.

***

It was a few weeks later, in September when the CD she'd ordered arrived. She wrapped it and that evening when she saw Will's ute in his driveway, she clipped the lead on Molly and walked across the road. It was early Spring and the evenings were getting brighter. She intended to leave the CD in Will's letter box, but as she crossed the road to his house, his front door opened and Will appeared. 'Oh!' he exclaimed, 'Hello, Elizabeth, were you coming to see me? I was about to check my mail.'

Elizabeth held out the package. 'I was just going to pop this in your letterbox.'

'Oh?'

'Just a little gift to thank you for all your help with Molly and the vet.'

'It was a pleasure to be able to help. Eh, Molly?' He took the small package, then bent and stroked the dog's head.

'Won't you come in?' Will said as he moved to check his letter box.

Elizabeth scanned the other houses in the street.

Will followed her glance and laughed. 'I don't think the neighbours are watching.'

Elizabeth cursed her fair skin, as she felt her cheeks get hot. 'I'm just about to take Molly for a walk.'

'Just for a moment? I wanted to show you the paint cards I've got and get your advice.'

'Of course. Is it all right to bring Molly?'

Will went towards Elizabeth and took the dog's lead from her hand. 'Come on Molly.'

'Molly seems to like you,' Elizabeth said as Molly trotted after Will without a backward look. 'Usually, she's nervous of men.'

Inside the house, Elizabeth followed Will into the kitchen where he unwrapped the CD and stared at it. She suddenly felt uncertain.

'Um, well you said you liked the piece of cello music I was playing one day when you came over. It's the whole piece. Dvorak's cello concerto. I thought you might enjoy it.'

Will smiled. 'Thank you so much! I'll enjoy listening to it. Have you time for a cup of tea? Or a glass of wine? I'll put the CD on.'

She nodded. 'Well, I really shouldn't stay.'

'Just a few minutes?'

'All right, then. Thanks, a glass of wine would be lovely. White if you have it.'

'Great. Sit down while I get my laptop. I don't have a CD player anymore.'

Elizabeth sat and watched as he went out of the kitchen, followed by Molly. He returned, set up the laptop and inserted the CD, then filled two glasses with wine and sat opposite her.

The sound of music filled the room. After the first movement, Will paused the CD. 'We should sit somewhere more comfortable to listen,' he said.

Elizabeth blinked and started to stand. 'I ... I'd better take Molly for her walk ...' she mumbled at the same time as Will continued, 'outside on the veranda, now I've got some comfy chairs.'

Elizabeth felt the heat rush to her face. She'd stupidly jumped to the conclusion that "somewhere more comfortable", meant, well, meant what? Snuggling up on the sofa?

He must have seen her discomfort for he bent down to clip Molly's lead on. 'Thank you for the CD, I'll enjoy listening to it. I know Molly likes her evening walk.' He smiled and handed her the lead. 'It's always nice to see you, Elizabeth. And Molly.' He walked with them to the front door.

Outside Will's house, Elizabeth walked briskly down the road, her cheeks burning. How could she have thought he meant anything by "sitting somewhere more comfortable." For goodness sake, she was much older than him ... she must be losing it ...

***

The next evening, when her doorbell rang, Elizabeth opened the door to see Will with paint cards in his hand. He held them out to her and smiled.

'Come in Will.' She led him to the kitchen.

'Sorry, I'm interrupting you.' He indicated the open laptop on the kitchen table.

'I've been reading more about my ancestor, Edward Turner after he was arrested. Would you like to read it?'

Will nodded as he sat at the table; he took his reading glasses from his pocket and looked at the screen, then he started to read about the trial and the beheading of Brandreth and the other two men.

'That was pretty brutal,' Will took off his glasses and watched Elizabeth, who was placing two glasses of wine on the kitchen table.

'Yes, and Edward, along with ten others, was offered a plea bargain that if they pleaded guilty their lives would be spared and their charge commuted to transportation for life to Australia.'

'So they came to Australia?'

'Yes, but first those who were fit enough were sent to a prison hulk, *Retribution,* which was docked at Sheerness to wait for the next ship to Australia.'

'Prison hulk?'

'Yes, they were decommissioned sailing ships, mostly from the Napoleonic wars, used as floating prisons. There are different accounts but it seems the prisoners were kept in appalling conditions.' Elizabeth grimaced and shook her head. 'I don't know if I would have been able to bear it.' Her face darkened. 'I imagine the women convicts would have been subjected to the same fate.'

Will was silent.

Elizabeth studied him. He seemed far away, a slight frown on his face.

To change the subject, she showed him a letter she'd found online. 'Look, I discovered this letter that Edward's eighteen years old nephew, Manchester Turner, wrote to the Derby Mercury. His name was actually Joseph, but he was called Manchester because he'd been working there, and to distinguish him from some of his relations, who were also called Joseph Turner.' She turned the laptop towards her and pressed a few keys, then read out:

'We are put in irons and go out to work; we were told our sentence on Tuesday night by the chaplain of our ship. We have barley and oatmeal night and morning and beef for dinner four days a week and the other days, bread and cheese. There is a school and chapel in the hulk which are regularly attended and it is far from being a reprobate place as we were led to believe at Derby, for, if a person is inclined, every encouragement is allowed him to improve his morals.'

Will's brows drew together. 'That smacks of censorship! I can't imagine an eighteen-year-old boy being inclined to improve his morals ...'

Elizabeth considered. 'Hmm, perhaps you're right.' She didn't know anything about eighteen-year-old boys, the thought of the letter being censored hadn't occurred to her.

'And why would he write to the Derby Mercury? I could understand him writing something like this to his mother, to reassure her that he was okay ...' Will looked up at Elizabeth, then at his watch and smiled. 'I'd better go before it gets dark. Don't want Merv to have a heart attack!'

Elizabeth flushed.

'Sorry, Elizabeth, have I embarrassed you?'

'No, no, not at all,' she lied. To cover her confusion, she picked up the paint cards. 'I really need to see the rooms and furnishings to decide on paint colours.'

'I should have thought of that,' Will replied. 'The furniture and furnishings are all old.' He frowned and stood. 'They were in the house when I moved in.'

'I could come over tomorrow...' Elizabeth hesitated. 'Or another day.'

'Tomorrow would be good. Okay, I'll be off then.' He walked towards the front door.

'Bye, Will.' Elizabeth closed the door behind him and leaned against it. Will was right. *Why would young Manchester Turner write to the Derby Mercury?*

***

'Did you discover anything more about Edward Turner?' Will asked as he followed Elizabeth into his kitchen.

Elizabeth put the paint cards on the kitchen table. 'Yes, quite a lot. A letter from him to his wife. It was printed in the Caledonian Mercury in 1820. Would you like to read it?'

'Yes, indeed.' He smiled at her. 'I'm getting quite hooked on your family history stuff.'

'Well, why don't we go back to my place and you can read all about it.' She was amazed by her temerity at giving the invitation.

Will grinned. 'That will give the neighbours something to gossip about! In broad daylight!'

Elizabeth hadn't thought of that, but then she laughed. 'Yes, Merv keeps an eye on you and Iris keeps an eye on me.'

'Oh, my next-door neighbour, little Iris! I think she's still slightly suspicious of me. She's probably afraid I'll start keeping goats! Or performing some kind of voodoo rituals.'

Elizabeth had to admit to herself that she'd been a bit taken aback the first time she'd noticed him across the road. Now, she saw him regarding her, his eyebrows raised. She wondered if he'd read her thoughts. To lighten the moment, she suddenly said, 'Yes! Shall we go arm in arm to really set the tongues wagging?'

Will laughed. 'No, let's save it for another time.'

Elizabeth gave an inward sigh of relief. She'd only been joking and was glad Will hadn't taken her remarks seriously. They made their way across the road.

After a joyous reception from Molly, Elizabeth led the way to her kitchen.

'I'll just fire up my laptop. Have a seat,' Elizabeth indicated a chair at the kitchen table. When she had the details of the letter on the screen, she turned it towards Will. 'Glass of wine?'

'That would be lovely.' Will put on his reading glasses, and read:

Sydney, New South Wales, June 23, 1819

Dear Wife,

We have had a pretty good passage, and have been middling well treated; much better than the general run of those that were with us. We are all much disappointed in not having our freedom on our arrival, as was promised us. I am working for Government from daylight, till two o'clock in the afternoon; after that time I work for myself, and can earn as much as I could get for a whole day in England; therefore, was I on my own hands, I could get a very pretty living. I am very well, considering my situation, as I live with an old man, who is constable to the Governor, and his woman; they treat me as one of themselves. Indeed I have partly agreed with them for a thirty acres farm.

Now, my dear wife, if you wish for us to meet again and end our days in happiness, let me advise you to apply to the Secretary of State, to give you an order for a passage to this country free of all expense, and I shall be restored to you on your arrival.

If it be agreeable to my brother, Joseph, to apply likewise to come as a settler, I should much urge him to it. He would be granted a farm, and provisions from the stores for six months; but however; he would not want that and he would be able to gain a little fortune in a few years as our business is one of the best in the country and farming is good.

The natives are very slender people, Swedish Iron is six pence a pound, sheet one shilling and three pence. If you can get the works of any eight day clock, it will fetch a good price here.

We are building a Methodist chapel and I am engaged for the cutting of the stone. The stone of the country is remarkable white, and works kindly.

We have plenty of fruit; peaches in abundance; lemons and oranges and quantities of vegetables.

The passage is nothing to what it used to be as they reach us in about four months; very few die in passage. Enquire for me at John Dow's near Government Stores, Sidney NSW.[1]

Edward Turner

Elizabeth busied herself with the wine, then put two glasses on the table and sat beside Will, who had gone silent. 'What do you think?'

Will appeared puzzled. 'Isn't that a bit strange?'

'What?'

'The Caledonian Mercury. I thought Caledonia was Scotland. And didn't Edward's family live in Derbyshire? Wasn't that where the trial was held? Derby?'

'That's a point, I hadn't thought of that. Wait, let me check where the Caledonian Mercury was published.'

Elizabeth turned the laptop to face her and quickly typed in a Google query. After a few minutes, she smiled. 'You're right. Look at this.'

---

1. Extract of a letter received by the Caledonia Mercury 24th January 1820

Will read aloud, '*Founded in 1720 and published 3 times a week in Edinburgh, the Caledonian Mercury focused on news of local affairs*.' He took off his glasses and rubbed his eyes. 'Focused on **local** affairs! A letter from a convict in Australia to his wife in Derby isn't exactly local. At least I don't think Derby is near Scotland. I only have a vague idea where Derby is but I think it's somewhere in the North of England.'

Elizabeth turned to the laptop and started typing. 'Look,' she read, '*Derbyshire is a county in the East Midlands of England*. This is strange!' She frowned. 'Well, I've ordered a book about the Pentrich Revolution. It might throw some light on the subject.'

'And why would a wife who hadn't seen her husband for two years give the first letter she'd received from him from the other side of the world to a Scottish newspaper? That's really weird.'

They stared at each other. 'I'd like to read the book when you get it,' Will picked up his glass of wine. 'So, what happened to Edward's wife, Sarah?'

'I'm not sure but I read somewhere the Duke of Devonshire, who owned most of Pentrich, evicted the wives and families of the revolutionaries and demolished some of their homes,' Elizabeth said. 'But Edward lived in South Wingfield, I don't know if she stayed on there.'

Will shook his head in disbelief. 'It just gets worse.' He frowned. 'Maybe his wife never got the letter, if she'd been evicted.' He lifted his glass to Elizabeth. 'Cheers.'

'Cheers.' Elizabeth studied her glass of wine. 'Hmm, perhaps. But in those small villages where the postman knows everyone – at least, from TV shows that I've seen – surely the postman would know where to deliver the letter?'

'It certainly seems strange,' Will agreed. 'So, what happened to Edward after he arrived in Australia?'

'Well, it seems he prospered in Sydney. Apparently, because they were not the common run of convicts, that is, they were educated, hard-working and religious, and also had trades, the Pentrich men were treated better than felons. I must do more research.' She smiled at Will. 'I'm getting quite obsessed with this family history stuff.'

Will stared into his glass. 'Yes, indeed.'

Elizabeth's brow creased. She didn't like to pursue the issue of helping him with his ancestors. Time to change the subject. 'What about those paint cards?'

'Oh, yes, I'd forgotten about them in the excitement of your discoveries.' Will smiled at her. 'It's getting late now. How about coming over and having a bite with me on Saturday evening and we can look at them then. And bring Molly, of course.'

Elizabeth felt herself colouring. 'Why yes, that would be lovely!' *and this time she wouldn't be stupidly misinterpreting Will's intentions.*

Will stood, 'I'll be off then. Thanks for the wine.'

'A pleasure. You've given me lots to think about!' She accompanied him to the front door. 'See you on Saturday.'

Will waved a hand in acknowledgement as Elizabeth shut the door and leaned against it for a few seconds. Then she took a deep breath, walked to the kitchen, rinsed Will's glass and refilled her own.

She sat at the window watching the gathering dusk as she sipped her wine and reflected on the evening. Will was smart. She never would have thought of questioning the letter purportedly from Edward. She sighed, still cringing inwardly at the memory of her reaction to Will's suggestion of sitting somewhere "more comfortable".

What was wrong with her? She could see now how her domineering mother and hen-pecked father hadn't helped her self-confidence.

She'd loved her father but most of the time after their evening meal, he'd retire to his so-called study, and listen to classical music on his record player. The only time she could remember him going against his wife was when Elizabeth wanted to study music.

'What nonsense!' her mother had cried, when Elizabeth said her music teacher wanted her to apply for a scholarship to the Sydney Conservatorium of music. 'How will that find her a husband with money? She'd probably marry a poor violinist! No! She must go to a secretarial school, become someone's Personal Assistant!'

Elizabeth had winced at this but her father had stood up to her mother. At what cost she often thought.

When she'd met Graham, she'd been flattered by his attention; it was the first time in her life someone had said they loved her. Many years later she realised that he'd only pursued her in order to get access to her father's circle of business colleagues. Graham was a property developer and although Henry Turner had never actively helped his son-in-law, his position on the council had given Graham an advantage. And Graham was happy to have a pretty, intelligent wife to accompany him to social functions. He always introduced her as "my wife, Elizabeth, the well-known cello player." Of course, she hadn't been well-known! She played in a quartet, at weddings and the odd evening classical music event.

Elizabeth felt it was the turning point in their marriage when Graham eventually realised Henry Turner had no influence on the council,

It was many years after her marriage that she acknowledged how Graham had isolated her and undermined her confidence. She'd had a suspicion he was being unfaithful, but on the one occasion when she'd drummed up the nerve to confront him, he'd been piously outraged. 'How would I have the time or the opportunity to see another woman,' he'd demanded. 'And I have a wonderful wife who is everything to me.' He'd taken her in his arms and she'd been reassured. Graham had been extra attentive for a few days.

Everything crumbled when his secretary had become pregnant with Graham's child. He'd always wanted a son, but after Bronwyn's birth, Elizabeth had never conceived again.

Elizabeth took another sip of her wine. At the time she'd been devastated; she moved out and went to live with her mother; her father had died several years before. Of course, her mother had blamed Elizabeth. 'You should have been more loving, made more of an effort,' she'd grumbled. 'Instead of being a shrinking violet. Men don't go out for a hamburger when they can have steak at home.' Elizabeth had been startled by her mother's comment. Did she mean Elizabeth obviously hadn't been sexually satisfying? She hadn't wanted to ask.

At least Graham had been generous with the divorce settlement. He wanted to keep the grand house he'd built and she certainly didn't want to stay there. She'd never felt comfortable in its interior designed opulence. She was free to move out of the city and get a dog and have a big garden. But then her mother had had a stroke and she felt obliged to stay and care for her. Now she relished her freedom. Although not well off, she was financially independent, loved her cottage and new way of life. She bent down and patted Molly.

'We love our lives now, don't we Moll?' The dog opened her eyes, thumped her tail and went back to sleep.

She thought about Edward's wife, and the letter in the Caledonian Mercury. Then she hit the side of her head with the heel of her hand. *You dolt!* She exclaimed. *Of course!* She glanced at her watch. Too late to ring Will with her brainwave. She'd tell him on Saturday.

***

The following Saturday Elizabeth waited until after they'd eaten before telling Will her idea.

'That was lovely, thank you, Will.' She smiled. 'Sorry Molly, nothing for you.' She glanced at Molly, who was lying at her feet, drooling.

'It's all right, Molly, see? I have something for you.' Will threw a piece of chicken breast to the dog.

'She inhaled it! I don't think it even touched the sides going down!' Elizabeth laughed. 'Now Will, I had an idea about Edward's letter to his wife. You remember we wondered why it was published in the Caledonian Mercury?'

Will nodded. 'What have you come up with?'

'Well, anyone who has read Regency novels, like those of Georgette Heyer or Jane Austen, would know that at the time, unless it was sent by a polician, it was the person who *received* a letter who had to pay the postage, not the person who *sent* it, and the postage was based on the number of pages and distance covered. Goodness knows what a letter from Australia would have cost, and if Edward Turner's wife was destitute, she would not have been able to pay for it.'

'Hmm,' Will rubbed his chin. 'So perhaps the postal service kept the letter until it reached the end of their run, most likely Edinburgh and sold it to the Caledonian Mercury to recoup the costs.'

Elizabeth's eyes lit up. 'Another mystery solved! We're doing well. And that would explain why Manchester Turner wrote to the Derby Mercury so his mother wouldn't have to pay the postage. This is getting really interesting.'

'Or else his mother couldn't pay and Derby was the end of the post run.' Will smiled. 'More wine?'

'Maybe we should look at those paint samples before I have any more to drink,' Elizabeth responded.

'Okay.' Will started clearing the table.

'Let me help.'

'No, you sit and look at these paint cards. I was going to start on the bedrooms. No point in painting in here until I get council approval and can start knocking down that wall to open up the space like you've done.'

Elizabeth studied the paint cards. 'I'd need to see the rooms first.'

'Go ahead, you know where the bedrooms are, same layout as yours.'

Elizabeth went down the hallway and stood with her back to the front door. The main bedroom was on the right and to the left was the second bedroom. Next to it was a smaller bedroom, which, in her house, she used as a study. Opposite it, and next to the main bedroom was a bathroom and toilet. Further down the hall was the living room to the left and to the right the dining room and kitchen.

She opened the door of the main bedroom and glanced around. It was obviously Will's room. It was neat and tidy, quite spartan actually, she thought. When Will followed her, she remarked: 'This is the same as my bedroom, faces the street. Nice high ceilings. I had the old carpet taken up; lovely timber floors which I had polished.'

Will considered the worn carpet - a depressing grey colour. 'I guess I could do the same. Hire a sander and varnish the floors myself. But I'd need to do that before painting.'

Elizabeth smiled. 'Maybe we should revisit the paint cards after you've done the floors. That's a lot of work. But this is a nice room. It must get the morning sun. My bedroom gets the western sun, makes it quite hot in the evenings.' She turned to Will. 'Lovely antique furniture.' She indicated a carved oak wardrobe. 'That's beautiful.'

Will frowned. 'Hmm, not so keen on old furniture myself, and the wardrobe is too narrow to hang jackets in. My grandfather must have had very narrow shoulders.'

There was a sudden silence.

Elizabeth said nothing, just raised her eyebrows in a silent query as their eyes met.

Will sighed. 'Come into the kitchen. I'd better explain everything to you.' In the kitchen, he put the kettle on. 'Cuppa?'

'Yes please.'

'I'd better start at the beginning.' Will busied himself making tea.

Elizabeth sat at the kitchen table and studied Will. 'You don't have to explain anything, Will, if you don't want to.'

Eventually, he put two cups and saucers on the table. He poured the tea, stirred his, then indicated the milk and sugar and grimaced. 'My mother only told me the full story when she was dying of cancer; that was a few years ago. Apparently, when she was young, she won all these scholarships and her father wanted her to go to University and become a doctor. But she had no interest in medicine and was determined to be a teacher. Her father was a bit of a tyrant and got very angry with her. But mum got a grant and went to teacher training college in Sydney. She spent a year teaching in Sydney. That was the 1960s and England at the time was crying out for teachers. She was twenty-one by then and off she went, to London.'

He scowled. 'Her father was furious. Anyway, she had no problem finding a job, in a disadvantaged part of London. She made loads of friends with other Australians and was having a great time. Then she met my dad,' he paused and smiled. 'Apparently, she was walking back from work – it was winter and pouring rain - when she slipped and fell flat on her face. She made a joke about it, about lying face down in the gutter when a lovely soft voice said "let me help you" and this big black man picked her up as if she was a feather, and suggested they go to a nearby café. She laughed about it, said with her face so dirty, he probably thought she was coloured too!'

'Oh, Will!' Elizabeth said softly as she took one of his hands. She saw his eyes begin to fill with tears.

He gulped. 'Well, Mum said it was love at first sight. They were married a few months later, and then, the following year I was born. Apparently, it was difficult to find places to rent in those days, especially as a lot of the houses had signs up "Room to Let. No Irish. No Coloured." Mum was lucky to get something. She moved in and told them her husband was coming the following week. When my dad turned up it was too late, they couldn't turn her out. They rented two rooms. One had a tiny kitchen in it and they had to share the bathroom with people on the next floor. They were incredibly happy.' He paused. 'I can just remember this big black man coming home from work and roaring, "Where's ma woman? Where's ma chile?" and my mother laughing at his fake accent. He'd pick us both up and swing us around. My mother was so happy!'

'What happened Will?' Elizabeth whispered when Will grew silent.

'He already had a wife in Jamaica, and she wrote that she was coming over to be with him. My mother found the letter. He tried to tell her he'd been too young and it didn't mean anything, it was just a common-law marriage, and he hadn't seen her for years, but my mother wouldn't listen.'

'Oh, Will!' Elizabeth squeezed his hand. 'That must have been devastating for your mother!'

Will nodded. 'Her marriage to my father wasn't legal.' He scowled. 'Which makes me a bastard ...'

Elizabeth shook her head. 'No! Will!'

He looked at her and gave a weak smile. 'Sorry, Elizabeth. I didn't mean to bore you with all this.'

'Will, you're not boring me! What happened next?'

'Well, Mum brought me back to Australia. I was about six by then. She contacted her parents, but they didn't want to know her. At least, her father didn't. Her mother did. I remember just after we came to Australia Mum brought me here to meet them, she thought if they saw me, they'd welcome us both. Her mother came to the door and when she saw us, she shouted, "Oh, Christine!" and opened her arms wide, but then her father appeared, elbowed her mother aside and shouted, "Get out, and take that black bastard with you" and slammed the door.'

He grimaced. 'I thought he said "black basket" and on our way back to the bus I asked Mum what it meant. She just squeezed my hand and said to hurry or we'd miss the train back to Sydney.' He scowled. 'Anyway,' he continued, 'Mum managed to rent a flat in Sydney and got a job teaching in a school nearby, and I went to school there. They called me names, called my mother ...' his voice broke.

Elizabeth felt the hand she held clench into a fist.

He stared at her blankly as she murmured, 'Oh Will, it must have been horrible for you.'

He shrugged. 'Anyway, I got on okay at school, and when I was old enough, I left and started work for a horticulturist, digging and laying pavers, hard work, but I was very strong in those days.'

And you still are, Elizabeth thought, looking at his muscular physique.

Will was silent. Elizabeth was quiet too, still holding his hand.

He raised his eyes, 'Then I met this wonderful woman, Isabelle. We were married and so happy.' His voice caught. 'A year after our wedding she was cycling to work and was knocked down and killed in a hit and run accident.'

'Oh, my God,' breathed Elizabeth.

'I'm sorry,' Will said, 'I really don't know why I'm telling you all this.'

'No, no! Sometimes it helps to get it all out.'

'Anyway, I threw myself into work and started to build up a landscaping business, I was doing well, working night and day to stop myself thinking about Isabelle. Then a few years later I met Fiona. I thought she was nice and eventually, we married.' He glowered, unspeaking.

Elizabeth said nothing and after a few minutes, Will continued, 'Things went bad; we got divorced.' His frown deepened and he was silent, then continued 'I haven't seen my d ...' He stopped and swallowed hard, 'Anyway, at the same time, my wonderful mother was dying of breast cancer. I nursed her as best as I could, and when she died, four years ago, I found her birth certificate, which had the name and address of the person who registered her birth, her father. I didn't know if they still lived at the same address, but I wrote and informed them of her death, and heard nothing until three years ago when I got a letter from a solicitor to say my grandmother had died and left everything to her daughter's child. Me.'

'Oh, Will!' Elizabeth breathed.

He gave a watery smile. 'No one except you knows that this was my grandparent's house. I just can't face all the questions.'

She nodded. 'No one will ever hear any of this from me.'

He turned to her. 'Yes, actually I believe you. You're a good person, Elizabeth.' A slow smile spread across his face. 'Even if you do steal building material in the dead of night!'

Elizabeth gasped. 'Oh!' she exclaimed. Her hands flew to her face. 'Oh Will, I didn't, I mean, I did, but I thought no one would notice!'

He threw back his head and laughed. 'I saw you the very first night, I thought you must be some crazy old biddy from across the road! I'd rented a tipper truck to take the stones to a job I had a contract for. Big project in Sydney, cobblestone driveways. Well, the owner went bankrupt; when I got to the site it was all boarded up and a security guy told me what had happened. I didn't know what to do. The owner already owed me a lot of money; money that I'll never see again.' He looked rueful. 'And the stones were a special order and I'd paid for them and the rent of the truck. I was at the end of my tether, didn't know which way to turn.'

He lifted his cup with his free hand, took a sip and made a face. 'This has gone cold.'

He put down his cup and continued, 'Then I thought of this place – it seemed like an omen. So, I drove down. Hadn't seen it since I came down to do the paperwork and get the keys from the solicitor. Dumped the setts – that's what they're called, by the way, Belgian Setts, not cobblestones. They were taken up from the roads in London and replaced by tarmac then used as ballast on the ships coming to Sydney. Anyway, it was too late to go back to Sydney, the truck rental place would be closed and I'd been couch surfing at a mate's place and he wouldn't have appreciated a truck blocking his driveway.' Will rubbed his eyes and sighed. 'I didn't have the keys with me, so I went round the back and saw some flower pots outside the back door. I took a chance and lifted them up and under the last one was a key! A bit rusty, but I managed to open the back door. It was so dusty and damp smelling inside.' He smiled at Elizabeth. 'Well, then I drove to the local pub for a meal and had a few drinks. I left the truck there and walked back here and dossed down in the bedroom for the night. I heard a noise, peered out the window and saw this woman in fluffy slippers sneaking across the road and taking my rocks!'

'Oh, Will, what must you think of me?'

He took her hands, which were still clasping one of his. 'That you are a delightful, enterprising woman, and not a crazy old biddy, but a crazy, actually a very nice-looking biddy ...' His eyes crinkled with amusement and he squeezed her hands. 'And then, when I fixed your mower and you invited me for a cup of tea, I immediately noticed the rocks around your pond. I watched you as you brought out the teapot, and I could sense your anxiety – you were hoping I hadn't noticed them. You looked so shifty! I was going to make a comment, but I didn't know you then and didn't want to embarrass you.'

'Will!' Once again, she cursed her fair skin which caused her to blush so readily.

'Then I thought I'd keep quiet until an opportune moment arose where I could tease you,' he grinned. 'Okay, I think we need a drink after all this!'

'Just a small one, Will, it's getting late.'

'Give Merv something to talk about if he sees you inebriated and sneaking out of my house late at night!'

Elizabeth laughed. 'Don't care,' she said and was amazed to realise it was true.

'What about you, Elizabeth, what's your story?'

'Oh, nothing really. Got married young, had a daughter; my husband was unfaithful, got divorced when he got his secretary pregnant. Cared for my mother when she had a stroke, then moved here when she died.'

Will nodded. 'You're happy now?'

Elizabeth smiled. 'Yes, as much as anyone can be happy in this crazy world, but I'm very content with my life. I have everything I need, and can do all the things I enjoy without someone criticizing me or telling me what to do.' She stood up and put her glass on the table. 'Better sneak out and shock the neighbours,' she smiled. 'Thanks again, Will. Come on Moll.'

Back in her own house, Elizabeth took Molly out into the garden, then sat in one of the outside rocking chairs while she waited for Molly to sniff and find the perfect place to pee. It was a clear moonlit night, her garden eerily beautiful. Elizabeth went over in her mind all Will had told her. His mother must have been a wonderful woman. And it was sad about his father. Perhaps she could do some investigation and find out if Will had half brothers or sisters in England.

Her thoughts moved on to her own mother. She'd never been happy with anything Elizabeth did or achieved. And those last few years when Elizabeth had nursed her, she'd grumbled about everything: she "couldn't digest" the meals Elizabeth cooked; Elizabeth "was rough" when she washed her; never dressed her appropriately; and if Elizabeth had to go out to shop, she complained about being left to moulder away on her own. In fact, Elizabeth now realized, her mother had been a miserable old woman. Elizabeth's father, who she'd adored, had been the classic hen-pecked husband. Gentle and quiet, he'd gradually faded away and died in his sleep, as if the burden of his life had been too much.

Graham had been much the same as her mother, domineering and wanting everything his way. Making all the decisions, even as to where they would go on holidays, what car Elizabeth should drive, and the car had to be a status symbol. She'd only wanted a small, easy to park car, but he'd insisted on a Mercedes station wagon, big enough for her cello to go in the back. Not that she'd ever had to go anywhere with her cello. Well, she still had the Mercedes, part of the divorce settlement. At least he'd been generous with that. Which was lucky as her mother had left everything to Bronwyn.

With a sigh, she stood up. 'Come on Moll, bedtime.'

Molly wagged her tail and followed Elizabeth indoors.

Sydney - 1820

Edward Turner had been working as a stonemason for the last twelve months. He was hardworking; labouring outside of his required hours to earn extra money. Being of a thrifty nature, he'd managed to save a bit of money, but he missed Sarah, his wife. It was hard for a man not to have the comfort of a loving woman. It had been so long ... he hadn't had a reply to his letter asking her to come with the children to New South Wales. Had she received his letter? Why hadn't she replied?

Time passed. Another year gone by and still no sign from his wife.

One Sunday morning, Edward was sitting in a pew in the local church. He pondered on his family back in England, closed his eyes and said a prayer for them. He opened his eyes and became aware of a girl sitting at the end of the pew across the aisle from him.

From half closed eyes, he glanced at her. She returned his gaze then lowered her eyes and turned her head towards the preacher. Edward thought it had been a provocative glance. He looked over at her again; thick brown hair caught up under a hat, a lone curl escaping and covering her ear. She peeped sideways at him again and he was aware of full lips and blue eyes. She quickly turned her gaze back to the preacher. Edward was entranced. It had been over three years since he'd been with his wife. He felt a stirring in his loins and reached for his hat, nonchalantly putting it over his groin to hide his swelling erection. He studied the preacher, as he made a conscious effort not to look at the girl.

After the service, he hurried outside and waited until he saw her come out with what he assumed were her parents. He moved towards them and doffed his hat. 'Good morning,' he said, 'Good sermon, don't you think?' He hoped they wouldn't ask him what he liked about it because, to be truthful, he'd barely heard any of it.

The man lifted his hat. 'Yes, excellent sermon,' came the reply. 'Don't think we've met before? John Cawson is my name, my wife, Mary, and this is our daughter, Ann.'

Edward inclined his head towards Mary Cawson. 'Edward Turner,' he said. 'How do you do?' and then towards Ann. 'How do you do?'

Ann, keeping her head lowered looked up from under her eyelashes and said something indistinct. Then she raised her head and smiled; a rosebud mouth and laughing eyes.

Edward's heart thumped. However, he didn't want to appear too keen. Ann seemed to be about fifteen. He nodded at the family, lifted his hat and strolled away. He thought of his eldest daughter, Sophia, back in Derbyshire. She'd been thirteen when he'd been transported, now she would be sixteen, nearly seventeen. About the same age as this Ann Cawson. And he was still a convict – and as such had to be assigned to either a free settler or the government.

He'd been lucky … staying with the old couple - they'd been kind to him - he'd repaid their kindness by working hard, and helping them, doing extra work beyond what he was supposed to do. He'd been assigned to Dennis Bryan's convict gang where he worked as a stonemason on some of Sydney's early buildings, sometimes using the local sandstone and other times using the cobblestones from the ballast the ships coming into Sydney harbour. This was unloaded along with the convicts. Timber brought from the settlement was taken onto the ships for the return voyage back to England, beautiful cedar from the South Coast, and shells from what came to be known as Shellharbour. He liked working with the cobblestones, although strictly speaking, they weren't cobblestones, but setts, rocks hewn into rectangular blocks - perfect for building.

He managed to get work outside his indentured hours and started to earn money. More than he'd earned in South Wingfield or Pentrich. He often thought about building a public house. When his back gave out – as it eventually would, it happened to most stonemasons – he'd be able to run a public house and employ a boy to do the heavy work.

Every Sunday he attended the local church and managed to chat with the Cawson family. After a few weeks, John Cawson invited him back to their house for a meal.

Edward was thrilled. It started to be a regular event - Sundays with the Cawsons and the more that he saw of the young Ann Cawson, the more he became entranced. Eventually, he sought out her father and told him about his situation.

'I have a wife in England,' he announced. 'But I've heard nought from her in three years. I know the normal thing is to wait for seven years and if no word or contact from a wife is received then I would be free to remarry.'

John Cawson nodded. 'Our Ann is a good girl, but I don't think she can be kept waiting for four years.' He paused, looking at Edward, 'But I've heard good things about you. You're God-fearing, sober and a hard worker. I don't think our Ann could do better. Between you and me, I think she has a soft spot for you.'

Edward's heart soared. 'I'll find out if I can remarry before the seven years,' he said.

John Cawson nodded. 'I'll say nothing to our Ann until you find out, but I still don't think she should be made to wait four years ...'

Edward got the necessary permission. He married Ann Cawson on the third of December 1821. She was seventeen years old and illiterate; she signed the register with an 'X'. John Thorn and Hannah Booth were witnesses.

Eleven months later Ann gave birth to a son, John.

Edward blinked away tears as he held his first son in his arms. He'd told Ann about his wife in England and his two daughters there. She'd made sympathetic noises, but he felt she didn't understand how it felt. How could she? He'd never heard from Sarah, didn't know if she and their girls, Sophia and Sarah, were even still alive. At times it bothered him that his new wife was the same age as his daughter, Sophia, would be now. If she was still alive that was.

By February the following year, Edward had been promoted as an overseer to his own gang of stonemasons. This was a relief to him as at thirty-seven years old and after suffering the depredations of life as a convict, he wasn't as strong as he had been.

By 1828 Edward was the father of four children with Ann and had obtained his ticket of leave with his wife as surety.

Wambecarra - November 2020

Elizabeth continued with her ancestry research and when the book about the Pentrich Rebellion that she'd ordered, arrived, she settled down with a mug of coffee to read it. At only eighty-three pages it wouldn't take her long.

Suddenly she jumped up and started to pace around. 'Oh, goodness, how exciting, Molly!' Molly stirred and raised her head. 'Molly, I must ring Will!'

When Will answered Elizabeth said, breathlessly, 'Will, guess what?'

'You won lotto.' She could tell he was smiling.

'What? No, I don't gamble.'

'Why am I not surprised?'

'Oh, Will, I received the book I ordered about the Pentrich Rebellion. I simply had to tell you, I'm so excited! It's got a section on George Weightman, and guess where he lived in NSW?'

'Wambecarra.'

'No! but close. Kiama! And there's a commemorative plaque there.'

'Wow! That's only a short drive from us!'

'Yes!'

'I'm in the ute at the moment, just finished a job.' There was a pause, then he continued, 'it's only three o'clock. I should be home in ten minutes or so. How about I come and get you in about half an hour and we drive to Kiama and have a look?'

'Oh, Will! Really! That would be great! Thank you! See you then.' She went to her bedroom, changed into fresh clothes and combed her hair. She looked in the mirror, then found an old tube of lipstick and applied it to her lips. *Trying to make yourself appear younger, Elizabeth?* She rubbed it off.

Thirty minutes later she was at the door waiting when the bell rang. She couldn't help smiling and felt like hugging Will.

'Ready?' he asked.

'Yes, can Molly come too?'

He nodded. 'Of course!'

When Elizabeth and Molly were squeezed in the front of the ute, Molly curled up at Elizabeth's feet, Will started the engine. 'Now, remind me again who was this George Weightman,' he said.

'He was the one with the "borrowed",' she paused and made a gesture with her index fingers to indicate the questionable borrowed, 'Pony. He'd galloped ahead to Nottingham to see what was happening there. He came back to Langley Mill to tell them Nottingham had been taken and that the soldiers would not stir from their barracks – I think that bit was a lie - and there was a party of men waiting to join them, but what he didn't know was that after he left Nottingham the men there waited for ages and then because the Pentrich men hadn't appeared, they thought they'd been delayed with the weather and all went home!'

'Right. I remember now.' Will nodded.

'And he was with Edward Turner in the prison hulk, and I think on the ship as well.'

'And you say there's a plaque to him?'

'Yes, by the railway bridge.'

'I know where the railway bridge is, there's a height restriction for big trucks.' Elizabeth saw Will's sideways look, as they drove through Kiama.

He parked by the railway station, helped Elizabeth out, and took Molly's lead. 'The bridge is down this way.' They walked along, Molly delighted to have new scents to stop and sniff.

'Here it is!' exclaimed Elizabeth, pointing to a plaque set in a rock.

They studied it for a few moments. 'It's just such a co-incidence!' Elizabeth said. 'That I should be doing this research and then stumbled across this, and nearly next door!'

Will smiled. 'Going to take a photo?'

'Oh, yes, of course. Will you hold Molly for me?' Elizabeth took her phone from her handbag.

'Like me to take one of you beside the plaque?' Will offered.

'No, thanks, I hate having my photo taken.'

Busy with her phone Elizabeth appeared not to hear him murmur: 'Why am I not surprised, yet again?'

'All done, great!' Elizabeth smiled up at Will. 'Now, would you like a coffee?'

'Love one. Come on Molly, this way.'

They walked along the crowded main street until they found a café with an outside vacant table and chairs. 'This okay?' Will asked.

'Perfect, what would you like?'

'Flat white, please.' Will sat down with Molly while Elizabeth went inside to order. She could see him watching the holiday-makers and tourists thronging the streets as she waited her turn.

'I ordered a lemon tart for us too,' she smiled as she returned and sat opposite him. She hung her bag on her chair just as her mobile phone rang. 'Excuse me,' she said to Will as she took it out of her bag and glanced down at it. 'Oh, it's my daughter.'

'Answer it,' Will said.

'You don't mind? It's a bit rude.' She looked up at him.

He smiled. 'Go ahead.'

'Hello, Bronwyn.'

'Hi Elizabeth, how are you?'

'Good, I'm having coffee with a friend, so can't talk at the moment.'

'Oh! Well, um, good to hear you're making friends at last. Right, well just want to say we'll be coming down to stay with you for Christmas. Can't go to Bali as we usually do, due to the restrictions and everything's booked out all the way down the coast.' She sounded disgruntled.

'Oh! Right! Yes, okay, that would be lovely. Well, we can talk about the details another time. Better go, bye dear.' She hung up and grimaced. 'My daughter, Bronwyn,' she said, unnecessarily. 'They usually go overseas for the Christmas holidays, and the odd times when they do come down to visit me, they stay in a motel in town. Bronwyn doesn't like Molly, says she's allergic to dog dander.'

She put her phone back in her bag and smiled as a girl brought out the coffee and cakes. 'Thank you.'

Will picked up his coffee cup. 'How will you manage?'

Elizabeth sighed. 'I only have one spare bedroom with two single beds, and another room I use as a study. Same as your layout. I guess I'll have to let Bronwyn and her husband sleep in my bed, my two granddaughters can sleep in the twin beds and I can bunk down in my study.'

'I have a spare bedroom; your granddaughters could sleep there. It doesn't seem right turning you out of your bedroom.'

Elizabeth didn't reply. She took a sip of coffee. 'Have a lemon tart. They look nice.'

'Thanks.' Will took one and studied her.

'I don't think Bronwyn would let her girls sleep in the house of a strange man.' She gave a mischievous smile, 'Or, Molly and I could come and camp at your place!' *How could she have said that? The words just slipped out!*

He laughed. 'Wonderful idea! Well, then, I'd better get a move on and start sanding the floors! I'd love to have you and Molly stay.'

Elizabeth blushed. 'I was actually joking,' she stammered.

'Why? I think it would solve all your problems, and I'd love to have Molly.'

Elizabeth grinned. 'Okay it's a deal, and perhaps I can do something for you, like make new curtains or something. And I can't wait to see Bronwyn's face!'

Will's smile faded. 'What do you mean?' He frowned.

Elizabeth's face went a deep red. 'Um, I ...'

'Do you mean, you can't wait to see your daughter's reaction when she realises you'll be staying at the house of a coloured man?'

'No, Will! Truly! She's always on to me to make friends, but I think she means women friends. I just meant when she sees me being friends with a man, staying in a man's house ...' She bit her lower lip and twisted her hands in her lap. Tears came to her eyes. 'Will, I'd never do or say anything to hurt you. It didn't even cross my mind!'

Will's expression didn't change.

She looked down at her hands.

Will replaced his cup. 'Perhaps we'd better go. Thank you for the coffee, Elizabeth, and the cake.' He stood up and started to walk towards where he'd parked the ute.

Elizabeth took Molly's lead and followed him.

Back at the ute, he opened the passenger door and helped her into the seat, and then Molly into the space beside her.

They were both silent on the drive back.

Will stopped outside Elizabeth's house, and before he could turn off the engine, she'd opened the door of the ute and jumped out, saying, 'Thank you for taking me today, Will. Come on Molly.' She'd opened her gate and was at her front door before he had time to answer.

Sydney - 1828

Edward was pleased with life. He and his wife, Ann, had four children, John the eldest at six, followed by Mary-Ann, James and the newborn Elizabeth Esther. Edward had managed to save enough money to buy a horse and two head of cattle and was working for himself.

Convicts were returned to the Government Barracks after each assignment and then reassigned. A lot of convicts were assigned to free settlers on farms around the district. This suited the Government as they didn't have to provide lodgings for the convicts and also provided the free settlers with cheap labour. Any convicts who caused trouble were usually put in irons and sentenced to hard physical labour. Edward considered himself lucky to have been assigned to his wife for a few years. This legally made her the head of the household, but that was better than his previous assignments.

Edward found out his nephew, Joseph, who'd been a clerk in Manchester had been fortunate enough to get clerical positions, first at the building of the Liverpool Hospital and then at the Longbottom Stockade.

Ann was a good manager, despite being unable to read or write. He'd tried to teach her to at least sign her name. It amused him to see her practicing her writing, with the tip of her tongue between her lips. He resolved he would send their children to school when they were old enough.

But now Edward had his ticket of leave, which meant he was free to work for himself. He was keen to use his stonemasonery skills to build a house for them all. Perhaps build a public house. Masonry work was hard on the back and at forty-four years old he was already beset by aches and pains.

By 1833 the couple had built a home in Upper Kent Street Sydney, where Edward's first attempt at becoming a publican failed. He and Ann had been living in the six-room house since the late 1820s, and he'd applied for a publican's license for the property in July. The application was refused, because the premises were unfinished.

Undeterred, Edward purchased (again in Ann's name) a property in Parramatta Street. Once more, he applied for a publican's licence and this was granted in 1834. He called the public house The Stonemason's Arms.

By the time Edward received his absolute pardon in 1835, he was operating a prosperous business. The Stonemason's Arms was on the main thoroughfare to Parramatta and caught all the passing trade. Edward was content. He and Ann now had five children and a sixth on the way.

The sixth baby was a girl, Ellen and she was followed two years later, in 1836 by another boy who they named Edmund.

Ann was now thirty-one and beginning to feel worn down by constant childbirth. When Edmund was only eighteen months old, she became pregnant yet again. This time she appeared to be much bigger than with her previous pregnancies. By the start of the new year of 1838, she could hardly lumber around. The summer heat made her feel worse and she was no longer able to help Edward in the pub.

She lay fanning herself and instructing the twelve-year-old Mary-Ann what to do to help out. Edward had a convict woman, Ann Smith, assigned to him and she helped with the washing and cleaning. The midwife for Ann's previous pregnancies was predicting twins.

Her prophecy came true. Ann was delivered of a boy and a girl, Edwin and Hannah. Ann was exhausted. Fortunately, her older daughters were delighted to have small babies to cosset and mollycoddle. Breastfeeding two babies further depleted Ann's reserves of energy.

'I hope this is the last of them,' she confided to the midwife.

'Ha!' came the reply. 'No chance of that, your man is too lusty, and what age are you now?'

'Thirty-three, nearly thirty-four,' Ann sighed.

'Plenty of time for at least another eight! Ten if you have another set of twins!'

'God forbid!' groaned Ann.

Wambecarra - November 2020

After leaving Will's ute, Elizabeth let herself into her house and went straight into the kitchen, poured a glass of wine and sat in her easy chair by the window, gazing out at the birdbath and her pond. Tiny apples were forming on the newly green branches of the apple tree. Spring had arrived. She'd been so happy walking down the street in Kiama with Will. Now it was all spoiled. She'd noticed a few women looking at them. Looks of envy she'd thought to herself.

She sighed, got up and went to her study and sat at her cello. After half an hour of playing her favourite piece of music, she felt calmer.

Had what she'd said been so insensitive? She felt close to tears. The day had started so well, and now she'd hurt the only friend she'd made since she'd moved to Wambecarra. Molly came and put her head on her knee, staring at her with soulful eyes. Elizabeth stroked the dog's ears. 'You understand, Moll. What would you do?' Molly wagged her tail and licked Elizabeth's hand.

'You think I should try and make amends? Hmm. Maybe you're right. Okay, we'd better go for our afternoon walk, maybe it'll clear my head.'

As she walked briskly along with Molly, Merv popped out from behind a rose bush near his gate. 'Nice day,' he remarked. 'See you and Will across the road are getting on *very* well.' He smirked and winked.

'Indeed,' replied Elizabeth, not stopping. 'He's a nice man.' Merv made his usual rude gesture behind her back.

Will *is* a nice man, she thought. And she'd hurt him. She'd have to go and say sorry. But what exactly for? What would she say? '*Sorry I made a crass statement?*' No, that didn't seem right. '*Sorry I hurt you?*' Maybe simply front up to his place. When she got home, she fed Molly and then fetched a bottle of wine, taking care to wrap it so Merv wouldn't see it. 'Come on, Moll.' She clipped the lead on her dog and walked out and across the road to Will's, her heart thumping. She could hear a lot of noise from inside as she rang the bell.

After a few minutes, the door opened and Will stood there, covered in dust. He sneezed.

'Bless you.'

'Oh. Elizabeth.' He hesitated, seeming unsure what to do.

'Can I come in?'

'Of course.' He held the door open. 'The thing is, it's very dusty, I've been taking up the carpet in the spare bedroom.' He indicated the rolled-up old carpet blocking the hallway. 'Um, I wanted to get the floor varnished and ready for you at Christmas.' He lowered his eyes and frowned at the carpet.

Elizabeth studied the carpet, his words going round in her head. *So he still wanted her to come at Christmas!*

'Will. I came to say sorry.' She held out the wrapped bottle. 'I brought this as a peace offering. Um, Molly said I should.'

Will looked up and laughed, then grew serious. 'Elizabeth, I must apologize to you. I totally over-reacted.'

'Will, I'd never say or do anything to hurt you.'

Will's expression softened. He leaned over to her 'Elizabeth Turner, I think you are one of the nicest women I've ever met.' Gently he turned her face to his and kissed her cheek, leaving a dusty mark on her nose. 'Even if you are descended from a convict.'

She felt her face grow hot as a feeling of relief washed over her. To hide her confusion she replied sharply, 'Technically, he wasn't a convict, as he'd never actually been convicted, he pleaded guilty.'

He smiled at her swift retort. 'Touché! Now, I've just finished taking up the carpet. Would you and Molly like to sit outside on the patio while I have a shower and get changed? Won't be long.'

Elizabeth managed to navigate around the carpet as Molly jumped over it. They made their way to the kitchen where she left the bottle of wine and went out onto the patio. She couldn't help smiling to herself. 'You were right, Molly,' she said, sitting on one of the lounge chairs. 'We had to come and say sorry.'

When Will appeared ten minutes later, she remarked, 'Will, I love what you've done with the cobble-stones, sorry – Belgian setts.'

The garden was transformed; paths made of the setts and raised garden beds with stone walls.

He smiled at Elizabeth. 'I ran out of the stones ... about a dozen short ...'

'Oh! Really?' Elizabeth's shoulders slumped. 'You can take back the ones I, er, borrowed. I can get something else.' She bit her lip.

Will burst out laughing. 'Just teasing you! Have you eaten?'

'No,' she admitted. 'I was too upset to think about eating.'

His smiled faded. 'I'm so sorry, Elizabeth.'

'No, no!' She sighed. 'Will, can we just forget about it? It was all a misunderstanding.'

He nodded. 'Well, I'm starving, except for a lemon tart, I haven't eaten since breakfast, because someone was so excited about going to look at a plaque!'

'Oh Will, I'm sorry!'

He laughed. 'How about I do a barbie, I've got steak in the fridge, and there's salad stuff in the garden.'

Elizabeth's heart flipped. 'Lovely!' she smiled, 'I'll go and forage in the veggie patch, shall I?'

***

Some days later and Elizabeth had managed to find out more about Edward Turner from the 1828 Census. She kept an eye out for Will's ute, gave him an hour to shower and eat, then, eager to discuss what she'd learned she took her laptop and Molly and hurried over to Will's house.

'Okay, what have you found out?' Will's eyes twinkled when he opened the door. 'Come on in.' He followed Elizabeth into the kitchen. 'Just a minute while I clear the table.' He moved the paper he'd been reading and made room for her laptop. 'Right. Now, tell me the latest in the saga.'

'Oh, Will, when Edward was aged forty-four, he had his ticket of leave and was working as a stonemason in Kent Street, Sydney. He owned a horse and two head of cattle.'

'What's a ticket of leave?'

She consulted her laptop. 'It allowed convicts to work for themselves, provided they remained in a specified area, reported regularly to local authorities and attended divine worship every Sunday, if possible. Oh, and they were not allowed to leave the colony,' she paused and looked at Will, then she continued to tell him how Edward had been refused a publican's licence at his first attempt.

'But then he built and licensed a two-storey house in Parramatta Street in June 1834 and called it The Stonemason's Arms. It was probably a better proposition, as it lay on the road leading from Sydney to Parramatta. His wife, Ann was listed as the proprietor. Probably because Edward still had not received his freedom.'

'I guess there would have been heaps of settlers and traders using that road,' Will said thoughtfully. 'But wow, he was a go-getter all right!'

Elizabeth thought about her gentle father, directly descended from this Edward. He hadn't been a 'go-getter'.

'So which one of his children are you descended from?

'Well, that's a bit of a puzzle. When I work backwards from my father, Henry, to my grandfather, William, his father seems to be an Edmund Joseph Turner. And his parents were Edmund Turner and an Annie Marchant. And that Edmund Turner's parents were Edward Turner and Ann Cawson.'

'I can't quite figure it all out. Too many Edwards and Edmunds.'

'Okay, look. I did a little diagram, as I was a bit confused too.'

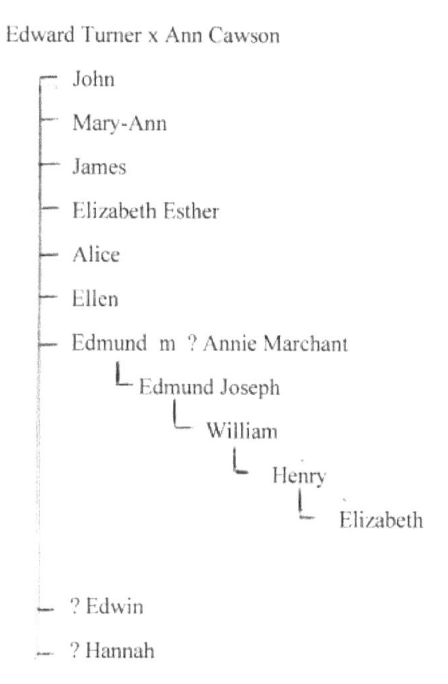

'Right, well that looks straightforward.'

'Yes, Going back to Edmund Joseph, everything is clear. But then things get a bit murky.'

'In what way?' Will looked puzzled.

'Well, you see, some records say Edward's third son, Edmund, died in 1841 when he was five.' She paused. 'But this is the thing, Will. I wrote to the church where Edward and Ann were buried, and they found the grave, but the inscriptions were so worn they're indecipherable. But they have a book called *Grave Reflections* which was published in 1996. And according to the book, from their records, it says on the headstone, Edwin, not Edmund. And it also says, Hannah, daughter of Ann and Edward Turner, 3 years 11.6.1841. And the book says "Headstone Inscription" for both of them, which means there was no entry in the burial register for them. Look, I took a photo of the page to show you.' She held out her phone.

Edwin, fourth son of Ann and Edward Turner, 3 years 12.6.1841 (3). Headstone inscription.

Hannah, daughter of Ann and Edward Turner, 3 years, 11.6.1841 (3). Headstone inscription.

'What does the three in brackets mean?' Will asked.

'That's the row number in the graveyard.'

Will made a face. 'But it's weird, that there was no record in the burial register.

'I thought so too,' Elizabeth paused and then continued, 'but it's strange that on the genealogy site I've found, it says Edmund was born in 1836, but no mention of an Edwin or Hannah being born. See how the *Grave Reflections* book says Edwin, **fourth** son of Ann and Edward Turner, 3 years old, died on the twelfth of June 1841 and Hannah, on the eleventh of June 1841. And I can find no records of Edwin and Hannah's births on the New South Wales births, deaths and marriages family history website. But it lists all the others.'

'Hold on a minute. Can you write that down, I can't get a picture in my head.'

Elizabeth did so 'Ok, well these are Edward's children with Ann according to some ancestry sites.'

Will studied the diagram.

Son	John	1822 – 1876
Daughter	Mary-Ann	1824 –
Son	James	1826 –
Daughter	Elizabeth Esther	1828 – 1849
Daughter	Alice	1831 –
Daughter	Ellen	1833 – 1906
Son	Edmund	1836 -

'And see,' Elizabeth pointed to the diagram, 'there are three sons mentioned here, but the headstone at the graveyard says Edwin, *fourth* son of Ann and Edward...'

'When did their father, Edward die?'

Elizabeth studied her documentation. 'September 1841'

'Hmm.' His brows drew together as he stared at Elizabeth. 'So that was just after the twins. Can you check on your laptop if there was a plague or something similar in Sydney in 1841?'

'That's a thought, Will.' She tapped away, while Will kept studying the diagram and thinking.

Suddenly Elizabeth exclaimed, 'Wow! Look at this, from the *Sydney Morning Herald*, the twenty-eighth of May 1841!'

She turned the screen towards Will and they both read the transcript of the article.

According to the best information we can procure, the march of this severe epidemic is by no means yet arrested in Sydney, and we do not say this with any wish, but the contrary, of creating unnecessary and unfounded alarm. It is much better, that the public should be properly cautioned, than that they should be lulled into thoughtless security by reports, unsupported by facts, of the decrease or disappearance of Scarlatina. The only known means for preventing the spread of this or any other infectious epidemic, are cleanliness and the chlorinated alkalies, soda, potass, and lime.

Every species of dirt and filth more particularly when moist is certain to attract and retain the poison, and hence the absolute necessity for rendering houses scrupulously clean ; and as animal textures are more apt to catch and retain the infectious matter, all garments of woollen or silk ought to be kept very clean.

Chlorinated lime, (Calx chlorinata) improperly and ignorantly called chloride of lime, for this term properly designates a widely different article, formerly termed muriate of lime ; or solution of chlorinated soda (Liquor soda chlorinata) are the only known disinfectants, and these are so certain and so powerful, that a daring and fearless French Surgeon actually put on and wore for a fortnight a shirt first steeped in the matter (Pus) of plague and then disinfected by chlorination, without catching the disease. Chlorinated lime is a very cheap article in England, and the dry powder only requires to be slightly moistened and sprinkled about a house, or set on shallow dishes in rooms, several times a day, to prove effectual in destroying all infection or contagion. Some years ago it was announced in Germany, and caught at by some in England, who run headlong after every absurd novelty, that extract of deadly-night-shade (Atropa Belladonna) is a certain preventive, (or as we often see it vulgarly spelled preventative) of scarlatina. This nonsense has been repeated here ;-nonsense we call it, for it is founded on no principle, and we cannot see how it could be proved.

We would upon principle infer, that so far from preventing, Belladonna would increase, the chance of infection, by its narcotic effects on the system, in the same way as infection is more ready to take effect the sleeping than in the waking state. There cannot be a doubt, that the disgraceful puddles of dirty water drained off from every sink and every pump into our streets, tend greatly to continue the infection of scarlatina, by actually floating it out from the houses into the public pathways, and rendering no person safe from the contamination.

This ought to be attended to without delay, and it would be well to appoint a Board of Health to inspect the houses in the quarters where the disease is most prevalent. One word more and we have done. Let every person watch for the first symptoms of sore throat and difficulty of swallowing, with languor or disinclination to walk or move, and send immediately for good medical advice. Any attempt to treat the disease by the unskilful may end fatally in a day or two. Particular caution indeed ought to be paid to abstain from all spirits and all stimulants unless ordered by a medical man, as spirits will be certain to increase the inflammatory symptoms of the throat, or drive a rush of blood to the head, and the patient may die delirious. [1]

'Oh my god, Will, can you believe this bit!' She pointed to the paragraph in the paper, where a French surgeon had steeped his jacket in pus. 'Well,' she continued. 'I guess that proved the efficacy of Chlorinated Lime. They dampened it and sprinkled it around the house,' Elizabeth shook her head in wonder.

Will smiled, and then his eyes lit up. 'So scarlet fever was rampant that year in Sydney!'

'Yes, and it started from an immigrant ship coming from England.'

Will nodded. 'Hmm, sounds familiar. But I thought scarlet fever was just a rash and not fatal.'

---

1. Funding for digitisation contributed by Vincent Fairfax Family Foundation

Elizabeth did another search. 'Apparently, it was pretty serious in the days before antibiotics.'

'Okay, so Edward and those two must have died of scarlet fever.' He paused. 'But, Elizabeth, see the pattern of births. Every two years, good old Ann pops out a baby. There's John in 1822, Mary Ann in 1824, James in 1826, Elizabeth Esther in 1828, Alice in 1831, Ellen in 1833, and Edmund in 1836. Yet on their father, Edward's gravestone, according the *Grave Reflections* book, there are two extra children, Hannah and Edwin, aged three, who both died within a day of each other in 1841.' He paused. 'If they were both aged three in 1841, it would mean they were born in 1838. Just two years after Edmund.'

'You're right Will!' Elizabeth looked at him with admiration. 'They must have been twins, and that means Edmund didn't die in 1841!'

Will grinned. 'Next question. What happened to Edmund?'

SYDNEY - 1838

When Edmund was born in 1836 there were four older sisters. Mary Ann and Elizabeth were old enough to mind their young siblings while their mother was kept busy, not only with the normal household duties but also with helping to manage The Stonemason's Arms, where they all still lived.

The young Alice and Ellen threw away their rag dolls and fought over Edmund. They took turns to rock and cosset him, play with and amuse him.

When he was nearly three years old, things changed. Their mother gave birth to twins, Edwin and Hannah. Suddenly Edmund was no longer the pet. Alice and Ellen each had a new baby to mother. Edmund was ignored. The two girls only relinquished little Edwin and Hannah when they took them to their mother, where they watched in fascination as she put a baby to each breast to suckle.

Disgruntled, Edmund sought out his eldest sister, Mary-Ann, 'Play with me Mary-Ann,' he said with a childish pout, tugging on her skirt.

'Ed, I've no time for play! I've got to help while Mammy's still laid low. Ask Elizabeth.'

However, at eleven, Elizabeth Esther was also busy. The birth of the twins had been hard on Ann Turner. Elizabeth was kept occupied taking care of their mother.

Edmund went off in a sulk to find his ten-year-old brother, James. But James wasn't interested in playing with a three-year-old.

Edmund became very jealous of these two new arrivals. Mary-Ann eventually took pity on him. When she could spare time from working in the pub, she would take him on her lap and read to him, teaching him the words as she read. Then, after an hour she would push him off her lap and shoo him out into the garden at the back of the pub. 'Go and help Doug in the garden, he needs a hand.' Doug was happy to show off his gardening skills to the young Edmund.

Edmund felt more and more excluded. He began to detest the twins, their whimpering and colicky screaming got on his nerves, and no one had any time for him. Why did his mother have to have them? He thought. Weren't there enough Turner children?

It got worse as the twins got older, everyone thought they were so acute, and so clever when they said their first words and took their first steps... He sat in a corner sulking.

'Look at little jealous boy!' Alice said one day, pointing at Edmund, and they all turned to look at him. He jumped up and ran out of the room into the garden with Doug. 'Wish they'd never bin born,' he told Doug.

Doug stared at him. 'They'm sweet little bubs,' he said. 'But youse is my favourite!'

Edmund had to be content with that.

Then when Edmund was five Sydney was brought low with an epidemic of Scarlet Fever. Edmund caught it and was up and about within days, only a rash and a sore throat to show for it. When the twins caught the disease a few days after him, he was blamed for giving it to them. He felt only slightly guilty about that, but after a short illness they both died within one day of each other. Everyone except Edmund was distraught. His mother and sisters sobbing and wailing, and his father and brothers going around with long faces. But then his father succumbed to the same fever - three months later he too was buried - in the same grave as the twins, in St. Peter's Anglican church cemetery.

Somehow Edmund felt he was to blame for these deaths.

His grief-stricken mother took over the running of The Stonemason's Arms. Edmund didn't know what was wrong with her, but she seemed to always be tired and taking to her bed. Edmund tried to crawl into bed with her for a cuddle but Mary-Ann said no, leave our mother alone, she's not well. Two years later, she died at their pub and was laid to rest in the same grave as her husband and the twins. Edmund never found out her cause of death, but he felt a lingering guilt that he was to blame.

Ann's death at forty years old on the thirty-first of January in 1843, left seven children without parents.

The orphaned seven-year-old Edmund was left to the care of his nineteen-year-old sister, Mary-Ann. Fortunately, Edward Turner had made a good living over the years and had several properties and left enough to provide for his family. The portfolio included twenty-seven acres of land on the Liverpool Road, known as Brighton farm and at least five other houses, including The Stonemason's Arms.

Wambecarra - December 2020

Elizabeth continued her research. Pleased with what she had discovered about the orphaned Turners, she texted Will to see if he'd be interested in what she had discovered.

Of course! Come over.

She hurried over to Will's with her laptop and Molly.

'So what's new?' Will grinned as he opened the front door.

'Apparently, a trustee, John Douglass, was left to administer the estate and took on the license of The Stonemason's Arms after Ann's death.' She smiled and went on, 'This is weird, he advertised an unusual promotional event for Saint Patrick's Day 1843. During the evening pub-goers were treated to "the largest" exhibition of Montgolfier Balloons, ever seen in the colony. The Sydney Morning Herald advertised that "an artist of great experience in aeronautics" would put flight to two balloons. The admittance to the event was one shilling.'

'Goodness, I didn't know they had those balloons in Australia!' Will exclaimed.

'And then,' Elizabeth continued, 'The license and goodwill of The Stonemason's Arms were put up for sale in September 1843. It seems controversy erupted, ending in a civil case when Douglass agreed to sell the business to a Mr Curtis.'

'And?' prompted Will.

'Well. Douglass agreed to rent the premises to Mr Curtis for £2 per week, as well as selling the remainder of the license and goodwill to him for £22 10s. About three days after the agreement, Douglass let the house to a Roger Murphy, who took possession of The Stonemason's Arms on the second of October, paying a weekly rent of £4 – double the offer made to Curtis.'

'Gazumping!' said Will.

'But,' continued Elizabeth, 'At the Supreme Court, Douglass said although he made arrangements for Curtis to buy the business, the "young Turners", who he managed the property for as a trustee, would not give up possession of the premises. The "young Turners" believed the offer made by Douglass to Curtis was too low and they refused to allow the deal to proceed.' She looked up at Will.

'What happened then?'

Elizabeth read out, 'On Tuesday, the twentieth of February the Supreme Court gave a verdict for the plaintiff. Douglass and the "young Turners" were forced to pay damages of £20.'

'Goodness. That was a lot of money in those days,' Will remarked, then scowled and muttered something about corrupt courts.

Elizabeth studied him. His face had become sombre. 'Yes,' she replied. 'It doesn't sound fair to a young orphaned family. She tried to lighten his mood. 'Well, now I've brought you up to date with the Turner Saga, I'd better leave you in peace!' She stood up and closed her laptop. 'Come on Molly. Back home.'

***

The week before Christmas, Will invited Elizabeth to come and see the finished rooms. He'd sanded and varnished the wooden floors and Elizabeth had chosen the paint.

'This must have been my mother's room and bed when she was growing up.' He surveyed the room which was to be Elizabeth's during Bronwyn's visit.

'It's lovely, Will,' Elizabeth exclaimed. 'You've done a great job. I just love the brass bed.'

'I hope it will be comfortable enough for you. I bought a new mattress.'

'Oh, Will! You needn't have done that just for me!'

Will gave a wry smile. 'You didn't see the old one,' he said. 'Now I must get new bed linen; I don't know if what's here will still be ok.'

'Show me,' Elizabeth said.

Will took her to the linen cupboard in the hall.

'Oh, this stuff is wonderful,' Elizabeth exclaimed, smoothing a set of sheets. 'I don't think you can get beautiful linen sheets like these anymore, and wow, a lovely patchwork quilt! It looks handmade!'

'I was going to take it to the charity shop,' Will confessed.

'What! No, this is perfect.' Elizabeth stroked the patchwork quilt. 'Do you think your grandmother made it?'

'Possibly, it would be nice to think so.'

Elizabeth considered the pillows on the bed. 'But you need new pillows, these look like they've been stuffed with chicken feathers and must be pretty old.' She hit one of the pillows with her fist, releasing a small cloud of dust 'It would be like resting your head on a concrete block,' she smiled. 'I'll buy you new ones next time I'm in town. I'll have to go and do a big shop anyway before

Bronwyn arrives.' She grimaced. 'Knowing Bronwyn, whatever I buy will be wrong anyway.'

She looked at the bed linen in her arms. 'I'll take these home and wash them. Just to give them a freshen up.'

'So, you're still happy to move in over Christmas?' Will took out a handkerchief and polished the brass knobs on the end of the bed.

'Yes, if you're happy with the arrangement. But I must pay you rent!'

'Don't be ridiculous, Elizabeth, after the way you've advised and helped me.'

'Bronwyn is coming down on Wednesday, I guess it will be the afternoon by the time they arrive, so is it all right if I bring my stuff around early in the morning?' She grinned. 'Before Merv gets up. Iris mustn't sleep very well; she always seems to be peering out her window whenever I go out.'

'I think she's lonely,' Will said. 'I never see anyone going to her house. Do you think we should invite her round one evening?'

Elizabeth thought about it. 'Hmm, that's a nice idea.'

'I thought about it before, but maybe she wouldn't like coming to my house when I'm on my own, but perhaps if you say I've invited you both, she might agree.'

Elizabeth laughed, 'Good idea, she'd probably think she would be chaperoning me!' Then she blushed.

***

On Wednesday morning, Elizabeth was up early and took a suitcase over to Will's. She left it on the porch and went back for both of Molly's beds. Will opened the front door as she returned. He took her suitcase.

'I thought it might be a good idea if Molly stayed at your place during the day to avoid dander issues, and of course all the hair which Molly sheds,' Elizabeth said, rolling her eyes. 'That's if you don't mind?'

'Of course not! I love Molly.'

'Okay, well, I'll bring her over after her morning walk, then I can clean up any fur and fluff around the place, and make up the beds. I'll just pop back home for the bed linen and Molly's bowls. And Molly.'

Molly had seemed a bit surprised to see her beds disappear and then her food and water bowls. She followed Elizabeth across the road to Will's and watched as Elizabeth made up the spare bed with the new pillows and put Molly's night bed in the room and her day bed in the kitchen.

'I've got two lawns to mow this morning, will Molly be ok do you think, staying here on her own while I'm out?' Will turned to Elizabeth.

'Should be. Just give her a treat from this packet, and explain.' She indicated a packet of dog treats on the kitchen table. 'I'll listen out and if I hear her whining, I'll come and get her.'

Will took a key from one of his pockets. 'Front door key,' he said and grinned. 'So you can creep in clandestinely at night ...'

Elizabeth laughed. 'Merv will have an apoplexy! Okay, I'd better fly.'

'See you sometime tonight,' Will said. 'Don't worry if it's late, I'll take Molly out the back for a wander in the garden. You won't disturb me.'

***

Elizabeth wondered if other mothers felt daunted at the prospect of a daughter and grandchildren coming to stay. She certainly felt apprehensive. She flew around her small house, dusting and vacuuming and making beds. Then the Christmas tree. Only a small one. She hung a few ornaments on the branches and put her presents underneath. She stood back and surveyed the effect. It would have to do! At last, when she felt everything appeared clean and tidy, she had a shower, taking care to meticulously clean it afterwards. She dressed and put her dirty clothes in the washing machine, along with the linen from her bed. She'd just hung out the washing when she heard the car outside. She hurried to the front door and opened it.

'Hello girls!' she said to the two young girls one of whom was getting out of the car.

'Hi, Nana,' said Chloë, the eldest at eleven.

Elizabeth went to hug her granddaughter, but Chloë had already turned back to the car and dragged out a backpack. Then Bronwyn got out.

'Hello Elizabeth, good to be here, what a nightmare drive! The traffic!' She gave Elizabeth a perfunctory hug and then went around to the driver's side.

'Darren, can you get my stuff out first, I need a shower after that journey.' She turned to Elizabeth, 'I'm so tired, been a hellish time at work with the Covid, I'm exhausted. Come on Alison, get out and help your father.'

Elizabeth's other granddaughter still sat in the car. 'Dad turned off the engine!' she wailed, 'just when it got to the interesting bit on the DVD!' She pouted and hunched up in the seat.

'Daddy, will you turn on the engine again so Alison can watch the end of the DVD,' Bronwyn ordered her husband.

Meekly, he obliged.

Elizabeth noticed the small screen in the centre of the car. She was stunned by the behaviour of her youngest granddaughter, and by the response of her daughter.

'Come inside,' she said.

'I hope that dog isn't around,' Bronwyn said, 'my asthma's been really bad lately.'

'No,' Elizabeth said soothingly. 'Molly's staying across the road with a neighbour.'

'Hmm,' muttered Bronwyn.

'I'm staying there too,' continued Elizabeth, 'so you and Darren can have my room and the girls can have the spare bedroom.'

Bronwyn followed Elizabeth to her bedroom. 'I thought you'd be more comfortable here,' Elizabeth said, 'and no doggy smells.'

Bronwyn looked around the room and wrinkled her nose. 'It still has a doggy smell, but it'll do, I suppose,' she said grudgingly.

Elizabeth took a deep breath to dispel the anger rising in her chest. 'The girls can share the other bedroom; the twin beds should be okay for them.'

Bronwyn gave a small sniff of disapproval. 'Of course, they have their own rooms at home, and en-suites and the same in the place in Bali where we usually go.' She turned to her husband who was lugging in two heavy suitcases. 'In here, Darren.'

Elizabeth heard her granddaughters following their father. 'Where's my room, Nana?' called Chloë.

'Just here.' Elizabeth led her to the spare bedroom.

Chloë glanced in the door at the two beds. 'Don't tell me I have to share a room with Alligator!'

'I'm not an Alligator!' wailed Alison.

'You smell like one!' retorted her sister.

'Girls!' Their mother appeared. 'We all have to make the best of the situation.'

Elizabeth's heart sank. Just then Darren came in with another two suitcases. 'Girls, here are your cases.'

'That's mine,' Chloë grabbed one and Alison managed to take the other.

No word of thanks to their father, Elizabeth noted. She was beginning to feel very grateful to Will for his offer of accommodation. She looked at her watch, ten past four. 'I expect you'd like a cup of tea and something to eat,' was all she said.

'We stopped in Kiama for fish and chips,' Bronwyn said. 'The girls were starving.'

Elizabeth thought of the lamb tagine she'd made, thinking it would be easy to heat up whenever they arrived. Anyway, it was in the fridge.

Darren came in with the last of the luggage. 'How are you, Elizabeth?' he gave her a peck on the cheek. 'You're looking well.'

'Thank you, Darren. You too.' But he didn't, she thought. He appeared pale and a bit puffy.

'Well, I'll put the kettle on and let you all settle in.' Elizabeth moved towards the kitchen.

'What's for dinner, Nana?' Alison demanded.

'Well, I've made a Moroccan Lamb Tagine,' Elizabeth replied.

Chloë looked up from her mobile phone. 'Yuk! Meat! I don't eat meat anymore!'

Elizabeth took a deep breath. 'That's all right, there are lots of vegetables in the fridge, perhaps you can prepare a salad for yourself.'

'Elizabeth!' Bronwyn suddenly appeared. 'Chloë's too young to be using sharp knives. For goodness sake!' She was interrupted by the doorbell.

Darren moved towards the door and opened it, revealing the figure of Will blocking the doorway.

Bronwyn frowned at him. 'We don't need anything, thank you, whatever it is you're selling,' she said. 'Darren, close the door.'

Darren started to obey as Will took a step forward. 'Just wanted to ask Elizabeth what I should give Molly for her dinner.'

Hearing the doorbell, Elizabeth had come out of the kitchen. 'Oh, Will!' she exclaimed, then turned to Bronwyn. 'Bronwyn, this is my lovely neighbour, Will. I'm staying at his place while you're here. Will, this is my daughter, Bronwyn and her husband Darren. My granddaughters are in the kitchen. Girls!' she shouted. 'Come and meet my neighbour.' She turned back to the kitchen.

Bronwyn's jaw dropped. Darren stepped forward. 'Nice to meet you, Will.' He made to put out his hand, then suddenly remembered. 'Keep forgetting this social distancing stuff, and bumping elbows seems slightly silly.'

'I agree,' Will smiled at him.

Bronwyn made a humph sound and stood rigidly in the bedroom doorway.

Elizabeth emerged from the kitchen with a bag of dog biscuits and a tub of meat, reluctantly followed by her granddaughters. 'Will, this is Alison and this is Chloë. Girls, this is Will.'

The two girls stared at Will for a moment, then mumbled a 'Hi.'

Will nodded at them all. 'Right, I'll go, Molly's anxiously waiting for her dinner.' He smiled at Elizabeth. 'See you later, Beth.' He turned and left, leaving Darren to close the door.

Elizabeth started. Will had never called her "Beth" before. *Was he deliberately stirring things?* She smiled inwardly, suddenly feeling calmer.

Bronwyn came away from the bedroom door. 'You're staying with *that man* tonight?'

Elizabeth raised her chin and held her daughter's eyes. 'Yes, he thoughtfully offered to have me and Molly stay with him so you wouldn't have to put up with doggy dander and I won't have to sleep on the floor.' She moved back to the kitchen, followed by Bronwyn.

'But, he's ... he's ...' Bronwyn's voice trailed off.

'He's what?' Elizabeth demanded, turning to stare defiantly at her daughter.

'Black,' supplied Alison, not looking up from the television where she was trying to get the remote to work.

There was an awkward silence.

***

The atmosphere was charged. Bronwyn sulky and distant, the girls obnoxious, fighting over who was going to sleep in which of the twin beds, and then barely speaking, after they'd been separated by their father, who made them draw lots for the beds. Now they were occupied with their iPads, once they'd discovered Elizabeth didn't have any entertainment channels like Netflix.

Darren had tried to smooth things over, but after a few attempts, he disappeared out into the garden with a book until it got too dark to read.

It was after eight before they all eventually sat down to eat. Elizabeth couldn't believe her eyes when Chloë, having lined up the meat from her plate to one side, then put an elbow on the table, rested her chin on her hand and used the fork held in her other hand to push the rest of the food around, picking out the odd chickpea and eating it.

'Aren't you hungry, love?' asked Bronwyn, her voice filled with concern.

'I'm starving,' pouted Chloë, 'but I can't eat this stuff.'

'What would you like to eat?' Bronwyn glared at her mother. 'Chloë has a delicate stomach.' She turned back to her daughter. 'Nana might have a nice dessert for us?'

'There's ice cream in the freezer,' Elizabeth said, 'and fresh fruit.'

Chloë gave a slight shrug. 'That'll do, I 'spose.'

Elizabeth was astounded Bronwyn was letting her daughter get away with such bad manners. She looked at Alison, who was steadily working her way through her meal, but when she heard of the ice cream, she stopped eating and dropped her knife and fork with a clatter. 'Yummy,' she said. 'Can I have a double portion, 'cos I've eaten most of my dinner?'

Darren seemed embarrassed at the behaviour of his daughters. 'That was lovely. Thank you, Elizabeth.' He frowned at the girls.

Bronwyn stood and started to collect the plates. She placed them on the kitchen workbench and then sat down again. 'I see you still haven't got a dish-washer, Elizabeth.'

'No, dear, it's not worth it for just me,' Elizabeth replied.

After a moment of silence, Elizabeth got up and put dessert bowls on the table and fetched the ice cream and bowl of fruit. Silently, she served the dessert. They finished eating, and Elizabeth expected Bronwyn to tell the girls to clear the table and wash up, but they didn't move and it was Darren who stood and collected the plates.

Bronwyn eyed her mother and made a dismissive noise, then she frowned. 'I need to talk with you, I brought some nice wine, maybe we could sit outside now and have a glass.' She emphasized the 'nice', the implication being the wine Elizabeth had given them with the meal wasn't up to her standard.

As soon as they were both sitting outside, Darren still in the kitchen washing dishes, Bronwyn turned to her mother. 'I'm very worried at the way you've taken up with this Will person,' she said.

Elizabeth felt her hackles rise. 'Oh?'

'Well, it's just not appropriate, especially in front of the girls.'

Elizabeth swirled the wine in her glass and took a sip. 'Oh? In what way?'

Bronwyn's frown deepened. 'Elizabeth! For goodness sake, you know very well what I mean.'

'No, I don't, actually.'

'Carrying on with a coloured man, who's obviously much younger than you, and *calling you Beth*! So familiar.'

Elizabeth felt herself flushing. 'I'm not carrying on with him, whatever you mean by that! He's a nice man and just a friend.'

'Are you sleeping with him?'

Elizabeth choked on her wine. 'How dare you! What business is it of yours anyway?'

Bronwyn looked shaken. 'I don't know what's got into you, Elizabeth. You've changed. There's no need to get narky. If you'd only bought a decent new house close to us and big enough, this deplorable situation wouldn't have arisen. This man has obviously been manipulating you. Buttering you up with a sob story. He probably thinks you've got money; and like I said - he's so much younger than you!' She stopped and took a breath. 'Is he renting that house?'

Elizabeth stared at her daughter. She finished her glass of wine and stood up. 'It's getting late. I'm tired. I hope you all sleep well. I'm going over the road now. Goodnight. Oh, and by the way, I'll be going into town early in the morning to get seafood and other food. Perhaps you'd move your car so I can get mine out of the garage in the morning.'

Bronwyn's mouth fell open; for once she was speechless.

Elizabeth took her wineglass to the kitchen, rinsed it and said goodnight to Darren. 'Hope you sleep well, Darren.'

'I'm sure I will,' he replied. 'You too. Goodnight Elizabeth and thank you for having us. I'm sorry we've upset your routine.'

She smiled and nodded.

***

Elizabeth turned the key in the lock of Will's front door and tried not to make any noise. She heard Molly bark, and the next thing the kitchen door opened and Molly came rushing out to greet her.

'Hello, Moll!' Elizabeth bent and hugged her dog.

Will came out from the kitchen and leaned against the door frame, his arms folded, watching. 'Family all gone to bed?' He enquired.

'Don't know, don't care,' she replied.

'Hmm.' He went over and gently took her arm. 'Come into the kitchen and have a drink and tell me all about it. That's if you're up to it.'

Elizabeth sank into one of the kitchen chairs and buried her face in her hands. 'I've probably had too much to drink already this evening.'

Will sat down opposite her.

'It was awful, Will, I'd forgotten how Bronwyn is like a mixture of my mother and her father, my ex-husband. Bossy and domineering and she's totally spoilt those girls.'

'What about their father, Darren is it?'

'Yes. Darren. He acts just like my father did, says nothing, just does as he's told, well, like I did in my marriage.'

Will stood. 'I think you need either a cup of tea or a small glass of something.'

She managed a weak smile. 'A small glass of something, please.'

Will poured two glasses of red wine, gave her one and sat down with the other.

Elizabeth told him most of what had happened, omitting the bits about him.

'I hope I didn't stir things up,' he said.

She grinned and gave a shaky laugh. 'Well, you did actually, calling me Beth!'

'I'm sorry.'

'Don't be! I think I've surprised Bronwyn; she's never seen me so belligerent.'

'Belligerent, oh no, not you, Beth! That's the last thing I'd call you!'

'Well, assertive then.'

It was sometime later when Will stretched and said, 'We'd better call it a night. Would you like to use the bathroom first?'

Elizabeth nodded. 'Thanks.'

'Oh, and I'll show you where the tea and coffee are, just help yourself whenever you wake up, forage around in the fridge and pantry for breakfast.'

'Thanks again, Will. I don't know how I would have coped having to stay at home. Oh, by the way, it's Christmas Eve tomorrow and I'll be going into town early in the morning to get seafood. Can I get anything for you?' She suddenly had a thought. 'Oh, Will, what are you doing for Christmas Day?'

Will grinned. 'Just having an easy day, pottering in the garden, might head to the beach and have a swim. I could take Molly if that's okay with you. There's an off-leash area.'

'Molly would love it.' She lowered her eyes and hesitated. 'I was wondering, if you would like to come over for Christmas lunch?'

Will laughed. 'Thank you for asking, Beth, but I think I'd feel like the elephant in the room, so, um, no.'

She nodded. 'I'm sorry, Will, but you're probably right. 'Goodnight then.'

She smiled to herself when she went to her room to get her wash bag. She looked at the single bed with its brass bed ends, thinking Bronwyn was probably visualizing her and Will in bed together. She chuckled. Molly's tail thumped. 'Goodnight Molly.'

***

The next morning, after Elizabeth had left, Will was outside in his garden with Molly when he saw Iris hanging out her washing. He went over to the fence and called out, 'Hello Iris!'

Iris turned in confusion; when she saw him, she hastily pegged a towel to hide her undies on the line.

'Can I have a word, Iris?'

Iris nodded and came over to the fence. 'Good morning, Will.'

He smiled at her, she was so tiny and frail. 'Iris, I was wondering if you would do me a favour.'

She started and then said, 'If I can.'

'Well, as you know, I live on my own, but at the moment I'm looking after Elizabeth's dog, and Elizabeth is staying here at night, just while her family are here. Well, I'll be having Christmas lunch on my own, and it's a bit lonely, I was wondering if you would join me? And I think I've bought too much food ...'

Iris's face went pink.

'You'd be doing me a favour. But you might be too busy.'

'Well, I always seem to be busy,' Iris's dignified tone belied the smile of pleasure which lit up her face. 'But that's most kind of you, are you sure?'

He nodded. 'Oh, that's lovely of you Iris! You won't mind Molly, will you?'

Iris looked dubiously at Molly. 'No, no, of course not.' Will made a mental note to curb Molly's enthusiastic welcome to visitors.

'That's settled then, about two o'clock? Is that all right with you?'

Iris nodded and beamed at him. 'Thank you. What can I bring?'

'Why nothing. As I said, I always buy too much and you'll be doing me a great favour.'

***

All was quiet at her house when Elizabeth left Will's next morning. She decided to go straight to town, she'd remembered to put a big esky in the back of her car.

She returned home several hours later, exhausted after battling the queues of people at the fish market and the other shops.

She parked her car in the garage and noticed Bronwyn and Darren's big four-wheel-drive car had gone from the roadside where Darren must have moved it the night before.

Great, she thought, she'd be able to put her feet up and have a cup of tea before unpacking everything.

She opened the front door to be confronted by clutter. Damp towels were strewn around the bathroom. In the spare bedroom, it seemed the girls had emptied their cases on the floor and the beds. The door to her bedroom was thankfully closed. She'd had the foresight to take all the clothes and underwear she'd need for the week to Will's.

In the kitchen, dirty cups and bowls crowded the sink. On the kitchen table, a note read "Gone into town for breakfast".

Elizabeth looked at her watch. It was now eleven o'clock. She felt the electric kettle. It was warm. So they mustn't have been gone long. She filled the kettle, put it to boil and started to unpack her shopping, then realised there wasn't room in the fridge for all the seafood. Perhaps she'd gone overboard with the amount she'd bought. Living on her own for so long she found it hard to estimate quantities for five people.

She put some of the seafood back in the esky. Will might have room in his fridge for some of it until the next day.

With a deep sigh, she took her tea outside and sat under the veranda watching the birds and enjoying the peace. She missed Molly. She'd noticed Will's ute was gone from his driveway, so Molly was probably having fun at the beach with him. Maybe she'd spend half an hour with her cello to calm herself. *Her cello!* She jumped up and hurried to her study. It was still in its case propped against the wall. She heaved a sigh of relief, picked it up, took her keyring with Will's key on it, and went across the road.

She'd just placed the cello in a corner of Will's spare bedroom when she heard his ute returning and the next thing Will's voice calling Molly to come round the back. She walked out to the kitchen in time to see Will hosing Molly and Molly leaping and frisking to avoid the jet of water.

She opened the sliding door and watched until Will noticed her. He turned off the hose just as Molly spotted her owner. With a joyful woof, she leapt at Elizabeth and then shook herself, giving Elizabeth a cold shower. 'Hey!' Elizabeth exclaimed.

Will laughed. 'We've been in the water, Molly had a great time, but she was all salt and sand so I had to hose her down. You're early, I wasn't expecting you until this evening.'

'Oh, I'm not stopping. I had a sudden thought about my cello. I don't trust those granddaughters of mine not to go trying to play it and damaging it. So, I brought it over here.'

'Great! I'll have a live cello concert this evening?'

Elizabeth grinned. 'Probably not! By the way, can I put some food in your fridge, I think I've gone and bought too much so there's plenty if you'd like some. It's in the esky here.'

'I've asked Iris to have Christmas lunch with me tomorrow. I bought a small turkey that I thought I'd roast, but a little bit of seafood would be nice. Thanks.' Will took the esky and started transferring the contents to his fridge.

'Iris accepted?'

'Yes, I told her I'd bought too much food and that I'd feel very lonely spending Christmas Day on my own, and she graciously accepted.'

'What a manipulator you are!' she exclaimed but then her smile faded, Bronwyn's words suddenly coming back into her mind.

'She's such a sweet little lady, and looked thrilled when I asked her.'

'Yes, she is. Well, I'd better go back, lots to do.' Elizabeth expected her dog would try and follow her, but after noisily slurping at her water bowl, Molly flopped down beside Will and fell asleep. 'Moll looks exhausted.'

'Well, she's swum and run and played all morning.'

'Thanks, Will.'

Elizabeth went back to her own house in a thoughtful mood. *Who was Will? Was he what he seemed? Did the story about it being his grandmother's house ring true? What did she really know about him?*

Sydney - 1851

In 1851 Victoria broke away from New South Wales and became a separate colony. By coincidence, at that same time, gold was discovered near Clunes. Some people thought the discovery of gold had been covered up until after the formation of Victoria as an independent colony. They didn't want the gold mines to be taken over by New South Wales.

At just sixteen years old, Edmund Turner read about both events a few days later in the newspaper. In a thoughtful mood, he finished reading and started to think back over his life; back to his twin brother and sister, Edwin and Hannah. He'd been five when he'd caught Scarlet Fever. He barely remembered it, but the twins who caught it from him both died. He'd been sure it was his fault, and everyone thought it should have been him who died, not the family favourites, Edwin and Hannah. He still felt guilty that he'd wished they'd never been born, and then suddenly they were gone. A few months later his father, Edward, had died of the same sickness. He, Edmund, had probably given it to him too. His mother had taken on the running of The Stonemason's Arms, the public house their father had built. It had been a difficult period. No one had any time for him, they were all busy helping their mother. Two years after the epidemic, she'd also died. He'd been seven years old. There had been a few bad years and a lot of toing and froing. Someone had taken over the public house as a trustee for the young Turners. But there had been problems - the trustee hadn't done his best for the orphaned children.

Mary-Ann, his eldest sister, had married two years after their mother's death, followed just a month later by the marriage of his eldest brother, John. That was when the family started to crumble. A year later Elizabeth married, but she'd died in childbirth.

Ellen married in 1850 when she was seventeen; another one to leave the family home. A year later James had married.

Now, here he was, on his own, well, he was living with Mary-Ann and her husband, Nat, but she'd lost a few babies and she wasn't the same jolly sister she used to be. He felt in the way and he didn't want to live with James and his wife, Elizabeth. She was only two years older, and he had feelings for her. He couldn't bear the thought of her and James sleeping together. He picked up the Sydney Morning Herald and scanned the shipping news for boats leaving for Melbourne ... he started to daydream ...

A few months later he was ready. He began visiting the wharves every day until the masters of the vessels moored there got tired of him. The smart brigs and schooners with their sails excited him. Eventually, he found the *Bluebird* going to Melbourne with a cargo of tea, oats and potatoes.

The skipper, a burly man with a grizzled beard raised his head as Edmund approached.

'Any chance I can come with you to Melbourne? I can work my passage,' Edmund asked.

'Work yer passage!' the skipper scoffed. 'And what do you know about sailing? I lose half my crew to the gold mines on every trip to Melbourne. I can take you on the return trip all right, when I'm missing a few men!' He turned back to the ropes he was checking.

Edmund sighed and started to walk away. 'Thanks anyway,' he said.

The master turned back and looked up at Edmund. 'Hold on a minute, lad,' he said. 'What's yer name? You're too young to be goin' to the goldfields.'

'Edmund Turner and I'm eighteen.' Edmund puffed out his chest and tried to appear taller and older than his sixteen years.

'Any relation to Edward Turner? Used to keep The Stonemason's Arms?'

'My father, but he's been dead these ten years.'

The master straightened and studied Edmund. 'Yes, I heard and yer mother too.' He stroked his beard. 'Hard-working family. Yer dad did me a turn once. You look just like him.' He held out his hand. 'Captain Bruce. Well, if the weather's favourable we'll be leaving tomorrow. You can scrub the decks and help. Be here at eight.'

Edmund let out a yelp of delight. He took the captain's hand. 'Thank you, captain! I must go to the stores in King Street now and get a tent and other equipment.' As he turned to go, the captain put a hand on his shoulder.

'Not so fast, laddie. You won't need to buy any gear here; you can buy it all cheap at the goldfields from men who've been lucky and are going home. Maybe get a canvas and ropes. That way you can make a tent and a hammock when you get there. There's a spare hammock here you can use on board.'

'Oh! Thank you.' Edmund's face fell. He'd been several times to the King Street stores examining all the accoutrements for gold mining and planning what he'd buy. Perhaps the captain was right.

'Do you have a trade, laddie?' The captain fixed his gaze on Edmund.

'Um well, I've been working with a farrier, helping hold the horses when they're being shoed, and helping the local blacksmith ...'

The captain nodded. 'Both useful trades on the goldfields. Right then, laddie, I'll see you tomorrow.'

Edmund headed straight into Sydney to Waterloo House in King Street. He'd been saving hard for the past year. Although tempted by the range of goods for prospectors in the store, he was mindful of what the captain had advised.

He couldn't wait to tell Mary-Ann, he was sure she'd be pleased to have him find his feet and strike out on his own.

'Mary-Ann! Mary-Ann! Where are you?' he shouted as he went into her house.

'In the garden.'

He raced out to find her bent over a row of cabbages, busy squashing caterpillars. She straightened, holding her back and grunting. 'What's up? A fire?'

'No, no, I've got a place on a boat going to Victoria. I'm going to prospect for gold!'

She looked puzzled, 'Gold? There's no gold in Victoria, California yes, not Victoria.'

'Yes, there is, I've read about it in the papers, you're behind the times, Mary-Ann.'

She shrugged. 'Got no time to be reading newspapers. Anyway, I'm not letting you go. You're too young to be going off by yourself, mixing with all kinds of low life.' She turned and resumed her quest for caterpillars. 'You can help me in the garden if you've nothing better to do.'

Disappointed at her lack of support, he went inside and started gathering up a few things he'd need. Unable to stay still he wandered out and around to the blacksmith and told him his news.

***

Mary-Ann watched his retreating figure. He looked just like their father, she thought. He'd be tall and handsome in a few years, with those kind brown eyes and dark hair.

***

At last, Edmund was on board the *Bluebird*. He gazed at the two square-rigged masts. He knew brigs were fast and manoeuverable but difficult to sail into the wind. He stored his sack and said a quick prayer that the winds would be favourable.

The captain called one of the sailors over. 'Show yon laddie where he can sleep,' he ordered.

'Here!' The sailor tossed a hammock over to Edmund, who nearly fell over with its weight as he tried to catch it.

He was given a pail of water and a scrubbing brush to scrub the decks. Two hours later and he ached all over. He thought of the maids who'd worked in The Stonemason's Arms. They scrubbed floors for hours ...

His red hands and aching muscles were the least of his worries as the brig faced the open sea and his stomach spewed up his latest meal.

One night, wrapped in his hammock, he overheard two of the sailors, Jake and Joe, whispering plans about jumping ship at Melbourne and walking to the goldfields to try their luck at prospecting. He leaned closer to catch what they were saying and tumbled out of his hammock.

'You listenin' in on us, laddie?' one of the men growled.

'No, no, I just turned over, I'm not used to sleeping in a hammock.' Edmund climbed back in and wrapped himself up and turned away from the men.

'Better not.' The other man coughed, hawked and spat onto the floor.

Edmund thought of his father, who'd died when he, Edmund, had been only five years old. He barely remembered him. Mary-Ann, twelve years older, had told him about their father. How he'd come from England as a convict and had been a lovely kind man, making sure his children all went to school. Now Edmund thought how awful it must have been for his father on the voyage out from England, months at sea, crammed in with other men.

The weather worsened and the *Bluebird* made for Two Fold Bay, where they sheltered for three days. The captain had taken a liking to Edmund and gave him lots of advice about gold prospecting - things he'd heard from diggers returning after having found enough gold and wanting to go home. Edmund listened politely; he was sure it wouldn't apply to him.

By the time they'd rounded Green Cape Edmund had found his sea legs and the crew had accepted the puny young boy who seemed to be trying his best to fit in and be useful.

At last, they reached Melbourne.

Wambecarra - December 2020

Elizabeth managed to survive the Christmas period. The weather was good, so Bronwyn, Darren and the girls went out most days, Elizabeth didn't know or care where. They came back in the evening telling her all about the places they'd been. Places Elizabeth would have liked to have gone to, but they never invited her. Anyway, she consoled herself, the thought of being cooped up between her two granddaughters and having to endure Bronwyn's lectures was reason enough not to regret it.

On the fifth day, the weather changed and it started to rain. Bronwyn complained about the lack of amenities in Elizabeth's house - no en-suite, small rooms, no Netflix and nothing worth watching on the television.

Elizabeth watched Darren's reaction to his wife's whining. He simply nodded and tried to placate her. The girls spent hours on their electronic devices until they got cranky and started picking fights with each other.

Eventually, Bronwyn decided there was no point in staying any longer. The weather forecast didn't look good for the rest of the week. 'We might as well go home,' she announced after dinner. 'At least we have a decent entertainment system and there's no dog smell.'

Elizabeth was affronted, but she kept quiet. As far as she was concerned, the sooner Bronwyn left, the better. Then Bronwyn frowned.

'What about the ancestry stuff, Elizabeth? What have you found out?'

'Quite a lot,' replied Elizabeth. She paused, waiting for everyone's attention. 'We're actually descended from a convict.'

Bronwyn's brows drew together, 'A common felon?'

'Yes,' replied Elizabeth, deciding not to correct her. She saw Darren trying to hide a smile.

Alison looked up from her iPad. 'Golly, was he a thief? Or a murderer?'

'Can't be right,' Bronwyn said, dismissively. 'You've obviously gone down the wrong line. I'm sure our ancestors must have been free settlers!'

'Possibly,' acknowledged Elizabeth. If she let Bronwyn keep thinking that way, then she might stop bugging her.

Bronwyn stood up. 'Right. We'll head off in the morning. Girls! You can make a start on packing.'

Her daughters didn't move.

Darren stood and started clearing the table. He smiled at Elizabeth.

***

By eleven o'clock the next morning, Bronwyn, Darren and the girls were installed in their four-wheel drive and Darren was backing out the driveway. Elizabeth heaved a sigh of relief as she waved goodbye.

She went back indoors and surveyed her little house. Slowly she started collecting towels and bedlinen and filled the washing machine. Then she started on the kitchen. By midday, she had restored some kind of order. She looked at her watch. Time to go and get Molly and her stuff from Will's.

Will wasn't at home when Elizabeth let herself into his house and started gathering up her belongings. First, her cello, and Molly, who didn't seem to mind being led back across the road.

'I've missed you, Moll,' Elizabeth said, bending down to pat her dog. 'What can I give to Will to thank him for having us, do you think?'

Molly wagged her tail and licked Elizabeth's hand. As Elizabeth was walking down Will's path on her second trip with her suitcase and Molly's food and water bowls, Iris peered over the garden fence.

'Oh, Elizabeth,' she exclaimed, 'you're moving back home! Will so enjoyed having you and Molly. He told me so. What a lovely man, he is.' She paused. 'Even if he is, you know ...'

Elizabeth nodded and smiled. 'Yes, my family have all gone home, so I have peace and quiet again.'

Iris nodded. 'Peace and quiet is nice. But sometimes it's good to have company.' Her tone was wistful.

Elizabeth smiled at her. 'You're welcome to come over anytime, Iris. I'd love your company.'

'Really?' Iris beamed.

'Yes, indeed. I know I seem busy all the time, but I'd love to have the odd cup of tea and chat with you. Why don't you come over tomorrow morning for a coffee?' Elizabeth thought she'd probably regret it in the morning, but the look on Iris's face made it worthwhile.

'About eleven?' Iris said, tentatively.

'Perfect.' Elizabeth smiled. 'See you then.' She thought Iris seemed to have a spring in her step as she disappeared into her garden.

Elizabeth went back to Will's house and stripped the bed she'd been sleeping in, taking the sheets and pillowcases to wash. Carefully she covered the bed with the patchwork quilt.

At six-thirty that evening, her doorbell rang. She hurried to the front door eagerly followed by Molly. She opened the door to reveal a smiling Will. Molly immediately jumped up and joyously welcomed him.

'Come in, Will.'

'I see you've moved back home,' he smiled. 'I missed you.'

She didn't know if he meant he'd missed her presence, or been out and missed seeing her leave.

'I liked having you there, even if it was only at night, and I loved having Molly.' He bent and stroked the dog's head and she immediately fawned all over him.

'Come in and sit down, Will. How can I ever thank you? I'd have gone nuts if I'd had to be here with Molly, and Bronwyn complaining all the time about dog dander and the doggy smell. Not to mention having to sleep on the floor in my study.'

Will shook his head. 'No, the pleasure was all mine. If I hadn't made up my mind to move to England after all this Covid stuff dies down, I'd get a dog like Molly.' His tone was wistful, but his words made Elizabeth start.

'You're going to England?'

'Didn't I mention it?' Will frowned. 'I'm thinking of going to England to try and find my extended family.'

'Oh.' Elizabeth's mind did a somersault, 'Where will you start?'

'Don't know yet.' Will grimaced, then grinned. 'So how did your daughter react when you told her she was descended from a convict?'

Elizabeth laughed, trying to shake herself from her doubts about Will. 'She wasn't impressed. I didn't disabuse her of her impression that she was descended from a common felon! I think she was hoping her ancestor was someone on the First Fleet, or a free settler.'

'Hmm,' Will smiled then was silent. Elizabeth watched him, he seemed miles away.

'Iris enjoyed her Christmas lunch with you.' Elizabeth changed the subject.

'Yes. She told me things about my grandmother. Kathleen.'

'Oh?'

'Yes. She was very discreet, though. Didn't mention my grandfather, except to say he was a bit difficult.' He sighed. 'I wish I'd known her.'

They chatted for a while and then Will stood up. 'I'd better get going. Busy day tomorrow.'

Elizabeth saw him to the door and then sat deep in thought. When she was with Will, she felt so at ease, but once on her own, Bronwyn's words kept going round in her head. What did she really know about Will? Apart from the fact he said his name was Will Barnes and he'd had a landscaping business in Sydney and his grandmother had left him the house. It all sounded suss. Perhaps he'd bought the house and Kathleen and her husband were no relation, but why would he invent such an outlandish story as that? Then she suddenly remembered when she first met Will, outside Merv's house when she was putting out her bin, Merv had told them about Kathleen and the runaway daughter. What if that had been the first Will had heard about the daughter and he used it to make up the story about his parents? And if the house wasn't his, why would he be spending money and effort doing it up? Perhaps someone was letting him live there, rent-free on condition Will renovated the place and landscaped the garden, but who would do that?

How could she find out more about him? Then she felt guilty about doubting him.

***

Elizabeth woke in the night with the solution. Jolly old Google! She couldn't wait until morning. She slid out of bed trying not to wake Molly and went to get her laptop. Molly opened one eye and regarded her owner as Elizabeth got back into bed and opened up the search screen. She typed in Will Barnes. Nothing. She tried William Barnes. She tried Wilfred Barnes. Then she typed Landscaping Sydney Barnes. Nothing.

Maybe Will's landscaping business had another name. Elizabeth racked her brains to think of other search elements but couldn't think of any. With a sigh, she shut down her laptop and tried to get back to sleep. *Blast Bronwyn! Why did she have to come stirring up everything?*

Eventually, Elizabeth drifted off to sleep, waking early in the morning feeling exhausted and cranky. She was no further forward!

At eleven her doorbell rang. Exasperated, Elizabeth went to answer it. If it was someone selling religion, she'd slam the door in their face. She threw open the door, to reveal little Iris, standing there with an expectant look on her face.

'Oh! Iris!' Elizabeth had forgotten all about her invitation. She restrained Molly who was eagerly welcoming the visitor. 'Come in, through here.'

Iris clapped her hands when she saw Elizabeth's kitchen. 'Oh, it's just like Will's!' she exclaimed, 'so nice!'

Elizabeth didn't want to launch into a long explanation as to how Will had used her plans to remodel his kitchen.

'Sit down, Iris. Now, what would you like, tea or coffee?'

'Whatever you're having dear.'

Elizabeth put the kettle on and started to prepare coffee.

'Will is such a gentleman, isn't he dear? Such good manners. I wish more men were like him. Mind you, my Albert had lovely manners ...' Iris rambled on about her late husband, and Will, and the lovely garden he'd made.

Elizabeth set two cups of coffee on the table. 'Help yourself to sugar and milk, Iris.' She suddenly felt so tired. The week with Bronwyn and the girls and tidying up the mess after they'd left and now the sleepless night had taken its toll. She yawned. 'Sorry, Iris, it's been a busy time and I'm not sleeping very well.'

Iris's eyes filled with concern. 'Oh, I'm sorry to hear that, dear.' She smiled shyly, 'I find a cup of hot milk with a dash of brandy helps me to nod off.'

Elizabeth made an effort to smile. 'Thank you, Iris, I might try that.'

Iris finished her coffee. 'Thank you dear, that was very nice, and I've enjoyed our little chat. I won't keep you as I know you're busy. Perhaps you'd like to come and have a coffee with me one day?'

'That would be lovely, Iris.' Elizabeth smiled at her. 'Maybe next week? What about this day next week? Eleven o'clock?'

Iris's face lit up. 'That would be perfect!' she exclaimed as she got to her feet.

Elizabeth went to the front door with her; Iris seemed such a tiny, fragile little woman. As she waved goodbye, the thought came to her that Will had won Iris over, she couldn't stop talking about him. *Had Will manipulated Iris?*

VICTORIA 1852 - ON THE WAY TO THE MOUNT ALEXANDER GOLDFIELDS

The captain of the *Bluebird* shook Edmund's hand. 'Good luck, laddie,' he said. 'Mind now and meet up with some chums. You can't do it alone.'

'Thank you, Captain,' Edmund replied. From the corner of his eye, he saw the two sailors who'd been planning to leave the *Bluebird* going ashore. The bags over their shoulders suggested they wouldn't be returning to the ship anytime soon.

'Don't bother looking for gold, laddie, you'll make more money sharpening picks!' the captain chuckled.

Edmund nodded. 'Thank you, Captain. I'll bear that in mind.' Of course, he had no intention of doing so, he would strike gold!

After leaving the captain, and his cargo of oats, tea and potatoes, Edmund scanned the crowded wharves with a mixture of excitement mingled with alarm. He knew no one. He pulled his sack of belongings closer to his body and touched the slight bulge under his jacket where his savings were safely sewn into his vest.

Not knowing where to go he saw a troop of women and young girls disembarking from a schooner. Thinking they must know where they were going, he started to follow them. As he caught up with them, he saw the two sailors, Jake and Joe, in front, heading in the same direction as the women.

Jake turned around when he sensed someone behind him. 'Well, well, if it's not the young laddie!' he exclaimed. Joe stopped and peered at Edmund. 'Where are you off to then?'

Edmund shrugged. 'Dunno. Just following the crowd into Melbourne.'

Jake gave a wink and a gap-toothed smile. 'Well, I'm going to get me a "wife".' He indicated the column of women 'They're the latest band of Chisholm women. Ten pounds and take your pick.'

Edmund was puzzled. 'I don't understand.'

'Woman called Caroline Chisholm. Thinks the men on the goldfields need the softening influence of women, so she's been rounding up destitute women in England and shipping them out here. So, I'm going to get me a nice big buxom one who can wash and cook and knows how to please a man.' He winked and leered.

'Not a young, pretty one?' Joe asked.

Jake smirked. 'All look the same in the dark. Come on laddie, you might as well tag along with us.'

Edmund didn't really feel like joining the two sailors, however, they seemed to know what they were doing. He sighed and followed them.

They trudged on until they came to a rise in the ground. Edmund caught his breath and blinked. Spread out before them was a vast array of tents. 'What are all these tents? Is this the goldfields?' he managed to stutter, 'and what's that in the distance?'

'Nah, just people on their way to the diggings,' replied Jake, 'and that's Melbourne over there.'

'How do you know all these things?' Edmund's eyes narrowed.

'Talked to lot of men,' Jake coughed and spat. 'Last trip down from Sydney wiv the *Bluebird*. Few men returning with their gold. Told me how to go about it,' he paused and surveyed the scene.

'Now we keep going until we get close to Melbourne. We can buy everything we need there.'

The three men trudged on until they reached the outskirts of Melbourne, where Jake stopped and turned to the other two. 'Right. First of all, pitch our tents. You got a tent, laddie?'

Edmund shook his head. 'No, but I've got a strong canvas and some tools.'

Joe was impatient to get going. 'Do we have to stop here? Why don't we keep going? How far is it to the diggings anyway?'

'About eighty miles, so I've heard. I reckon we camp here for two nights, get ourselves sorted with what we need and then start early the following morning. Come on, let's find a spot to set up.' Jake scanned the area. 'Then I'm going into town to get a few things and sound out a few people.' He pointed to a spot at the edge of the tent city near a huge gum tree. 'Right lad, help us put up the tent, then you stay and guard it while we go for a few things. Got any money? We need to buy food and gear.'

Edmund hesitated. He didn't want to get his money out of his vest and let Jake see how much he had. Luckily, he had a sovereign in his inside pocket. He took it out and showed Jake, who looked at it scornfully.

'Hope you got more than that.'

Edmund was silent. Jake took the coin and turned to Joe. 'Come on Joe. We'll leave yon laddie to put up our tent.'

The two men set off.

Edmund watched them leave. This wasn't how it was supposed to happen. After a few moments, he turned to the men's kit bags and started to take out the canvas tent. He'd need some timber stakes and props. He looked around, most of the site had been denuded of trees but he spotted one not far away which would yield a few likely pieces of timber. He took a small axe from his kit bag and soon had some poles cut and two with a 'Y' shaped end which he managed to get into the ground with a longer pole resting on each 'Y'. With difficulty he got the canvas tent erected which cheered him up a bit. He decided to get some coins from his vest in the privacy of the tent; he'd need money not only for food but also, apparently, for the licence to dig for gold. His stomach rumbled as he carefully folded his money bag back into his vest pocket. *When would the two men return with food?* Also, it was getting cold, the weak spring sun had disappeared and the temperature had suddenly dropped. Edmund went off in search of kindling. It was difficult to find any, seemed everyone else had the same idea.

He had a few abortive attempts at lighting a fire when he heard a voice say, 'Need help?'

He looked up to see a girl carrying a pail of water.

'Just trying to get a fire going.'

She put down her pail and went off, coming back a few minutes later with handfuls of dried grass. 'See, this is how you do it.' She scooped out a hollow in the dirt and placed a few twigs across it. Then put the dried grass on top and the remaining twigs Edmund had gathered. 'Now, light it.'

Edmund did as she said, and in no time at all, there was a steady fire going. 'Thank you.'

She smiled, picked up her pail, strode off and was soon lost to sight in the hundreds of tents.

Edmund watched her go. He could see out of the corner of his eye Jake and Joe coming along the muddy path. Both were somewhat inebriated, and a tall, plump woman stumbled after them. Two men pulling a cart brought up the rear.

'Ho! Laddie!' Jake threw down a sack in front of Edmund. 'Spuds and mutton. Get the tucker on.' He ogled the woman, who had fair hair carelessly caught up in a knot at the back of her head. Her long skirts were encrusted with mud and she carried a bag made of pieces of patchwork. 'Cum 'ere, lass.' He shoved her towards Edmund, who tried not to show his distaste. 'Sally, this here is Eddy.' Then he turned to Edmund and winked at the woman. 'She's me wife now. We did the jumpin' over the broomsticks to make it all official.' He gave a snorting laugh. 'Hope you got a seprit tent fer us, Laddie.'

'Er, hello Sally,' Edmund managed to say. Sally didn't smile, just nodded.

Edmund didn't know what to do. He'd only erected the one tent, not expecting to have to share with a woman. 'Umm,' he mumbled. 'I'll be all right wrapped in my canvas.' He took the sack Jake had thrown down on the ground and opened it. Potatoes and a lump of mutton fell out. Fortunately, he'd fetched water from the creek, murky as it was, and had it boiling over the campfire. He dropped the meat and then the potatoes into the pot.

The other two men stood watching, saying nothing as Jake gestured towards them. 'We're all "chums" now,' he laughed, looking sideways at them. A little mockingly, Edmund thought, wondering what the two men were doing with Jake.

Jake turned to them. 'This here is little Eddy; hard-working lad. Come on now laddie, keep the fire going,' Jake said, then jerked his thumb towards the two men. 'An' this here is Harold and Jasper, they're joining us. They've just come off the boat from England. Got this grand billy cart and are going to help us. We'll help them too,' he added hastily.

Edmund stepped forward and held out his hand to the first man. They looked like they'd come from prosperous families and knew nothing of roughing it.

'Edmund Turner,' he said.

'Jasper Smith,' the first man replied, taking Edmund's hand.

The other man followed suit. 'Harold Bennet.'

Jake lost interest in them, moving towards Sally. 'Cum 'ere lass,' he tried to pull her towards the tent. She hesitated and scanned the area, her face showing her dismay, but she said nothing.

Joe stood dumbly to one side, a picture of misery. Suddenly there was an almighty volley of sound. Terrified, Edmund jumped up. 'Wh...what was that?'

Jake gave a sneering laugh. 'Just all the diggers testing their ammunition! Happens every night apparently. Never know when you'll need to shoot someone coming to steal yer gold. Or yer wumman ...' He looked suggestively at Sally and made to pinch her bottom, but she moved out of the way. 'Hope you lot have pistols,' Jake continued. 'You'll need them when we go through Black Forest. Bushrangers.' His words were slurred. Edmund watched Joe, who averted his gaze.

Harold pushed their billy cart near the tent. 'We've got our own tent,' he said, then turned to Edmund. 'There's room for another person if you want.'

'Thanks.' Edmund nodded, grateful not to have to share the tent with Jake, Sally and Joe.

By the time Edmund had helped Harold and Jasper put up their tent, the potatoes and mutton were cooked. The Englishmen had brought a camp oven and flour and Sally made damper. They sat on the ground around the fire and helped themselves to the food. Edmund noticed Jasper daintily picking at the food, pushing bits of ash out of his dish, and thought Jasper must have had a desk job back in England as his hands were slender and uncalloused. Edmund filled the billy kettle to make tea.

All around them was noise and confusion as campfires burned and arguments between the diggers erupted. Edmund was glad when eventually Jake stood up and announced he was going for a piss and then turning in. 'Come on Sal.' He grabbed Sally's arm and pulled her away from the fire out into the darkness. A few minutes later they reappeared and went into the tent. Joe shrugged and followed them.

Edmund turned to Harold and Jasper. 'Guess we'd better do the same,' he said. 'Might be a long day tomorrow.'

Harold nodded. 'How did you get to know Jake and Joe?' He asked as he and Jasper went into the tent.

Edmund followed them. 'They were sailors on the ship I came in from Sydney. Where did you meet them?'

Jasper sighed. 'We were given a list of items to bring but when we got to Melbourne, we realised we'd brought too much of the wrong things, then we saw others like us along Flinders Street, selling their stuff. So we decided to do the same.'

'What kind of stuff?' queried Edmund.

'Oh, clothes; I had beautiful white linen shirts, dress shoes, books, my violin ...' Jasper sniffed and swallowed. 'Other things.'

'It's all right.' Harold patted Jasper's hand, 'I'll buy you a lovely new violin when we settle here.'

Edmund blinked at the familiar gesture.

'Anyway,' continued Harold. 'Jake and Joe came along looking at our gear. We'd bought a kind of barrow, to carry our things in, billy carts I think they call them here. Jake wanted to buy it, but we said no, so then he said why didn't we come with them to the diggings and all help each other.' He frowned. 'It seemed like a good idea at the time, and then Joe started shouting out to people about the fine things we were selling, and in no time, most of the things we didn't need had been sold. Jasper didn't want to sell his violin, but Jake convinced us it would be a liability on the goldfields.'

He lay down on the rough bed he'd made for him and Jasper. 'Goodnight, Edmund,' he said. 'Good night,' Jasper echoed and lay down; Harold covered them both up with a coarse woollen blanket.

'Goodnight,' Edmund said, as he tried to ignore the noises coming from the other tent. He spread out a blanket, bundled up his remaining clothes to form a pillow and lay down. Eventually, he managed to get to sleep, waking at dawn to the smell of a fire and the remaining mutton chops and potatoes cooking in the campfire.

He breathed deeply. Here he was at last and no one knew where he was. He'd told Mary-Ann he was going to Melbourne to prospect for gold. She'd been dismayed, but as she'd just miscarried again, she seemed too wrapped up in her grief to pay much attention to him. He looked over at the other two men, who were still rolled up in their blankets, snoring softly. 'Wake up lads,' he said, prodding them. He put his head outside the tent, it was still early dawn, the sun hadn't yet risen. Sally was bent over the fire.

'Get a move on Laddie, and get yon lads up too and pack up the tent.' Jake's voice came out of the gloom.

'I thought we were going to camp here another night?' Edmund queried.

'Change of plan. We got everything we need now. Got my woman, got chums, sooner we get that gold the better,' Jake turned to Sally. 'Damper cooked yet?'

She shook her head and poked the fire. A shower of sparks landed on her skirt.

After the meal, when they'd finished eating, Jake threw wet tea leaves from the billy over the fire to douse it. As they were about to leave, Jasper spoke up. 'Um, I need to find a toilet.'

Jake narrowed his eyes. 'If you want to shit, just go and shit then.' He pointed to a tree. 'That's where I went.'

Jasper paled and glanced at Harold, who nodded.

'And don't take long,' Jake called after him. 'We're leaving soon.'

Twenty minutes later they were on the road.

They walked all morning, catching up with other prospectors. '"Chums" they call them,' Joe reported after chatting with some of the men headed towards the diggings at Mount Alexander.

'We know all about "chums". You pal up with them and share the digging.' Jake considered. 'Need someone to stay behind, mind the tent and get the vittles ready while the others go and find the gold. Get a dog if we can find one. Take it in turns.' He stared at Edmund. 'You would've been best at minding the tent. Too puny for digging. Now we have Sally.'

Edmund was incensed, he was as strong as any of them. He'd worked for a blacksmith in Sydney, and although he might appear weak, he was actually very strong. He took turns with Jasper and Harold at pulling the billy cart. Joe, Jake and Sally walked in front, Jake often spotting items previous travellers, weary with the weight they were carrying, had discarded. He picked up the more useful articles and piled them onto the billy cart.

'First stop, Five Mile Creek,' announced Jake. 'Lincolnshire Arms. We can get cold meat and beer there.'

After their short break, they trudged on through the Keilor Plains, until they came to a collection of tents. People had stopped and were lighting campfires. 'Must be Diggers Rest,' said Jake. He dropped his kit bag and turned to the others. 'Okay, *chums*, we'll camp here for the night. No need to put up the tents, takes too long. It's a fine evening. We'll sleep under the stars.' He winked at Sally. 'Got a spare hammock for you Sal.'

Edmund was relieved to take off his pack and stretch his shoulders. He reckoned they must have walked twenty miles and his feet hurt. People were milling around; campfires were being lit and there seemed to be an atmosphere of jollity. He looked over at Sally. She'd been silent most of the way. Now she was busy getting the pots and pans out of the billy cart.

'Stop daydreaming - go and find kindling, boy.' Jake scowled at Edmund.

Edmund scurried off.

Jasper and Harold decided they would put up their tent despite Jake, who had strung two hammocks side by side from the sturdy branches of two trees. Joe also put up a hammock, but as far away from Jake as possible.

Edmund returned with firewood and got a fire going. Sullen Sal, as he called her in his mind, soon had a camp oven over the flames with their evening meal cooking; the usual: mutton, potatoes and damper, followed by sweet black tea.

They sat around the fire eating their meal, to the accompaniment of the surrounding blast of guns being fired, dogs barking, the muted sound of bullocks' bells and raised voices. Afterwards, Jake gave them a lecture. 'I gotta few tips from diggers going back to Melbourne. Seems we gotta get going fast in the morning.' He paused to pick his teeth with a grimy fingernail, then continued, 'In case we get stuck in Black Forest where the bushrangers hang out.' He glowered at Jasper who had clutched Harold's arm at the sound of bushrangers. 'I reckons we get past the Bush Inn and as close as possible to Black Forest camp tomorrow night, camp there, then the following morning make an early start and try and get through Black Forest before dark. Make sure youse has got ammunition before we leave the Bush Inn.'

The next morning, they trudged on, managing to get through the notorious Black Forest before dark, and made camp at what they called Woodend. Three days later, they heard a dull rumble of noise which gradually got louder, then, just before sunset, they rounded a hill to see the promised land of Mount Alexander and stopped in amazement. Spread out before them was a sprawling vista of tents separated by dirt tracks, deep holes and piles of dirt. *There must be hundreds and hundreds of tents!* Edmund thought. The whole area had been denuded of trees and vegetation and the scene was a cacophony of noise - barking dogs tied to posts driven into the ground outside tents, the din of cradles being rocked back and forth over open diggings, the sounds of picks and shovels hitting rock and the curses and shouts of men. A few women wandered around. Blacksmiths could be seen beating the points of picks. But the worst thing was the smell. Not only the decaying carcasses of animals rotting outside tents which must have been used as slaughter yards but also the animal and even human faeces with their attendant retinue of flies.

Jasper put his hand over his mouth. 'I think I'm going to be sick,' he mumbled, doubling over.

Even Jake seemed surprised by the conditions. 'No time for that,' he growled at Jasper. 'Got to get our camp going before dark. You lot stay here while I go and have a scout around.'

Harold shrugged and took an axe out from the billy cart. 'Come on Jasper,' he said and the two men walked off towards a distant thicket of trees.

A feeling of utter defeat swept over Edmund. Somehow, he hadn't envisioned the diggings like this. He hadn't realised thousands of men had swept into Mount Alexander lured by the thought of gold. There were dozens of tent shops selling anything and everything. *What chance did he have to find gold?* The words of the master of the *Bluebird* came back to him. *Get work with a blacksmith laddie!*

Boiling inside, Edmund set off with a pail, making his way past deep holes that had been mined and left open, some filled with water and floating, bloated, dead animals. The smell was overpowering. His heart sank when he got to the creek and found only a murky brown sludge contaminated with gold washings and debris. This was even worse than he'd expected. He mentally shrugged and started walking further up the creek until the water appeared less putrid, then he filled his bucket, and walked back, dodging the snarling, mangy dogs tethered to tent poles, and eventually managed to find his companions.

Joe peered into the pail. 'That the best you can do, laddie? Took you long enough.'

'Yes,' replied Edmund. 'I had to walk along the creek to find some clear water.' But his words were drowned by the sudden explosive sound of many rifles being fired which made him jump, spilling half the murky water. He remembered Jake had said this happened every night.

Sally tossed potatoes into the camp oven, poured in the liquid from Edmund's pail and set it over the fire.

The smoke-filled area all around was lit up by campfires, as men returned from the diggings to their tents. Edmund noticed most tents had some kind of marker on them, a national flag or sign, enabling the diggers to each find their own tents.

While the food was cooking Edmund and Harold set up their tent with the poles they'd found.

***

The next morning as they were eating breakfast, Jake looked at them all. 'Now then mates, we have to stake out a claim and each of us buy a licence. I noticed yesterday a long queue at the Commissioner's tent, so I reckon we'll give Jasper our thirty bob and he can buy five licences while the rest of us go out and claim a site. One licence gives each of us an eight feet by six feet claim.'

'Thirty shillings? That's daylight robbery!' exclaimed Harold.

Jasper's eyes widened. 'Um, where is the commissioner's tent? And how do I find my way back here?'

Jake shrugged as he made a scoffing noise and pointed to the far distance. 'You'll find the Commission Tent,' he sneered. 'It's the biggest tent and has smaller tents around it all enclosed by a fence and there'll be guards there with rifles. And there'll be a queue of men. Now,' he stroked his beard. 'Finding our tent. We'll have to put up a flag.' He thought for a moment. 'We could use a pair of Sally's bloomers!' He turned to Sally and sniggered.

Sally cast her eyes down and grimaced. 'Don't have none.' Edmund heard her mutter.

'Well,' Joc mumbled, 'I've got a Jolly Roger flag we could use.'

'A Pirate flag!' Jasper exclaimed, a hand going to his mouth.

'Yeah, Joe used to be a pirate,' Jake grinned.

Jasper looked horrified.

'Nah,' Joe shook his head. 'Found it in a gutter somewhere. Thought I'd use it to wrap up my gold.' He made a face. 'When I find some ...'

Jake moved impatiently. 'Give it to Eddy, he can put it on the tent pole. Right. So, everyone must give thirty shillings to Jasper for a licence. 'Cept you, Sal. You'll be minding the tent.' He took his pick and shovel. 'Once we get our licences, we have to carry them at all times, mind.'

Edmund was pleased he'd taken money from the purse in his vest without the others watching. Jasper and Harold appeared embarrassed.

'Um, I'll just go into the tent to get some money,' Harold said.

Edmund took a gold sovereign and ten silver shillings from his purse and handed them to Jasper, who appeared slightly scared as he took the coins.

'We have to find a cradle to buy, can't just use pans according to some diggers I spoke to,' Jake said. 'Unless one of youse is handy with the old carpentry?' He glowered at each of them and sniffed. 'Hmm, don't look like it. Well, once we have our claims, I'll scout around to find one to buy.' It seemed he didn't put much faith in his chums' carpentry skills. 'Right, now Sal, put the rest of them chops and damper in a basket fer our lunch and we'll be off looking for a claim.' Harold reappeared from their tent and handed over his thirty shillings. Jake stared at Jasper who stood, petrified, holding the coins. 'Don't just stand there like a stuffed wallaby, get yer own thirty bob and off you go to the Commission tent!'

The others quickly gathered their gear and followed Jake, Edmund bringing up the rear carrying the pannikins of food.

***

They soon got into a routine; going off to their claim every morning with mutton, damper and cold tea, coming back at dusk tired and dusty. Their claim was some way off from their campsite, a good walk to be carrying picks and shovels. It fell to Edmund to take the picks to the nearest blacksmith – there were several at the diggings – to get the points remade. The heavy rocky ground soon blunted their tools.

Before long, Edmund became friendly with the blacksmith nearest to them. On a few occasions, he stayed longer than necessary, watching the process. One evening the smith raised an eyebrow at Edmund. 'Fill up the slack tub, laddie,' he growled, indicating the large tub of water used to quench the heat of the metal. Edmund hurried to oblige.

Soon Edmund was spending longer each time he had to go to the forge, helping in small ways and then making the excuse when he returned to their camp that the blacksmith was very busy.

Sullen Sal, as Edmund still thought of her, had food prepared and water boiled for when they returned at night. No digging was carried out on a Sunday, and the diggings seemed strangely quiet on that day.

Each night, Jake would bury their gold under his sleeping pallet. By the end of the month, there was nearly a pound of gold. They planned to share it out once they had a sizeable amount.

On the first of each month, Jasper was once more dispatched to buy their licences. This time he took roughly half an ounce of gold for each man, instead of coins. Jake carefully weighed out the precious metal.

Disaster struck two months later when, tired and hungry they returned from the diggings to find the tent in darkness, no fire, no Sally and no gold.

Jake was furious, 'Fucking bitch!' he stormed, 'fucking whore! I do her a favour, getting her away from a life of misery working for some old bastard squatter, and this is how she repays me!' He stormed out of the tent, looking for something on which to vent his anger. 'Out of my way,' he roared at Jasper, pushing him roughly aside. They watched him make his way to a nearby tent which purported to be selling lemonade but which was actually a sly grog tent.

Edmund wasn't too sure about the so-called favour Jake had done Sal. He'd noticed she had a black eye one day after he'd heard shouting and screaming coming from their tent; Joe had emerged appearing shaken and stumbled to the other tent. 'Bit noisy in there,' he jerked his thumb back behind him. 'Is it all right if I bunk down here?' But it seemed Sally gave as good as she got - Jake sported a swollen cut lip the next morning.

Now the four men looked at each other. Joe shrugged and turned to Edmund. 'Get the fire going laddie and termorrow you'd better stay here and mind the tent.'

Edmund was happy with the arrangement. Somehow the endless scrabbling in the dirt, digging and washing for very little reward had lost its appeal.

The four men sat around the camp fire eating the usual mutton and potatoes followed by a billy of tea. The atmosphere was more relaxed without Jake. They all seemed to sense it.

After a while, Joe studied Harold. 'So what brought you and Jasper to Australia, then, Harold?'

Harold glanced at Jasper and then gazed into the flames of their camp fire. 'Don't know if you'd heard about John Smith and John Pratt?'

Joe and Edmund shook their heads.

'Hmm, maybe before your time, 1835. In England. Famous case.' Harold looked at Jasper who sat with downcast eyes frowning into the fire.

There was a long silence. Then Jasper spoke up. 'You see, Harold and I ...'

Harold took Jasper's hand and squeezed it. 'John Smith and John Pratt were hung for the crime of sodomy. A few years ago now. But Jasper and I didn't feel safe in England. We thought we could come to Australia, find gold and make a new life here.'

Joe cleared his throat and spat into the fire. 'Nothing new under the sun,' he grinned. 'Happens all the time on long sea voyages. Anyways, we kinda guessed it was the case wiv youse two, didn't we Eddy?'

It had never actually occurred to Edmund, but now he thought about it, he remembered Mary-Ann making a vague reference to being careful with men. He nodded sagely. He liked Harold and Jasper. What they did between themselves wasn't his business, he thought.

They sat in silence for a while, until Joe said, 'better bunk down before Jake gets back and starts a fight ...' Drowsy from the food and the heat of the fire, no one moved for a while, each occupied with his own thoughts.

Jake staggered back to their camp after the guns had been fired. Luckily Edmund had saved him a plate of potatoes and mutton. Wordlessly he offered the plate to Jake who sat on the gound and shovelled the food into his mouth, belched, then slumped down beside the fire and fell asleep. Edmund had thought of suggesting Jake put an advertisement in the Melbourne *Argus* Missing Friends section, advertising for Sally, but when he saw Jake's face, he changed his mind and followed the others, who were glad of the opportunity to get into their tents. Edmund thought he heard Jake and Joe arguing at some stage during the night, but he turned over and went back to sleep.

WAMBECARRA - MARCH 2021

Why would Will be cultivating older women? Elizabeth didn't think Iris was well off, and neither was she. Perhaps Will thought she had plenty of money when he saw her driving an up-market Mercedes car. The story about his grandmother leaving the house to him ... perhaps the woman he claimed was his mother was another older woman whose confidence he'd won and when she'd died, she'd left the house to Will. Perhaps that woman had been Kathleen's daughter ... And the story about Kathleen's daughter being his mother! He could have made that up after Merv told him about Kathleen's daughter running away the time when they were putting out their bins, she mused. Maybe that was the reason he was renovating the house. He'd sell it and move to another place and do the same. Where, though did the story about the cobblestones fit in? None of it made sense.

She'd try and put it out of her head and concentrate on what happened to Edmund.

She opened her laptop to make a start when the doorbell rang. Molly raced ahead of her, and when Elizabeth opened the door, Will stood there grinning.

'Hi Elizabeth, hi Molly!' He bent to pat Molly. 'I'm going to the beach for a swim. Thought you'd like to come and bring Molly too. You'd like that Moll, wouldn't you?'

'Um.' Elizabeth struggled to think of something to say. 'Well, I haven't swum for years, and actually, I don't even have a swimming costume.'

'Come anyway, you can throw sticks for Molly. And it's too nice a day to be inside.'

Elizabeth hesitated. It sounded tempting and she hadn't been to the beach for ages.

'I'd love you to come.' Will looked at her. 'Molly wants to go.' He gestured towards the fawning dog.

'Okay then. Come inside a minute while I get ready.'

Five minutes later and they were in Will's ute, Molly at Elizabeth's feet.

When they reached town, Will pulled up outside a shop. 'It's the Surf Shop,' he smiled, 'Hop out and go and buy a cossie.'

'No, really!'

'Yes, really!'

'I don't have a towel.'

'I've got two ... come on, Molly's getting restless. Please, Elizabeth.'

Elizabeth hesitated, then got out of the ute. Will seemed so earnest, as if he really wanted her to go for a swim.

'Take your time,' he said.

Will smiled when she returned with a small carrier bag. 'All set?'

She nodded. 'I kept the costume on, just put my undies in the carrier bag,' she said, then blushed.

***

At the beach, Elizabeth sat on a towel until Will had stripped off; she watched him race to the water with Molly joyously following him. She cast her eyes around the others on the beach, mostly lithe young women in bikinis and athletic-looking tanned men. A couple of overweight women basked on towels, totally oblivious to what others thought. Elizabeth slowly took off her clothes, carefully folded them and put them in the carrier bag, along with her phone. She covered the bag with the towel Will had brought for her. She turned towards the ocean; it seemed so inviting. She hugged her knees and wriggled her toes in the sand, remembering the few times when her parents had brought her here. Actually, it had only been her father. Her mother had sent them off to the beach while she had a rest. Her mother didn't like getting sand in her clothes, didn't like the ocean. Elizabeth had been happy, just having her father to herself. He'd helped her make sandcastles ...

She took off her sunglasses and sunhat, put them on top of her clothes, then rose and walked towards the surf feeling so very conscious of her middle-aged body. She stood at the edge of the surf, the lacy waves washing over her feet.

She squealed as Molly came splashing towards her, 'Oh Molly! It's cold!'

Will swam over, 'It's fabulous once you're in!' Then he smiled at her. 'Nice cossie, Beth, you look good in it.'

Elizabeth felt her face go hot. Quickly she dived under the water to hide her confusion and started to swim. She soon felt tired after the unaccustomed exercise and went back up the beach to her towel and sat down, watching Will swimming along the beach with Molly paddling after him. The swim had been lovely, she didn't know why she'd never thought before to take Molly the twenty-minute drive to the ocean, and this was such a beautiful place, with amazing rock formations at one end of the beach and rolling green hills at the other.

Eventually, Will came out of the water, Molly behind him, her tongue lolling out. 'That was awesome, Beth, did you enjoy it?'

She smiled and nodded. 'I think Molly is thirsty.'

Will went to the beach bag he'd brought, and produced a bowl and a bottle of water. 'Voila!' He poured water into the bowl and offered it to Molly.

'You think of everything, Will.'

He smiled. 'I try. Now, I'm starving, are you? Fish and chips sound good? I noticed a chipper as we came along the beach road.'

She nodded and smiled. Her costume had dried while she'd been waiting for Will, so she put her clothes on over it and followed Will up the beach.

'You wait here with Molly.'

Elizabeth sat on the sea wall watching the waves and the boys with their surfboards running down the beach paths.

'So how is the ancestry research going?' Will enquired when he returned with the fish and chips. He handed Elizabeth a package.

'Thanks, Will.' She smiled at him. 'Smells good. No Molly, none for you.' She bit into a chip. 'Umm, so good. How am I going? Well, at a bit of a standstill at the moment.' She swallowed. 'I've found a record of Edmund's death but nothing since his birth, oh, except for the birth record of my great grandfather, who must have been Edmund's son. But no marriage records or anything else.'

'Where did he die?'

'Inverell, apparently, in 1874'

'Inverell in New South Wales?'

'Yes. I've never been there, so I've decided to drive there and do some research, check the church records and gravestones, that kind of thing.' Elizabeth put a piece of fish in her mouth and chewed it, a frown furrowing her brow.

Will watched her. 'That's a good idea, when were you thinking of going? I could look after Molly for you.'

'Thanks, Will, but I've found a motel that's pet friendly. You just have to pay extra for cleaning.'

Will was silent for a few minutes, then he said softly, 'I wouldn't mind going to Inverell. Never been there.'

Elizabeth's heart started to thump. *Was Will angling for an invitation to go with her?*

'It's a long drive, Elizabeth. Were you thinking of stopping for a night on the way?'

'I thought I'd leave early in the morning and have a few stops on the way for Molly. I think it's about an eight-hour drive ...' her voice trailed away.

'Hmm. Would you mind if I came with you? That's if the motel has a spare room.' Avoiding her eyes, Will studied his hands as he spoke. 'We could share the driving ...' He raised his eyes.

Elizabeth didn't know what to say. 'Well.' She hesitated, 'I can ring the motel, see if ...'

'Only if you'd like me to come along,' Will added hastily, 'I'm really getting hooked on your ancestors!'

Elizabeth's thoughts were all over the place; she took a deep breath and smiled. 'That would be nice. But what about your work?'

Will shrugged. 'If you're going at the weekend, it'll be fine.'

'I thought of going the weekend after next.'

'Suits me. But only if you're sure you'd like me to tag along.'

She nodded as she finished her chips and screwed up the paper. Will took it from her and went to the bin. 'Better make a move, I guess. You right?'

Elizabeth nodded. 'Yes, thanks.'

***

Back home Elizabeth felt invigorated after the swim. 'That was so good, Molly, wasn't it?' She chatted away to Molly on her way to have a shower. After rinsing out her new swimming costume and hanging it outside on the clothesline, she poured herself a glass of wine and went into the garden. She lowered herself onto a garden chair and put her feet up on a stool and thought about the day. She so enjoyed Will's company - didn't feel pressured to talk, and he seemed happy to stay quiet as well. *Stop it!* She told herself. *Get back to work on the ancestry stuff - try and find out more about Edmund.* But her mind kept sliding back to the vision of Will running into the ocean.

Stop it! She told herself again. *Think of something else! Go and ring the motel in Inverell, see if they have another room vacant.*

Molly nudged her knee. 'Okay, Molly, it's your dinner time, come on then.' Elizabeth finished the rest of her wine and hauled herself to her feet.

***

Elizabeth was carrying Molly's bed out to the car when Will met her two weeks later. She put the dog bed down and opened the rear door. 'I usually put Molly's bed in the back if I'm going very far,' she explained. 'Moll likes to look out the window in comfort.'

Will indicated the small backpack he was carrying. 'Shall I put it on the back seat?'

'Yes, I've already put my travelling bag and Molly's stuff in. I'll just lock up and we can go. Hopefully, before Merv pops out to see us off.'

Will smiled. 'Maybe I'll ring their doorbell to make sure he sees us.'

'Don't you dare!'

'Only joking! I'd better get in and keep my head low.'

Elizabeth smiled with relief. She knew Will had been joking, but she really didn't want Merv making all kinds of remarks and innuendos.

'Have you discovered anything new about Edmund Turner?' Will asked as Elizabeth drove out of their street. His voice was muffled as his head was on his knees.

Elizabeth laughed. 'You can lift up your head now, we've passed Merv's house.' *It's so nice being with Will,* she thought.

'I hope Iris didn't see us,' Will grinned and pushed his fingers through his short curly hair. 'But I think seven o'clock in the morning is a bit early for her.'

Elizabeth bit her lip, *was that why he wanted to leave so early?* But then she remembered she'd originally planned to leave early and make the trip to Inverell in one day. *Why was she always thinking of things to doubt him?*

'Have you discovered anything more about Edmund?' Will repeated as they left the village and drove onto the Princes Highway.

'No, I've reached a blank wall. Apart from the NSW Births Deaths and Marriages records, which I think I told you about. It shows an Edmund Turner with parents Edward and Ann, and that he died in Inverell in 1874.'

'Hmm. So how old was he when he died?'

'Born on the 6th July in 1836, so I suppose that would make him thirty-eight.'

'That's very young, don't you think?'

'Yes, but life expectancy wasn't great in those days. I wonder was there another epidemic, like the scarlet fever one that took the twins and Edward Turner...' Elizabeth paused as she concentrated on overtaking a learner driver. 'I'll check later.'

'Would you like to stop for a coffee somewhere before we get to Sydney?' Will asked as they approached the city.

Elizabeth glanced at the car clock. 'It's only nine-thirty, I'm okay for a bit but we can stop if you like. Actually, it might be a good idea to stop somewhere so I can get Molly out to stretch her legs. Next servo?'

Will nodded.

***

It was late afternoon when they arrived in Inverell and found the motel. 'Apparently, this is the centre of town and within walking distance of most things,' Elizabeth said, as she stopped the car in front of the motel.

Elizabeth checked in first. She waited while Will did likewise and was relieved Will's room was at the other end of the block from hers.

'Shall I carry Molly's bed to your room?' Will asked as they left the reception area.

Elizabeth looked at her watch. 'Yes please, and I don't know about you but I could do with a drink!'

Will grinned. 'How about we park our stuff and take Molly for a walk and see if there's somewhere we can sit and have a glass of something?'

They found a pub not far from the motel. 'Sit down, Beth. What would you like to drink? I'm going to have a beer.'

'You know what, I think I'll have the same, but only a small glass please.'

She watched him walk into the bar and thought how nice it was to have a companion with whom to share the trip. Much nicer than being on her own. 'Apart from you, of course, Molly,' she said to her dog as if Molly could read her mind.

'Talking to yourself or Molly?' Will's voice broke into her thoughts.

'I was thinking how nice it is to have your company,' she said and felt her colour rising, the words had just slipped out.

'I was thinking the same,' Will smiled and handed her a glass of beer. 'Now, what's the plan of action?'

Elizabeth took a sip of her beer and set her glass down on the table. 'I thought maybe relax this evening and then tomorrow go and visit the church and see if there's any information about Edmund there. Burial record or headstone for example.'

Will nodded. 'Sounds good.'

'I think there's an Inverell Historical Society based in the Public Library. Maybe go there first. They're open on Saturday mornings.'

Will stretched. 'Now,' he said. 'I noticed there's barbeque facilities at the motel. How about I go and buy food and cook for us tonight?'

'Oh!' Elizabeth didn't know what to say for a moment. 'Well, that sounds lovely. Thanks, Will, I was just going to get a takeaway or something, but your idea sounds much better!'

Will finished his beer and stood. 'Okay. I'll go shopping and I'll see you later. Say about seven at the barbeque area?'

Elizabeth nodded. 'Great! I'll go back to the motel and feed Molly and get myself organised. Anything I can do?'

Will smiled. 'No, you did all the driving, you must be tired.'

Elizabeth blinked. She did feel tired and even though Will had offered to share the driving, she wasn't a good passenger and anyhow, she admitted to herself, she didn't like other people driving her car. *Stupid, she knew, but there it was!*

***

The next morning Elizabeth was up early and after a mug of instant coffee, she dressed, clipped on Molly's lead and went out the door of her room.

It looked like being a lovely day, she thought as she strode past the other rooms in the motel block. The sun lit up the agapanthus on the driveway to the motel, some late flowers shining like blue jewels against the strappy green leaves. Passing Will's room, she wondered if he was still asleep, but then she saw the flickering light through the curtains and heard the sound of the television.

She walked on, picturing Will in bed drinking coffee and watching the news on TV. Her heart beat faster at the thought.

Back in her room, she texted him '*Out walking Molly, passed a nice place for breakfast. Interested?*'

The reply came back almost at once. '*Yes! Starving. Ready now?*'

Elizabeth smiled to herself. 'Come on Molly, breakfast calls!'

After their meal, they strolled into the main street of Inverell.

'The Library's in Campbell Street, near the river,' Elizabeth said. 'This way.'

'Can we tie Molly up outside?'

'Yes, she's getting very good at waiting outside places for me.'

Inside the Library, Elizabeth enquired at the desk for the Historical Society.

'I don't know if there's anyone there at the moment,' the librarian put a finger to her lips and looked around just as the main door opened and a pleasant, smartly-dressed woman walked in. 'Oh! You're in luck! Here's Dianne! She'll be able to help you.'

The librarian beckoned Dianne over. 'These people were enquiring about the Historical Society.' She indicated Elizabeth and Will.

Elizabeth stepped forward. 'Hello, I'm Elizabeth Turner and this is Will Barnes. We're interested in a certain Edmund Turner, who I believe died in Brodies Plains in 1874.'

Dianne smiled. 'Pleased to meet you. Let's go into the Historical Society section and see what we can find.'

Just then they heard Molly barking. Will looked at Elizabeth. 'You stay here, I'll go out and take Molly for a stroll. He indicated his watch. 'Send me a text when you're ready. Don't rush.' He smiled at her.

Relieved, Elizabeth gave a half-smile. 'Thanks, Will. That would be great.' She glanced at Dianne. 'Molly's a rescue dog, she gets a bit anxious if left for any length of time, especially if she hasn't been there before.'

Dianne nodded and smiled. 'Quite understand. Okay, let's see what we can find out.'

It was an hour later when Elizabeth emerged from the library and texted Will.

Just finished. Where are you?

A reply came back a few seconds later.

Stay at the library, we'll meet you.

It was about ten minutes later when Elizabeth saw Will and Molly coming towards her. Will appeared to be swinging a pickaxe.

'Sorry it took so long, I didn't realise we'd walked so far,' Will apologized. 'I stopped at a garage sale ...' He indicated the pick he was carrying. 'Couldn't resist it, it must be hand-made, very old; you can't buy quality tools like this anymore.' He studied it. 'The old guy selling it said it belonged to his grandfather. It'll come in handy for taking out tree roots.'

Elizabeth smiled, 'It looks a really good one, I might borrow it to dig up some old tree stumps along my back fence if that's okay?'

Will grinned. 'I can do it for you. Now, tell me did you find out anything interesting?'

Elizabeth grimaced. 'Lots but I don't know if it will be useful. Come, I'm hungry, it's nearly lunchtime, how about we find somewhere to eat and I'll tell you everything?'

They bought a takeaway pizza and went to a nearby park to eat it. They'd just finished eating when Elizabeth's phone rang. She glanced at it. 'It's Bronwyn.' She rolled her eyes, 'I'll ring her back.'

'Take her call,' Will said. 'I'll wander off with Molly. I'll leave the pick here if that's okay?'

Elizabeth nodded then sighed and pressed the answer button on her phone. Molly looked back at Elizabeth as Will led her away.

'Elizabeth! Where on earth are you?' Bronwyn sounded angry.

'Um, I'm in Inverell.'

'Inverell? What on earth are you doing there? The girls and I came down specially to give you a birthday surprise and find an empty house! The old woman across the road from you said she'd seen you going off with THAT MAN early yesterday morning.' Bronwyn paused for breath, *'I mean, what on earth are you doing? I've warned you about him!'*

Elizabeth took a deep breath and exhaled slowly. 'I'm here researching for the ancestry project you gave me.' She made her voice sound calm; she'd totally forgotten it was her birthday.

'Hmm.' Bronwyn sounded disgruntled. *'Lucky I booked rooms in a motel; the girls were so disappointed you weren't here. They were both so excited about giving you a surprise.'*

Elizabeth found that hard to believe. 'How's Darren?' she asked, anxious to change the subject.

'He's okay, his usual self. Now, Elizabeth, what were you thinking of, going away with THAT MAN! The neighbours will all be talking about you!'

Bugger Iris! Thought Elizabeth, trust her to have seen them leaving yesterday. 'Doubt it, Bronwyn,' she said. 'Anyway, I'm making good progress with the ancestry stuff. Can't believe it's a year since you gave me the project. I'm really into it now.'

Bronwyn sniffed. *'Hmm well I suppose you won't be back today, we'd better head home instead of staying another night.'*

'That's a good idea. Beat the traffic.'

'Anyway, why are you with that man?' Bronwyn was like a dog with a bone, Elizabeth thought, she wouldn't let the subject go.

'He's probably telling you all sorts of things to make you feel sorry for him. That's how those people operate.'

'Who? Will?' Elizabeth pretended innocence. 'He's just minding Molly for me while I do research. It's hard leaving her ...'

'You could have put her into kennels!'

Elizabeth let out a deep breath. *As if she could leave her dog in kennels! Molly was only just getting used to being left alone in the house while she went shopping.*

'So, the girls are well?' Elizabeth rolled her eyes.

'Yes, all good, disappointed at not seeing you, of course. They were so excited.' Bronwyn's voice faded, Elizabeth could hear her calling the girls ... *'Come and talk to Nanna Turner, girls.'* Then louder. *'Oh, they've just gone off to the ice cream shop. You've missed them.'* Her voice was accusatory.

'Oh, dear, never mind. Give them my love. Bye dear, say hello to Darren for me. Love you!' With a sigh, Elizabeth pressed the end call button on her phone and looked up to see Will walking back with Molly.

He raised one eyebrow in a query, 'Hm, apparently that wasn't a happy phone call. Come on Molly, sit down.'

Elizabeth sighed. 'That was Bronwyn. It's my birthday today and she and the girls went down to Wambecarra to give me a surprise birthday present and found an empty house, then apparently Iris came over and told her you and I had gone off together yesterday!'

Will grimaced. 'Good old Iris, she doesn't miss a trick!'

Elizabeth laughed. 'Well, anyway I'd rather be here than having to entertain those girls! I do love Bronwyn and the girls,' she added hastily, 'It's just sometimes a bit overwhelming!'

Will sat down beside her. 'You're lucky to have a daughter who cares about you.'

Elizabeth gazed at him. His shoulders had drooped and he was staring down at his hands which were clenched in his lap. 'Will?'

'Happy birthday, Elizabeth!' He raised his eyes and tried to smile, but his smile didn't reach his eyes. 'I didn't know it was your birthday. Many happy returns. We must celebrate! I'll take you out for dinner.'

Elizabeth was puzzled. Will seemed so sad. She indicated Molly, whose ears had pricked up at the word 'dinner'.

'Ah,' Will said, 'well, I'll get a nice takeaway and we can share it with a bottle of something. Sound good?' He raised his eyebrows.

'Sounds great!' But she was still a bit mystified. Will didn't seem his usual self. Something to do with Bronwyn?

Will sat upright. 'Now, tell me all you've learnt about Edmund Turner.'

'Hold on a minute, Will. What did you mean about me being lucky to have a daughter who cares about me?'

Will stared straight ahead and shrugged.

'Will! Please! What is it?' She turned and saw him blink away tears. 'Will! Tell me.'

Slowly, Will put his hand inside his jacket and pulled out his wallet. He took out a photo and held it out to her.

'Will, what a beautiful little girl!'

Will swallowed. 'My daughter. Caitlin.'

'Oh Will!'

'My ex-wife told lies in court. Said I'd abused Caitlin.' He scoffed. 'As if I would ever do such a thing as to hurt a little girl.' He glowered and was silent.

'Will?' Elizabeth said softly. She took one of his hands. 'Tell me about Caitlin.'

Will took a deep breath. 'She's fourteen now. I haven't seen her since she was ten. This photo is of her on her tenth birthday. I send her presents and birthday cards but never get a reply. Her mother has another partner now.' His fists clenched. 'The courts won't let me see my daughter, but some fucking bloke no-one knows can live in the same house with her! How does that work? Eh? Eh?' His eyes blazed, then focused on Elizabeth. Slowly he calmed down. 'I'm sorry, Elizabeth. It's just so cruel. Fiona ruined my life; her lawyers cleaned me out and all the time she had this other guy ...' He stood and paced around; Molly regarded him anxiously.

Elizabeth watched him and said nothing. She wondered why he had never mentioned a daughter before. Perhaps it was too painful ...

After several minutes he sat down and put his head in his hands. 'I'm sorry, Elizabeth,' he mumbled. 'Sometimes it just gets to me.'

Elizabeth put an arm around his shoulders. 'I understand,' she whispered.

'No. No, you don't,' his head jerked up. 'No-one who hasn't been through this can understand. My daughter has been brain-washed into thinking I'm a bad person, someone who has abused her. I've missed out on her childhood years, fighting to get access to her, all to no avail.'

'No Will! She'll find out for herself and come and find you!'

Will covered his eyes with his hands, shook his head and mumbled something.

Elizabeth stroked Will's back and said nothing.

After a while, Will took a deep breath, dropped his hands and straightened. He stood up and walked away. After a few minutes, he came back. 'I'm sorry, Elizabeth. You don't need this, especially on your birthday. Um, tell me what you found out about Edmund,' he managed to say.

Elizabeth looked at Will. Obviously, he wanted to change the subject. 'Well, it's all rather mysterious. As you know, I found from the Australian births, deaths and marriages site that Edmund had died in Inverell in 1874. Dianne at the Historical Society found a notice in the Australian Town and Country Journal for Sat 22nd Aug 1874. See, she printed it off for me.' Elizabeth held out a piece of paper. 'Look, halfway down the page.'

Jane, the beloved wife of William [illegible], Esq., aged [illegible] years, deeply regretted by a large circle of friends.

On August 13, at her residence, Pacific Lodge, Ocean-street, Woollahra, Sarah, the beloved wife of James Fussell aged 78 years, leaving six children, eighteen grand children, and one great grandchild

On the 4th August, at the residence of his parents, Chatham, Manning River, after a lingering illness, caused by a fall from a horse, Alexander James, eldest son of the late Mr. James Kidd, aged 17 years, a native of the Manning River.

At his residence, Brodie's Plains, near Inverell, on 9th August, 1874, Mr. Edmond Turner, aged 70 years. Deeply regretted by a large circle of friends.

At Wellington, on the 19th instant, Mr. D. S. Miles, superintendent of the hospital, and late of Goulburn, and brother of Mr. J. R. Miles, Telegraph-office, Sydney.

At his residence, Regent-street, Sydney, August 9th, E. Heydon, father of G. T. Heydon, Tenterfield, aged 57.

On the 9th August, at Brodie's Plains, Mr. Edmund Turner, aged 70.

On the 8th August, at his residence, Sale Plains, James Murdock, Esq., late Crown lands bailiff.

On the 11th August, at his residence, Geelong, Victoria, in the 80th year of his age, the Rev. Samuel Hewlett.

Will scanned through the cutting, then read out '*At his residence, Brodie's Plains, near Inverell, on 9th August 1874, Mr. Edmond Turner, aged 70 years. Deeply regretted by a large circle of friends.*'

Will frowned. 'Aged seventy years? That's weird! I thought you said he was thirty-eight when he died?'

Elizabeth studied the cutting again. 'You're right, and if he was seventy, and he died in 1874 then that would mean ...,' her eyes swivelled up to the right as she thought, 'he would have been born in 1804 ... and that was before Edward had even arrived in Australia. I hadn't twigged that!'

'And look! It says Edmond not Edmund! And missed by a large circle of friends. Nothing about family ... but hold on Elizabeth,' Will paused, 'see, a bit further down, it says '*On the 9th August, at Brodie's Plains, Mr. Edmund Turner, aged 70.*', and this time Edmund is spelt with a 'u' not an 'o'!'

They stared at each other. 'I don't understand.' Elizabeth frowned. 'Why is the death notice in twice?'

Will stood up and stretched. 'Let's have a break,' he said, 'sorry, Elizabeth. I can't concentrate at the moment.'

Elizabeth stood too. 'That's Okay, Will. Why don't we have a drive to Brodies Plains. See what's there?'

'Good idea. Let's go back to the motel and get the car.'

***

An hour later and Elizabeth was driving along the Gwydir Highway towards Brodies Plains.

'Apparently the population is fifty-eight, and it seems to be called Brodies Plains with no apostrophe now,' she said, with a quick glance at Will who was sitting beside her in the front passenger seat of the car.

'Hmm.'

'Dianne, in the Inverell History Section of the library said there had been a big homestead here, with their own church, cemetery, etc., Newstead Station.'

'Hmm.'

'Will, I don't think you're really interested in Brodies Plains, are you?' Elizabeth said, turning her head slightly to look at Will

Will sighed. 'Sorry, Elizabeth, my mind was elsewhere.'

'Well, there doesn't seem to be anything of value here for my research,' Elizabeth said, indicating the flat, sparsely populated landscape. 'Let's go back.' She squinted at the clock on the dashboard of the car. 'It's nearly four o'clock; Molly will be getting hungry soon.'

Molly lifted her head at the sound of her name.

Will nodded. 'Okay by me. Can you drop me off at the shops in Inverell, please, Beth?'

Surprised, she nodded, her mind going ahead to the evening. What could she have for her dinner? She didn't really feel hungry but there were a few bits and pieces in the motel fridge, some nuts and yoghurt. It would do ...but then she remembered Will was going to get a takeaway, maybe he'd forgotten when his mind was on Caitlin. She'd wait and see.

***

Later that evening, Elizabeth fed Molly, had a shower and was about to get a glass of wine from a bottle she'd bought and put in the fridge earlier when there was a knock on the door. Molly scrambled to her feet and went to the door, wagging her tail.

'Hello?' Elizabeth said. 'Who is it?'

'Elizabeth, it's me, Will.'

'Oh', she exclaimed as she opened the door.

Will stood there, grinning, a bottle of champagne in one hand and two champagne glasses in the other.

'Will!'

'Can I come in?'

'Of course!'

'Happy birthday, Elizabeth!' Will bent over and kissed her.

Elizabeth's heart missed a beat. 'Oh!' She could think of nothing to say, then burst out, 'Where did you get champagne glasses?'

'From the op shop! Don't worry, I've washed them thoroughly!' He put the glasses on the table, bent to pat Molly, smiled at Elizabeth and undid the wire holding the cork on the champagne. A satisfying 'Pop' ensued. Carefully Will poured the champagne into the glasses and held one out to Elizabeth. 'Happy birthday, dear Beth!'

Her heart raced as they clinked glasses and she took a sip of the wine, bubbles going up her nose. 'Thank you, Will, this is such a nice surprise.' Just then there was another knock on the door. Will opened it and went out. Elizabeth heard the murmur of voices and then Will came back in with two bags.

'Hope you like Thai?' He raised his eyebrows.

'Love it!' Elizabeth shook her head in bewilderment.

'Just a moment, I'll be back, drink your champagne,' Will ordered as he disappeared out the door.

Elizabeth sat down at the table; the tantalizing smell of the Thai food made her suddenly realise she was hungry.

Will returned with a packet of paper serviettes and a bottle of red wine.

'Just a little birthday celebration for you, Beth.' He went to the motel kitchen cupboard and found plates and cutlery. 'Come on, help yourself.' He opened the tubs of food.

She blinked away tears. 'Thank you, Will,' she managed to say. 'This is such a lovely surprise.'

Mount Alexander – The Goldfields - 1853

The day after Sally's disappearance, the men left for the diggings leaving Edmund behind to mind the camp. He cleaned the pots from the breakfast, aired the bedding and fetched water and kindling. With all the chores done, he wandered over to the blacksmith and stood watching him making horseshoes.

The smith regarded Edmund. 'Got another pick to sharpen then?'

'No,' replied Edmund. 'I'm just interested, I'd like to learn to be a blacksmith.'

The smithy laughed. 'Then you'd better put a bit of meat on you, laddie.'

'I'm stronger than I look.' Edmund squared his shoulders and lifted his chest.

'Left you to mind the tent, did they?' The smith swung his hammer onto the piece of metal he was bending into a shoe.

Edmund nodded, and started to recount the story of Sally, but the smith was focused on his work.

Five minutes later the smith turned round. 'You still here?'

Edmund nodded again.

'Well make yourself useful then. Go and fetch water for the slack tub.' He nodded towards an empty wooden bucket.

Edmund grinned and ran off to the creek with the bucket.

On his return, he gave the tents a quick check and then took the bucket of water to the blacksmith's forge and filled the slack tub. He watched as the blacksmith dipped a red-hot horseshoe into it. 'Better get another one.'

'Hold on lad,' the smithy shouted. 'Take two buckets! Then you'll be balanced coming back.'

Edmund's cheeks reddened. *Why hadn't he thought of that!* He picked up another bucket and set off.

On his way back, he passed their camp again and saw a girl coming from behind Joe and Jake's tent. He put down the buckets. 'What are you doing here?' He narrowed his eyes. Then he recognized her as the girl who had helped him light the campfire the first day they'd arrived.

'I was hoping to see Sally,' she said.

'Ha!' exclaimed Edmund. 'She took off two days ago with all our gold.'

The girl appeared surprised. 'Oh ...'

'Why did you want to see her?'

'Um ... she was one of the few women around here. Someone I could talk to. She helped me when I ...when I ...' her voice trailed off. 'Better go.'

'Just a minute. What's your name?'

'Annie.' She gathered up her skirts and ran off.

Edmund watched her go. Strange person, he thought. Yet she was oddly attractive - pretty. Maybe she'd wanted to talk to Sally about women's troubles. With four older sisters, he knew all about the "rags" and monthly bleeding.

He took his buckets and walked on towards the blacksmith's tent. The smithy smiled when he saw him. 'Took yer time, laddie. All right, you can make yerself useful. Turn the handle of the hand crank to fire up the furnace.'

Edmund beamed with pleasure, emptied his buckets into the slack tub and went towards the furnace.

The days turned into weeks and the weather got warmer and drier. The whole tent city was a dust bowl. Every tent was covered in dust, their food tasted of dust and water got scarcer. The men's beards were encrusted with dust. Tempers frayed. Jake spent more and more time at the "Lemonade" tent.

The conditions were appalling, excrement from the dogs and horses, not to mention the human waste, littered the site. The blow flies were so bad that meat would be covered with maggots within hours of a carcass being hung.

Jasper got thinner and thinner; they all had bouts of dysentery but Jasper seemed to suffer the most. Harold had brought a case of medicine with him and dosed them all with Holloway's pills and Senna leaf, but it didn't seem to help Jasper.

Joe developed sandy blight in his eyes, and they streamed with pus and made him half-blind. One morning he got up and stumbled out of the tent. 'Gotta shit, Eddy. Oh, gawd, me eyes are so itchy,' he muttered.

Edmund gaped at him, appalled to see maggots crawling around Joe's eyes.

'Stay still, Joe, I must wipe your eyes, there's maggots in them. A blow fly must have laid its eggs in your eyes overnight; it's so hot and your eyes are humid with the pus, well, they must've hatched out while you were asleep.'

Joe shuddered as Edmund dipped a rag in water and wiped the maggots away then threw the rag into the fire.

'Hate this life,' Joe mumbled as Edmund led him around to the hole in the ground they used as a latrine.

'Careful,' cautioned Edmund, 'the hole is just here.' He positioned Joe so his buttocks were over the hole.

'Jasus, what has it come to? Thanks, Eddy.'

INVERELL - MARCH 2021

Will gathered up the empty takeaway containers and took them outside to the bin. 'Come on Molly, I think your owner is too merry to take you out before bedtime.'

Elizabeth smiled. She did feel happy. It had been such a lovely evening, Will made her laugh, he was so nice to be with. She watched him take Molly out the door, returning after a few minutes. He unclipped the lead, patted her, then came over to where Elizabeth was sitting in the one easy chair in the room.

'Good night, Beth,' he smiled. 'Hope you enjoyed your birthday. Sleep well.' He bent as if to kiss her then must have thought better of it because he straightened and instead patted her shoulder. He opened the door, waved and left.

'Good night, Will,' she echoed, 'and thank you for such a lovely evening.' She rose and watched his figure retreating along the pathway to his room.

That night she lay awake thinking about Will. He'd had such a hard life. Her thoughts turned to Bronwyn. Yes, she was a good daughter. Will was right. Even if she could be annoying. And Will had a daughter. Why hadn't he mentioned her the time when he had explained about his marriage to ... What was her name ...? Frances? Began with an 'F' ...Bronwyn would probably say he'd made up the story about his daughter to win her sympathy. Bugger Bronwyn. Now she was doubting Will again. But he'd seemed so genuinely upset ... and the photo of the beautiful little girl. She'd be one-quarter black. What were they called? Quadroons? Was it even politically correct to use that word these days? Probably not. Her thoughts went round and round until she eventually fell asleep.

***

She was woken by the sound of rain pounding on the roof. She groaned and turned over in the bed. Molly's cold wet nose nudged her chin.

'Oh, Molly, okay! I'm getting up.' She looked at her watch. Seven-thirty. Maybe she'd had too much to drink last night. She hauled herself out of bed and had just dressed when there was a knock on the door.

'Elizabeth? Are you ready?' It was Will.

'Nearly!' They'd arranged to have breakfast together at the café down the road at eight o'clock before heading back home.

She opened the door, 'There's an umbrella in the car. I'll just get it out.'

Molly stood in the doorway peering out. 'Come on Molly, I know you don't like the rain but needs must!' Will crouched down and patted the dog.

An hour later and they were on the road, stopping for lunch near Newcastle. Elizabeth yawned. Will glanced at her. 'Are you okay to drive, Beth?'

'Oh, I'm just tired,' she replied, stifling another yawn. 'Maybe I had too much to drink last night.'

'Pull over and I'll drive.'

Elizabeth waited until the next pull in, indicated and parked. 'Thanks, Will.' They swapped seats. She settled into the passenger seat as Will adjusted the driver's seat. She glanced over at him before drifting into a pleasant doze.

'I think Molly might need a comfort break, Beth.'

Will's voice broke into her dreams. Startled, Elizabeth jumped up. 'Oh! Will! Where are we?'

'Nearly in Sydney. You want to stop, or carry on?'

Elizabeth glanced back at Molly. 'Carry on. Molly's sound asleep.' She sank back into her seat and slept.

***

'Wake up Elizabeth!'

She shook her head and tried to come around. 'Where are we?'

'Back home.' Will had stopped the car outside her garage. It was nearly dark. Elizabeth sat up and rubbed her eyes.

'It's okay, no sign of Merv or Iris,' Will grinned. 'Come on, poor Molly is desperate for a pee.' He got out and opened the back door of the car. Molly jumped out and went straight to her favourite spot on the lawn.

'I can't believe I slept most of the way,' Elizabeth said. 'Thanks, Will, for driving.'

'No probs. If you open your front door, I'll bring in Molly's bed.'

Elizabeth got out of the car, stretched and blinked. 'Thanks, Will.' She unlocked the front door as Will followed her with Molly's bed. She wondered if she should ask Will to come in for a quick drink They hadn't eaten since lunchtime and she didn't have much food in the fridge. 'Um, Will, you must be hungry, but apart from Molly's food and a few eggs, my fridge is bare.'

Will smiled, 'It's okay Beth. I won't stay. Got a few things to do and there're some leftovers in my fridge that need finishing.' He moved back to the car, took out her suitcase, his overnight bag and the pick. He carried her case to the front door then slung his bag over his shoulder. 'Nearly forgot my pick! Thanks for the trip, Beth, I really enjoyed it.'

'Thank you, Will. It was great having your company.'

Will turned, lifted up her chin, leaned down and gave her a quick kiss. 'That's in case Iris is looking,' he whispered. Then he laughed and strolled across the road to his own house.

Elizabeth's heart gave a flip as she watched him go; she parked her car in the garage and went indoors.

That night, she found it hard to get to sleep. Probably after sleeping in the car most of the way back, she thought. She lay awake thinking about the past few days. Somehow Brodies Plains kept coming into her mind. But most of the time her thoughts were of Will and his daughter. Then she wondered if perhaps they should have stayed an extra day and made it to Brodies Plains. Maybe she could contact that nice Dianne in the Historical Society in Inverell. She'd been so helpful. Find out more about the history of the place.

Mount Alexander - 1853

Edmund was happy when it was his turn to mind their camp. It seemed he and Jasper were the ones usually assigned to tent duties. Jasper confided in him one day, 'I'd really rather stay back at the tent, Eddie, I like tidying the tents and making the meals.'

Edmund had stared at him. 'So would I,' he'd muttered, looking longingly towards the blacksmith's tent.

However, Jasper was mainly the one to be left behind, for not only was he getting too weak to be of much use at the diggings, but he also spent most of his time doubled up in pain and squatting over the latrine.

Joe's eyes slowly healed but Jasper got so bad that eventually, he couldn't even get out of the tent to go to the latrine. The smell was gut-wrenching. Edmund moved out and just slept outside. It was becoming too hot in the tent anyway.

Early one morning, Edmund woke to the sound of Harold, staggering out of the tent and sobbing. 'What's up?' Edmund asked.

'Jasper's gone!'

'Gone? Gone where?' Edmund looked all around, he could only see other diggers coming out of their tents and preparing for the day.

'Dead!' gasped Harold.

Jake came stumbling out of his tent. 'Who's dead?'

'Jasper.' Edmund nodded towards the tent. 'Harold just found him.'

'Hmm, no big loss,' Jake said.

Harold turned to him, 'How dare you!' he spluttered, 'How dare you!' He raised his fists.

Jake pushed him aside and went behind the tent for a piss.

Joe emerged from the tent, 'Heard the news,' he said. 'Sorry to hear that, Harold. Know he was a good mate of yours. Well, I guess we'd better dig a grave for him.'

They all turned their eyes towards the area set aside for burials. It was a rocky gulley that drained into the creek when it rained.

'I'll make a start,' Harold managed to say. Edmund didn't feel like breakfast so said he'd join him.

They went with picks and shovels and spent several hours trying to dig. There were other men digging graves and one called over to Harold and Edmund, 'We reckon four feet is deep enough.'

Edmund eyed the hole they'd dug so far. It was about two feet deep. Sometime later, Joe came and found them and helped. 'Jake stayed to mind the tent, in case any dogs came round and started in on poor Jasper,' he said.

Harold paled. 'Didn't think of that.' He began to dig with renewed energy.

When they'd finished, Edmund and Harold returned to the tent while Joe stayed behind to dig deeper. Edmund helped Harold roll Jasper up in the soiled sheet in which he'd been sleeping. The stench was so overpowering that Edmund had to hold his breath and try not to think. There was no water to spare to clean the corpse.

'We should never have come here,' Harold sighed as they laid Jasper to rest. 'He missed his violin.'

Edmund thought it was a strange thing to say.

***

The time came when it appeared the Mount Alexander diggings had yielded all the surface gold. The men were having to dig deeper and deeper shafts to find gold.

'I reckon it's time to move camp to the Ovens[1],' announced Jake one evening as they sat around the campfire after their evening meal. 'Anyways, I'm going there. You coming, Joe?'

They all watched Joe. 'Um... dunno,' he mumbled, lowering his eyes.

Jake shrugged and glowered at Harold, who since Jasper's death seemed to have lost interest in the diggings. 'No,' Harold shook his head. 'I'm going back to England.'

Jake scowled. 'Me and Joe can do it alone,' he said brusquely. He looked over at Edmund and sneered. 'An' you can stay with yer blacksmithing chum! Yes, I know how you've been hanging around the smithy.' He stood up and went to his sleeping bunk and started to dig up the store of gold. The others all watched him, each wondering what to say. At last, Jake stood up, slightly unsteadily – he'd been to the lemonade tent – and surveyed them all. 'Here you go.' He began sharing out the gold. Edmund was content with his share, but he could see Harold thought he deserved more, at least Jasper's share, but none of them was prepared to challenge Jake, who threw the final lumps of gold at Joe. 'Termorrer we're off to the Ovens,' he growled, and staggered back into their tent and collapsed onto his bed.

Harold turned to Joe. 'What about it, Joe? Going with Jake?'

---

1. The Ovens Valley, a gold mine near Beechworth in Victoria

Joe shook his head. 'Nah. Think I'll go back to Melbourne, get on the next boat to Sydney. Got enough gold to buy me a bit of land. I'll find me one of them nice Chisholm girls and settle down somewhere near the sea.' He smiled. 'Get out while the going's good.' He turned to Edmund. 'What about you, laddie? Is Jake right? You like the old blacksmithing?'

Edmund nodded. 'Yes. I reckon if I can get a smithy to take me on, I'll learn the trade.'

***

The next morning, Edmund helped Harold pack up his tent. 'Thanks, Edmund.' Harold held out his hand. 'It's been great having you to help. If ever you come to England, look me up.' He took a card from his wallet and gave it to Edmund.

'Thanks,' Edmund said, taking a quick glance at it. He thought it was improbable that he would ever make the voyage to England.

Jake and Joe finished packing their tent. 'You won't need the billycart if you're going back to England,' Jake said to Harold. 'So, I can take it off your hands. Won't charge you nothing.'

Harold stared at him. 'I think I might need it to take our gear back to Melbourne.' He stood stolidly in front of Jake.

Jake shrugged, 'As you wish. No skin off my nose. Just trying to do you a favour.'

Joe intervened. 'Harold said he'd take my gear in his billy cart, Jake.'

Jake knew when he'd been beaten. He shrugged and hoisted his pack onto his back. 'Good luck, *chums*,' he growled, then shrugged, took his pick and shovel, raised a hand and walked off, watched by the other men.

Edmund thought he heard Harold mutter under his breath, 'Good riddance.'

Harold turned to Edmund, 'How will you manage Edmund? What will you do?'

Edmund smiled. 'Redmond, the smithy over there,' he raised his hand and pointed, 'is going to take me on.'

***

Edmund moved his tent close to the blacksmith, happy to be working and doing something he enjoyed, not like digging deeper and deeper down into the earth, getting covered in muddy clay when it rained and breathing dust when it didn't. The panning for gold, washing the silt looking for that glint of gold became boring and monotonous after a while. Somehow, he didn't have the lust for gold that made the diggers keep going day after day.

Annie came regularly to the blacksmiths with one of her husband's picks to have the point remade. Edmund thought she seemed to get prettier each time he saw her, with her large blue eyes and curly fair hair. One day he asked her how she had come to Australia.

'Oh,' she said, 'well, I was working as a maid in a big house in London.' She picked at her skirts and lowered her eyes. 'But the master of the house kept getting me into a corner on the back stairs,' her expression darkened, 'then the mistress found him, I was struggling to get away from him – but his wife blamed me, said I was encouraging him and dismissed me without a reference.' A tear rolled down her cheek.

'What did you do then?'

'I had no choice but to go to the poor house. I had no money, and I couldn't get another job without a reference. It was horrible.

Then the government thought it would be a good idea to send a lot of us young healthy girls to the colonies. I was put on board a sailing ship with all these other girls. It was appalling.' Annie shuddered. 'There was eight of us in one small makeshift cabin, and no fresh air and when it was stormy, we were shut in for hours at a time.' She frowned at the ground. 'Anyway, when we reached Sydney, I got put in a house run by a Mrs Chisholm. People came there looking for servants or wives. No-one wanted me for a servant,' she paused and her cheeks coloured. 'They said I was too pretty.' She hung her head.

'Well, you are,' Edmund said.

Annie gave a half-smile. 'Then a woman came and said she'd take me to marry her son. She said that I was so pretty, I might keep him at home.'

'And did it?'

Annie sighed. 'Not for long. Not that I minded; I didn't like him. He was nasty when he'd drink taken. Then he decided we'd go to the goldfields. His mother was furious. Blamed me.'

'That wasn't fair.'

'No. But I felt a bit sorry for her.'

Edmund shook his head.

'What about you?' Annie asked.

'Nothing to tell,' Edmund replied, 'came from Sydney to look for gold.'

The blacksmith interrupted them. 'Here's your pick, Missus. Put it on Sam's tab, will I?'

'Thank you, mister.' Annie took the pick and walked off.

'Beautiful girl,' Redmond said. 'You fancy her?'

Edmund blushed. 'She's married,' he said, sharply.

The blacksmith nodded. 'I know, and her husband's a waster. I've noticed on a few occasions she had bruises on her face and arms.'

Edmund had noticed them too but hadn't liked to remark on it.

***

By the time he was eighteen Edmund was tall and muscular, his beard had progressed from the initial thin tufts into a thick lush growth. He felt he'd learned all he could from Redmond, who had taught him lots of skills but there was little opportunity to practise them. He was getting a bit bored making horseshoes and sharpening picks. He wanted to practice more of the trade, things like knife making and wrought iron. There wasn't much call for wrought iron at the goldfields.

One morning, as Edmund was getting the fire ready, Redmond stretched and studied his young apprentice. He scratched his beard. 'Eddy, lad, you seem a bit restless lately. Do you feel like moving on?'

Edmund started. Did Redmond want to get rid of him? He stared at the blacksmith. 'Um, well, I appreciate what I've learnt from you, Redmond, but I'd like to be able to put all you've taught me into practice. Seems to be mostly sharpening picks and horse-shoes here.'

Redmond sighed. 'You're right lad, but the money's good, and I'm getting old and tired. I just want to last out a few more years and then move into town, maybe just make a few horseshoes but get away from the rough company here on the diggings.'

Edmund nodded.

'But you still have to make a living, boy, and the goldfields is the place to do that. Maybe try the Ovens, or Bendigo goldfields, or even New South Wales. You've learnt all you can from me.'

Edmund nodded again. 'I appreciate what you say,' he said, choosing his words carefully. 'I've saved a bit so maybe in the next week or two I'll make a move.'

'Your lady friend is here,' Richmond nodded towards Annie. 'Reckon she fancies you.'

Edmund blushed. 'I keep telling you, she's married,' he mumbled.

'Doesn't stop her fancying you and if her husband's a brute; well, nice young chap like you ...' He winked at Edmund and moved away.

'Hello, Annie.' Edmund turned to her and smiled. She smiled back, making his heart thump.

'Hello, Edmund. Just come to settle Sam's tab 'cos I might be leaving soon.'

'Oh? That's strange so am I. Where are you going?'

She brushed a curl from her face. 'I don't know yet. My man died last week. Coming back from the lemonade tent, late at night, he must have slipped and fell into one of the diggings that had filled with water. They found his body the next day.' She shivered.

'Oh. I'm sorry to hear that.' Edmund didn't know what to say. She'd never mentioned children so he assumed she had none – unusual for a woman at the diggings.

'Don't be. He wasn't a nice man.' She smoothed her skirts and lowered her eyes.

'So where will you go?'

'Dunno yet, but I have to get away, there's a couple of men who've started pestering me. Where are you going?'

'Dunno either. Maybe Melbourne first then Sydney, see my family.'

'It's not good for a woman travelling on her own.' Annie peeped up at him., 'Would you let me come with you as far as Melbourne? I was thinking of perhaps renting a place there and starting a boarding house. I've got enough money from Sam's gold that I managed to hide away from him.' She frowned.

Edmund's heart beat faster. He didn't know what to say.

She must have taken his silence as a refusal for she continued, 'It's all right, you don't have to. I'll manage.' She turned to go.

'No, wait, Annie. Of course, I'll escort you to Melbourne.'

She turned and beamed at him. 'Thanks. I'll come back tomorrow and we can arrange things.'

'What was all that about?' Redmond appeared from inside his tent.

'Er,' Edmund coughed. 'Her husband died last week and she's leaving. She said she came to settle her husband's account, but I think she must have forgotten, but she's coming back tomorrow.' He kicked a loose stone. 'Um, I'm going to escort her as far as Melbourne.' He blushed.

Richmond raised his bushy eyebrows and grinned. 'Lucky you! You'd better get sorted out then. How will you travel? Get a bullocky? You've got a lot of tools now.'

'Haven't thought that far ahead.' Edmund frowned. He thought about the drays that several bullocks pulled – the standard method of transport on the rough unmade roads. Not a comfortable ride; in fact people usually stacked their possessions on the cart and walked alongside.

'Or, wait, there's the new Cobb & Co coaches. That would be safer for a lady.' Redmond winked.

***

A week later, Edmund and Annie were sitting inside a Cobb & Co coach, their baggage on the top.

'I feel like a lady,' smiled Annie.

'Well, you are!' replied the gallant Edmund.

In Melbourne, they were set down at a hotel and their luggage stored. 'I'm going to the bank to exchange my gold for currency,' Edmund told Annie, 'If you want to come with me.'

The storekeepers at the diggings would exchange gold for currency or goods, but Edmund had noticed some storekeepers sifted the gold to remove any "dust" before weighing it. They then swept the dust into a container under the counter. He was sure they would then sieve it through a finer sieve and keep any gold.

Annie was thrilled with the money he got in exchange for her gold. 'I'm a rich widow!' she exclaimed.

Edmund was thinking fast – with his money he'd be able to build a nice house and set himself up as a blacksmith, maybe get married. He looked over at Annie. 'Will we have dinner together at the hotel tonight?'

'Yes,' Annie smiled, 'that would be ever so nice.'

Later that evening Edmund sat at a table in the dining room and waited for Annie to join him. His heart thumped when she came into the dining room. He stood and pulled out the chair opposite his and gestured towards it. 'My lady,' he said, bowing.

Annie giggled, but then they were both silent, neither knowing what to say.

Annie turned her gaze to him, 'I was thinking of going to Sydney instead of opening a boarding house in Melbourne. It seems a bit rough here with all the gold diggers.'

'Yes,' agreed Edmund. 'I was going to go down to Port Phillip tomorrow and see if I could get a passage back to Sydney on a sailing ship ...'

'Would you take me with you?' Annie looked at him from under her lashes.

Edmund gulped. 'Well, yes, if it's what you want to do.'

Wambecarra - April 2021

The days passed; Elizabeth didn't see much of Will, he must have a lot of work on, she thought when she saw his ute driving off early in the mornings, and not returning until the evening. Not that she was keeping tabs on him, *of course!* She knew the recent rains and the sun made everyone's lawn grow so he must be busy mowing. As was she.

'I dunno, Moll,' she grumbled to her dog. 'I seem to be cutting the grass every week lately. And I haven't made much progress on my ancestry research.'

Molly's tail thumped.

Elizabeth finished her mowing, showered and sat out in the garden with a cup of tea. She had to admit to herself she missed Will. It was now over a week since they'd returned from Inverell and she'd had no contact with him. Did he regret to have revealed so much about himself and his daughter? Then Bronwyn's words came back to haunt her. Was he once more telling her things to make her feel sorry for him? She tried to recall exactly how he'd looked when he told her about Caitlin, but he'd appeared genuinely upset. You couldn't act that sort of thing.

Iris must have told Merv about their trip, because the first day back, when she'd been taking Molly for her afternoon walk, Merv had bobbed up beside his gate and winked at her. 'Is it true then, what they say about bla ...' he'd started to say but she'd marched straight past him pretending not to notice him. She was sure he knew the times she walked Molly and lurked around waiting for her.

Since then, she'd put Molly in the car and driven to an off-leash area a few kilometres away for her afternoon walk. She was safe on the early morning walks; it seemed Merv was a late riser. *Bugger Iris,* she thought. And she couldn't think of an excuse to go and see Will ... Her thoughts went round in her head. Maybe Bronwyn was right. She should make more friends, not just rely on Will. Perhaps she should join something. Learn a language, what was that organisation called? U3 something? She'd look it up later. She needed to return her library books; they'd know. Perhaps she could volunteer for something ...

'Come on Moll, into the car, walkies time.'

***

The following Saturday afternoon she had a text from Will: *I just remembered you needed some stumps removed from around your back fence. I could come over this arvo if that's a good time for you?'*

She couldn't help smiling. She immediately replied with a thumbs-up emoji.

Molly went rushing to the door at the sound of the doorbell that afternoon.

'Hi, Will!' Elizabeth greeted him with a smile as she opened the door.

He swung the pick. 'All ready to test it out,' he grinned. 'I've put linseed oil on the handle, and see what I found ...'

He showed her a mark on the head of the handle. Elizabeth peered at it.

'It's a blacksmith's trademark,' Will said. 'It would have been handmade. It's very clever, see,' he pointed to the mark. 'I think it's a **T** with the top rounded to look like a pickaxe and just under the left arm of the T is a smaller E.'

Elizabeth studied it more closely. 'I think you're right! Come in Will, before Merv spots you.'

'Oh, he already has,' Will replied. 'Waved at me and tried to find out where we'd been last weekend. I pretended I didn't hear him, just said, "Yes, lovely day, Merv" and hurried to your front door.'

Elizabeth laughed. 'He's dying to find out...' she stopped when she remembered what she thought Merv was trying to find out and she blushed.

Will didn't seem to notice. 'Okay, show me these old tree stumps you want removed.'

'It's lucky there's a high fence along the back or Merv would be peeping over spying on us,' she laughed.

He grinned, 'Yes, but he's probably lurking behind it listening to us.'

She watched him using the pick to break up the stumps. 'I need to fetch my crowbar to finish getting them out,' he said after a few minutes. 'Won't be long.' He disappeared around the side of the house followed by Molly.

'Come here Molly!' Elizabeth called, but Molly took no notice and kept following Will. Elizabeth sighed.

She took the discarded pick and frowned. Maybe she could take a swing with it. Then her eye was caught by the brand mark burnt into the end of the handle. Like Will had said, it was a T with an E under the left arm of the T. She smiled, and looked up as Will returned with the crowbar.

'I think this is my pick,' she grinned. 'See, it's got my initials, ET, Elizabeth Turner.'

Will appeared thoughtful. 'Or Edmund Turner,' he said slowly. He regarded Elizabeth. 'Wouldn't it be weird if Edmund had been a blacksmith and made this pick.'

'It'd be more than weird,' replied Elizabeth, 'it would be a one in a million chance.'

'I guess so. But truth is stranger than fiction. Right, let's get this sucker out of the ground!' Will drove the crowbar into the ground and lifted half the rotten tree stump out.

Elizabeth watched him. It was so good to be with him again, she thought.

'There you are, all done.' Will's voice interrupted her thoughts. 'What are you going to do with this bit of ground?'

'I thought of putting a raised vegetable bed there,' Elizabeth replied.

'Great idea. If you can wait until after Easter,' Will said, 'I can build it for you. Just a bit busy at the moment, everyone seems to want things done before the holidays.'

'Would you? That'd be great.'

Will stroked his chin. 'Hmm, pity I ran out of cobble stones, I could have built it with them.'

'You're never going to let me forget that, are you?'

His eyes twinkled. 'Nope! It's my secret weapon!'

'Have you time for a beer?' Elizabeth asked.

'Beer? I didn't think you drank beer.'

Elizabeth blushed. She'd noticed what Will had drunk when they were in Inverell, and had bought a six-pack and put it in her fridge. *Just in case,* she'd told herself.

'Oh, I just thought it might be handy to have a bottle in the fridge,' she tried to make her tone casual.

'For tradies doing work?'

Elizabeth took the pick and pretended to swing it at him.

'Yes!'

Will laughed, took it from her and grasped his crowbar which he'd stabbed into the ground. 'Sounds good to me.'

They walked back up the garden to the house.

'Sit down and I'll fetch it.' Elizabeth indicated the outside table and chairs.

Will stretched out his long legs and sighed as she came out with two glasses and two bottles.

'That's nice, you're joining me.'

She nodded. 'I might develop a taste for beer.' She held out a bottle and a bottle opener. Will shook his head at her offer of a glass. 'I'll drink out of the bottle. The Aussie way.'

He opened the bottle and raised it. 'Cheers.' He took a swig. 'So, what are you doing for Easter? The family coming down?'

'No,' Elizabeth carefully poured some beer into a glass and took a sip. 'Bronwyn and family are going to Byron Bay for the school holidays.'

'So, you'll be footloose and fancy-free ... Will you miss them?'

She considered. 'Don't know. Bronwyn keeps on to me to go up and stay with them, but Molly's a problem.'

'You know I'd mind Molly, don't you?'

She nodded.

Then Will gave her a sideways look. 'Actually, Elizabeth, I have a favour to ask you.'

She caught her breath. *Here it comes! Was Bronwyn right? What favour could he want?* 'If I can.' She tried to keep her voice casual.

'Well, I was thinking that it seems I won't be able to go to England any time soon, with the government travel restrictions ...'

'Hmm ...' Elizabeth's heart started to race. She took a deep breath and waited.

'Well, you did mention once you could look up my ancestry for me. I might be able to find relations if they exist. Would you do that for me?'

She let out a long breath. 'Yes, of course. When?'

'Whenever it suits you, I could come later today. Would that be okay? After dinner?'

She nodded, not knowing what to think. Afterwards, she thought she should have invited him to dinner, but she had nothing much to offer, she'd intended to just have scrambled eggs on toast.

'What do I need to bring? Birth certs, that kind of thing?'

'Yes, that would be good.'

***

A few hours later, Elizabeth sat beside Will in her kitchen, her laptop open on the table.

'I've brought all the documentation I thought might help.' Will opened a folder. 'My birth certificate and my mother's, her bigamous marriage certificate ...'

Elizabeth could hardly breathe. Her eyes scanned Will's birth certificate. It was as he'd said. He'd been born in Lewisham, on eighth February 1968. Mother, Christine Barnes formerly Watson. Father, Wilberforce Barnes. And Will's name was actually Wilberforce! No wonder she couldn't find him on Google. She'd thought Will was short for William. She did a quick calculation, he was fifty-three – eight years younger than her.

It all added up! She was so overjoyed she felt like hugging him. Why had she been doubting him all these weeks? Bloody Bronwyn! She smiled inwardly and then studied his mother's marriage certificate.

Wilberforce Barnes aged twenty-eight married Christine Watson, aged twenty-two on the 4th March 1967. The certificate showed Christine's father's name, James and occupation as carpenter and Wilberforce's father's name also Wilberforce and occupation as a labourer.

She typed the details into the ancestry site.

'What now?' Will asked, looking at Elizabeth, his brow furrowed.

The computer screen showed a family tree with Will's mother and father and himself as an offspring.

'So, it only shows me as my father's child. He had no other children then.' He gave a sigh of disappointment.

'I think you have to click on your father and then put partner unknown and check for offspring,' Elizabeth replied.

Will nodded. 'Please.'

A few minutes later two new entries appeared on the screen.

Will blinked. 'So my father had two other children, besides me! Look, a girl, Tamara Barnes and a boy Delroy.'

Tears came to his eyes as he stared at Elizabeth. 'Oh my god,' his voice broke. 'I have a family.'

He appeared so shaken that Elizabeth put her arms around him and hugged him to her. Gently she released him. He sat up and put his hands to his face, covering his closed eyes. After a few deep breaths, he managed to mutter, 'Can we contact them?'

'I think it's only possible if they're also on this particular ancestry site. You send a message to them via the site. They forward it to them anonymously.'

'Would you do that for me, Elizabeth?'

'Of course. What shall I write.?'

'Whatever you think.'

Elizabeth could see Will still seemed shaken. 'I think we should have a break and think about it. How about a glass of wine?'

Will nodded. Then smiled. 'Sounds good.'

Elizabeth stood up. 'Come out onto the veranda, we can relax for a bit. And think what to write. Probably something simple, like "I believe I am your half-brother and would like to get in touch with you," and then give them details of your date of birth.'

Will stood up and stretched. 'Yes, that sounds about right. Thanks, Elizabeth.'

Elizabeth nodded, as she watched Will go out onto the veranda and start strolling around her garden. She brought out a bottle and two glasses.

Will turned and came over to her and took her hands. 'Lovely. Thank you, Elizabeth.' He looked into her eyes. 'I'm so glad I met you.'

Melbourne - 1856

Edmund managed to get a passage on a brig sailing from Melbourne to Sydney, with a tiny cabin for Annie and a hammock for himself. He enquired about Captain Bruce and the *Bluebird* but no one seemed to know what had happened to him.

Annie went shopping for new clothes, suitable for Sydney. When Edmund saw her that evening, he caught his breath. 'Oh my! Annie, you're beautiful,' he couldn't help exclaiming.

'Fine feathers make a fine bird,' she grinned. 'Must make a good impression for when I get to Sydney.'

The weather was favourable and they made good time to Sydney. Edmund had written to Mary-Anne to tell her he was on his way back, but his letter hadn't reached her when they arrived.

Mary-Ann's eyes widened when she opened her door. Then her mouth fell open. 'Oh, my word! It's Edmund!' Mary-Ann clutched her chest then threw her arms around him. 'Oh, my goodness, you left a boy and have come back a man, and you look the image of our father! And who is this pretty child you've brought with you?'

'Oh, this is Mrs Annie Marchant. She's a recent widow, her husband died on the goldfields.' He turned to Annie, 'Annie this is my sister, Mary-Anne, um, Mrs Wallis.'

Mary-Anne bobbed her head. 'Pleased to meet you, Mrs Wallis.'

'And pleased to meet you, Mrs Marchant.'

Edmund smiled at Mary-Ann. 'I've just escorted Annie from Melbourne, now I must find her accommodation.'

'Well, I'm sure I can find room for you both here.'

'Thank you, but I don't want to inconvenience you, Mrs Wallis,' Annie spoke up.

'Well, let's not stand on the doorstep for everyone to gawk at us! Come in, Edmund.' She turned aside and shouted, 'Nat! Look who's here! Edmund and a friend.'

Her husband came hurrying from the back of the house. 'Edmund! What a surprise! Welcome, we didn't expect you! Well, you've filled out, that's for sure.'

'I did write, but it seems the letter didn't reach you yet,' Edmund said.

Mary-Ann turned to her husband. 'I'm just telling Edmund they can stay here; we have plenty of room.' Her voice sounded sad.

Edmund grimaced, remembering Mary-Ann had miscarried several times and now he couldn't see or hear any evidence of babies being born since he'd been away.

'Yes, yes, come away in.'

Edmund introduced Annie to Nathaniel Wallis, and again Annie said she didn't want to be a nuisance and could easily find a hotel in the city.

'Nonsense!' replied Mary-Anne, 'now you come and sit down and I'll get Milly to prepare rooms for you both while I put the kettle on.' She led Annie to a prettily furnished drawing-room.

'I'd rather come and help,' Annie said, following Mary-Ann to the kitchen, 'if you don't mind?'

Edmund smiled at Mary-Ann. 'Annie likes to keep busy,' he said.

Mary-Anne nodded.

'Come, Edmund.' Nathaniel tugged Edmund's sleeve, 'See what I'm building now.' Edmund followed him into his workshop where Nathaniel, a carpenter, was making window frames.

In the kitchen, Annie sat and watched Mary-Anne. When the kettle was filled, and on the hob, Mary-Ann busied herself with cups and saucers and then turned to Annie. 'A widow, Edmund said. So, have you children, Mrs Marchant?'

Annie looked down at her hands. She'd noticed there was no sign of any children in the house. 'Um ... no ... um, I lost a baby and I didn't fall after that ...' She didn't mention she'd lost the baby she'd been carrying when her husband had come back drunk to the tent and hit and abused her. Whatever he'd done, she'd never conceived again, but she didn't mind, the thought of children fathered by him filled her with horror. Sally at the diggings had bandaged her up and helped her. Then Sally'd gone round to Annie's tent when she knew Sam would be there and threatened him that if he ever touched Annie again, she would go round and cut his balls off. Annie had been taken aback at Sally's rough language, but grateful for the result. Sally was a large woman with powerful arms and Annie's husband was a skinny little man; he'd tried to bluff and whinged he'd done nothing, but Sally had held up a fist. 'I have ways,' she'd growled.

Now Mary-Ann mistook the dark look on Annie's face for sorrow. She went to the table and took Annie's hands in hers. 'Oh, you poor darling!' she said. 'I know how you must feel. I've lost several babies and now I'm in my thirties and I don't think I'll ever bear a child.' She sniffed and wiped her eyes. 'Poor Nat is so disappointed but he doesn't show it. He's a good man.'

Annie nodded. 'I'm sorry, Mrs Wallis.'

'Please call me Mary-Ann!'

'And I'm Annie.'

'Now tell me all about how you first went to Melbourne, you sound English.'

Annie had started to tell Mary-Ann about her experience coming out on the ship from England when Edmund and Nat came into the kitchen.

Mary-Ann raised her eyes. 'You must both stay here, Edmund. That's to say, I don't know what your plans are ...'

Edmund glanced at Annie, 'Well, I'm thinking about going to the goldfields around Bathurst and starting up a forge, there always seems to be plenty of work for a blacksmith on the mines.'

'A blacksmith!' Mary-Ann's eyes widened. 'Whatever made you take up that? I know you used to like hanging around the forge here before you left for Melbourne.'

Edmund smiled. 'Dunno, I just like making things with metal, and Annie is thinking of setting up a boarding house here in Sydney.' He turned to Annie. 'Unless you've changed your mind, Annie?'

'A boarding house!' Mary-Ann exclaimed. 'My dear, you're far too young to be setting up a boarding house. You could have all kinds of rough men living there.'

Annie smiled. 'I was thinking of only taking in females. But someone on the quay said there are lots of them here, so if you wouldn't mind, Edmund, I'd like to come with you to Bathurst and rent a house there.'

Edmund's heart lurched. He'd enjoyed her company on the sea voyage from Melbourne.

Mary-Ann frowned, she glanced at her husband, who was looking thoughtful.

'Well, you're an enterprising young woman, that's for certain,' was Nat's only comment.

'Mary-Ann,' Edmund said, 'it would be good if we could stay here until we sort things out, transport and so on. I think Annie must be tired after the sea journey from Melbourne.'

'Plenty of empty rooms here,' Mary-Ann sighed.

'I'll help you bring in the rest of your bags, Edmund,' said Nat. 'Good to see you again, lad.' He patted Edmund's shoulder as they went out the door.

'Let me come and help you,' Annie said to Mary-Ann, who smiled and nodded.

***

Edmund managed to find a bullock team going to the town of Bathurst in New South Wales that would take his bags and the blacksmithing tools he'd made with Redmond on the goldfields. It would take about three weeks for the journey, so he left Annie with Mary-Ann with instructions to put her on the mail coach once they received a letter from him to say everything was arranged. He'd go with the bullocky and find accommodation for her and then meet her at the coach stop.

Mary-Ann and Nat were happy to agree.

Wambecarra - April 2021

Two weeks later, Elizabeth had a reply to her Ancestry message. She couldn't wait to contact Will. She picked up her phone and called him.

'I know it's late, Will, but I just got a message from England. Your sister.'

There was a silence, then Will's voice came through. 'My sister ...'

'Yes, she wants to know more about you. Wants to do a Skype meeting.'

'Skype? I don't know how to do that, Beth. Can you help me?'

'Be thrilled. When?'

'As soon as you can show me how. Can I come over now?'

Elizabeth glanced at her watch. It was nine o'clock in the evening, but she could hear the urgency in Will's voice. 'Okay. Yes. I'll unlock the door. Just come in.'

She'd hardly had time to unlock the front door and go back to her laptop in the kitchen when she heard Will coming in.

'She's here now.' Elizabeth turned to Will, then looked back at her laptop screen. 'Can you see me, Tamara?'

'Yes,' came the reply.

'I've got your brother, Will, here now.' Elizabeth turned the screen towards Will.

'Oh my God, you look just like Daddy!' Elizabeth heard Tamara cry.

Will was speechless for a moment, then his voice came out in a squeak, 'You're my sister?'

'Yes, indeed. I can't believe it. Daddy never made a secret of your existence, and Mum didn't mind. She died a few years back. Dad isn't too good at the moment, he's in hospital. I wish you could come over and we could all meet up.'

Elizabeth stood. 'Tamara, I'm going to leave you and Will to chat, I've got a few things to do.'

'Okay, Elizabeth. Nice to meet you, thanks for getting Will and me together. Wait until I tell Delroy!'

Elizabeth went out of the kitchen to her bedroom and sat on the bed. She had nothing in particular to do but wanted Will and his sister to be able to talk together in private.

She heard the rumble of Will's voice and the faint murmur of Tamara's. She'd always known Bronwyn had been wrong about Will. He was who he'd said he was. And she could understand how he hadn't wanted to spill everything out to her in the beginning.

She lay back on the bed and closed her eyes. It had been a pretty busy day ...

She must have dozed off because the next thing she heard Will's voice and a knock on her bedroom door.

'Are you there, Beth? Can I come in?'

She jerked awake and blinked. 'Yes, come in, Will.' She combed her hair with her fingers and sat up as Will pushed open her bedroom door.

'That was amazing, Beth, I'm blown away.'

He certainly seemed shaken, Elizabeth thought. She swung her feet off the bed and onto the ground. 'Come out to the kitchen, I'll make a cuppa, or maybe a glass of wine?'

Will nodded. 'Thanks.'

'So, what did Tamara have to say?' Elizabeth led the way to the kitchen. Her laptop was still open on the kitchen table. She closed it and busied herself getting glasses and a bottle of wine.

Will sat at the table. He took off his glasses and rubbed his eyes, then gave a watery smile. 'I can't believe it, Beth. She wants me to come over to London. Apparently, our dad hasn't been well - in and out of hospital. He's over eighty now. She said he'd be thrilled to hear about me.' Will picked up the glass of wine Elizabeth had placed before him. 'Thanks,' he said and took a big gulp. He studied her. 'I've got to go, Beth.'

Elizabeth nodded and took a sip of her wine. 'But how can you with the restrictions?'

'I'll get permission somehow.' Will scowled. 'Can you look up what I have to do please, Beth?'

'What, now?'

'Would you mind?'

Elizabeth could see the wall clock out of the corner of her eye. Nearly midnight and she was tired. She stifled a yawn. 'Of course!'

Five minutes later and she turned from the laptop screen. 'You need to comply with condition 8570,' she read, 'and you need to complete and submit Form 1454 – 'Request for Approval to Travel' under visa condition 8570 ... no, hold on that's for people on a temporary protection visa.' She frowned. 'It seems very complicated.'

'I've got a British passport as well as an Australian one,' Will said. 'That might help; last year, when I decided to go back to England, I renewed the one I had when I came over when I was six.'

'Hmm.' Elizabeth suppressed another yawn.

Will must have noticed because he stood, 'Beth, it's late,' he glanced at his watch. 'I'm sorry, I've kept you up. I can try and look into this myself in the morning.' He went over to her and hugged her. 'Thank you, Beth, for all you've done.'

Molly jumped up and nudged him. 'And you, Molly.' He walked to the door. 'I hope Merv is keeping watch!'

Elizabeth smiled and followed him. 'Goodnight, Will. I hope you can sleep after all this excitement.'

'And you, good night, Beth, and thanks again.' He bent and pulled on his boots.

Elizabeth gently closed the door behind him and locked it. She got ready for bed but then couldn't sleep. She lay awake thinking about Will and his sister. Tamara seemed nice ...

She got up at three o'clock and peeped out from behind her bedroom curtains. A light was on in Will's bedroom which also faced the street. Poor Will, he probably couldn't sleep either ...

***

Early next morning Elizabeth groaned as Molly nudged her. 'All right, Molly, I know, you want to go out ...' She dragged herself out of bed and went to the kitchen and opened the sliding door. Molly ran out. Elizabeth yawned and went to put the kettle on. She needed coffee. She turned on her phone as she waited for the kettle to boil and found a message from Will.

Managed to find all the instructions, Beth. I need to find a JP as I have to make a Statutory Declaration as to the reasons why I want to leave for longer than 3 months. Do you know a JP?

Elizabeth replied that the local library had a JP and to ring the library to get details. Then she realised the implication of Will's text. Longer than three months? Did he mean to stay longer? Her heart sank. But then, he had said at some stage he was only doing up his house with the intention of selling it and moving to England …

It was three days later when she heard from Will again and that was a text asking her to come over for a drink that evening. Lots of news, he'd said. And have a bite with me, he'd added.

She sent a message back asking what time, and he'd said about six, and bring Molly, of course.

She put a bottle of red wine into a paper bag and casually strolled across the road with Molly, for all the world as if she was taking Molly for a walk. Taking a quick look around and seeing no one, she opened Will's gate and went to the door which Will had left ajar. A tantalizing smell greeted her.

She went in, calling out to him, 'I'm here, Will.'

'In the kitchen,' came the reply.

'Umm, smells good, Will,' she smiled.

'Just a chicken curry,' Will turned to her, 'glasses on the table, help yourself to wine. Cold white in the fridge.'

Elizabeth gazed at the kitchen table which was set with plates and cutlery and a small vase of flowers. She was about to remark he must be expecting someone special when she stopped herself. 'Thanks, Will.'

'Won't be long,' Will continued stirring the curry. 'Rice is done if you'd like to put it on the table.'

'Wine for you Will?'

'Yes please.' He smiled at her.

A few minutes later they were seated at the table. 'Help yourself, Beth,' Will indicated the bowl of rice and the wok.

'Thanks.'

They ate in silence until Elizabeth could contain herself no longer. 'So what's been happening, Will?'

He finished chewing a mouthful of food then placed his fork on his plate.

'I've sent off my request for a permit to leave Australia. I think I've done it all correctly. Went to the library as you suggested and got a Justice of the Peace to witness my affidavit saying I needed to go and see my long-lost father who's eighty-three and seriously ill in hospital.'

'Is he seriously ill? I didn't realise,' Elizabeth interrupted.

'Well, I don't know, but at that age and if you are going in and out of hospital, it must be pretty serious.'

'I guess so.' Elizabeth said.

'I also went to see a real estate agent in town about letting this place while I'm away. He said he'd have no problem. Apparently, lots of people want to live in this area and rent while they look for somewhere to buy. That would be good as I can let it furnished for a short-term rental.'

Elizabeth's heart sank.

'I have another favour to ask of you.' Will looked into her eyes.

'Anything I can do, Will.'

'I've taken a post office box in town and getting all my mail delivered there. I was wondering if you'd collect my mail whenever you're in town. Shouldn't be much, maybe a few invoices, most of my stuff I get online, but in case something comes in. Just open the letters and let me know what they contain.'

'Of course. Not a problem, Will.' He looked so excited, she thought.

'I can't book a flight until I know if my application has been accepted, but I'm hoping it won't be too long. Oh, and while you're here, could you show me how to get on to Skype?'

'Of course, Will.' Her mouth felt dry, she was finding it difficult to swallow. She took a sip of wine. 'This is delicious Will.'

'Thanks,' he smiled at her.

'So you think you'll be in England longer than three months?' She tried to make her tone casual.

'I think so, it's not worth going all that way just for a couple of weeks,' Will said, 'and I have a lot of catching up to do with my new-found family.'

'Of course.' Elizabeth took another mouthful of wine and swallowed.

'I'll probably be able to get work over there.'

'Indeed.' Elizabeth suddenly felt bereft. 'Maybe you won't want to come back ...'

'Hadn't thought that far ahead.' Will concentrated on his food. 'Eat up, Elizabeth, you've hardly touched your food.'

'Had a big lunch,' she replied. 'If I'd known you were going to cook such a lovely meal, I would have only had a snack.'

But Will was preoccupied and not really listening.

'Have you heard from Tamara since the other evening?'

'Yes, she's been texting me and eager to get onto Skype with Delroy.'

Elizabeth tried to imagine what it must be like to suddenly find a family you never knew you had.

'She's done a lot of research into our family history, apparently our great great grandparents were taken to Jamaica as slaves and ended up working on the sugar cane fields. Then our dad came to England after the war, as part of the *Windrush* emigrants.'

'The *Windrush*?'

'Yes, I looked it up after Tamara told me about it. Britain needed workers after losing so many men during the war and they were happy to have Jamaican workers.' He frowned. 'It seems it wasn't quite how the Jamaicans envisioned England. They weren't really accepted by the British people and found it hard to get accommodation. Well, so much of England had been bombed and destroyed there was hardly anywhere for the English to live either.' He fell silent.

Elizabeth watched him.

'Anyway, he did get work and lived with other Jamaicans, who were on shift work. It seems when one of them went off to work, the other one went straight into the recently vacated bed …' Will gave a rueful smile. 'I think times must have been hard for everyone then.'

'Hmm,' Elizabeth murmured. It didn't sound very hygienic.

'At least during the winter, the bed was warm …' Will smiled. 'I guess Tamara will fill me in with more when we get onto Skype.'

Elizabeth's spirits sank even more as the evening progressed. She showed Will how to get onto Skype on his laptop and when he had it all sorted, she got up from the table. 'I'd better go and leave you to it, Will. So pleased the way everything is working out for you.'

'Thank you, Beth. You've been brilliant. I can't thank you enough.'

Elizabeth nodded. 'Pleasure.' She looked down at Molly. 'Come on Moll, we must leave Will to it and go home.' Her dog hauled herself to her feet, shook herself and followed Elizabeth to the front door.

Will held the door for her, then glanced outside. 'This is for Merv,' he said and gave her a quick peck on the lips. 'Goodnight, Beth, and thank you again.'

'Goodnight Will.' Elizabeth went across the road, conscious that Will was watching her until she'd opened her door and was safely inside. She waved to him and he waved back. Then she went into her bedroom, threw herself on her bed and cried.

Molly came and rested her head on the bed and appeared so sad. 'What was all that about, Molly?' Elizabeth gave a tearful laugh. 'I'll miss Will, but so what? I'll have to make more friends. Bronwyn is right.'

***

Elizabeth didn't see much of Will over the next few days. She had a few text messages keeping her up to date with his progress, but he was busy sorting out his place, getting it ready to let and finishing off jobs he'd committed to. She invited him over for dinner the following week.

'This is lovely, Beth,' he said when he came in. 'I really felt too tired to cook tonight.'

'Help yourself to a wine and sit down,' Elizabeth said. 'Pour me a glass too, please.' She turned back to the cooktop where she was stirring a sauce. 'So, what's been happening, you seem to have been busy,' she tried to keep her tone light.

'Yes, well, it's all coming together. I think I've told you most of my progress.'

'And you managed to get a flight?'

'Yes, it's very difficult, I've got an open return ticket, but from what I've heard people are having problems getting flights back into Australia. All being well, I leave in three weeks.'

'Oh! How will you get to the airport? Can I drive you? We'd have to have Molly in the back of the car, I couldn't leave her alone for that long.'

'No, Beth, I'll get the train from Kiama, if you wouldn't mind taking me to the station.'

'Of course. A pleasure.' She served the meal and watched as Will tucked into the food.

After a short time, Will looked up at her. 'I wanted to ask you to come over and see what stuff I should leave for the letting and what I should put in storage,' he said.

'Storage?'

'Well, I thought a few things, like my printer and some of my more expensive tools, for instance, that I don't want to leave in the house. I've managed to get tenants to rent the house – a short term lease, so I thought it best to rent a small storage place in town. Put stuff in there.'

Elizabeth's heart sank at this news. She pretended to consider. 'Hmm, well, that lovely patchwork quilt and maybe your bedlinen, most people wouldn't expect that to be in a furnished letting, and it might get damp in storage. I could keep it here for you if you like.'

'Thanks, Beth and would you come and help me with the other stuff? Have a quick look?'

'Of course. Anytime.'

'Oh! And another favour, Beth.'

'Yes?' She raised her head.

'Well, it's Caitlin's birthday next month. I always send her a card and put some cash in it.' He sighed. 'I doubt if her mother ever gives it to her, she probably keeps the money and throws out the card. But if I leave the card with you, would you post it a few days before her birthday?'

'Of course.'

Bathurst, NSW - 1857

Edmund arrived in the town of Bathurst – over one hundred and twenty miles of rough terrain - after nearly three weeks on the bullock dray which carried his trunk with the blacksmith tools that he'd fashioned for himself under the guidance of Redmond, and another trunk with his personal belongings. The journey had been wearying, often having to help the cursing and swearing bullock driver pull the team of bullocks up steep parts of the road.

He hoped Annie would have a more pleasant journey on the mail coach. It was expensive but worth it for her. He wondered if she'd marry him. She'd never said much about her husband, except the very first time Edmund had met her – he wasn't sure how old she was, he thought maybe older than him. She'd been a skinny little waif of a thing but very pretty even then. At the time he'd paid no attention when she said she'd been bought from Mrs Chisholm's hostel. He knew the man hadn't treated her well. But she must have been a careful manager as by all accounts she now had enough money to rent a property to run a boarding house.

He hadn't had much to do with females, apart from his sisters, of course. There weren't many women at the Mount Alexander diggings, and they were all married, or at least with men folk. He'd never had a mind to seek out prostitutes. His sister, Mary-Ann had frightened him when he was young with gruesome stories about men who went with fallen women. 'Find yourself a nice wholesome girl and marry young, like your brothers,' she'd advised. Well, he was nineteen now.

He was attracted to Annie. In fact, he acknowledged now, he was in love with her, couldn't stop thinking about her. Even if she was a few years older than him, it didn't matter. And also, Mary-Ann liked her. He made up his mind. When she arrived in Bathurst, he'd ask her to marry him. Having made this decision, he dreamed of her, of spending nights in her arms ...maybe they could do the jumping over the broomsticks until they could find a priest to marry them formally.

He'd asked around and heard that gold had been discovered in a place called Sofala about thirty miles from Bathurst, but most of the miners had moved on to the Upper Turon, so there would most likely be places to rent. Even with the smaller population, he thought it might be a good place to start up as a blacksmith. And much pleasanter for Annie than a new goldfield with no facilities. He managed to get a ride with a bullocky to Sofala. There was room for another forge; he'd spoken with the one other blacksmith who had a forge there and he was inundated with work. Edmund mentioned he was thinking of starting up, and would the smithy object, and the man had seemed happy enough. Shrugged and said, 'Plenty of work for two smiths, lad.' Edmund managed to rent a small two-roomed cottage with space for a forge. Happy to have achieved so much, he went back to Bathurst and the post office and, using the newly opened morse telegraph line, sent a telegram to his sister in Sydney.

Please put Mrs Marchant on next passenger coach to Bathurst. Stop. Edmund. Stop.

He'd built up in his mind the scenario of Annie being so happy to be asked to marry him, that the day before the coach bringing

Annie was due to arrive, he moved from the room he shared with two other men in a boarding house, to a hotel with a double bed. They could get married, and then he'd take her to Sofala. He wasn't sure about the legal requirements for getting married, but he was pretty certain from what he'd seen at Mount Alexander it was an easy process and they could do it the same day.

When he met the weekly passenger coach in Bathurst and helped Annie down, he couldn't wait to tell her his plans. He thought she looked prettier than ever, with her shining blue eyes and fair curls.

'Hello Edmund,' she said.

He put an arm around her and kissed her. She drew back. 'Oh! Edmund!'

To cover his confusion, he took her bags and led her to the hotel.

'I thought we could stay here tonight and tomorrow go to Sofala where I've rented a place with two rooms and a space for a forge,' he said, proud of his achievements.

Annie seemed puzzled. 'But I want to rent somewhere in Bathurst to have a boarding house,' she said. 'I told you. I have some money, but it won't last and I need to have an income. I thought this was the best way. And Bathurst would be cheaper than Sydney.'

Edmund led the way to the hotel. Outside, he stopped, put down her bags and turned to her. 'Annie, my dear, I thought it would be a good idea for us to get married, and I could look after you and you wouldn't need to run a boarding house.'

'Married?' Annie exclaimed, 'But I don't want to get married! I've been married once and never again.' Her eyes darkened.

Edmund's face fell. He'd assumed she'd be delighted. At Mount Alexander, Redmond had insinuated Annie fancied him and she'd given every indication that she liked him, especially on the journey from Melbourne. He thought of the double bed in the hotel. He'd better try and get another room for himself and let Annie have the double bed.

'I'll take your things up to your room.' He picked up Annie's bags and led the way into the hotel and up the bare, wooden stairs. He opened the door to a small wood-panelled room. It was indeed small – just big enough for a double bed, one chair and a few wooden pegs set into the wall for hanging clothes. Annie walked in, her footsteps echoing on the timbered floor. She went to the small uncurtained window and peered out. The room was at the back of the hotel, overlooking the outhouse and privy. 'Seems nice,' she said, then turned around, 'but whose stuff is this?'

Edmund had left his bag on the floor and his coat flung over the chair. He flushed. 'Mine, I, er, I thought, I mean, I must go and see if I can get a room for myself. I'll go now and let you settle in.'

'Thank you, Edmund, you've been so kind to me. Um, do you think I could get a cup of tea? And,' she paused and cleared her throat. 'The lav?'

'Yes, comc down to the bar.' He put her bags down.

The bar was very basic. On the sawdust-covered floor were several wooden tables, with a chair on each side. 'The lav's out through here,' Edmund told Annie, showing her the door.

He turned to the bar where the proprietress, a plump blousy looking woman, was wiping the counter with a dirty wet rag.

'Er, Missus McDonald, could I have a pot of tea for the lady, please?' he asked. 'Oh, and have you another room, um, a single room I could have for the night?'

The woman cackled. 'You got the last room this morning, son; you'll have to share with yer lady friend I'm afraid.' She slapped down the damp rag and turned away, disappearing through a door. 'I'll make the tea,' she said over her shoulder.

Edmund was in a dilemma. He couldn't go back to his old lodgings; another man had moved in before Edmund had barely had time to move out. There was nowhere else. He'd been lucky to get the double bedroom in this place.

Annie emerged from the back of the hotel as the proprietress came out from the kitchen with a tray. 'Here you are, ducky,' she said to Annie, as she banged the teapot on one of the tables. 'I've brought two cups, thought yer man might like a cup too.' She gave him a wink. 'Build up yer strength for tonight,' she leered.

'Thank you,' Annie smiled at the woman who gave a gap-toothed smile back.

Edmund had noticed Annie only had to smile at someone and they were instantly charmed. The thought depressed him. She could marry anyone, why would she bother with him? Then he remembered the room.

When the woman had gone back to her kitchen, he turned to Annie, who was pouring out the tea.

He cleared his throat. 'Annie, there's a problem. There're no more rooms in the hotel, and everywhere else is full. I was lucky to get the room you're in. So ...'

Annie raised her eyebrows, then smiled. 'Well, I suppose we'll have to share the room.'

Edmund coloured. 'I'll sleep on the floor, of course.'

'Of course,' echoed Annie. She took a sip of her tea. 'Oh, this is so good!'

***

Edmund left Annie to settle in while he went off trying once more to find a place to stay, but again he had no luck. He returned as the hotel was livening up with men returning from the goldfields.

He went up to Annie's room and tapped on the door. 'Annie? It's Edmund.'

He heard the key turn in the lock and Annie opened the door.

She smiled that radiant smile of hers. 'Hello Edmund, I was hoping you'd be coming soon. I'm very hungry and I can smell something cooking in the kitchen below.'

'Yes, are you ready now?'

She nodded and went back to fetch a shawl and threw it around her shoulders.

At the bottom of the stairs, she took his arm as they went into the smoke-filled, noisy bar.

The noise died down as the men all turned to stare at her.

Edmund felt proud to have her on his arm.

Mrs McDonald came out from the kitchen. 'Over there, ducky,' she addressed Annie, pointing to an empty table.

'Thank you, Mrs McDonald,' Annie smiled.

The men's heads all swivelled in Annie's direction as she passed by, swishing her skirts between the tables to the empty one.

'Lucky sod,' one of the men muttered as Edmund followed her.

Edmund ordered ale and then sat opposite Annie. He couldn't take his eyes off her.

The pot boy brought ale and tankards, his eyes so drawn to Annie he nearly spilt the ale.

Edmund wracked his brains to think of something to say. 'A change from mutton and damper at Mount Alexander, 'eh Annie,' he eventually said, as he started to eat the mutton stew with potatoes, carrots and onions one of the maids brought out.

Annie nodded. 'Mary-Ann made some very nice meals while I was there. She's lovely.' Annie took a sip of porter. 'I was talking to Mrs McDonald while you were out.'

'Oh?' Edmund looked up.

'Yes. She said there wasn't anywhere in Bathurst I could rent to start a lodging house. Said I'd have to buy land and build something and being a woman, I probably wouldn't be allowed,' Annie sighed. 'And anyway, I don't have enough money to buy land and build. So, I thought maybe I'd better come to the place you mentioned. I might be able to rent somewhere there.'

'Sofala,' he said, suddenly feeling more optimistic.

'Yes, that place. Mrs McDonald didn't know much about it but she said to give it a go. Otherwise, she'd give me a job behind the bar. Reckoned I'd draw in business.'

Edmund frowned. He didn't think much of that idea.

At last, they finished eating. 'I think I'll go up to my room,' Annie said as she rose from the table. 'I'll just go to the lav first.' She disappeared out the door to the back of the hotel.

Edmund waited for her, then followed her up the stairs. 'It's a bit early for me,' he said as he opened the door to their room. 'I'll go for a short stroll and come back after you've gone to bed. Oh, and the chamber pot's under the bed.' He pointed to a china pot whose handle could just be seen and he blushed.

Annie nodded. 'Thank you, Edmund.'

'Right, well I'll be back in about half an hour, then.' He thought that might be enough time for her to get into bed and fall asleep.

'Good night, Edmund and thank you for everything.'

He didn't quite know what to do for half an hour, he wandered back down to the bar, which was already getting noisy and smoke-filled.

'Wot you doing down here, then, should be up wiv your lady friend,' one man said to him.

'Reckon she'd be getting herself ready for him,' cackled another.

Edmund went outside to the toilet. It was the usual long drop, just a hole in the ground covered with a plank with a hole cut in it supported by two oil drums. He thought it was lucky Annie was used to the goldfield shit holes or she'd be horrified by this smelly 'lav' as she called it.

He hung about for a while then went around to the front door of the hotel to avoid the crowd in the bar. He went up the creaky wooden stairs to their room, his heart thumping. He turned the handle of the door as quietly as he could and crept inside. Annie had left a candle burning on the one chair in the room. He picked up the candle holder and held it up. Annie lay on her side, her hair spread out over the pillow. She seemed to be breathing slowly as if asleep.

He took off his clothes as quietly as he could, leaving his underpants and stockings on, then bundling up his shirt and pants to make a pillow, he lay down on the floor and covered himself up with his overcoat. The floor was hard, cold and draughty. He could hear the noise from the bar below. Not much chance of sleeping, he thought.

The noise from below got louder as the night wore on. As he was wondering how Annie could sleep through it, he heard her getting out of the bed and pulling out the chamber pot. He tried to ignore the sound of her pissing into the pot, then it stopped and she came over to where he lay. There was no curtain on the small window so he could see her outline in the moonlight.

'Edmund,' she whispered. 'Are you asleep? You must be frozen down there on the hard floor. Get up and come into bed with me.'

Dazed, he sat up. 'Are you sure?' He whispered back.

'Yes.'

He felt her put out a hand to help him up. 'Thank you, I couldn't sleep with the noise, could you?'

'No.'

'I must use the pot,' he said, regretting all the ale he'd drunk that night in the bar.

'All right.'

He heard the bedsprings creak as she got into bed and he soon followed her. The bed was pushed against the wall and she lay close to it. He tried to take up as little space as possible, but couldn't avoid touching her.

'You're freezing, Edmund. Come and cuddle into me.'

She pulled him towards her and wrapped her arms around him.

He felt dizzy as her hands moved down his body ...

Wambecarra - June 2021

The day of Will's flight arrived. With a heavy heart, Elizabeth reversed her car out of the garage. She saw Will wheeling a large suitcase across the road, a backpack slung over his shoulder. His flight wasn't until later that night, but he wanted to be at the airport in plenty of time.

She stopped the car and Will opened the rear door and heaved his suitcase in.

'Never know what the weather will be like in England,' he smiled. 'I'm prepared for every eventuality!'

She returned his smile. 'Good plan.'

'I've got my laptop in my backpack and all the important stuff in a safety wallet around my neck.' He raised his eyebrows. 'I hope you're impressed?'

'Yes! But I don't think you can take any hand luggage in the cabin with you because of all the Covid stuff.'

'Dunno. Have to wait and see. Oh! By the way, as soon as I get a UK SIM card for my phone, I'll send you a message.'

She nodded. 'That'd be good.'

They drove the rest of the way in silence.

At the station, Elizabeth dropped Will at the entrance. As he got out, she said, 'I'll park and come back and see you off.'

'No need. I'll be okay.'

She drove further down the road, found a parking space and walked back to the railway station. She could see Will waiting on the platform as she walked down the steps.

'Oh, Beth, there was no need to come!'

Just then the train pulled up and passengers started to get out. Suddenly the platform was crowded with people and suitcases. Will stood back until the platform was clear, then turned to Elizabeth. 'Beth.'

Overcome with emotion, she tried not to cry. 'Safe journey Will,' she managed to mumble.

He bent down and picked up his suitcase, then put it down again. Slowly he lifted her chin and met her eyes. 'You take care, Beth.' He bent down, gathered her to him and kissed her. After a long moment, he released her, took his case and boarded the train.

Elizabeth saw him mount the stairs and move to a seat near the window. He waved.

Thinking she was going to start crying, she waved back and hurried from the station. Back in her car, she had to wait a few moments until she felt able to drive home.

***

Two days later she had a text from Will telling her his new mobile number and saying he'd Skype her that evening, about seven Australian time.

At half-past six she went to her bedroom and combed her hair, wondered about putting on lipstick and then chided herself. *For goodness sake, Elizabeth. Get a grip!*

It was so good to see Will's face on her laptop screen. 'How are you, Will?'

'Good, bit tired from the jet lag but all good. Seen my father. Oh, Beth, it was amazing.' He wiped his eyes and his voice grew husky. 'He's not been well, he's got diabetes, but he was so pleased to see me. He wanted to know all about my mother. He looked all round to make sure no one was listening and then he leaned towards me and said in a low voice, "She was the love of my life, Will. I never would have hurt her." I said, "I know, Dad and you were the love of her life, she never re-married." He got a bit upset then, but I told him we'd had a happy life and that seemed to make him easier.'

'That's good,' Elizabeth said.

'And do you know what's amazing, Beth?'

'What?'

'Delroy has a horticultural business! He said I can work with him whenever I like when I'm not visiting Dad.'

'Wow! That's so good.' Elizabeth repeated and tried to make her voice sound pleased, but she couldn't help thinking Will would never return to Australia if he had a ready-made job and family over in England.

'Well, I'd better sign off and go and visit Dad.' Will's words jerked her out of her reverie.

'Okay. Well, thanks for getting in touch, Will.'

She signed off and sat back in her chair. 'I dunno, Molly. Think I need a glass of wine after that.'

SOFALA, NSW - 1861

Edmund slowly built up his smithy. Thomas Miller, the other blacksmith who had his forge just opposite the imposing new brick-built Bank of New South Wales, often had so much work he couldn't cope, and when that happened, he sent those customers round to Edmund.

Edmund was happy, he adored his Annie, who had made their little timber cottage into a cosy home; she'd started a garden and grew most of the vegetables they needed.

Annie was a good cook and while men were waiting for Edmund to complete a job, mainly putting a point on a pick, she would sometimes provide tea with home-made jam and scones. Word got around and Annie started selling her jams and pickles. Edmund felt blessed to have her. A few times he'd mentioned them getting officially married, but Annie had just laughed.

'We've jumped over the broomsticks[1] , that's legal, isn't it?' she replied 'And anyway why bother, everyone thinks we're married, I'm always called Mrs Turner. It would only cause gossip if we were to have a wedding now.'

---

1. Jumping the broomsticks was an old custom thought to have originated in Wales among the Romany people who were not allowed to marry in a church. On the goldfields where a priest or clergyman may only have occasionally visited, jumping the broomsticks was a valid marriage ceremony

'I suppose so, but one day when we go to Bathurst, we'll get the vicar at Holy Trinity to make it regular.'

It became harder for miners to find surface gold, and many left the town, however, there was great excitement when on the twenty-fifth of June that year, two nuggets of gold, one of 54 oz and the other of 9 oz were found by Chinamen at Bullock Flat. These finds were not repeated, but then alluvial mining – gold deposited by water movement - took over so there were still well over a thousand people living there; plenty of work for two blacksmiths.

Edmund and Annie had been living in Sofala for five years when Annie became pregnant. Edmund was delighted when she told him. 'That's wonderful,' he said, hugging her close, he'd begun to think they would never have a child.

'I hope so,' said Annie. 'I hope it will go well.'

'Why wouldn't it?'

But Annie said no more. Edmund thought she meant she might miscarry, like his sister Mary-Ann. He remembered when he was living with her and Nathaniel, she always seemed to be crying over the loss of yet another baby. But then, he had a letter from her a couple of years ago to say she'd been delivered of a healthy baby girl, at long last. Rachel, the baby was called. His other sisters had healthy children. Ellen had five or six as he recalled. Elizabeth Esther had only one boy, and she'd died soon after, but the boy was healthy enough, and his brothers also had several children. He dismissed Annie's fears as natural for a first-time mother.

'Right. I'd better get the fire going in the oven.' Annie moved to the tinder beside the oven.

'I'll chop more firewood for you.' Edmund hastened to the door.

The year wore on and Annie became more tired. Edmund had suggested again that they get properly married but Annie said it was too hot and the journey to Bathurst would be too much for her.

They employed a young girl to help, fetching water, doing the washing and cleaning while Annie kept making jams and chutney until the day she went into labour.

She'd engaged the services of a midwife, Mrs Flynn, who lived close by and had several children of her own, the latest only two months old.

'I don't know how she keeps going,' Annie said to Edmund.

'Well, she's a big strong woman,' he replied. He studied Annie and her protruding stomach which seemed to dwarf her small frame and he grimaced.

Annie's labour was long and painful. Edmund tried to keep working at the forge, but after making a few mistakes he closed the forge and went to the back of the house and started chopping firewood.

Late in the afternoon, Mrs Flynn came out and called to him. 'You have a fine son, Mr Turner!'

Edmund beamed as he threw down his axe and rushed indoors into the room leading off the kitchen which was their bedroom. Mrs Flynn blocked his way. 'Just a minute Mr Turner. I have to clean up a bit.'

Edmund tried to peer over her shoulder and was horrified to see Annie lying in bloodied sheets, her eyes closed.

'Let me in.' He shouldered Mrs Flynn aside and went towards Annie. 'Annie,' he murmured. 'Annie, are you all right?'

Her eyelids fluttered and she managed to smile. 'A boy,' she said and looked at the small bundle resting on her breast. 'A little Edmund. Edmund Joseph.'

Edmund brushed away tears. 'My darling Annie.' He leaned over and kissed her, then pulled aside the swaddling in which his son was wrapped and gazed at the tiny baby.

Mrs Flynn came bustling in with towels and hot water. 'You can leave now,' she ordered. 'Mrs Turner's very weak. Go and fetch more water and put it on to boil.'

Edmund went to the pump for water, his heart singing. He wanted to shout to the world that he had a son, but after drawing the water, feeding the fire and putting more pots on the stove he couldn't settle to anything. Mrs Flynn was still in with Annie. He'd just thought of writing to Mary-Ann to tell her the good news when Mrs Flynn came out of the bedroom.

'I don't like the look of Mrs Turner.' She made a face 'She's losing a lot of blood and the afterbirth hasn't come out yet. I think you'd better try and get a doctor.'

Edmund panicked. The nearest doctor was a Dr Meynink from Tambaroora and that was about thirty miles away. There was no possibility of reaching him and getting him to come to Sofala at such short noticc.

'But who?' he asked, 'It would take me a day to get to Tambaroora and another day for the doctor to come back here, that's if he was able to come.' His voice shook.

Mrs Flynn considered. 'Well, there's Dr Evenett. He's an animal doctor,' she said with a slight shrug. 'He'd be better than nothing, I 'spose.'

Edmund raced around to the veterinary surgeon's house.

'Doctor's out with a cow,' the vet's wife said. 'I'll send him round as soon as he gets back. You're the other blacksmith, aren't you?'

'Yes, yes,' Edmund replied. 'My wife, she's just given birth, our first baby; Mrs Flynn said to see if your husband could help.'

Mrs Evenett nodded. 'Mrs Flynn knows what she's doing, she delivered all my ones.'

That was no consolation to Edmund, who raced back to his house.

Mrs Flynn met him at the door, holding his baby in her arms. She held him out to him. 'I have to go home now and feed my baby. I'll come back later.'

Edmund took his son and hurried inside to Annie. He put the young Edmund into the crib Annie had prepared, then turned to Annie. He was shocked at her appearance, she looked like a ghost, no colour at all in her face. 'Annie, darling,' he said softly.

She made no movement; he thought she was scarcely breathing. Then he saw the blood seeping from the towels Mrs Flynn had wrapped around Annie's legs.

He cursed himself for dragging Annie out to Sofala. If they'd stayed in Bathurst there would have been doctors who could have helped. A few minutes later there was a knock on the door and a voice.

'Dr Evenett,' it announced. 'My wife said you were asking for me.'

'Come in, come in,' called Edmund, 'in here.'

A tall dark-haired, bearded man appeared in the doorway. His clothes were stained and rumpled. He grimaced when he saw Annie.

'I'm more used to dealing with animal births,' he said, as he pulled back the bloodied sheets from Annie. He caught his breath and tutted. Then gently parted Annie's legs.

Edmund could see the trickle of blood.

'Where's the afterbirth?'

'Um,' Edmund didn't know what to say. 'I think Mrs Flynn said it hadn't come out.'

The vet exhaled sharply. 'It has to come out,' he said. He tried massaging Annie's stomach but she merely groaned and nothing happened. 'In a cow, I'd try and pull it out, or else leave it and often it comes out eventually.' He scratched his nose. 'But in this case, your wife seems too exhausted. Maybe put the baby to the breast. That sometimes helps cause a contraction.'

'I think Mrs Flynn already tried that,' Edmund said.

'Well, we can try again,' Dr Evenett said and looked around. He saw the crib and picked up the baby, who started to mewl.

Edmund tried to suppress a shudder at the sight of the vet's large dirty hands touching his tiny son.

The vet drew aside Annie's nightgown, pulled out one of her breasts, squeezed the nipple and pushed it into the baby's mouth. He frowned at Edmund who was appalled at the cavalier treatment of Annie's breast. 'Sorry,' the vet muttered and looked away.

Baby Edmund Joseph started to suckle. Annie groaned in pain but the placenta still didn't emerge.

'Maybe put hot cloths on her stomach,' Dr Evenett suggested, 'not much else to do.' He bent over Annie's parted legs.

Edmund started towards the kitchen, but he turned as Annie suddenly gave a huge moan and the bloody placenta shot out and hit Dr Evenett in the chest. 'Good girl!' Dr Evenett sounded pleased. 'That's a relief,' he said, standing up. 'Well lucky I hadn't changed my clothes since pulling out that calf! She should be all right now.' He moved towards the door. 'I've got a horse needs shoes, maybe you can make me some in exchange for my fee.'

Edmund nodded his thanks then turned back to Annie. The baby had slipped from her breast and Edmund just caught him from sliding onto the floor. Annie didn't even seem capable of holding her baby, in fact, she appeared to have lost consciousness. Baby Edmund Joseph started to whimper as the door opened and

Mrs Flynn came into the room. She saw the placenta which still lay at the end of the bed.

'Good! It's out, go and dig a hole and bury it,' she told Edmund. She took the baby who was crying in earnest now. She started to open her bodice and Edmund averted his eyes and hurried out as she flopped a large, blue-veined breast out and guided a nipple to the baby's lips.

***

February 1862

My dear Sister,

It is with great sorrow that I write to inform you my darling Annie passed away last week after giving birth to our son, Edmund Joseph.

At the moment a Mrs Flynn is taking care of him but I am writing to ask if you and Nat would take Baby Edmund and raise him as your own. I am unable to care for him as a mother would. Mrs Flynn is very good but she has several children of her own as well as being the local midwife.

If you are agreeable, please inform me as soon as possible and I will bring baby Edmund Joseph to Sydney on the mail coach.

I have decided to leave Sofala, I cannot bear to stay here without my beautiful Annie.

Your loving brother,

Edmund.

Edmund blotted the letter and sealed it. He blew his nose and wiped his eyes. Gathering his coin purse, and jacket, he took the letter to the Sofala post office. Then he went to the cemetery and stood and stared at the mound of fresh dirt covering Annie's grave. His heart was breaking. Annie had been buried in the dress she'd bought in Melbourne. 'My posh dress' she'd called it. He sobbed. 'Forgive me, Annie, I should never have brought you here, never have asked you to marry me.'

He turned back and went to see Mrs Flynn, to tell her of his decision. He found her out the back of her cottage, up to her armpits in a tub of washing.

She nodded when she saw him. 'Come to see young Edmund?'

'Yes. Please. And to tell you I've written to my sister in Sydney to ask her to take Edmund. They only have the one child, a little girl. She must be about two years old by now. I know he'll be well cared for.' His voice broke. 'Annie liked my sister, Mary-Ann. She would be happy with that arrangement,' his voice was muffled as he turned away to hide his tears. 'I'll take him on the mail coach.'

'Hmm, and will you be coming back to Sofala?'

Edmund shook his head. 'I'll pack all my tools and put them on a dray.' There were too many reminders of Annie in Sofala.

A week later Edmund received a reply from Mary-Ann. She and Nat offered their condolences and baby Edmund would be more than welcome in their home.

Wambecarra - July 2021

Elizabeth had put a note in her calendar when to send Caitlin's birthday card. Will had put a stamp on it, but she thought it best to put her address on the back of the envelope. There was money in it – she didn't know how much – but just in case it wasn't delivered at least it would eventually be returned. She posted it early – with the lockdowns happening she wasn't sure how long it would take to arrive.

The weather that week had been dismal; wind and rain. Well, it *was* winter, Elizabeth thought, but it meant she hadn't been able to get out in the garden, or go for long walks. She sighed. The day dragged. She lit the fire in the wood heater – at least that made the place look more cheerful. She glanced out the kitchen window at her garden, barely visible through the rain. She poked the fire, raising a shower of sparks, then sat in front of it and opened her latest library book. After reading a few pages and realising she had no idea what she'd just read she rested the book on her lap and studied Molly. 'I'm feeling a bit forlorn, Moll,' she said. 'Winter blues.' She looked at her watch – half past four. She put the book down and stood. 'Come on Molly, time for walkies. Put on your rain jacket.'

Elizabeth fetched the jacket from the laundry and fastened it around her dog. 'It's too wet for Merv to be out so we can just have a short walk.'

Outside, Elizabeth managed to get soaking wet trying to juggle an umbrella, Molly's lead and open a poo bag to pick up after her dog.

Back home she put more timber on the fire and changed her wet clothes. She gave Molly her dinner, turned on her music system and selected some Beethoven, then poured herself a glass of wine and settled down in front of the now roaring fire.

'What will I have for dinner, Molly?' she asked the sleeping dog. Molly's ears perked up at the mention of dinner. Elizabeth gave a big sigh. She felt lonely. She had to admit it, she missed Will. She'd just taken a sip of wine when there was a ring at her front door. *Who would be calling at this time of the evening?*

Molly jumped up, barking, and raced to the door. Annoyed, Elizabeth put down her glass and followed her dog. She nudged Molly back with her knee as she opened the door. A bedraggled looking girl stood there, rain dripping off her long hair. Elizabeth frowned. 'Hello? Can I help you?'

'Um, I'm looking for Will Barnes.'

'Will Barnes?' Elizabeth's tone was curt. 'He doesn't live here.' The girl's shoulders drooped and she half turned away.

'The address on the back of the envelope was this one ...'

'Wait!' Elizabeth had a sudden thought. She put out her hand. 'Are you by any chance Caitlin?'

The girl turned back, with an appearance of surprise. 'Yes ... I ...'

'Come in! Don't mind Molly.'

The girl moved into the hall. 'I'm very wet.'

'That's okay.' Elizabeth could see a puddle forming on the floor. 'Come into the warm.'

Caitlin dropped her backpack onto the floor. 'I'm sorry. I got the train to Kiama and then a bus and I had to walk the rest of the way.' She shivered.

'Right. Let's get you out of those wet clothes and then we can talk.' Elizabeth led Caitlin to the bathroom. She pulled out a towel and handed it to Caitlin. 'Jump in the shower while I find you something warm to put on.'

Mutely, Caitlin obeyed.

Elizabeth went to her bedroom and thought. She pulled out a T-shirt and a cardigan, warm socks and her thick dressing gown. She heard the shower running and went to the bathroom and opened the door slightly. 'I've put some things here for you,' she called out, putting the clothes on the side of the washbasin. Her head in a whirl, she went back to the kitchen and took a gulp of her wine.

She heard the bathroom door open. 'In here,' she called, getting up.

Caitlin appeared, wrapped in the dressing gown, with the towel around her head. 'Thank you, what will I do with my wet clothes?' she whispered and started to cry.

'Come and sit by the fire, I'll hang them in the laundry to dry, and then I'll make us a cup of tea and you can tell me everything. By the way, I'm Elizabeth. Now, are you hungry?'

Caitlin nodded then shook her head. 'This is nice, by the fire,' she murmured.

Elizabeth mentally went through what was in her fridge. There was some homemade chicken soup, she could add a few more vegetables to it ...

'I've got some soup,' she said.

Caitlin nodded. 'Thanks.'

As she prepared the soup, Elizabeth half-watched Caitlin.

After a while, Caitlin looked up. 'So, are you Dad's new girlfriend? Where is he?'

'No,' Elizabeth said, 'I'm not. And your father has the house across the road.'

Caitlin made to get up, 'So why am I here, I don't understand!'

'Just a minute! I'll explain.' Elizabeth poured the soup into a bowl and put it on a tray. 'Here, have this, while I tell you.'

Caitlin sat down, rested the tray on her lap and started to eat, all the while taking quick glances at Elizabeth.

'Your dad's grandmother owned the house opposite and when she died, she left it to your dad. He moved here a year ago and I got to know him. He recently found out he's got relatives in England, and a father he hasn't seen since he was six. That would be your grandfather. Well, that grandfather is over eighty now and your dad was anxious to see him again, so he flew out to England a few weeks ago. He gave me your birthday card to post before he left and I put my address on the back. He said he'd sent birthday cards and presents to you every year but never heard anything ...'

'I've never heard from him,' Caitlin's brow puckered, 'perhaps my mother threw away the cards and didn't tell me.' She sighed and stood up. 'The soup was lovely. Thank you, Elizabeth.' She made to carry the tray to the kitchen sink.

Elizabeth took the tray from her. 'Now. Tell me what brought you here.'

Caitlin rubbed her eyes. 'My stepfather is horrible. He's been touching me and coming into my bedroom when I'm asleep or when I'm getting dressed. I told Mum, and she said I was imagining it, but she must have said something to him because the last few days he's been calling me a lying bitch and other horrible things. I could hear them arguing. I didn't know what to do. Then I went to the mailbox this morning and found the card from Dad. I think you must have posted it early, as it's not my birthday until tomorrow …' She sniffed. 'Have you got a tissue please?'

'Just a minute.' Elizabeth went to her bedroom, found a clean linen hankie, came back and handed it to her.

'Thanks.' Caitlin blew her nose. 'Then I thought I'd run away and find Dad. Mum always told me he'd abused me when I was young and that he was horrible and violent, she'd had to get an AVO out against him.'

Elizabeth frowned. 'An AVO?'

'You know, an Apprehended Violence Order.'

Elizabeth couldn't imagine Will being violent.

'So I thought, well he couldn't be worse than horrible Matt. Matt's my stepfather. I pretended to get ready for school. Matt had already left for work and Mum was busy getting Liam ready so as I was going out the door, I shouted to Mum that I was staying the night with a friend and left before she could say anything.'

Elizabeth's brow furrowed. 'Who's Liam?'

'He's mum and Sleaze Bag's son, my half-brother. He's five now.'

'Sleaze Bag?'

'That's what I call mum's partner.'

Oh, I see.' It was getting more and more complicated, Elizabeth thought.

'So, I got the bus to Central Station and then I was smart, I didn't use my Opal card, you know, the train pass, I bought a ticket.' She tried to smile. 'I found out I had to get a bus from the train station in Kiama to Warracamba and then walk from the bus stop to here. I turned location off on my phone when I left home, as I didn't want anyone to know where I was. I had to keep asking for directions.'

Elizabeth smiled. 'That was clever of you, but your mum will be worried tomorrow when you don't go home.'

Caitlin shrugged. 'Nah. I'm just a nuisance to her. Anyway, I don't care. I don't want to live with that horrible sleaze bag, Matt.' She looked anxiously at Elizabeth. 'Can I live with you?'

Elizabeth gave a start. 'Well, I don't know ...'

Caitlin seemed to shrink inside the dressing gown. 'Of course, you wouldn't want a complete stranger landing in on you ...' She patted Molly who was sprawled at her feet with her head on Caitlin's knees. 'I like your dog.' Molly licked her hand. 'I would have gone to stay with my grandmother, you know, Dad's mother, she was lovely, but Mum wouldn't let me see her after the AVO business and then mum said she'd died a few years ago.' She sniffed and wiped her eyes.

Elizabeth suddenly had an idea. Why hadn't she thought of it before? She looked at her watch. It was seven o'clock, that would be about ten o'clock in the morning in England. She got her phone and sent a message to Will. She hoped he was at Tamara's and not at the hospital.

Can you Skype me? It's urgent

She got her laptop and opened it up. Ten minutes later a there was a ping and a message. She saw Will on the screen.

'What's up?' he said.

'Um, I have an unexpected visitor. Are you sitting down?'

'Yes.'

She turned the laptop towards Caitlin. 'Caitlin, look. Here's your father.'

Caitlin gasped and turned around and studied the screen. 'Oh my God,' she exclaimed and burst into tears.

Will just opened and closed his mouth. 'Caitlin,' he eventually managed to say. 'Is it really you?'

Elizabeth suddenly thought that this hadn't been such a great idea. She turned the screen back to herself. 'Will, it's okay, Caitlin has run away and she's with me. It's all good. I'll explain later. I probably shouldn't have dropped this bombshell on you.'

'No, no! Does she want to come and live with me? I'll get the next flight back.' Will's words were tumbling out.

Caitlin wiped her eyes. 'Dad, it's all good. Don't worry about me. I'm going to live with Elizabeth for a bit.'

Elizabeth's brows drew together. How could she have a runaway teenager living with her? The police would be looking for her, her mother and the evil stepfather would be banging on her door demanding Caitlin come home. Then she saw Will's face on the screen and she knew she'd do anything for this man.

'Will,' she said gently. 'You must stay with your father for the time being, and anyway it's unlikely you'd get a flight back anytime soon. The government is talking about more restrictions on flights coming into Australia.'

'She could come over here. Tamara would love to have her.'

'Who's Tamara?' asked Caitlin.

'Your dad's half-sister,' replied Elizabeth.

Caitlin shook her head. 'It's all too much.'

Elizabeth turned back to Will. 'Will, this has all been a big shock to you both. Caitlin's very tired, she's been worried and upset and travelling all day. I'm going to make up a bed in the spare room for her and tomorrow we'll think of the best way to go about things.'

Will nodded. 'I guess so. But why has she run away?'

'Long story, Will,' Elizabeth said as Caitlin interrupted and started to tell him about Matt. 'Hush, now, Caitlin, this has all been a big shock to your dad.'

'Caitlin, darling,' Will said, 'I never abused you, never, ever would hurt you, please believe me! Your mother made up lies about me.'

'Yes, Dad, it's all coming clear to me now.' She started to cry again. 'I've missed you, Dad.'

Elizabeth could see Will getting emotional. He took out a hanky and blew his nose. 'Elizabeth'll take good care of you and I'll be back as soon as I can. I love you, dear Caitlin.'

'Right!' Elizabeth stood up. 'I think that's enough for tonight. Caitlin, come and help me make up the bed for you.' She had a sudden idea, 'and I have a patchwork quilt your great grandmother made. I'll put it on your bed.'

'Really?' Caitlin was distracted.

'Thanks, Elizabeth. It was good you took my linen stuff to store for me.' Will gave a watery smile. He seemed reluctant to go.

'Bye for now, Will. Just thought you'd love to see Caitlin. I'll send a text later explaining everything.'

She signed out of Skype and closed her laptop.

'Let's make up your bed now,' she said. She went out of the room followed by Caitlin and Molly. 'I'll find you a new toothbrush.'

Elizabeth put a hot water bottle in the bed for Caitlin.

'Thank you, Elizabeth,' Caitlin sniffed, 'and, Elizabeth?'

'Yes?'

'You won't tell anyone I'm here, will you?'

'No, I won't.'

'I'll have to stay hidden for a while because the police will come looking for me.'

'Why would they look for you here?'

'Because they'd be able to get Dad's address, wouldn't they?'

Puzzled, Elizabeth frowned.

Caitlin continued, 'I was thinking coming down in the train that Mum would ring the police and they would be able to trace Dad and find his address.'

Elizabeth nodded. 'Of course, I didn't think of that. But this isn't your dad's address. They won't come looking for you here.' She supposed Will would have been paying child maintenance all these years and the police would be able to get his details from that.

'If it's all right with you, I must stay hidden for a while.' Her eyes lit up. 'Don't suppose you have a secret hiding place in the walls by any chance?'

Elizabeth smiled. 'Unfortunately, no. All right now, it's getting late. I'll leave the bedroom door open a little bit and there's a torch on the bedside table if you wake up in the night. Try and sleep now.'

When Elizabeth got ready for bed, she realised Molly wasn't in her bed, 'Molly,' she whispered, 'where are you?' She heard the sound of Molly's tail thumping coming from Caitlin's room. When she peered, in Molly was on the bed, her head on Caitlin's stomach.

Elizabeth smiled. 'Right, you know you're not allowed on beds but just this once it's okay,' she said softly. She went back to her room and lay in bed thinking about the day's events. She kept seeing Will's face when he saw his daughter ...

***

'I must take Molly for her morning walk now,' Elizabeth told Caitlin the next day after they'd eaten breakfast.

'Oh! What shall I do if anyone comes to the door?' Caitlin asked anxiously.

'Nothing. Don't answer it. And no one will come.'

Caitlin looked perplexed. 'What about your friends?'

Elizabeth smiled. 'I don't have any friends. Well, only Iris across the road comes over sometimes. Your dad is really my only friend here.'

'That's sad.' Caitlin stared at Elizabeth. 'Not having any friends, I mean. Well, I'll stay in my room and I can peep out the window from behind the net curtains and see if anyone comes.'

'Good idea. Now, have a look in my bookcase and see if there are any books you'd like to read - in my study, through that door.'

'Okay.' Caitlin went into Elizabeth's study and then exclaimed, 'Oh do you play a double bass? Is it in that case?'

Elizabeth laughed. 'No, that's a cello.'

'Oh.'

'Well, I'm off now, Molly's getting restless. I won't be long.'

'Okay, well, I'll stay hidden.'

Elizabeth couldn't help smiling. When she returned from walking Molly, Caitlin bounced out from the study.

'Phew, you're back! I was getting nervous,'

Elizabeth smiled and said, 'Caitlin, I have to go into town to the shops and get food. What do you like to eat?'

'Why anything! I'm not fussy. But I can cook, you know.'

'That's great. Well, I might head off now. What were you thinking of doing?'

Caitlin screwed up her nose. 'Dunno. I 'spose I should do some school work, but I didn't bring much, only what I would have taken to school yesterday ...' Her voice trailed off.

Elizabeth suddenly had an idea. 'Tell you what,' she said, 'I've been doing ancestry research and writing it all down. Perhaps you'd like to read it.'

Caitlin seemed dubious. 'If you think so ... I'm not very good at history ...'

'Well, see how you go. Now, this is what I've done so far.' Elizabeth turned on her laptop and got the word document where she'd been recording everything she'd found out.

'Do you think we could talk to Dad again?' Caitlin fidgeted with her crumpled school blouse which she'd retrieved from the laundry.

Elizabeth frowned at her. 'I've just realised; you don't have anything else to wear except your school uniform ...'

Caitlin looked down at her clothes. 'Umm.'

'I'd better get you a few things while I'm in town. Undies and stuff. What size are you?'

Caitlin told her. 'But don't spend much on me, maybe the Op Shop?'

Elizabeth raised her eyebrows. 'Right. I'll see, and as for talking to your dad, well ...' She glanced at her watch. 'It's about midnight in England, so he'll be asleep. We'll wait until this evening.'

Caitlin nodded. 'Okay. I'll look after Molly while you're away.'

'Molly would love that,' Elizabeth smiled.

'Oh, Elizabeth?'

'Yes?'

'Dad put $100 in my birthday card. I only spent a few dollars on my train fare and something to eat, so I'll give you the rest. It's not fair you having to buy stuff for me.'

Elizabeth was torn, should she take Caitlin's money or say, no, it was okay. Then she thought Caitlin was acting responsibly so she smiled and said, 'Thank you, Caitlin. I'll try to spend it wisely.'

***

On her return, as Elizabeth opened the front door there was silence, then Molly came rushing to the door. 'It's only me, Molly,' she called out. When she went into the kitchen it was empty. 'Where are you, Caitlin?'

Her study door cautiously opened and Caitlin peered out. 'Are you on your own?' she hissed.

'Yes. Look, come and see what I've bought you.'

Elizabeth had enjoyed shopping for Caitlin, and Caitlin seemed grateful for what Elizabeth had bought, saying everything was great.

'Was everything okay while I was away?' asked Elizabeth.

'Yes, no-one came to the door, and I've been rapt with your ancestry stuff, Elizabeth! It's so interesting. Do you think you could find out about my ancestors?'

'I think your aunt Tamara has been doing exactly that,' Elizabeth replied. 'It's how your dad found her. He asked me to search for him.'

'Oh.' Caitlin put her head on one side. 'That's so nice. 'Praps I can talk to her tonight on Skype.'

'We'll see,' said Elizabeth. 'Now, how about some lunch?'

***

At the last minute at the shops, Elizabeth had remembered it was Caitlin's birthday. She'd gone into a cake shop and bought a birthday cake, and then found candles and a card.

After their dinner that evening, as Caitlin started to clear the table, Elizabeth said, 'Could you just check if I left Molly's lead outside?'

Caitlin appeared puzzled but went out through the kitchen door and started to look around. Elizabeth had purposely hidden the leash. A few minutes later Caitlin returned. 'No, Elizabeth, I couldn't see it anywhere.' Then she saw the birthday cake with the candles and an envelope on the table. She stared at Elizabeth.

'Happy Birthday, Caitlin!'

Caitlin ran round the table and hugged Elizabeth, then she took out her phone and took a photo of the cake. 'Thank you so much, Elizabeth.' Her voice thickened and she started to cry.

'Come on, blow out the candles and we can have a slice of cake,' Elizabeth said.

Later in the evening, when they were on Skype, Caitlin held out her phone, 'Look, Dad! Elizabeth got me a lovely cake! And a card.'

Will smiled, 'That's so nice of Elizabeth.'

After a long talk with her father and Tamara, Caitlin yawned. 'Good night, Dad, and thank you for the birthday card and money.' She turned to Elizabeth, 'Do you want to talk more to Dad? Because I think I'll go to bed now, Elizabeth, if that's all right. I think I'll be fine tonight by myself.'

Elizabeth smiled. 'I put a hot water bottle in your bed. These winter nights are chilly.' She turned back to her computer. 'Bye for now Will.'

***

The next day, Elizabeth returned from walking Molly and was making coffee when Caitlin crept out of her bedroom and breathed, 'The cops are across the road, Elizabeth!'

Startled, Elizabeth went into Caitlin's room, stood back behind the net curtains and peered out. There was a police car parked across the road and a policeman and woman standing at the front door of Will's house.

The door opened and a man came out, who Elizabeth recognized as the tenant. She hadn't spoken to him or his wife, just seen him taking out the bins.

She saw the man shake his head then disappear inside. He came out a few minutes later and handed the policeman a card.

Just as the police were leaving, Elizabeth saw Iris come out of her front door and seemed to be putting something in her bin. Elizabeth smiled to herself as she saw Iris give an appearance of surprise when she saw the police and after the police had driven off, Iris waved at the tenant. He went to the fence and she could see them talking.

'Who's the old woman across the road?' asked Caitlin.

'That's Iris. She's our local news reporter.'

'Really? She looks a bit old for the job.'

Elizabeth laughed. 'I'm joking! She and my next-door neighbour, Merv, like to know everything that's going on in the street. She'll probably be over later to tell me why the police were here.'

'Oh! I'll make certain I'm hidden then.'

Elizabeth smiled. 'Good idea.'

Sure enough, about eleven o'clock the doorbell rang. Caitlin jumped up from Elizabeth's laptop where she'd been reading more of the Turner ancestry. 'I'll go into your study and stay very quiet.'

Elizabeth checked there was no evidence of a teenager's presence in her kitchen, then went to the front door.

'Oh, hello, Iris, how are you? Will you come in for a few minutes? I'm rather busy at the moment so I won't offer you coffee ...'

'That's all right, dear. I just wanted to tell you the news.'

'Oh?' Elizabeth pretended innocence.

'Yes,' Iris's voice dropped. 'You'll never believe it, but the police came to Will's house looking for him!'

'Really? Why?' Elizabeth exclaimed.

'We don't know. But of course, the tenants, John and Georgina their names are, told them Will had gone to England and they were renting and didn't know where Will was but John got the letting agent's business card and gave it to them. I suppose the police will contact Will in England.' She peered at Elizabeth as if suspecting her of knowing something hidden in Will's past. 'I thought perhaps you might know his address, Elizabeth. Or why the police were looking for him ...'

'No, I don't,' said Elizabeth. She wasn't going to tell Iris she knew Will's phone number.

Iris nodded. 'Perhaps Will had to leave the country in a hurry!' Her voice trembled. 'I wonder why he left in a hurry. Do you know, dear?'

Elizabeth shook her head.

'Well, I'd better get going and tell Merv and Mabel, they'll be surprised too.' Iris pulled her cardigan around herself and turned to leave.

'Indeed. Well, thank you for letting me know, Iris.' Elizabeth walked to the door with Iris and watched her hurry out the gate and into Merv's house.

'You can come out now, Caitlin,' she called. 'It's safe.'

Caitlin peered around the study door. 'I heard it all,' she said. 'See, I knew it would happen.'

Elizabeth sat down and grimaced. 'But Caitlin, you can't stay hidden here forever! What will we do?'

Caitlin grinned. 'Dunno, Elizabeth, but it's exciting, isn't it?'

Elizabeth studied her. Caitlin was very beautiful. Her skin was a peachy tan and unlike Will's short grizzled curls, Caitlin's glossy black hair fell to her shoulders in waves. She had Will's brown eyes and full mouth and his grin.

'We'll have to think carefully about this, Caitlin. I could be charged with kidnapping.'

Caitlin's eyes widened. 'Really? Hmm.'

'Well, at least an accessory, or something like that.'

'We'll ask Dad tonight. He'll know what to do.'

'I certainly hope so.'

***

Later that night, when Elizabeth sought Will's advice, he had no answers.

'I've been thinking about it,' he said. 'I don't want you to get into trouble, Elizabeth.'

Caitlin interrupted, 'She won't get into trouble, Dad. I'll run away again if the police come here.'

Will shook his head. 'I think we need to get legal advice about this.' He blinked and then continued, 'I'm going to try and get a flight back as soon as possible.'

'No, you don't need to, Dad. You must stay with Grandad if he's very ill. I'll write to mum and tell her I'm living with a friend of yours and I'm well and happy and I'm not coming back because of Sleaze Bag Matt. I'll tell her if she doesn't agree I'll go to the police and put in an AVO against him and tell them he's been sexually molesting me. They won't make me go back then.'

Will was silent. Elizabeth could see his fists clenching. 'Has he been?' Will growled.

'He tried,' Caitlin said, 'but I managed to fight him off.'

Elizabeth heard Will mutter, 'I'll kill him ...'

Quickly she interrupted. 'Well writing a letter sounds like a good idea, and perhaps I could find a good child psychologist to see

Caitlin and assess her as being mature enough to make up her own mind about where she lives.'

Will's expression relaxed. 'That sounds like a good idea. But Elizabeth, having Caitlin living with you until I get back to Australia is a big imposition on you. Hopefully, it will only be a matter of a few weeks ...'

Caitlin shifted from foot to foot. 'Please, Elizabeth? I'll be really good,' she pleaded

Elizabeth smiled. She could see Will in Caitlin's expression. 'I'd love you to stay,' she said.

'Yippee!' Caitlin jumped up and enveloped Elizabeth in a big hug. 'Thank you, dear Elizabeth!' She turned back to the laptop screen. 'Dad, I've been reading all about the Turner family history. Elizabeth said Aunt Tamara has been doing the same for us.'

'She's here now, just waiting to see you and speak to you,' Will said, as Tamara's beaming face appeared beside him.

'Hello, Aunt Tamara! I really want to come to England and meet everyone,' Caitlin said. 'Perhaps we can live there, Dad.'

'We'll see,' replied her father. 'Your mum probably wouldn't give her permission for you to leave Australia. You'd have to wait until you're eighteen, I think.'

Elizabeth stood. 'Well, I'll leave you all to have a chat,' she said. 'I'll just go into my study and do some practice.'

'Elizabeth plays the cello, Aunt Tamara, she used to be in an orchestra.'

'No, no,' Elizabeth tried to protest but Caitlin was already bombarding Tamara with questions about their ancestry and did she have cousins. Elizabeth went to her study and gently closed the door, took out her cello and started to practice.

***

The next day she searched for a child psychologist in the area. They all had long waiting lists for appointments. She took a chance and made an appointment with the earliest date available. Then she called to Caitlin, 'Caitlin, I'm going to write to your mother and tell her you're with me, and safe. I'll outline your reasons.'

Caitlin nodded. 'Can I see it when you have it written?'

'Of course.'

It took Elizabeth over an hour to be satisfied with her letter.

Caitlin read it out:

Dear Ms Hastings,

This letter is to let you know your daughter, Caitlin, is living with me at the moment. She is safe and well. She has informed me of the circumstances of her decision to leave the family home, i.e., the unwelcome and persistent physical and sexual attentions of her step-father.

She hopes you will agree to her being with me. If not then she is prepared to go to the police with these accusations.

I am an elderly friend of her father and can provide character references if required. Her father is currently overseas but I have spoken with him and he is happy for me to become her interim guardian.

'You're not elderly, Elizabeth!'

'Sixty-one is elderly, my dear.' Elizabeth smiled. 'But it sounds better than just being a friend.'

Caitlin made a face 'I 'spose so.' She finished reading the letter and nodded. 'Yes, that seems good. I'll give you the address. When do you think I'll be able to come out of hiding?'

Elizabeth considered. 'Perhaps I should sneak you out tomorrow morning, and then in the afternoon bring you back and you jump out of the car as if you've never been here before. For sure Merv or Iris will spot you and want to know who you are.'

Caitlin's eyes lit up. 'Yes! And in the morning, you and Molly create a diversion while I get down low and creep out to the garage and go in the back door and get in the car. I'll curl up on the floor in the back!'

'Hmm. Well, that's Molly's place ...'

'Even better! I'll curl up with Molly! And Elizabeth?'

'Yes?'

'What will you tell the neighbours about me?'

'I'll tell them you're Will's daughter and staying with me, while he's in England visiting his sick father. Oh, and by the way, Caitlin, no one around here knows the house belonged to your dad's grandmother. He just couldn't face going into a long explanation.'

'Okay, I won't mention it if they talk to me.'

'Good, and next we have to get you into a school.'

'School! Oh, no!'

'Oh, yes!'

***

It took Elizabeth some time to organise a school for Caitlin. There were so many formalities to go through. At least Caitlin's mother hadn't objected to her staying with Elizabeth.

'They only wanted me there to babysit Liam,' Caitlin said when Elizabeth showed her the letter from her mother, who had reluctantly agreed to Caitlin staying with Elizabeth.

'Oh, your little brother! You must miss him.'

'He used to be cute, but now he's turned into a spoilt brat. They just give in to him all the time,' Caitlin said dismissively.

Most evenings they Skyped Will. He was trying hard to get a flight back to Australia but without much success.

'I'm exhausted with trying all the airlines,' he admitted to Elizabeth one evening. 'It's lucky I can work with Delroy to earn some money. I spend most evenings with Dad at the hospital. Tamara goes in the mornings and Delroy in the afternoons, so between us, he has someone with him all the time.' He sighed. 'It's been so good hearing about his life, and he keeps telling me about how he met my mother. He said she was the love of his life. It's lucky Tamara and Delroy aren't there to hear him tell me that.'

'Indeed,' Elizabeth murmured.

Will went silent, then suddenly looked up at the screen. 'Elizabeth, I contacted Social Welfare to get the child support I've been paying to Caitlin's mother, transferred to you. You must go to Centrelink and see them. Take Fiona's letter, agreeing to her staying with you.' He sighed. 'Are you sure it's not too much for you, Beth?'

She smiled. 'Actually, I love having her.'

Caitlin had come into the room and overheard the last few comments from her father.

'I love being here with Elizabeth and Molly, Dad.'

He smiled. 'That's good.'

'Well, I think, when you get back to Australia, you and Elizabeth should get married.'

'Caitlin!' Elizabeth exclaimed.

Will hesitated. 'Well, it's a good idea, but I don't think she'd have me.'

It took Elizabeth a few seconds to respond, 'Once was enough for me, Caitlin!'

'Fair enough!' Caitlin shrugged and changed the subject. 'Dad, what do you know about Calculus?'

Elizabeth got up and left them to it, but her heart was hammering.

***

Their days fell into a routine. Elizabeth would call Caitlin at seven o'clock and then prepare breakfast for them both. When Caitlin was ready for school, if it wasn't raining, they would walk to the bus stop with Molly. Caitlin would get the bus to Kiama and go to school and Elizabeth would walk home with Molly. On the odd rainy days, Elizabeth drove Caitlin to the bus stop. Molly wasn't keen on walking in the rain, just a quick run out in the garden was enough for her.

In the afternoons the reverse would happen. Elizabeth and Molly would meet Caitlin at the bus stop and they'd all walk back together.

'You don't have to come and meet me, you know, Elizabeth,' Caitlin said soon after they'd got into this routine.

Elizabeth halted. 'Oh! Perhaps you'd rather walk back on your own?' She asked.

'No, no, it's just that I don't want to be a nuisance to you.'

Elizabeth thought perhaps Caitlin felt a bit odd having an elderly woman meeting her, maybe the other teenagers on the bus had teased her.

'Hmm, well, maybe I can give it a miss for a few days,' Elizabeth said. She'd enjoyed the walk to the bus stop with Caitlin who was such a lively, entertaining girl.

Caitlin had become absorbed with Elizabeth's family history. 'It's like a detective story,' she said when she was thinking about what could have happened to Edmund. She stretched her fingers. 'I might be a detective when I leave school ...'

Elizabeth hadn't made much progress on her family history since Will had left. Somehow the motivation had gone. Maybe Caitlin would get her interested again.

Bronwyn and the girls had planned to come down for the weekend during the September school holidays – Bronwyn had found a nice Airbnb place, so she told Elizabeth – but then Sydney was put into lockdown due to the Covid Delta variant and those plans were cancelled.

Elizabeth hadn't told Bronwyn about Caitlin; she'd been putting it off and putting it off and then thought she'd introduce Caitlin when Bronwyn arrived. Now, she was relieved she could delay yet again. By the time Bronwyn eventually came down, hopefully, Will would be back, the tenants in his place moved out and Will and Caitlin could live in Will's house.

But Will still hadn't managed to get a flight back to Australia, and he was fretting about Caitlin being a burden on Elizabeth.

On their nightly Skype chats, Elizabeth tried to reassure him everything was fine, and it was, she thought. Initially, she'd felt slightly daunted by the prospect of having a teenage girl living with her, after living by herself for so long. Now she reflected on it, it was quite nice to have Caitlin's company, she was a sweet girl, quiet and unassuming but lively and funny at the same time, very different from how Bronwyn had been as a teenager. Molly loved her and Caitlin loved Molly and was always happy to take her for walks. Elizabeth looked out her bedroom window one evening as Caitlin and Molly walked past Merv's. Merv darted out and engaged her in conversation. Elizabeth held her breath, *what could they be talking about?* She hoped Merv wasn't giving her the third degree and that Caitlin wouldn't let slip about Will's house being his grandmother's.

'Molly's tired,' Caitlin announced, as she put fresh water in the dog's bowl on her return.

'I saw you talking to Merv ...' Elizabeth raised her eyebrows and paused.

'Oh,' said Caitlin, 'he started to ask me about Dad, so I said Dad was really pleased to have Merv living opposite to keep an eye on things for him, and Merv was all delighted so then I asked him if he'd been a detective before he retired and he started to tell me all about what he used to do. I asked him what was wrong with his legs, they're all bandy, and he said he was waiting to get new knees. I had a problem to get away, so I said, I'd love to hear more but I have to walk Molly and maybe he'd tell me next time I saw him.'

Elizabeth blinked. Why was she worrying about Caitlin saying too much?

'And then,' Caitlin continued, 'on my way back, Iris bobbed out and waylaid me. So, I told her how pleased Dad was to have her next door, that she'd been so helpful to him. Iris kind of perked up and smiled, then I asked her did she have any grandchildren and she said yes, but they were in America. Then she went on about them so I said I had to take Molly back for her dinner and help you. I memorised their names, so I can ask her the next time I see her.'

'How did you become so skilled at deflecting awkward questions, Caitlin?' Elizabeth just had to ask her.

Caitlin's eyes widened. 'Am I?' She thought for a while, then said, 'Oh, well, when I lived with Mum and Sleaze, I was always being asked questions about whether I was a throwback and who was my father and stuff like that, because I don't look like mum, and it's obvious I've got a black inheritance. Mum's blond with blue eyes. So I used to make up stuff, like I'd say my dad was in the

Diplomatic Service and I wasn't allowed to talk about him, secrecy laws and all that, and then I'd ask what did their parents do and say something nice about their hair. Stuff like that.'

'Hmm.' Was all Elizabeth could think to say. She felt like asking if Caitlin had read the book, 'How to Win Friends and Influence People' but she thought it might sound a bit nasty.

'Shall I give Molly her dinner?' Caitlin asked.

Elizabeth nodded.

A month later and Sydney, Wollongong and all the way down to Shellharbour were in lockdown due to the Covid Delta variant.

'What will they call it once it mutates and reaches Omega?' Caitlin asked.

Elizabeth sighed. 'I hope it all disappears before then and just be like the 'flu. Or die out like the Spanish Flu. At least Wambecarra isn't locked down and we can still go out.' She'd heard from Will and he was still trying to get a flight back to Australia; but he was sounding more and more despairing.

Caitlin nodded. 'I wish Dad could get a flight, but the good news is Mum and the Sleaze are in lockdown with Liam. Mum must be working from home with Liam doing homeschooling. I think Sleaze would be at home too. Wasn't it lucky I got here before the lockdown? Can you imagine being locked in with Sleaze?' She shuddered.

Elizabeth didn't want to imagine it.

Caitlin resumed reading what Elizabeth had written about her and Will's trip to Inverell, then she turned from Elizabeth's laptop, 'So, you didn't get to Brodies Plains?' She asked.

'No,' Elizabeth sighed. She tried to recall why not, and then remembered it was when Will had told her about Caitlin and had been upset, so neither of them had felt in the mood for driving.

'Do you think we could go there, Elizabeth? Maybe in my next school holidays?'

'We'll see. The whole of New South Wales could be in lockdown by then,' Elizabeth said. 'We can't make any plans. I'd certainly like to see Newstead Station.'

But Elizabeth did give it some thought. She'd meant to contact that nice woman in the Inverell Historical Society, and then so much had happened she'd forgotten. She made a note to remind herself.

***

Caitlin tapped her biro against her front teeth. 'So, Elizabeth, from what I've read, you're clear about your ancestors except for this Edmund.'

Elizabeth hid a smile. Caitlin looked so like Will when she was concentrating. 'Yes. I'll draw it out.' She took the biro from Caitlin and wrote:

Edmund Turner 1836 – 1874 (according to NSW births, deaths and marriages)

His son, Edmund Joseph 1862 – 1919

His son, William 1885 – 1970 (my grandfather)

His son Henry 1927 – 1998 (my father)

'So, I don't understand what your problem is.' Caitlin rubbed her nose. 'That all seems okay.'

'Well, I suppose there isn't really a problem, except there's no record of Edmund's marriage, but I did find a baptismal entry for an Edmund Joseph, born in 1862 in Sofala, NSW naming Edmund Turner as his father and an Annie Marchant as his mother. And there was also a death notice for Annie Marchant, two days before Edmund was baptized. So, this Annie must have died in childbirth.'

Elizabeth's brow furrowed. 'And the other mystery is when Edmund died. Look at this ...'

Elizabeth held out the newspaper cutting showing the death notices. 'See,' she continued, 'According to the New South Wales birth, deaths and marriages website, Edmund Turner, died in 1874 in Inverell and it states his parents were Ann and Edward Turner, however, he would have been thirty-eight, not seventy. And, the newspaper obituary has the notice in twice, first it spells his name as Edmond with an 'o' and the second time with a 'u'.'

'Hmm.' Caitlin frowned. 'Perhaps the newspaper made a mistake with Edmund's age, and the "70" was a misprint.'

'That's the only thing I can think of.' Elizabeth sighed. 'It's a pity because I've found out lots about Edmund's brothers and sisters. James moved to Fiji and was the proprietor of the Criterion Hotel in Levuka and had seven children.'

'Fiji!' Caitlin exclaimed.

'Yes, it's hard to imagine. John ended up in Moliagul in Victoria. It was a gold mining town, so he probably went prospecting for gold. He had two children. Mary-Ann stayed in Sydney, she married a man from Kent in England, Nathaniel Wallis. They had two children; apparently Mary-Ann was thirty-five when she had her first child, a little girl, and forty-two when she had a son in 1866. Another sister, Elizabeth Esther had only one son and sister Ellen had seven children.'

'Wow, imagine having seven children! Well, what's your next step, Elizabeth?'

'I'm working backwards from Edward Turner now; to find out my English ancestors. I've discovered a lot about his forebears from the Pentrich & South Wingfield Historical Group.'

'That's good.' Caitlin looked sombre. 'Aunt Tamara is sending me details about Dad's ancestry, apparently their father, that's my grandfather, came out from Jamaica after World War Two, and he's descended from African slaves who were taken to Jamaica by the Spanish and British. She's going to send me all the details. It sounds very complicated. There were runaway slaves who went to live in the forests and they were called Maroons.' Her brow wrinkled. 'At least, I think that's what they were called.' She sighed. 'I'd better get back to my homework.' Instead, she sat lost in thought.

'Good idea and I'd better get out in the garden and do some weeding.'

'Just a minute, Elizabeth. Edmund Joseph was born in Sofala, where's that? Why would Edmund have gone there?'

'I hadn't thought of that ...' Elizabeth said. 'Maybe the garden can wait. I'll get my laptop.'

Caitlin grinned.

Half an hour later, Caitlin stood up and stretched. 'Finished my homework, Elizabeth, come on, tell me what you've found.'

'Apparently, Sofala was a gold mining town. See, it says here Sofala began as a gold rush town in the 1850s when gold was discovered on the Turon River.'

'Wow!' Caitlin moved to look over Elizabeth's shoulder. 'It says by 1855 most of the population had moved on to newer goldfields,' She straightened. 'But, according to your records, Edmund Joseph was born in 1862. That's seven years after most gold diggers had left Sofala. So why did Edmund stay? Or did he stay? If his baby's mother had died?'

SOFALA, NSW - 1862

The week after receiving Mary-Ann's letter, Edmund was on the mail coach with his tiny son. Mrs Flynn had given him a beer bottle filled with her milk and instructions as to how to care for the baby on the journey. 'See, here's a piece of clean towel. Put one end in the bottle and tip it up, the milk will soak into it and the baby can suck on it. Might stop him crying for a bit.'

As it happened there was a woman passenger on the coach with a young baby and seeing Edmund's predicament she offered to feed baby Edmund. She gave Mrs Flynn's beer bottle to her child, who was six months old and well able to drink from a bottle.

Edmund was grateful but it meant he had to endure the woman's constant chatter about her husband, her family, and her life on the goldfields. But at least, after his initial explanation about the death of his wife, she didn't question him about Annie and where he was going with the baby.

He was glad to reach Sydney and the Post Office in George Street. Nat and Mary-Ann were there to meet him. Mary-Ann hugged him. 'We're so sorry about Annie.'

Edmund nodded. 'This is Edmund Joseph.' He held out the baby and looked around. 'Where's your little Rachel?'

Nat smiled. 'She's at home with the maid we have. Didn't want to bring her out into the crowd here.'

Mary-Ann took the bundle into her arms. 'Oh, he's so beautiful,' she breathed, stroking the baby's downy head. 'I've found a reliable healthy wet-nurse for him.'

Nat coughed and held out a hand to Edmund. 'Sorry for your trouble,' he said. 'Let's go home, I'm sure you must be stiff and tired after the journey.'

'Yes.' They walked in silence behind Mary-Ann who was rocking the baby and making crooning noises.

After a while, Nat cleared his throat and spoke, 'So what are your plans now, Edmund? Will you go back to Sofala?'

Edmund shook his head. 'No, Nat. I couldn't stay there without Annie. I hated leaving her there, but I couldn't bear it. I don't know what I'll do. Perhaps I could stay with you for a few days to think about things?'

'Of course! Delighted to have you.'

The wet nurse lived two doors away; Mary-Ann came back that evening with baby Edmund wrapped up in her arms. 'He's sleeping peacefully, now he's been fed,' she announced. She held the sleeping infant out to Edmund. 'Have a cuddle.'

'He's so perfect,' Edmund said, his voice thick with emotion.

'We'll take good care of him, won't we Nat?' Mary-Ann turned to her husband, who nodded.

Edmund handed his son back to Mary-Ann.

'I'll put him into bed now, Ed. Rachel's two and getting big. I've put her in a truckle bed so that Edmund Joseph can have her cradle,' Mary-Ann said.

Little Rachel Wallis tottered over to Edmund. He picked her up and watched by her adoring father, he tried to play with her. 'I hear you're a big girl now,' he told her, 'And sleeping in a big girl's bed.'

She nodded at him, then her eyes sought her father. She didn't know who this big bearded stranger was. Her lower lip pushed out. Afraid she might cry. Edmund handed her to Nathaniel.

Nat cuddled his daughter, who put a thumb in her mouth and regarded her uncle. Nat raised his head. 'James is in New Zealand. Last we heard he was thinking of going to Fiji.'

'Really? What about John?'

'He's in Victoria, Moliagul. Gold mines.'

Edmund frowned. 'Yes, I heard they'd found gold there. Didn't realise John was there. Should have gone there instead of Sofala.' His face darkened. 'Annie might still be alive if we'd gone there.'

Nat appeared anxious to change the subject. 'So how is the blacksmithing going?'

Edmund shrugged and was silent. Both men were relieved when Mary-Ann came back into the room.

'I'll make a pot of tea,' she said. 'Baby's settled down nicely. Come on Rachel, time for you to go to bed.'

***

Edmund moped around. Mary-Ann and Nat tried to keep out of his way, and the whole household seemed to be sunk in gloom. Then Mary-Ann confronted him.

'Edmund, Annie wouldn't like to see you like this. She was a lovely, lively girl. She'd want you to perk up and start to live your life again.'

Edmund scowled. How would Mary-Ann know what Annie would have wanted, he thought. Then he blinked and peered around as if coming out of a trance. He heard baby Edmund Joseph cry and Mary-Ann hurried to pick him up and get him ready for the wet nurse who would be coming to feed him in another few minutes.

Mary-Ann was right. He was infecting the whole house with his grief. He had to do something. The dray with his tools would be arriving in the next few days. He'd have to decide what to do with the remainder of his life. He didn't feel like joining James in New Zealand, or John back in Victoria. Although John wasn't at Mount Alexander, which would have reminded him of Annie.

He wandered down to the quays, vaguely looking at the sailing ships. He wondered what had become of Captain Bruce and *Bluebird*. It might be a good plan to get on a ship going somewhere. Better than moping around Sydney. A sea voyage might do him good. He asked around and eventually found a schooner going up the coast to a place called Shoal Bay, and thence to a township called Grafton. Rumours of gold having been found nearby drew prospectors, and on the return journey the ships brought valuable cedar timber back to Sydney.

Edmund applied for a berth leaving two days later. The dray could take his tools straight to the quay. He returned to Mary-Ann's feeling more optimistic. He found her in the kitchen jiggling baby Edmund Joseph on her knee and Rachel standing by her mother holding out a wooden toy to her new cousin.

'Look,' Mary-Ann said, 'He's smiling!'

Edmund's heart flipped. He was sure he could see Annie's smile in her baby. He caught the baby's hand. 'I'm going to a place called Grafton,' he told him, 'But I'll be coming back soon.'

'Really?' exclaimed Mary-Ann. 'Where's that?'

'It's up the coast, ships are bringing cedar timber from there, and there's talk of gold. So, I thought I'd go and see what it's like. Always work for a blacksmith if I don't find any gold.' He gave a wry smile.

Mary-Ann blinked. 'Well, that's good news.'

'At least I'll be out from under your feet.'

'No, no, Ed. You know you're always welcome here, and baby Edmund Joseph will always know you're his father. And I'll be sure to tell him all about his beautiful mother as he gets older.'

The ever-present tears came to Edmund's eyes. He nodded and took out a handkerchief. 'Thank you, dear Mary-Ann.' He blew his nose, and swallowed. He turned away. 'The dray should be here tomorrow with my tools and things; I can meet it and send it straight to the quays.'

'Nat can give you a hand,' Mary-Ann said.

'Nat's a good man. I'll go and tell him now.' He went out the door leading to Nat's workshop.

Mary-Ann watched him leave.

Wambecarra - August 2021

'Guess where I am?' Will's gleeful face on the Skype screen seemed surrounded by mist.

'Dunno. Looks a bit damp, where ever you are!' Elizabeth couldn't help smiling.

'Pentrich!' Will said and moved to one side, revealing a country road with a sign displaying REVOLUTION 1817 on it and in bigger letters PENTRICH Please drive carefully.

'Wow!' Elizabeth exclaimed.

'And this is Sylvia Mason, who's researched so much about the Pentrich revolution.' Will moved and Elizabeth could see a woman smiling through the rain.

'Hello Elizabeth!' Sylvia said. 'I've been doing a lot of research into Edward Turner's ancestors. Will, here said you're one of his descendants.'

'Yes, I believe I am.'

'Well, I've shown Will all around the place, South Wingfield and different sites, and I've printed off some information for you about Edward Turner's forebears. Will said he'd take it back to Australia when he can get a flight.'

'That's awesome! Thank you so much, Sylvia. I've seen your name in several of the books about the Pentrich Revolution, it's so nice to see you in person.'

Will's face appeared. 'Sylvia is going to take us to Derby now, to see the old courthouse and gaol. I'll take lots of photos to send you. I'll sign off now and talk again tomorrow. Oh, by the way, Tamara's here, she says hello, she drove me up here.'

Elizabeth managed to utter: 'Say hello from me.' before the screen went blank.

'Phew!' She exclaimed as Caitlin bounced into the room.

'Was that dad? Have I missed him?'

'Yes, I can't believe it, he and Tamara are in Pentrich.' Her voice rose. 'They've got lots of info about Edward Turner for me when your dad comes back.'

***

Since Will had left for England, as soon as she woke up in the morning - usually when Molly decided it was time to get up – Elizabeth would turn on her phone and check for messages.

She rubbed her eyes and looked at her phone. 'A message from Will,' she told Molly, who wagged her tail.

'Oh my!' exclaimed Elizabeth, making Molly jump. 'Will's got a flight!' She glanced at her watch, seven. Not too early to wake Caitlin.

She leaped out of bed and went to Caitlin's room. 'Caitlin! Your dad's got a flight!'

A sleepy murmur came from the bedroom, followed by silence, then the door flew open and a tousle-haired Caitlin emerged, a huge beam on her face. 'Yippee!' she shouted, flinging her arms around Elizabeth. 'When does he get here?'

'Oh, he's going to send more details, but he didn't text me until he actually got on the plane, in case it didn't happen. Then he had to turn off his phone. I guess we'll have to wait until he can tell us more. I don't even know which airline he's flying with.'

Caitlin started dancing around the hall, exciting Molly, who started to jump and bark.

Elizabeth smiled and thought how nice it was to have someone with whom to share good news.

***

Will had to quarantine in a hotel for two weeks when he arrived in Sydney.

Elizabeth worried as to what would happen when he arrived in Wambecarra. The tenants were still in Will's house – their lease had another few months to run – and Elizabeth had suggested Will stay with her and Caitlin until he could move back across the road, but Will was concerned it would add to her inconvenience.

'I think I should try and get an Airbnb somewhere,' Will said when he rang her one day from his quarantine hotel room.

'Nonsense. I can move one of the twin beds in Caitlin's room into my study and you can sleep there.' Elizabeth was adamant.

'But what about your cello and doing your music practice?'

'I can bring my cello into my bedroom and practice there,' she replied. 'I know the study is small, but I think you can manage. Otherwise, Caitlin could sleep there and you can have her room. It's bigger.'

'Hmm. Well, maybe we can try it that way for a few days ...'

'I'll get Caitlin to help me after school. I'll meet you at Kiama station. Text me when you know what time you'll be there,'

'Thanks, Elizabeth. I don't know how I'd manage without you.'

'So how are you coping with the quarantine?'

Will laughed. 'Lucky I've got my computer and can download books. I'm studying some of the research Tamara has done on our ancestry, and I've got a load of stuff from lovely Sylvia about Pentrich and Edward Turner to give you.'

'I'm looking forward to seeing it all,' she paused, 'and Caitlin is so excited. She can't wait to see you. She's delightful, Will.'

He sighed. 'I can't wait to see her again, either, Beth. It's been too long.'

Elizabeth ended the call and put down her phone, only to have it start ringing again. Bronwyn!

With a sigh, she took the call. 'Hello Bronwyn, how are you?'

'Oh, still in lockdown, it's ridiculous, I'm so over it! Trying to work and homeschool the girls is a nightmare. They never stop bickering and won't concentrate on their lessons. How am I expected to work in this environment?'

'Oh, dear, it sounds horrendous.'

'And Darren is no help. It's all right for him, banks are considered essential services, so he still goes off to work, leaving me to do everything ... '

Elizabeth found that hard to believe. 'Oh dear,' she repeated. Just then she heard Caitlin come in from school.

'Hello, Elizabeth! I'm home!' Caitlin called out.

'Who's that? I heard a voice.'

Elizabeth's heart sank, she didn't know what to say. 'Just a friend calling round.'

Caitlin came into the kitchen. Seeing Elizabeth on the phone, she smiled and whispered, 'Sorry,' and crept out of the room.

'Lucky you, being in Regional New South Wales, and you can have friends call round, we can only go out for exercise and essential shopping. The girls want to get a dog so they have an excuse to go out. As if we could, with my allergies!'

'Yes, I'm lucky,' Elizabeth managed to say.

Bronwyn droned on until she eventually had to break off to shout at the girls. *'Can't stay talking all day, the girls must finish their school work. Right, bye Elizabeth.'*

Elizabeth ended the call and sighed. She straightened her shoulders and filled the kettle.

'Just going to make a pot of tea, Caitlin,' she called.

Caitlin bounced into the kitchen. 'Great! How are you, Elizabeth? What have you been doing today?'

'Not a lot,' Elizabeth smiled. 'Just a bit of gardening, shopping, took Molly for a walk. How was school?'

'Okay.' Caitlin sat at the kitchen table and proceeded to tell Elizabeth about her day, accepting the tea and biscuits Elizabeth offered her.

SYDNEY, NSW - 1862

Edmund boarded the steamer *Agnes Irving*, heading for Grafton, on the thirteenth of December 1862. The weather looked promising. He remembered his first voyage on the *Bluebird*. So much had happened since then; he felt so much older than his twenty-six years. He paced around the small deck then finally stopped and leaned over the side, mindlessly regarding the ocean. He became aware of a man beside him. Edmund glanced at him, the man appeared to be about his own age,

'I've seen you walking the deck,' the young man said.

'Hmm?' Edmund raised his head.

'Patrick Anderson,' he said, holding out his hand.

Edmund stared at the outstretched hand for a few moments before taking it and shaking it. 'Edmund Turner,' he replied.

'Nice boat,' Patrick Anderson remarked.

'Yes.'

'Named after the eldest daughter of one of the directors of the company who owns it.'

'Hmm,' Edmund mumbled, because, really, he couldn't care less.

'Where are you headed?' asked Patrick Anderson.

'Grafton. The goldfields.'

'Been to Grafton before?'

'No.' Edmund didn't feel like talking to this man. He wanted to think his own thoughts, thoughts about Annie and young Edmund Joseph. He turned back to look at the ocean.

'I'm going further, after we land at Grafton, to a property near Inverell. Place called Brodie's Plains,' Patrick Anderson persisted.

'Oh?' Edmund tried to feign interest.

'Yes, my mother has a property there, Newstead Station. She's just built a church in memory of my father, who died a few years ago.'

'I'm sorry to hear that,' Edmund murmured.

'Two of my sisters, Mary and Margaret died of the scarlatina[1] the year after Father, and it was all too much for Mother, so she went back to England with us children.'

'Oh ...'

'Yes, but now she's back and trying to make a go of the place.' He studied Edmund. 'So, what's your line of work then, Turner?'

'Blacksmith.'

Patrick Anderson was silent for a few seconds. 'Well, there's a coincidence. Mother's looking for someone to make wrought iron railings and other fancy iron lacework.

Edmund's interest was piqued by the words. He turned to the other man. 'Oh?'

'I suppose you can do that kind of work?'

'Indeed, I can.'

'Oh! Well, if you change your mind about the goldfields, you could always come with me to Newstead.' Patrick smiled at Edmund.

'Indeed,' said Edmund slowly. 'Indeed, why not?' He stared at this Patrick. He was a nice enough fellow, and to be honest,

---

1. Scarlatina, the common name at the time for Scarlet Fever

Edmund couldn't care less where he settled, and this seemed an easier option than trying to start a new life in Grafton, finding work in new territory. He studied Patrick, and suddenly became more animated. 'Yes. I'd like that.'

'Good! Well, that's settled then!' Patrick Anderson grinned.

***

On reaching Grafton, Edmund, leaned over the gunwale and watched as the *Agnes Irving* docked.

'Big flood here last year.' Patrick Anderson came up behind him. 'Fishers wharf completely washed away. This is a new one, only just finished; it's large enough for ocean steamers.'

'Really?' Edmund studied the wharf as they disembarked.

Patrick soon had a dray down at the wharf. 'Get your tools and belongings,' he told Edmund. 'I've got to load all the materials I went to Sydney to buy for Mother.'

'I'll help.'

Two hours later and the dray was loaded. Patrick smiled at Edmund. 'Room for both of us on it.'

Edmund looked at the dray with its team of bullocks and the large man in charge who was already cracking his whip, cursing and swearing at the animals. Edwin nodded. 'Why not?' He said and suddenly smiled at Patrick. 'It's a long time since I rode with a bullocky!'

***

It took over three weeks for the bullocks to cover the two hundred odd miles to Newstead. Patrick and Edmund had to walk beside the dray for parts of the track, through mostly dense rain forest.

Every night they camped out, bringing back memories for Edmund. While Patrick Anderson and Tom, the bullocky, chatted away, Edmund stared into the flames of the campfire, and thought of his time at Mount Alexander and the nights around the campfire there with Jake, Joe, Harold and poor Jasper. He wondered if Harold got back to England and if Joe managed to settle down near the ocean. He remembered when Annie used to come to the blacksmiths with her husband's picks. *Was she somewhere watching him now?* He thought she would be pleased that he would be going to work for Patrick Anderson's mother, rather than having to find somewhere to live in Grafton and make a new start.

Patrick explained how the original bush track had been cut by wool hauliers and timber getters in the early 1840s. They passed parts of the road which was in the process of being improved by low paid labourers. The men ceased their work and waved at them as they went by.

Eventually they reached Inverell, where they stayed the night at an inn and to rest the bullocks.

'It's not much further,' announced Patrick. 'About another eight miles, but it's better to stop the night here and arrive at Brodie's Plains tomorrow around lunchtime.'

'Who was Brodie?' Edmund asked.

'Don't know, but Brodie's an old Scottish name, so perhaps it was named for one of the original settlers. Never thought about it before!' He slapped Edmund's shoulder. 'Lot of Scots came to this part of New South Wales.'

Edmund nodded. He was glad they were staying the night in Inverell. He welcomed the chance to appear fresh and groomed when he met his prospective employer, who, he reminded himself, didn't yet know of his existence or that he would soon be working for her.

The next day, as they neared the station, Patrick gestured to the open countryside studded with a few giant gum trees. 'All this is Newstead,' he said. 'Good pasture.'

Edmund surveyed the scene; he could see sheep grazing everywhere. An hour later they rounded a bend in the dirt track and he saw a long, low building with generous verandas all around, and flower beds beside the wide steps leading to the entrance.

Patrick watched his reaction. 'Roof is new stuff, corrugated iron,' he said.

'Yes,' Edmund agreed, 'it's become very popular. It looks a very nice property.'

Mrs Anderson must have heard the noise of the dray and the bullocks, because she came running out to meet them. The bullocky refined his language in the presence of a lady, simply calling 'Shtop, will ye!' to his animals, rather than the usual, 'Shtop ye bastards!'

Patrick jumped down from the top of the loaded dray and hugged his mother. 'Mother!' he said, 'This is Edmund Turner. He's a blacksmith and skilled at making iron lace and wrought iron. I told him he could get work here.'

Mrs Anderson extended a hand and nodded at Edmund. 'Pleased to meet you, Mr Turner.'

'And you,' murmured Edmund, bowing over her hand. She appeared very elegant, with her greying hair swept up into a bun.

'Well, won't you come in for refreshments after your journey?' Not waiting for a reply, Mrs Anderson turned and led the way.

'I've got all the things you needed, Mama,' Patrick said as he skipped up the steps to the veranda.

'That's good, son. Thank you. Now, Mr Turner, we don't have a blacksmith's house at the moment, and I would suppose you would like to build your own forge in the way you would prefer.'

'Why, yes,' Edmund replied. 'That would be ideal.'

'So, tomorrow Patrick can organise the men to start building for you. Are you married?'

Patrick quickly interrupted 'No, Mama, Edmund's wife sadly passed away a few months ago.'

'Oh!' Mrs Anderson turned around to Edmund. 'I'm so very sorry to hear that, Mr Turner, please accept my condolences. I know how painful the loss of a beloved spouse can be.'

Edmund bowed his head and mumbled something unintelligible.

'Well, I hope you will find peace and acceptance here at Newstead. I'll get a room prepared for you until you can be settled in your own place. Now, come and have some refreshment.'

***

Edmund soon settled in at Newstead. Within a few weeks, a simple timber cottage had been built for him - one room with a brick chimney and fireplace, furnished with a table and two chairs and a dresser. Off this room was a smaller one – really just a big cupboard – containing a box pallet with a feather mattress on it. A chair stood beside the bed and several timber hooks were set into the wall for hanging his clothes. There was an adjoining workshop for his forge.

Mrs Anderson had provided some cooking utensils and crockery. 'It's perfect,' he told her when she met him the day after he'd moved in.

It felt good to have his tools around him once again and to make a start on the detailed lacework Mrs Anderson wanted as a border around her husband's grave. A few days after his arrival, she'd led Edmund to a newly built small church on the property, surrounded by an area of ground that had been designated as a cemetery.

'This is the grave of my husband and two of my daughters,' she said. 'I want to make a nice railing around it.' She looked up at Edmund. 'Can you draw some designs for me?'

Surprised, Edmund said, 'Of course.' He was gratified to be consulted and asked to design a pattern. It took him several days, and after a few false starts he came up with just one design. He took it to show Mrs Anderson. 'Is it something like this you had in mind?' he asked.

She studied it for a few moments, then smiled at him. 'It's perfect,' she said. 'That's exactly what I want.'

Edmund was pleased. He was getting off to a good start.

As the years passed, Edmund realised he was coming to terms with Annie's death. He still missed her intensely, but he wasn't so totally overwhelmed with grief as he had been. He settled into a comfortable existence. He enjoyed his work and the Andersons were kind and generous employers. He'd written to Mary-Ann when he'd arrived at Newstead to inform her of his address, and he received regular letters from her about how young Edmund Joseph was doing. Mary-Ann told him that at forty-two years of age she'd been safely delivered of her second child, a baby boy they called Austin, in 1866. Edmund was pleased for her.

***

Edmund was making a name for himself in Brodies Plains and the surrounding district. He'd lately started branding the tools he made with his initials – a small E under a larger T. He made the T into the shape of a pickaxe, smiling to himself as he did so. He did a brisk trade with the picks he made. Some men thought there were valuable minerals around the area and his handmade picks were in great demand.

Wambecarra - August 2021

Elizabeth waited on the platform at Kiama station for the Sydney train. Caitlin had wanted to come with her, but Elizabeth insisted she go to school. 'You'll be home from school before I get back with your dad, and perhaps you could take Molly for her walk as the train will probably be delayed anyway,' she told Caitlin.

Caitlin pouted then thought about it and said 'Yes, of course, Elizabeth, you're right. Molly will be busting to go out.'

Now Elizabeth's heart flipped at the thought of seeing Will again. Would he have changed since being with his family in England? Maybe she should have let Caitlin come to meet him. She glanced at the overhead information panel. Train due in another eight minutes. Then it was seven minutes. She went to the ladies' room and checked her hair. When she came out there was still five minutes to go. Her phone beeped. It was a message from Caitlin.

Has he arrived yet? I'm walking Molly now. She was busting all right.

Elizabeth smiled to herself as she replied – *train running late.*

Two minutes to go.

Then she saw the train snaking around the bend in the tracks. She scanned each carriage as it passed and couldn't see Will. Her eyes prickled with tears as she walked down to the end of the platform, looking at each door hoping to see him emerge.

'Hello, Beth!'

She jumped and turned around. There he was, his nose and mouth covered with a face mask. Her lips parted, and then she was enveloped in a bear hug.

'I was right in the front carriage; I saw you and then you went racing down the other end of the train! Oh Beth, it's so good to see you.'

She nodded, 'And you, Will,' she managed to croak, blinking hard to stop those tears from escaping.

'Caitlin not here?' Will pulled off his mask and looked around.

'No, she had school and I asked her to go home and take Molly for a walk, in case the train was late. Which it was.'

Will's mouth turned down. 'Sorry, Beth. Have you been waiting long?'

'Not really.' It had been nearly an hour but she wasn't going to tell him that. 'Come on, I'll get the car from where I've parked it and drive round to the exit.'

Will grimaced. 'Thanks, this case weighs a ton, plus my other bags.'

The drive back felt awkward. Elizabeth didn't know what to talk about. Stupid of her as they'd spoken most days on Skype. Eventually, she said, 'You must be tired from the jetlag.'

'No ...'

Elizabeth could sense him smiling.

'No, I've had two weeks in Sydney to get used to the time difference.'

'Of course, how silly of me!'

'It's lovely to see you again, Beth.' He lightly touched her left wrist which was resting on the steering wheel. Her pulse raced.

'And you Will.'

They were silent the rest of the way. As Elizabeth drove through her open gates – she was sure she'd closed them when she left –

then realised Caitlin must have opened them, Caitlin and Molly came bursting out of the front door.

'Dad!' screamed Caitlin, throwing herself into his arms before he'd hardly had time to get out of the car.

Will hugged his daughter then lifted her up and away from him and stared at her. 'Caitlin, I can't believe it,' his voice was husky and his eyes filled with emotion.

'Dad! Look at Molly, she's welcoming you too!' She indicated Molly who was jumping up and down and barking.

Elizabeth turned, scanning the street, sure that Iris would be watching and Merv would be popping out any minute.

'Come on now, let's get inside. Will, can you get your luggage out and I'll put the car in the garage.'

Elizabeth noticed a certain shyness between Will and his daughter. They were each stealing sidelong glances at the other. Will wheeled his case and bags inside the house as Caitlin ran ahead.

'Dad, I've given you my room and I'm in Elizabeth's study.' She opened the door of the front bedroom opposite Elizabeth's. 'In here.'

'Thank you, Caitlin,' he studied the room. 'This is very nice and I like the patchwork quilt.'

'I think my great-grandmother made it,' Caitlin said proudly, smoothing the quilt with her hands.

Will nodded, then gazed at Caitlin again. 'Caitlin, my dear. You have no idea how wonderful it is to see you. I've missed you so much.'

Caitlin gave a sob. 'Same here Dad. I don't know how I was made to believe all the lies about you. I'm never going to speak to mum again.'

Will was silent for a moment, and then said, 'Well, things change, let's just wait and see.'

Caitlin made a humph noise and rolled her eyes, then smiled at Molly who was sitting with her liquid brown eyes fixed on Will. She pointed at the dog.

'See, everyone loves you, Dad! Molly, me, Elizabeth, Iris ...'

Will's eyes widened. 'Elizabeth?'

Caitlin grinned. 'Well, whenever she Skypes you, she always combs her hair and puts on lipstick and makes sure she looks nice, and she NEVER wears lipstick anywhere!'

Will smiled. 'Hmm ...'

'She's lovely. You do like her, don't you, Dad?' She chewed her bottom lip.

Will sighed. 'Yes. Very much.'

Just then they heard Elizabeth coming into the hall. 'Anyone hungry? Dinner's ready.'

Molly jumped up at the words "hungry" and "dinner".

Brodies Plains, NSW - 1874

Edmund had been over ten years in Brodies Plains, and had never in that time returned to Sydney. He often felt he should make the journey to see his son, but somehow, as he now admitted to himself, he hadn't had the courage. He'd made excuses: he had a lot of work to do for the Andersons and it was a long journey, but lately he'd been feeling exhausted and Patrick's mother, Mary, had noticed.

'Mr Turner,' she'd said. 'I really think you need a holiday. You must've been here a good ten years now. Why don't you have a break and go and see your family in Sydney?'

Edmund felt it to be an order. 'Thank you, Mrs Anderson. Perhaps I will.'

'Patrick can take you into Grafton to get the boat. Next time he's in there, I'll get him to check which vessels will be sailing to Sydney. Write and let your sister know.'

Edmund and Mary Anderson had grown close over the years, she always seemed to be coming up with new designs for iron lace around buildings on the homestead. He felt it could also be because they had both lost beloved partners. In the beginning, she'd tried to find a new wife for him, obviously thinking an unattached man needed a good woman. When he'd gently dropped a hint that no one could ever replace his Annie, she'd got the message.

Three weeks later and Edmund was on the *Diamantina*, a paddle-steamer headed for Sydney. He hung over the railings, watching the wash from the paddles as he remembered his previous journey when he'd left Sydney. Mrs Anderson was right, he did need a break, he'd never felt so weary. Bone tired in fact ...

When he arrived at the wharf in Sydney, he was surprised to see Mary-Ann and Nat waiting for him with two boys and a girl. Edmund gulped, he couldn't take his eyes off the older boy, his and Annie's son, who held out his hand to Edmund.

'Hello, Father,' the boy said.

Edmund felt overcome with emotion; he managed to mumble 'Hello, son,' before turning to the smiling Mary-Ann and Nat.

'Welcome, Edmund,' Nat said as Mary-Ann threw her arms around her brother and hugged him.

'This is Austin.' Mary-Ann pushed the younger boy towards Edmund. 'He's eight now.'

'Hello, Uncle,' the boy said.

'And of course, you remember Rachel.' Mary-Ann glowed with pride as she presented her children to Edmund.

Edmund nodded. 'Of course.' But he only had eyes for the tall, fair-haired boy that was Edmund Joseph. He studied his son who was now absorbed with watching the cargo being unloaded. He was like Annie in his features, Edmund thought. And he had her fair hair and blue eyes.

'He looks like Annie but he's very like you in other ways, Edmund,' said Mary-Ann as she watched him.

'See, Uncle Nat, Austin, over there.' Edmund Joseph pointed to something in the distance, then he turned to Edmund. 'See, Father, how they're taking the cedar off the ship?'

It felt so strange to Edmund to be called "father". 'I see,' he said.

'Well, we'd better get home,' Mary-Ann said, 'Come, children.'

'Yes, Aunt Man,' Edmund Joseph replied.

Edmund started, then remembered that Mary-Ann had written to him when Edmund Joseph was very young, telling him his son couldn't say Aunt Mary-Ann, it had become Aunt Man. He smiled now, thinking of it.

'You must be tired Edmund,' Mary-Ann's voice interrupted his thoughts.

Edmund nodded. As they walked along, Edmund Joseph and Nat went ahead with Austin and Edmund fell into step with his sister and Rachel.

'Thank you, Mary-Ann,' he said. 'You've done a wonderful job bringing up my and Annie's son, he's a fine boy.'

'Oh Edmund, it's been a pleasure, Nat and I have enjoyed every moment, he's been a gift.'

Watching Nat and Edmund Joseph, their easy comradeship, Edmund felt a pang of jealousy, then he chided himself. He would never have been able to bring up his son on his own. He'd given him the chance to be part of a proper family. And Annie would be pleased too. He wished she were here to see her child. Tears came to his eyes. He blinked them away and took Mary-Ann's arm, 'And how are you keeping, Mary-Ann? You look well.'

Over the next few days, Edmund could see his son covertly watching him. Edmund didn't quite know what to talk about to him. After the first stilted questions and answers about Brodie's Plains and his blacksmithing work, Edmund was at a loss. One day when he caught Edmund Joseph studying him, he smiled and said, 'You seem puzzled, son.'

'I was wondering if you could tell me more about my mother,' Edmund Joseph said hesitantly.

Edmund smiled. 'Well, she was very beautiful, with blue eyes and long curly fair hair and a wonderful smile, which enchanted everyone she met.'

Edmund Joseph nodded, not taking his eyes off his father.

'And she was clever and brave and looking forward to you being born.'

'And why didn't you keep me, Father? You could have stayed in Sydney and lived with Aunt Man and Uncle Nat.'

Edmund sighed. 'That's hard to answer, Edmund Joseph. I thought at the time you needed a motherly woman to care for you. You were only a few weeks old and I had to earn a living; I couldn't have looked after you properly. And there were already blacksmiths working here in Sydney – no room for yet another smithy.' He felt his son wasn't satisfied with his answer. 'And I thought it would be easier for Mary-Ann and Nat not to have me around.' He knew that sounded feeble.

'But you could have come to Sydney to see me before now! I'm nearly twelve!'

His son's angry words hit Edmund like a blow to the stomach. He couldn't meet his son's eyes and bowed his head. 'You're right, Edmund. I should have. I don't know why I didn't. Perhaps I was too afraid.' He shook his head and sighed. 'I'm sorry Edmund, I wish now that I had.'

'Too afraid? Afraid of what?' Edmund Joseph shot back; he stood, his fists clenched and his stance combative.

'I don't know,' muttered Edmund, putting his head in his hands. 'Of seeing your mother in you, perhaps; of having done the wrong thing, by leaving you, bringing back all those memories ...'

Edmund Joseph's shoulders suddenly drooped. He came over to his father and put a hand on his shoulder. 'I'm sorry, Father. I didn't mean to upset you.'

Edmund's head jerked up. 'I've always loved you, son. I thought by giving you up I was doing the right thing. It was the hardest thing I've ever had to do.'

'I thought perhaps you hated me because I was the cause of my mother's death.'

Edmund's face crumpled. 'No! No! Never. I hated myself for taking her somewhere where there was no doctor. I should have stayed in Bathurst where someone could have saved her.' He put his hand out to Edmund Joseph, who took it and wrapped his other arm around his father.

'I understand now. I'm glad I've met you at last, Father. Aunt Man has always said you were a good and lovely man. She used to read your letters to me. I was always pleased when you would write asking about me.'

'She's been wonderful, writing to tell me about your progress.' Edmund sighed. 'I wish with all my heart I had come back before now.'

'You're not like I imagined you.' Edmund Joseph said, his head on one side as he stared at his father.

Edmund didn't know what to say.

'I guess I thought you'd look like Mr Bennet, the old blacksmith down the road.'

Edmund managed a smile. 'Goodness, is he still going? I used to help him back when I was not much older than you!'

'Tell me about the goldfields, how you met my mother; things like that,' Edmund Joseph suddenly demanded.

'Well,' Edmund stroked his beard, 'Once upon a time there was a beautiful young girl ...' He paused, 'and an ugly old blacksmith ...'

Edmund Joseph giggled. 'Go on!'

WAMBECARRA - AUGUST 2021

Elizabeth turned on the television for the six o'clock news.

'Oh no!' She exclaimed. 'The whole of New South Wales is in lockdown because of Covid!'

Will and Caitlin turned towards the television screen.

'Can only go out for essential purposes, exercise, medical appointments, food shopping, maximum five kilometres from home,' Elizabeth said, repeating the message on the screen.

'What about school? I hated home-schooling in Sydney with mum and Liam.' Caitlin frowned and pursed her lips in a pout.

'Not sure. Probably have to stay home.'

Will grinned. 'So, you'll have to put up with me being here for a bit longer.'

Elizabeth stared at him.

When he saw her look, he said, 'I'll have to ring the letting agent, and see when is the earliest I can get back in my own house and give you some peace, Elizabeth.'

'Can't we all stay here?' Caitlin demanded. 'I like living with Elizabeth and I want you here too, Dad.'

Will raised his eyebrows at Elizabeth and grinned.

'We'll just have to wait and see,' Elizabeth said. She'd been getting anxious about the end of the Sydney lockdown when Bronwyn would be sure to want to come down and see her. What would she make of Caitlin and Will, living with her?

SYDNEY, NSW - 1874

Edmund stayed a month with Mary-Ann and Nat. He spent many hours with his son, whenever Edmund Joseph was not at school.

Did he regret leaving it so long to see Edmund Joseph? Yes, of course he did. He said as much to Mary-Ann.

'Of course, Ed!' she replied, 'But I know what you were going through. I've tried to tell Edmund Joseph that. Over the years, that is, but, he's a boy, he didn't really understand.' She grimaced, then smiled. 'But, Edmund, Nat and I have been privileged to have Edmund Joseph in our lives. Nat loves Edmund Joseph like he does Austin!'

Edmund sighed. 'Yes, I can see how close they are. Mary-Ann, somehow, I feel I don't have long left in this world, so I'm grateful, really grateful you've given Annie's son ...' He sniffed and wiped his eyes with the back of his hand. 'Given Annie's son a happy family life.' He swallowed.

Mary-Anne came and put an arm around him. 'Oh, Ed! Back in the day when the twins died, I knew how hard it was for you. For all of us! But especially for you and you only four or five! And then losing our mother and father ...' She hugged him. Then her brows drew together. 'What do you mean? Not long left in this life? Edmund? What do you mean?'

He shrugged. 'Oh, I've just been tired lately. Work has been hard. Mrs Anderson noticed it and suggested I take this trip.'

Mary-Ann studied him. 'Well, you do look pale. And thin. How old are you now, Edmund?'

'Thirty-seven, going on thirty-eight. But, Mary-Ann, don't worry. Ever since Annie died, I've never wanted to live.'

Mary-Ann sucked in a breath. 'Don't talk like that Edmund!'

He shrugged. 'It's true. I just want to be with her, and now I know Edmund Joseph is happy with you and Nat.' He shrugged again. 'I can go peacefully.' He smiled.

'Stop it, Ed! Stop it! Don't say such awful things!'

Edmund laughed. 'It's all right, Mary-Ann! I'll go when my maker is good and ready to have me!'

Mary-Ann wasn't consoled. 'Oh, Edmund, you were always my baby when you were little! Don't say things like that!'

'All right!'

Just then Edmund Joseph and Nat came in.

'What's for dinner, Aunt Man? I'm starving!'

Mary-Ann smiled at Edmund. 'Just like his father!'

Wambecarra - August 2021

'I can't believe what's happening here,' Will said at breakfast the next morning. 'England had Freedom Day last month. No masks, no lockdown, some people were saying that would be the end, it would be a disaster. No such thing! Now I come back here and there's this climate of fear!'

Elizabeth looked anxiously at Caitlin, then at Will. She made a face at him, hoping he would get her silent message to Shut UP!

'It must have been awesome to meet up with your family,' she said, to change the subject.

Will stared at her.

She glared at him with what she hoped was an innocent look.

'Yes, indeed,' Will responded, 'and to meet my father after all these years.'

Caitlin raised her eyes. 'Is he very black?' She asked.

Will considered. 'Well, he's pure Jamaican, so I guess the answer is yes.'

Caitlin nodded. 'Did you know Black is the new White, Dad?'

Will frowned. 'What on earth do you mean?'

'Well, it's the in thing to have black ancestors.' She nodded and smiled. 'For the first time in my life, I'm with it! Look at all the newspapers, well not the ones Elizabeth reads, but the others, they all have black models. I think I'll be a model when I leave school.'

Will's frown deepened. 'You're not black, Caitlin!'

'Well, anyone can see I have black ancestry!'

Once again, Elizabeth hastily changed the subject. 'Have you had the vaccine, Will?'

'No, and I won't.'

Oh dear, thought Elizabeth, not a good point to raise. 'Um, Will, what about the information Sylvia Mason from Pentrich gave you?' She asked.

'Oh, you'll be thrilled with it.' Will's face lit up. 'Such a nice woman, she's done so much research and would you believe she was in Kiama to celebrate the two hundred years since the Pentrich revolution?'

'Really?' Elizabeth was distracted. 'Did she give Kiama the plaque?'

'What plaque?' asked Caitlin.

As Will told Caitlin about it, Elizabeth remembered the disastrous day when she'd upset Will. She glanced at him, hoping he'd forgotten it, but he returned her look and she knew by his half-smile he was also remembering the outcome.

Elizabeth rose from the table. 'If everyone's finished, I'll clear the table.'

Caitlin jumped up. 'I'll help, Elizabeth.'

Will rose. 'Yes, you sit down, Elizabeth, you've done all the work.' He smiled, 'and tomorrow I'll make a start on the raised vegetable beds I promised to make for you. I did buy the sleepers for the sides ages ago. They're in my garage. Just forgot about it with all the excitement of going to England.'

Elizabeth gave a start. 'Oh! Well, thank you Will, but I must pay you for them.'

'Only if you accept payment for Caitlin and my board and lodging ...'

She raised one eyebrow, making him grin.

***

Elizabeth had to smile that evening at the kitchen table. Will was sitting with his open laptop doing whatever, she didn't know; Caitlin was frowning over her laptop and tapping her teeth with a pencil, apparently doing homework, and she, Elizabeth had her laptop open at the end of the table opposite Will trying to find out more about Newstead Station.

Caitlin waved her pen. 'Elizabeth, Dad. I was just thinking about Edmund Turner.'

'Hmm?' Will raised his eyes, not really listening.

'And?' Elizabeth said.

'Why did he go to Brodies Plains?'

Will blinked. 'Why did he go to Brodies Plains? Well, to look for work, I guess.'

'Good question, Caitlin,' Elizabeth smiled at her.

'I was wondering what kind of work he would have done. Newstead was a station, would it be a sheep station, do you think? Or a cattle station?'

'Where did you say Edmund's son was baptized, Elizabeth?' Will asked.

Elizabeth checked her records. 'Sofala in 1862.'

'Dad, you're behind the times. Elizabeth and I have determined Sofala was a gold mining town in the 1850s but most of the diggers left around 1855.'

'But hold on,' Will said. 'Why would he have stayed in Sofala after most of the gold diggers had left?'

'Apparently, there were shop keepers and other kinds of trades at the goldfields,' said Elizabeth, 'well, from what I learnt at school. Maybe he met this Annie Marchant there and decided to stay.'

'Can you see if there's a record of Annie Marchant being born in Sofala?' Will looked at Elizabeth, who nodded and started typing.

After a few minutes, she shook her head. 'No record of her being born there.'

'Where does that leave us?' Caitlin said.

'Well, we still don't know what took him to Brodies Plains.' Elizabeth said.

'What job would he have got at Brodies Plains?' Caitlin asked. 'I'd guess a carpenter, or maybe a stonemason like his father?'

'But his father died when Edmund was young, so probably not a stonemason,' Elizabeth said thoughtfully.

'A publican then? His father had a public house,' Caitlin persisted. 'What other jobs would you get on a station?'

'If it was a sheep station, then a job as a shearer, perhaps ...' Elizabeth smiled. 'I'll make a pot of tea and we can think of other trades. I'm sure Edmund would have had a trade; it seems all the family were literate and pretty well educated.'

Will nodded. 'Yes, and now I think we'll have to sleep on it. Caitlin, have you finished your homework?'

***

The next morning Will went across to his house and rang the doorbell. Elizabeth saw him talking to the tenants. Then Will went to his garage and she watched him reversing his ute, and loading it with some tools.

'Got my tools and the sleepers so I can start on your raised beds,' Will said. 'Spoke to the tenants. They seem nice; said they love the place and want to buy it. Just name my price!'

'Really?' Elizabeth's eyes widened.

'Yes, I was a bit taken aback. Said I'd think about it.'

Elizabeth was silent as Will started to take the tools he needed from the back of the ute.

'Umm. So, are you thinking of moving to England? Permanently, I mean,' Elizabeth tried to keep her voice neutral.

Will shrugged. 'Depends.'

Elizabeth didn't pursue the matter, but her heart sank. Just then Caitlin came bursting out the front door. 'Elizabeth! Guess what I've found?'

'Don't know,' Elizabeth smiled.

Will grinned. 'Gold?'

'Don't be silly, Dad! No, I've found out something about Brodies Plains!'

'I thought you were doing school work,' Elizabeth smiled.

'Oh, I am! But I just stumbled across this! Come and see!' Caitlin took Elizabeth's sleeve and pulled her inside. 'You too, Dad!'

Will raised his eyebrows and smiled at Elizabeth. 'Just stumbled in the middle of schoolwork!'

Caitlin ignored him. She pointed at her laptop screen. 'You know the painting of the sheep shearing shed that's everywhere?'

'You mean the one by Tom Roberts?' Elizabeth asked.

'Yes! Well, it was painted at Newstead Station! Look!'

Elizabeth peered over Caitlin's shoulder at the picture and the article which included it.

'Well done, Caitlin! See, Will.'

'So, Newstead was a sheep station, not a cattle station. But somehow, I don't think Edmund would have been a sheep shearer.' Will scratched his head. 'It doesn't tie in with Sofala.'

'What other jobs would there have been?' Caitlin frowned.

'A gardener?' Elizabeth suggested.

'They would have had horses on the station, so maybe a farrier? Possibly a blacksmith?' Will said.

Caitlin put her head to one side, thinking. 'Hmm. A blacksmith?'

'Well, if they had horses, they'd need horseshoes, wouldn't they? And blacksmiths made lots of other things they would have needed.'

Elizabeth glanced at her watch. 'Must be time to start dinner.'

***

The next morning, Caitlin was up early. Elizabeth was surprised to see her with her laptop open on the kitchen table. 'Look Elizabeth! Photographs of Newstead Station, Brodies Plains!' She scrolled down the screen. 'I woke up early and was thinking about Newstead, see? Photos of the house and all the surrounds.' She pointed at the screen. 'Someone called Gerald Steding took all these amazing photos! And look at the cemetery!'

Elizabeth pulled her dressing gown around her and peered at the screen. 'And?'

Just then Will came into the kitchen. 'What's all the fuss?'

'Look, Dad, look at the wrought iron around the graves!' Caitlin wriggled with excitement.

'Sorry. I don't get the connection.' Elizabeth was puzzled

Will suddenly said, 'You mean you think this is the work of a blacksmith and it could have been made by Edmund?'

'Yes! Remember the pick Elizabeth has with ET on it? You said you'd bought it at Inverell!'

Will grimaced. 'I think that's rather a long shot, Caitlin.'

Her face fell. 'Oh ...'

'But it's something to think about, Caitlin,' Elizabeth interposed when she saw Caitlin's dejection. 'Can you send me the link, please?'

Caitlin brightened. 'Of course, Elizabeth.'

A few moments later Caitlin suddenly exclaimed, 'Oh! Gross!'

'What?'

'Elizabeth, did you know that in Victorian times some people would pose their dead relatives for a photograph? Look at this ...'

Elizabeth peered over Caitlin's shoulder at an old photo of two boys sitting on a sofa.

'They're twins and that one on the left is dead! They did it a lot, yuk, they even had special stands made to prop up the corpse.'

'How on earth did you get onto this site, Caitlin?'

'Oh, I was researching what they did in the olden times for burials.'

***

The following morning, from her kitchen window, Elizabeth saw Will and his daughter in the garden, marking out the proposed raised vegetable beds. She couldn't help smiling at the pair of them, Caitlin was waving her arms and pointing to another part of the garden and Will was shaking his head and pointing up at the sun. Elizabeth could see Caitlin frown and then nod. Molly was watching them both, her head bobbing from side to side as she followed the conversation.

Elizabeth was keen to look at the photos of Newstead Station Caitlin had found. It seemed a remote possibility that Edmund had had a forge there but, like Will had said, 'truth is stranger than fiction'.

Since Caitlin had been sleeping in her study, Elizabeth had kept her laptop in her bedroom. She fetched it and set it up on the kitchen table. She scrolled down to the part about the cemetery and read:

'Sixteen grave markers survive east of church, the earliest of which is that of Colin Anderson who died in 1852. Its use has continued into the late twentieth century. The cemetery contains sandstone and marble, black and grey granite headstones. They include Celtic crosses, a simple cross, semicircular upright stelae with and without shoulders, a gabled upright slab, a low scroll, and desks with plaques. Some have wrought and iron surrounds with fleur-de-lys.[1]

Hmm, yes, wrought and iron surrounds with fleur-de-lys ... and the cemetery was only for the family. Which would explain why Edmund Turner had been buried in the Inverell cemetery. But how could she find out how and where that wrought iron was made? She looked at hundreds of photographs. *How sad, such a lovely old place has fallen to rack and ruin!* Caitlin was right, there were lots of photographs and fences around the cemetery and some around individual graves. She pursed her lips. Caitlin had done well to find these photos. Unfortunately, the cemetery in Inverell and the church had burnt down and no records remained. The newspaper entry was the only clue.

---

1. From Gerard Steding's notes

Brodies Plains, NSW - 1874

Edmund stepped off the paddle steamer at Grafton. He'd written to Mrs Anderson telling her his planned arrival date, but he was unsure if she would have got his letter in time. At least his journey had been quicker and more pleasant than when he'd first come to Newstead.

He took his bag and walked to the most salubrious public house in the town, where he managed to get a room. He'd have to get the mail coach to Inverell in the morning. For now, he lay down on the bed and tried to relax. He couldn't stop thinking about Edmund Joseph. His and Annie's son. She would be so proud of him. *Had he done the right thing giving her child to his sister?* His thoughts went round and round in his head. *Oh, Annie! Why didn't I stay in Bathurst? You would have got help there!'* He stayed awake for hours before falling into a fitful sleep.

The following morning, he was up in plenty of time for the mail coach to Inverell. As the coach trundled along the highway, he remembered the last time he'd come this way was with Patrick Anderson, all those years ago, when the road was only just being carved out through the countryside. At the Inverell coach stop, he was delighted to see Patrick Anderson waiting for the coach.

'Well, Turner! I didn't expect to see you here,' exclaimed Patrick, 'just meeting the mail coach to collect some things that mama ordered. I can take you back to Newstead. That's if you're going straight there?'

'Yes, indeed. That would be most gracious of you.' Edmund was relieved he wouldn't have to hang around and wait for some kind of transport to Newstead. He was weary. It had been an emotional farewell from his sister and Edmund Joseph.

'Take care, Edmund,' Mary-Ann had said as he'd boarded the paddle steamer.

Edmund Joseph had hugged him and seemed reluctant to let him go. 'Come back soon, Father,' he'd said. 'I want to hear more about my mother and your time in Victoria and Sofala.'

Edmund had turned away and wiped his eyes.

Now, Patrick Anderson clapped a hand on Edmund's shoulder. 'Throw your bag in the trap,' he said. 'Did you have a good time in Sydney? Feeling more chipper? Mama's been worried about you.'

Edmund looked around him. 'Thank you, Mr Patrick. All went well.'

'Jump up, we'll soon be back at Newstead.' Patrick indicated the smart new horse and buggy.

Edmund was relieved to be able to climb into the carriage, it had been a wearisome trip. He'd loved meeting his son, and now he could acknowledge that his decision to leave Edmund Joseph with Mary-Ann and Nat had been the right one. He would never have been able to rear his child as well as they had. He turned to Patrick. 'Thank you, Mr Patrick.'

Patrick Anderson peered at Edmund. 'You still look a bit peaky, if you don't mind me saying so.'

Edmund shrugged. 'Well, it's been a busy few weeks. Rather tiring.'

'How are your family? All good?'

Edmund nodded. 'Yes, thank you.' He'd never felt the need to explain about his son. As far as the Anderson's knew, he was childless.

Patrick chatted away telling Edmund all the news. Edmund barely listened.

Arriving at Newstead, Mary Anderson came out to meet the trap. She was taken aback to see Edmund. 'A nice surprise,' she said, greeting him. 'Come in and have a cup of tea, you must be tired after the long journey.'

'Thank you, Mrs Anderson. I won't trouble you; I'll just get back home.'

'As you wish. Patrick, drive Mr Turner to his home, I'll get one of the girls to bring you some provisions,' she said, turning to Edmund.

'That's most kind of you, Mrs Anderson.' He smiled at her.

'And your dinner tonight.'

'Thank you, that's very thoughtful.' Edmund bowed his head.

'Hmm. You still look rather pale,' Mrs Anderson remarked. 'Hope you're not coming down with anything. I hear the scarlatina is back in Sydney.'

Edmund smiled. 'No, I feel well, just weary, that's all.'

At his cottage, Edmund went inside and put his bag in the small room which served as his bedroom. He put a match to the fire he'd laid in the fireplace before he'd left. It seemed ages since then. By the time he'd unpacked his bag, the fire was roaring. He filled the kettle from the water barrel outside and put it on the trivet over the fire. There was a tap on the open door and one of Mrs Anderson's maids appeared with a jug of milk and a basket.

'Missus said to leave you a loaf and some butter and milk', she said.

'Thank you, Bridget,' he smiled, taking it from her. She bobbed a curtsey and scuttled off.

As soon as the kettle boiled, he made a pot of tea and poured himself a cup. He felt so exhausted he could barely stand. He took the cup into his bedroom and placed it on the chair beside his bed. He thought he'd just lie down for a while.

He drank the tea and lay thinking about Edmund Joseph and his trip to Sydney. Suddenly he was gripped by an intense pain in his ribs. He clutched at his chest. Must have been the tea, too strong, giving him indigestion, he thought.

He closed his eyes as the pain abated, then they flew open as an agonizing, crushing feeling engulfed him and brilliant white light surrounded him. Then to his astonishment, he saw Annie, dressed in her "posh" dress. She looked so beautiful. She held out her hands to him and smiled. 'Annie!' he gasped, trying to reach out to her. Then he lost consciousness as she disappeared into the intense light...

***

Bridget burst into the homestead clutching her breast. 'Oh, Missus Anderson! Poor Mr Turner has passed!'

Mary Anderson clenched the arms of her chair and half rose. 'Oh, dear, come and tell me.' She sank back into her chair. 'Patrick!' she called out.

At the urgency in his mother's voice, Patrick hurried into the room.

'Bridget says Mr Turner has passed!'

Bridget fidgeted with her apron, 'Yes, ma'am, I went into his kitchen with the tray of food and it was all quiet like,' Bridget's voice rose, 'I called out and then I saw him through the open door, all sprawled out on the bed, like.'

'Dear God, the poor man,' exclaimed Mary Anderson and blessed herself. 'Right, Bridget, go and make us all a pot of tea and Patrick and I will sort everything.'

'I suppose we'd better get Mrs Macpherson to lay out the body,' Patrick said. 'And I'll get Tom Ryan to make a coffin.' He appeared to think, 'And tomorrow I'll drive to Inverell and organize a funeral.'

Mary Anderson nodded. 'Thank you, son. He was a good man.'

'And I'd better put a notice in the paper. What should I say?'

'Fetch the latest *Australian Town and Country Journal* please, Patrick, we can check how other entries are worded. It's a while since I had to pen a death notice.'

'Good idea, mama.'

Patrick returned a few minutes later with the newspaper and spread it out on the writing desk. Mary Anderson rose and seated herself in front of it. She took up her pen and unscrewed the bottle of ink.

'There's one, quite simple, I think he'd like that. Just the date, his residence, name and age.' Her son pointed to an entry. 'How does this sound? "On 9th August, at Brodies Plains, Mr Edmund Turner aged 40 years."'

His mother wrote it down, then looked worried 'Was he forty? I thought he was younger than that. In fact, I vaguely remember him saying just before he went to Sydney that he hadn't been back since he was twenty-seven and that had been over ten years ago …'

'So that would make him thirty-seven.' Patrick crossed out the 40 and wrote 37 in front of it.

'Or maybe thirty-eight.'

Patrick waited while his mother thought, studying what she'd written.

'But that seems a rather miserly entry,' she said. 'How about something like "At his residence, Brodies Plains, near Inverell, on 9th August 1874, Mr Edmund Turner aged 37 years, deeply regretted by a large circle of friends"?'

Patrick nodded and Mary Anderson wrote down the words and blotted them.

***

A week after the funeral Patrick went into Inverell and brought back a copy of *The Australian Town and Country* newspaper.

'Here, mama, I know you like to read it first.'

Mary Anderson opened the paper at the death notices. Suddenly she exclaimed 'Patrick! What have you done! Mr Turner's death notice is in twice, and both with the wrong age and his Christian name is spelt differently!'

Patrick frowned and leaned over her shoulder. 'Oh, goodness, I gave them the piece of paper you wrote on, they mustn't have realized I only wanted the second better one. And I don't know how they got the age wrong. Sorry, mama.'

Mary Anderson gave a 'tsk' of annoyance and turned to the other news.

WAMBECARRA - AUGUST 2021

Will sent messages to the people with smartphones who he'd worked for before he'd left for England, letting them know he was back and available for work again. He rang the few people without mobile phones. Many of them were surprised he was back and also able to work during the lockdown. He explained that he could do urgent repairs or outside work.

Elizabeth was pleased when he was able to get back to work. After finishing her raised garden beds and doing a few minor things around her house he paced around the house, full of pent-up energy.

'Molly's walked off her feet, in fact, I think she's lost weight,' Elizabeth smiled at Will, 'Between you, me, and Caitlin, each of us trying to find an excuse to get out for exercise! It's good you'll be back working.'

Will laughed. 'I'm not made for sitting around. I've read all your books ...' He made a face, 'well, most of them.'

'You'll have to learn to play a musical instrument,' Elizabeth grinned. 'I've heard there's a vibrant ukulele club in the village.'

'Actually, that's a great idea! I must find out about it!'

Caitlin came in. 'I've left Molly outside,' she said. 'That's her third walk today.'

Elizabeth nodded. 'Thanks, Caitlin. I've just made a pot of tea if you'd like a cuppa.'

'Thanks, Elizabeth.' She poured herself a cup and sat at the table with Will. She cupped her chin in her hands and looked pensive.

'I guess we'll never know what really happened to Edmund Turner,' she said.

'Probably not,' Elizabeth replied.

Caitlin nodded and turned to her father. 'So, Dad, what do you think about this Extinction Rebellion?' She confronted Will.

Will immediately gave all his reasons why it was nonsense.

Elizabeth couldn't help smiling at them both, at the sudden change in Caitlin's thoughts and how Will had responded. Now, as the argument about climate change heated up, she suddenly became aware of Molly barking outside. She stood. 'That's not Molly's usual bark,' she frowned. 'I'll go and see what's happening.'

She opened the sliding door and went out into the garden where Molly was jumping away from something. Seeing the danger Molly was in, Elizabeth rushed forward to grab her dog's collar. 'No! Molly,' she screamed, 'Come away!'

Will and Caitlin came rushing out at the sound of Elizabeth's screams.

'A brown snake! Oh my god, it's bitten me!'

Will ran to Elizabeth who was holding onto Molly's collar. 'Caitlin!' he ordered, 'quick, go inside, take Molly with you and ring triple 0. Ask for an ambulance, brown snake bite; then go out to my ute, behind the driver's seat is a first aid box. Bring it here.' He turned to Elizabeth. 'Don't move,' he ordered. He looked around in time to see the snake disappearing behind Elizabeth's compost bin. 'Elizabeth, where did the snake bite you?'

She indicated her right ankle where two puncture marks could be seen. Will took a handkerchief from his pocket and pressed it against the bite. 'Don't move, Beth,' he whispered. He could see

Caitlin coming back with the first aid box, still with her mobile phone pressed against her left ear.

'Open it and take out bandages.'

With her right hand, Caitlin managed to extract bandages from the box, while still talking on her phone. 'Yes, brown snake bite, it's urgent.' She gave the address and the nearest cross street.

'Hold this handkerchief tight against the bite while I bandage,' Will said as Caitlin finished the emergency call, 'Then go and wait by the gate to show the ambos where we are. Shut Molly in Elizabeth's bedroom.'

White-faced, Caitlin ran off to obey.

Will turned to Elizabeth. 'Beth, my darling. You'll be fine. Don't move. Stay as still as you can.'

Elizabeth blinked. 'Will ...'

He leaned over and kissed her.

'Will ...'

'Don't try and talk, Beth darling.'

'Will ... darling ...' Elizabeth's eyes closed as the ambulance siren could be heard coming closer.

Caitlin came running out with the paramedics.

'I'm Jim,' said one of them, looking at Will's bandaging. 'You've done a good job, mate.' He turned to his companion. 'Jane here will get a stretcher and we'll get her into hospital. Need a few details, but we can get them later. You'd better follow us, mate,' he addressed Will. 'Seems your missus has passed out.'

Will followed them out to the ambulance, he could see Iris and Merv already at their gates. He turned to his daughter. 'Caitlin, Elizabeth will be all right. Just give Molly her dinner, maybe take her for a walk. I'm going to the hospital.' He gave her a quick hug, jumped in his ute and drove off after the ambulance.

Caitlin watched the ambulance disappear at the end of the cul-de-sac, then she turned back, tears starting to her eyes.

'Caitlin!'

It was Iris, hurrying towards her. 'What happened, Caitlin? Is Elizabeth all right?'

'I think so,' sobbed Caitlin, 'She was bitten by a brown snake, but Dad said she'll be all right.'

Iris put her thin arms around Caitlin. 'If Will said she'll be all right, then it means she'll be all right!'

Caitlin sniffed. 'Thanks, Iris. I must go and take Molly for her walk now.' She straightened her shoulders and tried to smile. 'All good, Iris.'

***

By the time Will got to the hospital, the ambulance had taken Elizabeth to the Emergency Ward. He put on his mask and went to reception where his temperature was checked. At the Emergency room, he said he was there to see Elizabeth Turner who had been admitted for a brown snake bite.

'Name?' Asked the receptionist.

'Will Barnes.'

'Relationship to the patient?'

'Partner.'

'Your phone number and details?'

Will told her.

'We need to know has she got private health cover and her Medicare card number.'

'Um, I don't have the information at the moment,' Will said.

'Okay, well please let us know as soon as you can.' The receptionist activated a button, 'go through that door, cubicle six.' She indicated a double-door.

Will obeyed. He walked through the Emergency ward. It was amazing, he thought, everything was buzzing yet there was an atmosphere of calm. He found the curtains around cubicle six, and pushed them aside.

'Can I help you?' A nurse was checking Elizabeth's temperature.

'I'm Elizabeth's partner, I'd like to know what's happening.'

'Well, we must monitor Elizabeth for a while, to check if it's a dry bite or did the snake release venom.' The nurse looked up at the monitor, wrote something on the chart, then bustled away.

Will sat beside Elizabeth's bed and took her hand – the one not connected by a cannula delivering fluids to her body.

'Beth ...'

Her eyelids fluttered and she appeared to focus on him.

'Will ...'

He thought she smiled.

'Oh, Beth, darling, you've given us all such a fright!' He sat holding her hand, watching her and the patients in the beds opposite. After a while, a nurse came into Elizabeth's cubicle, followed by a doctor.

'I'm Dr Shawabi, Elizabeth,' the doctor said, as she studied the monitor attached to Elizabeth. She smiled. 'I think she'll be fine. We're pretty sure it was a dry bite, so you could leave her now if you want. We'll keep her in overnight to be sure.'

Will straightened and nodded. 'Yes,' he said, 'if you're certain Elizabeth is out of danger, I'll head off and come back first thing in the morning. You have my phone number, in case of developments.'

He bent over Elizabeth and kissed her cheek. 'I'm going now, Beth, darling. You're going to be okay. I'll be back in the morning.' He looked at the doctor and nodded. 'Thanks for taking care of her.'

***

Outside the hospital in the car park, Will took off his mask and rang Caitlin.

'All good, Caitlin, love. Elizabeth will be fine. I'm just leaving the hospital now. You okay?'

'Yes, Dad, I took Molly for a walk and fed her, but Elizabeth's phone keeps ringing. I didn't know what to do, so I looked at it and it said Bronwyn.'

'That's Elizabeth's daughter.' Will started the engine. 'Right, Cait, I'll be home in about twenty minutes.'

He wondered about Bronwyn, should he ring her? Sydney was still in lockdown, so even if he did ring and tell her about Elizabeth, there was nothing she'd be able to do. Unless she got an exemption to travel ...

He parked his ute in the driveway; Molly must have heard the engine as she was bouncing around the front door as he went inside.

'Oh, Dad, Elizabeth's phone has been ringing and ringing, I think it must be Bronwyn again and she's leaving messages. I don't know what to do.' Caitlin held out Elizabeth's phone.

'Next time it rings, I'll answer it.' Will had just finished speaking when it rang again.

'Hello, Bronwyn,' he said.

'Who's that?'

'It's Will Barnes, your mum's friend.'

'Why are you answering? Where's Elizabeth? I've been ringing and leaving messages.' Her voice rose. *'I wanted to ask her to email stuff about her ancestry research, Chloë needs it for a school project.'*

'Bronwyn, your mother was bitten by a brown snake this afternoon. She's fine but they're keeping her in hospital for observation.' Will could hear her breathing hard.

'Why have you got her phone? This is ridiculous! Which hospital is she in? I'll ring them immediately!'

Will sighed. 'It's a long story, Bronwyn. I'll let Elizabeth tell you when she's fully recovered. In the meantime, rest assured your mother is being well cared for and will make a full recovery.' Then he pressed the end call button. A minute later the phone rang again. Will let it ring out and go to voice mail.

Caitlin stood, watching him. 'Dad, are you all right?'

Will smiled and put his arms around his daughter. 'Yes! Absolutely!'

'Dad,' Caitlin said, 'You love Elizabeth, don't you?'

Will was silent.

'Because I think you should ask her to marry you. She loves you, you know.'

Will blinked. 'What makes you think that?'

'Oh, Dad, you're so dumb! She can't take her eyes off you, the pair of you are like two lovesick teenagers!'

'And what would you know about lovesick teenagers, my girl?' Will grinned and stroked her cheek.

'Enough!' Caitlin smiled at her father. 'Seriously, Dad, you need to tell her. She thinks because she's older than you that that is an imp... an imp something.'

'Impediment?'

'Yes, that's the word.'

'So, she's told you that?'

'No, but I know how she thinks.' Caitlin broke free from her father's embrace. 'I'm starving, Dad, I think Elizabeth was going to make a curry tonight, but how about sausages and mashed potatoes instead?'

'Sounds good to me.' Will walked to his room. 'I'm going for a shower.'

***

The next morning, Will took Elizabeth's handbag with her wallet and phone with him when he went to the hospital. Donning his mask, he went through the routine temperature check and then to the emergency department and asked for Elizabeth.

'Beth!' He mumbled through his mask as he entered cubicle six, 'You look so well!'

Elizabeth put down the cup of coffee she was drinking and smiled. 'Hello Will. This coffee is yuk ... Come and sit down.' She indicated a chair beside the bed. 'Will, I believe I have you to thank for me being alive. Apparently, you did all the right first aid ...'

Will leaned towards her and pulled down his mask. 'Elizabeth Turner,' he said. 'I know you are still weak and recovering from a serious snake bite, and very vulnerable which is why I am going to take advantage of you and ask you something.'

'Oh?'

'Beth, um, Caitlin said it would be a good idea for us to get married. What do you think?'

Elizabeth blinked, then smiled. 'Well, I have great regard for Caitlin's judgement, but I'm too old for you, Will.' She lowered her eyes and plucked with her fingers at the sheet covering her.

'Age has nothing to do with it.' His eyes suddenly clouded. 'Oh, Beth, is it my colour?'

Elizabeth's head jerked up. 'No! of course not! I'm just too old for you.' She frowned at the sheet.

A nurse came in. 'Must check Elizabeth's blood pressure,' she announced.

Will stood up. 'Nurse. I've just asked this woman to marry me and she says she's too old. What do you think?'

The nurse looked at Elizabeth, whose face had gone pink, and then at Will.

'Age is just a number,' she smiled and turned to Elizabeth. 'Lucky you! Wish I had a handsome man like this one asking me to marry him. You're never too old for love!' She nudged Elizabeth and winked, then disappeared to the next cubicle.

Will stared at Elizabeth. 'Well?'

'What would Bronwyn say?'

Will laughed. 'She'd be thrilled! Really Beth, do you actually care what Bronwyn thinks?'

Elizabeth studied her hands. 'Are you really sure, Will?'

He took her hand. 'Yes Beth, I love you and I think we could have a great life together.'

She nodded. 'If you're sure ...'

Will laughed and shook his head, as a doctor came into the cubicle, followed by an entourage of nurses and assistants.

The doctor studied his notes. 'Ah, Elizabeth, and how are you today? You're looking well.'

'Yes, thanks to you all, I'm much better,' Elizabeth said.

'Well, you can go home this morning, but if you have any adverse side effects, get back in here straightaway.' The doctor nodded at Elizabeth and Will and moved to the next cubicle.

A few minutes later a nurse appeared, 'I'll get your discharge notes ready and then you're all set to go, Elizabeth. We'll need your Medicare details.'

Will gave Elizabeth her handbag and she rummaged inside and came up with her wallet. She extracted her Medicare and private health fund cards and gave them to the nurse.

'Will, I think my clothes are in that plastic bag by the side of the bed.'

Will sighed. 'Domesticity already! Not five minutes engaged and she's already ordering me around!' He leaned over to Elizabeth and grinned. 'Your wish is my command.'

***

In the ute going back, Will said, 'By the way, Bronwyn rang on your phone yesterday. I had to answer, because apparently, she wanted you to email some info about your ancestry research for Chloë. She was a bit disgruntled when she heard my voice. Anyway, I told her you were in hospital but out of danger and you'd ring her today.' He looked sideways at Elizabeth. 'I assume she doesn't know that Caitlin and I are living with you at the moment ...'

'Um, no. I didn't see any reason to tell her.'

Will let out a bellow of a laugh. 'Chicken! Well, now you can tell her we're getting married!'

When Elizabeth didn't reply, Will took his left hand off the steering will and caught her hand. 'You aren't having second thoughts are you, my dear?'

She lifted his hand and pressed her lips to his palm. 'No.'

***

'Can I be bridesmaid, Elizabeth? Please, please!' Caitlin jumped up and down when Will told her Elizabeth had agreed to marry him.

'Goodness, I hadn't thought that far ahead.' Elizabeth looked over at Will. 'I think it will be a very simple ceremony, don't you Will?'

Elizabeth's phone interrupted them. She glanced at it. 'Bronwyn,' she muttered and pressed the green button to take the call. 'Hello, Bronwyn.'

'Elizabeth! What's going on? THAT MAN answered your phone yesterday and I could get no information from him, except you'd been bitten by a snake!'

'Yes, that's right, dear. Yes, I'm fine. Um, thanks for asking ...'

'What on earth's going on, why did that man have your phone?'

'He had it because he's living in my house with me and we're going to get married, Bronwyn.'

There was silence and then a screech. *'You're WHAT?'*

'We're getting married, haven't sorted out the details yet, but I'm sure you'll be happy for me.'

'Elizabeth! I warned you! I knew you'd be taken in, taken advantage of! This is ridiculous! I'm coming down at once!'

'New South Wales is in lockdown, in case you've forgotten, Bronwyn, but in any case, I've made up my mind. And I forgot to mention, Will's daughter, Caitlin is living with us, so you'll have a step-sister ...'

There was a strange noise from the phone, then Elizabeth could hear her daughter shouting out to her husband. *'Darren! My mother's gone mad! She's talking about marrying THAT MAN! We'll have to go down and see her at once and put a stop to all this nonsense.'*

Elizabeth was about to hang up when she heard Darren's voice.

'Elizabeth, I understand congratulations are in order?'

'Yes, thank you, Darren. Will and I are engaged, plans not finalised at the moment.'

'I'm very happy for you, Elizabeth. Will seemed a very nice man from the little I saw of him.'

'Thanks, Darren. I've got to go now, I'm feeling a little tired, I got a nasty snake bite yesterday, I don't know if Bronwyn mentioned it …'

There was a pause, then *'Well, you take care and look after yourself and give my regards to Will. Let me know if there's anything I can do. Bye for now.'*

Elizabeth ended the call and smiled at Will. 'Phew. That's a relief to get that phone call over.'

'Who will give you away, Elizabeth?' Caitlin was jumping up and down again.

'Oh Caitlin, we haven't got that far in our plans.'

Will smiled at his daughter. 'It'll be very low key, Caitlin. Whatever Elizabeth wants.'

***

The wedding day dawned fine and sunny. Luckily weddings were now allowed to go ahead with a maximum of twelve guests. Bronwyn and family had arrived the day before; Darren said he'd be delighted to give Elizabeth away.

Elizabeth's heart fluttered with nerves, as she tried to get her hair to curl under her ears.

'I'll fix your hair in a mo,' Caitlin said, glancing at Elizabeth. 'I'm nearly finished Alison's.'

Chloë was already parading around preening herself in front of the mirror. 'I think I like my new aunt Caitlin.'

Elizabeth smiled to herself; Caitlin had won over the two girls in a matter of minutes. She was sure it would take a lot longer, if ever, for Bronwyn to come around.

'The celebrant is here, Beth,' Will called out, 'and Iris, Merv and Mabel.'

Mabel hobbled in, pushing her Zimmer frame, with Merv holding her elbow. Iris followed them in a slight drift of mothballs and lavender.

Will had made an archway in the garden and Caitlin had decorated it with spring flowers and ribbons, and prepared the outside table ready for their celebration.

'You look beautiful, Elizabeth,' Caitlin whispered as she handed Elizabeth her bouquet, 'You look young enough to be Bronwyn's sister, not her mother!'

Elizabeth studied herself in the mirror. She'd chosen a pale lilac tulle skirt and top for the wedding – with the thought in her mind that it would be suitable for other occasions – she couldn't think of any at the moment, but you never knew ...

The ceremony passed in a haze for Elizabeth, until Will turned to her, kissed her and everyone cheered. 'I love you, Mrs Barnes,' he mouthed.

Later, after toasts and speeches, Bronwyn, who'd had several glasses of champagne, approached her mother. 'Elizabeth, I hope you won't live to regret this.' She frowned, turned and waved her champagne glass at Will. 'Well, at least you've made an honest woman of her,' she said grudgingly.

Will smiled. 'I'll try and keep it that way,' he said, 'and stop her from sneaking out in the dead of night and stealing stuff from people's gardens.'

'Will!' exclaimed Elizabeth, her face turning a rosy pink.

Bronwyn's frown deepened. 'What?'

'A private joke,' Will smiled, putting an arm around Elizabeth's shoulders.

Afterword

Author's note:

The details about the Pentrich Rebellion, Edward Turner's sentence of transportation and his life are true, as are those of his children, except for Edmund.

There is a mystery about Edward's son, Edmund, as to whether he died aged five or aged thirty-seven in Brodies Plains. Edmund's story and all other characters are fictitious and any resemblance to real persons either living or dead is purely coincidental.

Acknowledgments

Laurel Horton for the book *Grave Reflections*.

Dianne Atkinson of the Inverell Family History Centre

Gerald Steding for permission to include extracts from his photographic work at Newstead Station

Robert Poxon for the photographs of the Pentrich plaque in Kiama

Nathan Cowley for the cover photo

Val Herbert and Patrick Cook for proof reading

Ian, across the road, who, by getting a delivery of cobblestones, originally from old London roads, got me started on this story.

Thank you to my wonderfully patient beta readers: Trish Behan, Shirley Gould, Sylvia Mason, Jennifer Smith, Barbara Spence and Paul Terry.

A special thanks to Sylvia Mason of the Pentrich & South Wingfield Revolution Group (www.pentrichrevolution.org.uk) who has been endlessly helpful and patient

Thank you to Trove and it's historical records – I hope the Government will continue to fund this valuable resource.

Resources

"Transported for Treason" by Ralph Hawkins
"The Pentrich Revolution: a brief history" by John Young
"England's last Revolution Pentrich 1817″ by John Stevens
"Grave Reflections" by St Peter's Church, Cooks River.
"Nothing But Gold" by Robyn Annear
"To The Diggings" by Geoff Hocking
Clarence river and paddle steamers: https://nla.gov.au/nla.obj-2383321940/view?partId=nla.obj-2383322265#page/n0/mode/1up

About the Author

Lyn Behan grew up in the English West Country. She spent her working life as a systems analyst and computer programmer in Europe and Australia.

She now lives on the south coast of NSW with a variety of chooks and dogs.

If you enjoyed this book, you may also enjoy her other books:

The Men and the Medium - based on a true story of the men who loved a spiritualist medium, set in England in the 20th century.

Seeking Samuel Goldberg – an Australian Jewish woman searching for family members caught up in the second world war.

Stolen Love, Fractured Lives – three generations of women, an incurable hereditary disease and a stolen baby lead to a web of lies and deceptions.

Discussion points for book clubs

1. The book mainly uses Elizabeth's voice. Do you think this works? Do the other characters seem real?

2. Did the swapping between the current time and the past work? Did it jar?

3. Were you surprised to read about the effect of the Mount Tambora eruption? If a similar event took place today how do you think it would affect the world and you personally?

4. Are there instances where the book is not "politically correct"?

5. Does the book have a central theme? If so what? Does it have many themes? If so how do they interlink? Is one theme more dominant than others? Do the themes blend naturally with the storyline or do you feel the author is using the characters to labor a particular point?

6. Did you find the author's writing style easy to read or hard to read? Why?

7. How long did it take you to get into the book?

8. Who was your favorite character? What character did you identify with the most? Were there any characters that you

disliked? Why?

9. What surprised you the most about the book?
10. Compare this book to other books you have read by the same author, or other books you have read covering the same or similar themes. How are they the same or different?
11. How would you adapt this book into a movie? Who would you cast in the leading roles?
12. Would you recommend this book to someone? Why or why not (or with what caveats)?
13. What kind of reader would most enjoy this book?

Did you enjoy this book? If so please write a review, even a brief one, as this would help other readers decide if they would like to read it.